CHASING
SHADOWS

Also by Swati Avasthi

Split

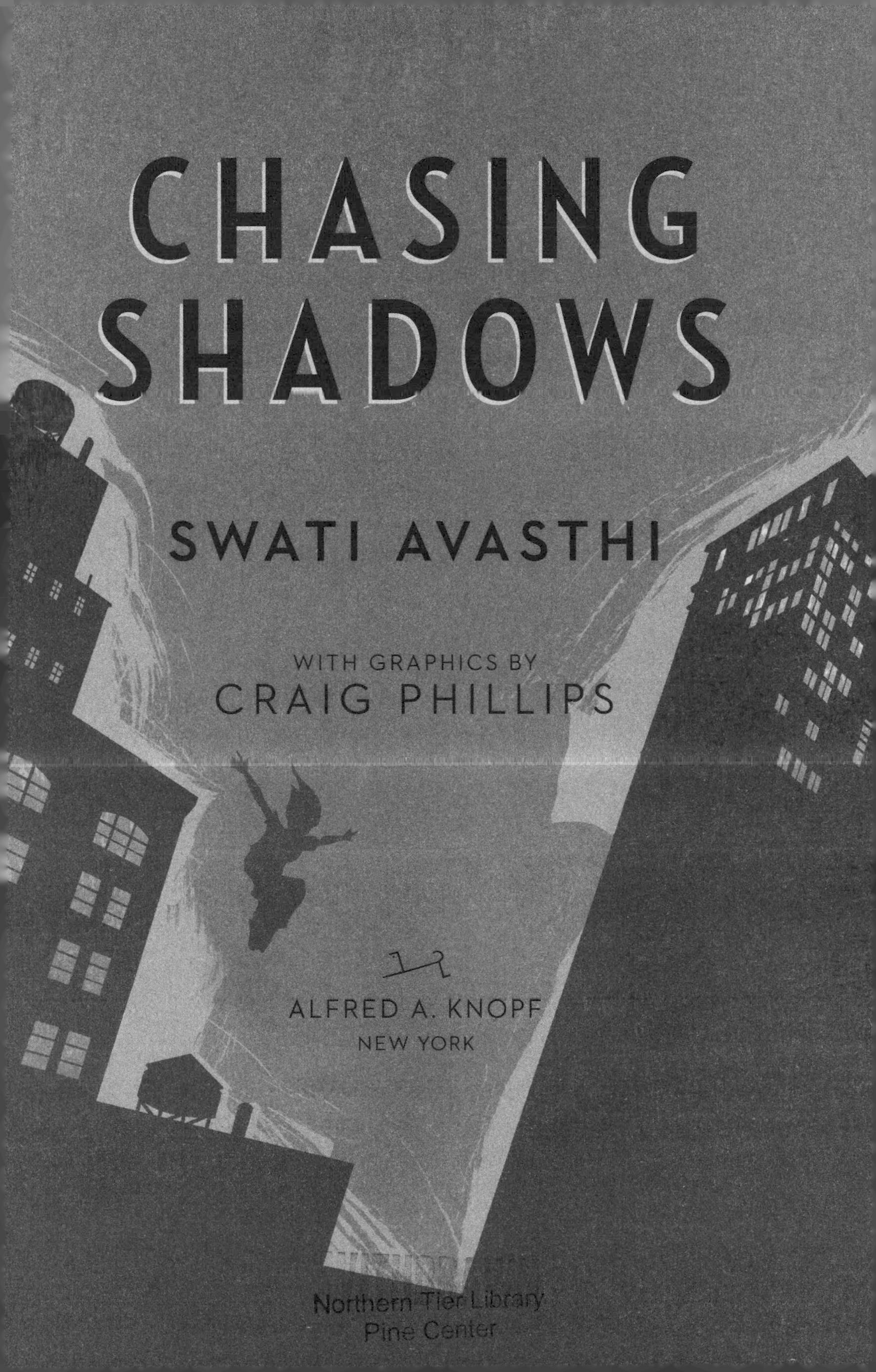

CHASING SHADOWS

SWATI AVASTHI

WITH GRAPHICS BY
CRAIG PHILLIPS

ALFRED A. KNOPF
NEW YORK

THIS IS A BORZOI BOOK PUBLISHED BY ALFRED A. KNOPF

This is a work of fiction. Names, characters, places, and incidents either are the product of the author's imagination or are used fictitiously. Any resemblance to actual persons, living or dead, events, or locales is entirely coincidental.

Visit us on the Web! randomhouse.com/teens
Educators and librarians, for a variety of teaching tools, visit us at RHTeachersLibrarians.com

Library of Congress Cataloging-in-Publication Data is available upon request.

ISBN 978-0-375-86342-4 (trade) — ISBN 978-0-375-96341-4 (lib. bdg.) — ISBN 978-0-375-89527-2 (ebook)

The text of this book is set in 11-point Goudy Old Style.

Printed in the United States of America
September 2013
10 9 8 7 6 5 4 3 2 1
First Edition

For my husband, John Yopp, who remains my compass—
All roads together.
Step for step.

MADNESS IS THE EMERGENCY EXIT.
—Alan Moore, *The Killing Joke*

PART I

Holly

I am not The Leopardess, but sometimes I wish I were.

As I dangle off the edge of this roof, I could use her steel claws. Superheroes get Wicked Toys, Cinematic Escapes, and Guaranteed Wins. If I could live in a comic, I'd be The Leopardess. And if I were The Leopardess, I'd be Fearless.

But I'm just Holly Paxton, so I have to run my fear ragged.

I tighten my grip on the cold edge of the roof, close my eyes, and open my breathing. Deep into my body. I sink into freerunning mode. Where my thoughts are dictated by the Morse code of footsteps and the flow from jump to jump. Where Fear Cannot Leash Me.

See your way to safety—my dad's advice when he trains rookie cops—rings through my head. *If you can see your way out, you can find your way out.*

It works for freerunners too. I force myself to ignore Hungry Gravity and the four stories of free space below, and picture my escape.

My right foot finds the wall. Followed by my left. I jump, jump, jump them up until they are crouched beneath me—and I'm in cat-grab position, hands gripping, legs tucked, ready to spring.

Savitri sails over me. Her th-thump landing—much heavier than she is—shakes my grip and I try to dig my fingers into stone.

"I've got you, Holly."

She grabs my wrist, but I don't loosen my grip; I can fix this on my own. More than fix it. Fast as I can, I muscle up, pulling my weight and tucking my feet until I'm crouched on the ledge. I go for a showy move to cover. An A-twist—big one-footed takeoff, flying cartwheel plus a half twist—should do the trick. Sav flattens herself against the roof and I twist over her. As if we'd planned it.

I land, soft as a cat. Sav laughs. Too loudly; she must have seen how my feet caught the edge of the roof instead of clearing it. A quick fall. And quicker grab. Good Reactions—Leopardess-pace reactions. Thank God.

I glance at Corey, my Twin Bro, who is on the far side of the roof already.

Sav gets up, her shirt polka-dotted with rooftop gravel. She squints at me, ever watchful.

"So?" she asks. Our way of checking in.

Options: Collapse and Cry, or Keep Moving.

"So," I say. "Close."

"Centimeters." Her voice quiet and as gravelly as the rooftop.

Sav has the best voice in the history of womanhood. Corey calls it sandpaper wrapped in silk. I try to concentrate on that, rather than on how her voice is shaking. *Must have looked bad. Must have been bad.*

"So." I deliberately unclench my hands. Never Let Fear Rule. "Ready?"

Before she answers, I take off and the world rushes at me. All speed. No hesitation. Just my own heat, pumped from my own heart, running my own blood.

Which helps stop the shaking and settle the stomach.

Corey is closing the distance to the front of the building, to the facade that upgrades its look: a fancy brick front to dress up the cheap sides and a short brick wall that rises above the roof in steps toward a capstone. On his way, he detours, jumps over a single forgotten planter, and then races up the steps to the capstone. I go after him. Sav—just a couple of seconds back—sprints to the far side and joins us. *Sav, be nimble; Sav, be quick.* When all three of us are gathered on the makeshift podium, panting out our own steam, we Survey Our Domain. I grab Corey's hand and he grabs Savitri's. We stand together for a Moment of Us—our training sign-off.

The Chicago wind kicks up, bringing us a sample of lesser scents from below: rotting apples and nicotine. Snow lies on the ground in half-melted lumps, like campfire-burned marshmallows: black pollution crusts with slashes of white. This false spring day turned the skies a shocking blue, drove the thermometer far above freezing, and Let Us Out. Into our city. So much better than training in a gym with soft mats and predictable obstacles.

When you freerun outside, a standard row of storefronts becomes a multilevel playground. We turn stoops into springboards, ricochet off walls, and throw flips off parapets. We scale buildings, using window ledges as complex ladders. Run outside and the city is no longer dead concrete and asphalt. It becomes an instrument—my instrument. Percuss-ive. I. Wake. It. Up.

Now Corey—who apparently has one more trick in him—scoots his feet back to the edge, prepping for a handstand fifty feet from the pavement. I steal Sav's smile: hers fades while mine grows. Sav worries too much; Corey's indestructible.

He places his palms on the platform and levers his legs over his head. Muscles over gravity. Complete control. His blond hair hangs and his face goes from cream to eggplant while blue veins bulge in his neck. His sneakers slice through the setting sun.

I let out a howl that gets Sav to startle and Corey to laugh—his body shaking. He pikes down and, seamlessly, flips backward. I throw a Webster—cartwheeling through the air. Sav just hops down. As Corey walks up to her, she shakes her head and walks away, toward the gardening shed that sits in the corner of the rooftop.

"What's wrong?" he calls to her back. "I'm okay, aren't I?"

"You're perfect," she says, her voice flat.

Corey and I exchange a glance. My turn. As I walk toward her, she is brushing off the gravel that is still clinging to her. She de-pebbles her palms, leaving pink dimples behind. I pick one from her ponytail. We become Monkeys of the City.

"Are you all right?" she asks me.

We've covered this already. Which means she isn't really asking. She's keeping the light on me to hide her own struggle in the shadows. *Tricky Sav, tricks don't work on me.*

"Better than okay. Great," I say, swallowing the leftover panic.

I hold out a fist and we bump knuckles. Once our hands meet, we unfold our fingers and whisper-hiss: *sssshhhaw,* the sound of steam power.

I'm about to ask her what's wrong when Sav turns on Corey.

"Did you notice that your sister nearly missed the roof? And here you are, four stories up and—"

"Whoa, whoa, wait a second," Corey says, and puts his hand up. He turns to look at me. I swallow hard.

I tell him about the stutter step that threw me off.

"Are you okay?"

"Obviously I'm okay; I'm standing here, aren't I?"

But then he says, "You knew it was wrong at the takeoff?"

And I realize he isn't worried about my Here and Now body—he's worried about how long I had to panic. A jump has three parts: takeoff, midair, and landing. You can control the takeoff, driving your muscles, and you can control the landing, channeling your flow. But in the air— those moments when you are Defying the Physical Laws of Gravity—you can't change your momentum, can't reverse your flow. You are In. That. Moment. And there's no going back. It would be a long time in the air to panic.

"No, it all looked good," I say. "I had the ledge in my hands before I even thought about the fall."

His face relaxes and he walks toward Sav, striding into a dive roll that comes up at her feet.

"See," he says, "it's all good."

She doesn't smile, but she lets him take her hand. Still, he has to do all the leaning to kiss her. Mid-kiss, she grabs his face and yanks him closer. Corey hesitates—startled—before stepping in, slipping his hand around her, and pressing on the small of her back.

Her move, his response means one thing: she hasn't mentioned Princeton.

She wasn't supposed to hear anything until April first, like everyone else. But yesterday she brought over a McDonald's bag loaded with fries, root beer, and cherry pie. Corey, who knows that this meal is code for Best Friends Only, vanished. She showed me a letter from Princeton that neither of us could make sense of.

So, this afternoon we brought it to Retired-from-the-Runway Richardson, our stick-thin college counselor. Turns out a few colleges will, very occasionally, try to "capture their best applicants' attention with a note like this to let the candidate know that admission is likely." *Likely, just likely,* I told myself, but Mrs. Richardson was wearing her Ivy League Grin.

Sav's options, revamped: Princeton alone, or Chicago with us.

I'm sure it will rock her world to turn down her dream school, but she won't go. She wouldn't leave us.

Would she?

I watch Sav as she watches Corey. He throws his foot over the parapet, getting ready to scale his way down. She lets out a soft sigh and smiles, as if recording this moment for posterity.

Shit.

* * *

While Corey walks Sav to her car, I am waiting inside The Dana, our zippy silver Mini Cooper. When our mom's parents died, they left a trust for Corey and me, which has translated into a private education and The Dana. Corey wanted to give our baby a woman's name. Fine, whatever. But Sav said he was "falling victim to an archaic, misogynistic thought pattern." He crossed his arms and said that it clearly wasn't archaic, and that whether he was "falling victim" to it or not, he was *not* driving a male car. So they met in the middle, and The Dana was born.

I could take off and let her drive him back to our neighborhood; I should take off, probably. But with Princeton in the mix, I don't know whether they're going to need Time Together or Space Apart. I drum my fingers on the steering wheel.

Stalker defined: a person who sits watching someone through a windshield? Maybe so.

I grab *The Leopardess: Origins* from the backseat and rub the spine where it has bubbled up, preparing to crack. Damn, I'll have to buy a third copy. Corey keeps telling me I should go digital, but I can't get the same visual rhythm on a screen.

I scooch down and disappear into how Larissa Powell goes from Ordinary Girl to Superhero. I get caught in a two-page spread: Larissa stands beside a mouth carved into the earth by the shovels and sweat of gravediggers. A single tear rolls down her cheek as a sea of black umbrellas keeps the rest of her dry. Next to her, her sister's face is obscured, but the stitches across her wrist poke up like barbed wire. Her dad—FBI Agent Extraordinaire—stands helpless on the other side, face of stone while they bury her mom, who was abducted and murdered.

I'm almost through part 1 of *Origins* when a rap on the window startles me back to the real world.

Corey. I put the book in the backseat while he gets in, locks his door, and straps on his seat belt. He sits upright, not looking at me.

Silence stretches out.

I shove The Dana into gear and we slide around corners, mazing through one-ways until we're heading the right direction. We drive past a burned-out empty lot with one tree standing on its own and Corey is still silent, still rigid. I hate not knowing what to say to my twin, the guy who has been finishing my sentences since sentences were an option. I nudge him with my elbow, and he looks at me.

"So?" I say.

"So," he says. "Princeton."

"Has she decided?"

"There she goes," he says, pointing at her Subaru as she glides in front of us. He shrugs. "She says she hasn't."

"But?"

"It doesn't matter," he says, his voice tight. "I'm sure we'll make it work."

I'm not so sure. When it comes to relationships, there is no halfway with Sav—a condition of her Lioness Loyalty. With Sav, you're either in or you're out. She's just like Corey that way. When Josh screwed me over last year, they froze him out so fast, he practically had icicles hanging off his fingers.

"Is that what she said? That you guys could make it work?" I ask.

"That's what I said."

The light turns yellow. I start to gun it, remember my two speeding tix, and hit the brakes. One more and my parents won't let me drive. Sav sails through. Her rear windshield wiper waves "So Long, Suckers," but then she pulls over, loyalty winning the day. *A good sign?*

"Do you think it's a problem?" he asks.

"Nope." I school my face to a Casual Expression that would fool anyone.

"Bullshit. You're worried too."

I roll my eyes. Can't keep anything from him. Might as well share the same brain.

He pauses and an SUV pulls up next to us at the light. "Well, there's another option, then."

"Which is?"

"Transfer. Princeton can't be the only school in New Jersey. Some place will accept me."

I frown. I'm nothing if not a Chicago Girl. And I'm not that into following Sav around the country. But I'm even less into the idea of

Corey and me separating for college. We're supposed to share an apartment, for one thing.

I won't look at him. I stare out the windshield—Two Disappearing Acts in One Night, first Sav, now Corey.

"Holly?" he says gently.

As he moves into my peripheral vision, I turn my head and look out my side window, taking in the street.

And I see . . . Everything Change.

Time sl-o-o-ws. Sounds stop as my brain captures images, frame by frame.

My mouth goes bone-dry. I can't manipulate my tongue to say anything, not even to scream.

All the words I've ever known . . .

       frac

         tu

           r

            e

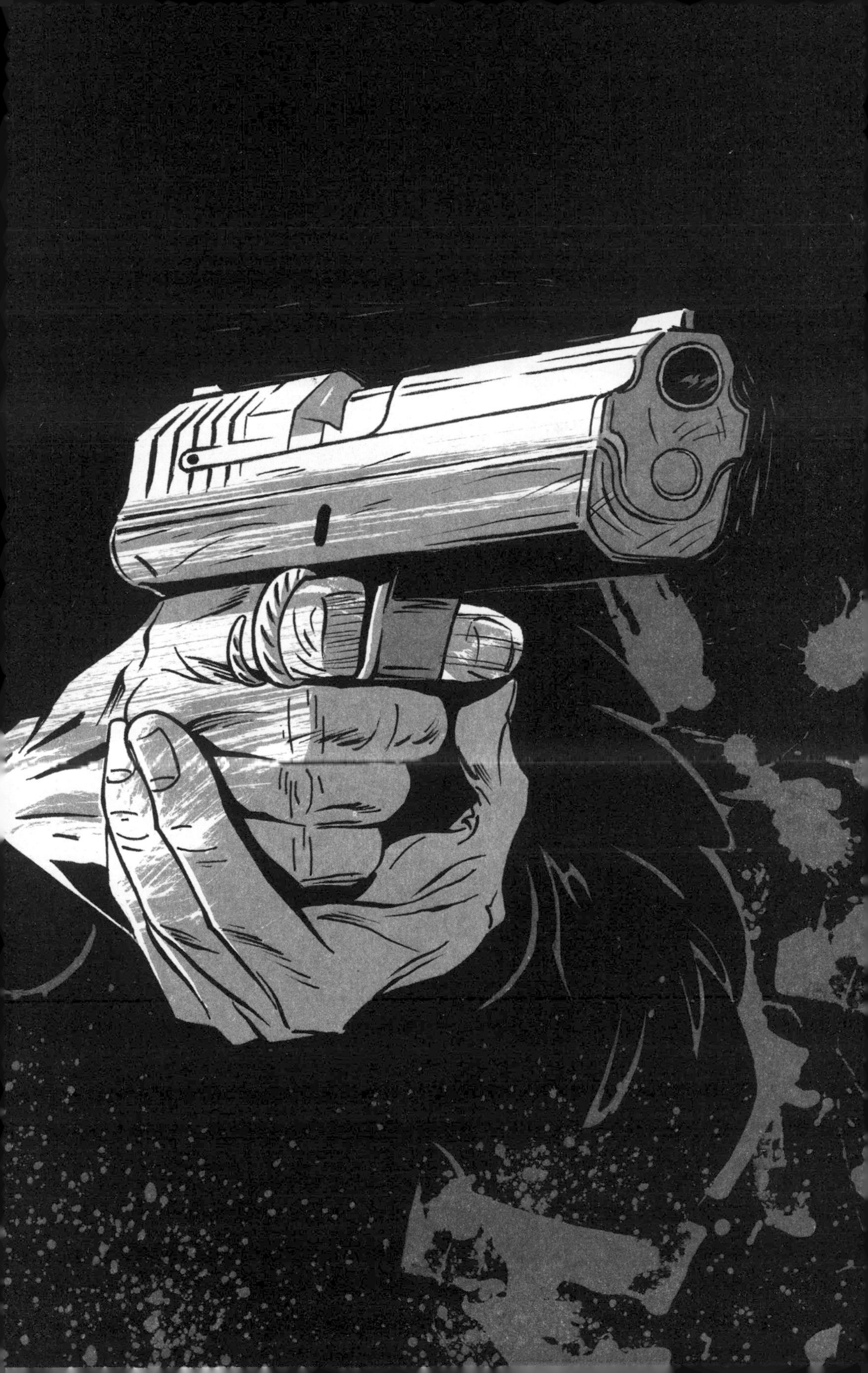

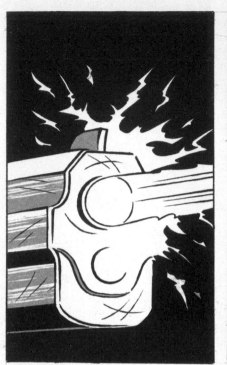
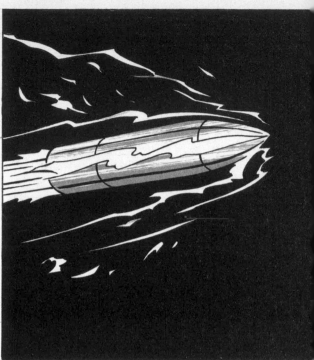

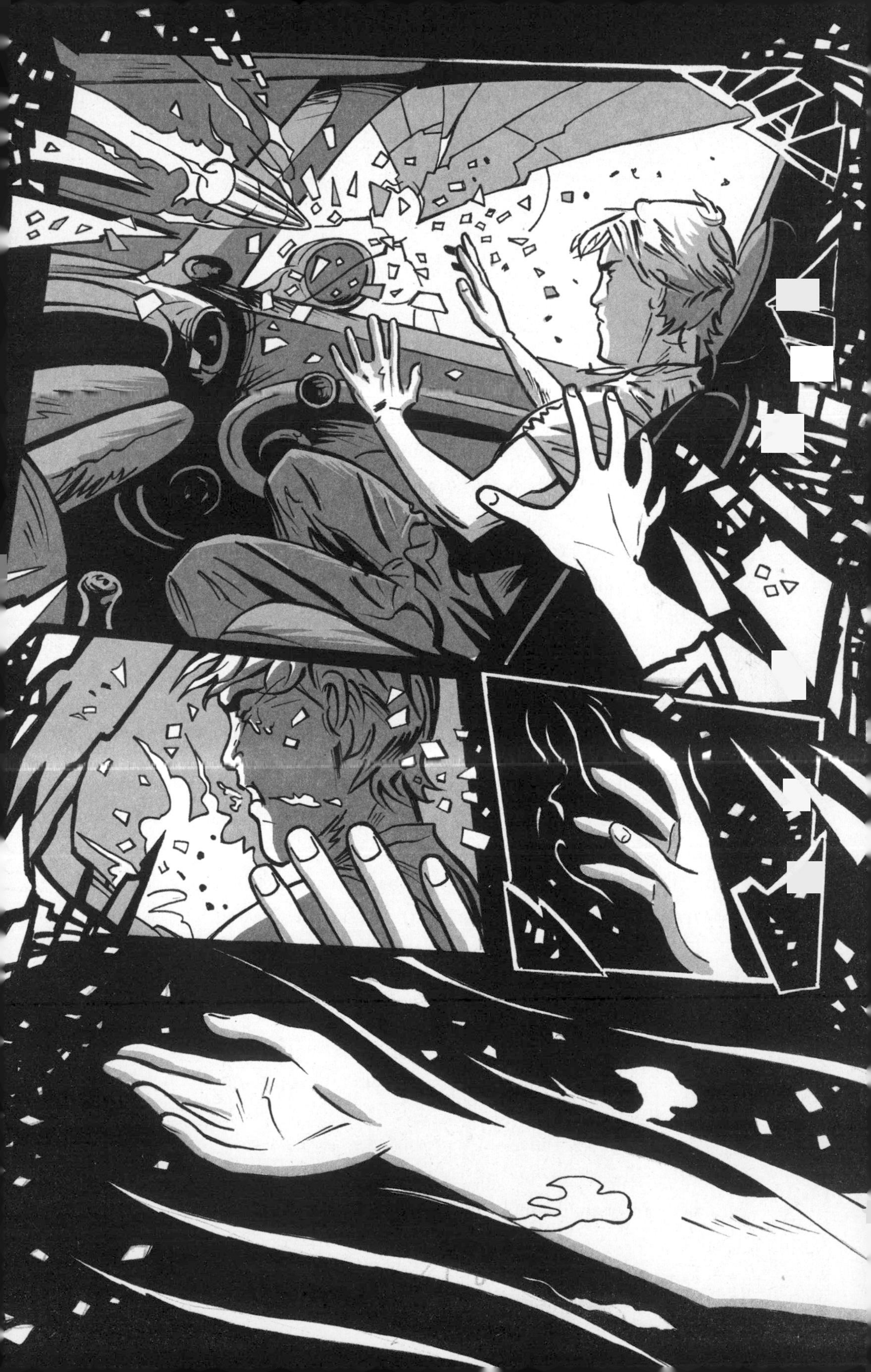

Savitri

While Corey walks me to my car, I keep my eyes down, trying to make an ordered pattern out of the random cracks on the sidewalk. Our shadows stretch beside us on the ground, sometimes merging, sometimes separating.

The day my family moved into the Morgan Park neighborhood, Corey and Holly were playing a game of Shadow Tag in their driveway. She chased him, braids bobbing, trying to make her shadow disappear entirely into his. It was a game that worked better with three, a game that started our eleven-year friendship. But now . . . ?

Well.

Our plan was to stay together for college. Chicago has a school for each of us: Holly at UIC for film and video, Corey at DePaul for comp sci, and me at Northwestern or U of C to major in thinking-too-much. Holly said we'd meet up for dinners, twice a week, no matter what. At Penny's, she said, and I knew she was picturing us sitting with overflowing plates of rice noodles while trains rattled above us.

It was a fine picture—a good picture, even. And since Princeton hung so far out of my reach, it seemed pointless to mention my late-night, quiet-in-the-dark fantasies: walking under the cherry trees, synthesizing Freud and fairy tales, sitting in a dining hall with people who don't sip grudgingly at knowledge but gulp it down, slam the chalice on the bar, and demand more.

But most of all, the fantasy of being someplace new.

When we get to my car, Corey hands me my bag, which he had grabbed out of the Dana's trunk—a spot to keep things safe, since our favorite freerunning place isn't in the best neighborhood and we often find parking in an even worse one, with gang territory grafitti and bars on the windows.

"Unusually quiet," Corey says softly, as if my silence needs to be handled with kid gloves. I'm not being fair.

"What's on your mind?" he asks.

I hesitate, searching for the right words. When I applied, I made a deal with myself: get into Princeton, say goodbye to Corey.

Distance ruined my parents. My father went to India for work for just a few months that stretched into just a few years that stretched into an unofficial divorce and a permanent change of address. When we Skype now on birthdays and holidays, long pauses break up our conversations. So. No slow, painful death for Corey and me. I'll rip off the Band-Aid fast; it's the only possible way we can remain friends. I hope.

He takes my hand, and my fingers rest in the hollows between his bones.

"Sav, seriously. Are you mad at me?"

"Never."

He half smiles. "Really. Was it the handstand? I was perfectly stable."

"Do you have to take chances like that?" I slide into the familiar argument—a strange sort of salve.

As much as he is my anchor to the edges of life, I'm his anchor to the middle. Balance and counterbalance. What risks will he take if I leave for Princeton?

He shakes his head slightly and leans a little closer. "Don't worry about me," he says. "Is it Holly? Was her jump that wrong?"

I know what he's trying to ask. Holly cures her worries by pushing the limits. Chronic bad dreams got her into freerunning. And after her pregnancy scare last year, when Josh told the whole school that her "maybe-baby" could have been anyone's, she moved our running to the rooftops.

I shake my head. "No, she's fine."

"So, then . . . ?"

"College admissions."

He makes a sound that is both a laugh and a sigh. A cloud of his breath dissipates into the air. "That's weeks away. I'll make you a deal: worry for the whole month of April. You can stress to your heart's content over which of your suitors to pick, and in exchange I'll—"

"I'm getting into Princeton."

He steps back and looks at me, his eyebrows drawn together—startled. "That's what I like to see. Confidence."

"That's not what I mean. I mean . . ."

In the silence, his smile withers.

"You heard?" he asks.

My head dips once in a semi-nod. He puts his hand on my car and leans into me, pressing me back against the window. He kisses me—mint and salt slide against my lips.

When we separate, he says, "Congratulations. I'm proud of you."

Formal. Distant. Already.

"You've worked hard for this, Savitri."

I've always loved that he pronounces my name correctly, that he bothered to learn how to roll his r's, to get the t: SAAV-i-three. After we started dating last year, he quietly read *The Mahabharata,* the entire holy text, just so he could know who I'm named after. When he told me he'd read it, I smiled and handed him one of the comic book versions of that particular story—*Savitri: The Perfect Wife.* He read that too and said my name fits me well, that I have Savitri-Devi's degree of loyalty. But now . . . Princeton.

I slide my hand around his neck, my fingers trailing on his skin, and close the distance. *What would be so wrong in staying like this forever? Forget everything else and just stay here. Four more years with him, and with Holly.*

"It's not official—yet," I say, and explain the email while he pulls back.

"We'll celebrate all weekend, okay?"

"O . . . kay."

He's taking this rather well. Maybe too well.

"I haven't decided for sure yet," I say.

He nods and then begins to laugh. "Yes, you have. I mean, it might take you a while to own it—make some known-unknown charts and pro-con lists—but you've decided."

"Hey, my lists give us indisputable insights."

"Oh, all hail."

I laugh.

He continues, "But factor us out, okay? We'll be fine." He says it so firmly that I suspect he's trying to convince us both. "We'll be fine. We can Skype and email and . . ." He keeps going and I just nod, not ready to tell him the rest.

I run the tip of my finger over the scar that divides his eyebrow, courtesy of a falling icicle when he was nine.

"What time is it?" he says.

"Three-fifty-two," I say without looking, consulting the clock that runs in my head.

He tells me we'd better go or I'll be late for my Speech Team prep. I say sure, but we both know that I'm the timekeeper in our trio and don't need to be reminded. Then he turns and jogs back the way we came instead of riding back to Morgan Park with me.

I curl my lips inside my mouth, tasting the mint Corey left.

I get in the car, turn the key in the ignition, and, after weaving through a labyrinth of one-way streets, somehow end up in front of the Dana. The light shines yellow and I head through, but the Dana stops. *That's strange; I thought Holly was driving.* I turn on my back wiper to wave goodbye, but maybe tonight a see-you-later shouldn't be conveyed with a mechanical arm. So I pull over to wait.

I can imagine how Holly will react once we're face to face again: *Here are your options, girl: Stay with Us or Move On.* Holly has a way of talking with mid-sentence caps.

I rest my head on the steering wheel.

Dear Breakup, enclosed please find high levels of anxiety. Would appreciate return of my peace and calm.

I lift my head and am popping my neck when a crack splinters the world.

My head whips around and I watch their driver's-side window shatter, glass spilling onto the street. The Dana shudders and stalls out.

What is happening?

I'm maybe fifteen yards ahead, but through my back window I can see a guy—small and wiry—striding toward the Dana. His hoodie covers his face and his hand is raised. Holding a gun.

My muscles lock.

He fires over and over—a fast spray of bullets. The Dana rocks with the impact. When he is a foot from Holly's shattered window, he squares his shoulders, steadies his aim, and fires again. At the same time he pulls the trigger, I scream—"NO!"—but the shot smothers my voice.

The guy—this wiry guy—slides the gun into his waistband. In one fast move, he pulls something from his pocket, snicks open a sleek blade, and yanks the Dana's door handle. He leans inside and comes back out carrying a silvery thing—like a tassel.

He hurries around the front of his SUV, his head down.

Oh, God, what do I do? Plate number? Get the license plate number. But no white square shines from the fender. Only more black.

He revs the engine and screeches out, the SUV leaning dangerously when he turns at the intersection. The sound of the engine dies away, leaving me on a silent street. All I hear is my own ragged breathing.

Then I am on the street. Fifteen yards to go. Sprinting, arms pumping for speed. Can't hear, can't breathe, can't think. How long does it take to cover fifteen yards? Seconds, but stretched seconds.

The windshield has splintered—spiderwebbed and bowed, but still intact. I can't see inside. My feet crunch down on diamonds of glass.

I'm close, so close. For a moment, I wish I could run past the Dana—not look—because you can't unsee. Because as bad as this moment is, the next will be worse.

I round the open driver's door and freeze.

A knot of bodies. Utterly still.

Corey is draped over Holly, one arm stretched toward me. Blond hair stained. His splattered cell phone peeks out from under his hand. Holly's seat belt has kept her lower half firmly rooted while her torso has fallen over into the passenger seat, her face next to Corey's knees. Blood slides down her forehead and forks at her eyebrow.

I inhale sharp gunpowder and rich blood, and finally, finally, my thoughts snap to: I grab Corey's phone and dial. Just three numbers, but the phone is shaking so hard I have to hold it with both hands. I watch red flow from Corey's head—paint spilling.

I tuck the cell phone between my ear and my shoulder and reach inside the Dana. Two fingers on his neck. Warm skin. *Thank God, thank God, thank God.*

But . . . there is nothing under my fingers. No pulse. I slide them up and pause, I slide them down and pause. Nothing. His back is still.

I scream his name. Nothing.

"911 Emergency. What is your emergency?" I hear through his phone.

My voice is uneven—fluctuating helter-skelter from a whisper to a scream, my sentences scattershot—but I manage to answer his questions: our location, what happened, Corey's age.

And then he says, "You said there are two victims?"

My stomach heaves as I force myself to look at Holly. She lies motionless; I haven't reached her neck or her wrist to check her pulse. I race around the other side of the car and try to pull open the door, but it is locked. Blood has pooled in the hollow of her eye.

Am I alone here with two dead bodies?

No, no, no. They cannot die. I am not going to let them. There must be a way to save them, to breathe life back into his still lungs. My mouth on his, the taste of mint.

My feet have taken me back to the other side and I'm with Corey again.

"What do I do? Do I move him? I know CPR."

"Is he breathing?"

After three tries that come out as whispers or whimpers, I finally manage a "No."

Three minutes. Three minutes without oxygen before brain damage ensues. Incongruously, I marvel: *CPR training actually works. You remember when you need to.*

"Should I move him?"

I know you shouldn't move head injuries, though I can't think of why.

A sound—small, inside this car—stops me. I pull the phone away from my ear and stare. Under Corey, Holly moans.

"Holly? Holly!" My voice breaks when I tell her she will be all right. "Don't move, Holly."

I can't move him, not without moving her, and I can't risk that. She has a chance.

And he . . . No, no, no.

The voice on the phone tells me to stop the bleeding if I can. A couple of comic books lie in the backseat, but nothing else. Holly, who maintains the Dana in binge-and-purge cycles, must have just cleaned it out.

My hands will have to do. I want to hesitate; I want the luxury of squeamishness, but Corey doesn't have the time for that, so I press down on his skull, palms matting the hair. His blood is hot against my palms, slippery under my hands. Alive. *Please.*

I can't hear the sirens.

"Where are they?"

"Two minutes away."

20

Two minutes—120 seconds, and if I breathe once per second . . .
One . . . Two . . . Three . . .

Holly makes a high keening sound and I tell her to hang on, that
they are coming. I start counting her breaths instead of my own, watching her side rise and fall, rise and fall. *One. Two. Three. Four. Five.*

My shirtsleeve wicks Corey's blood. Stitch by stitch, it crawls up
my arm.

Three. Four.

My shirt, I realize. Why didn't I think of it in the first place? I strip
it off, wad it, and press it against Corey's head.

"Keep breathing, Holly. Keep breathing."

Three. Four. Five.

"Miss, I'll hang up now. They should be there," says the operator.

"They aren't," I say. *Did they get the address wrong?* "We are at—"

"I can hear the sirens through the phone, miss," he says, and the
wailing cracks into my consciousness. A blue light blinds me.

"We've got them," someone says, and puts a hand on my shoulder.
"Miss."

A curly-haired EMT appears at my side and suddenly, inexplicably, I
want him to go away. *If he would just leave us alone, we'd be all right. I can't
leave them.*

But I back out of the car.

Lights and motion everywhere.

I watch as they tend to Holly and Corey in a flurry of movement and
sound. *They will be all right now; they are safe now.*

I start backing up, back and back, when something rolls under my
foot and I land hard on the pavement. I get on my hands and knees and
find what I slipped on. A metal shard that has writing on it. I pick it up
and read: s&w 9 mm. My hands jerk away from the bullet casing and it
clinks on the ground.

Somehow this—not the blood that is cooling and drying on my
skin; not how they have pulled Corey out onto the street and started

chest compressions, his body jerking under their hands; not how they strapped Holly's head between two cushions, her face framed in red—this shell lying on the pavement, this small piece of metal, takes me apart.

I start screaming and screaming and screaming.

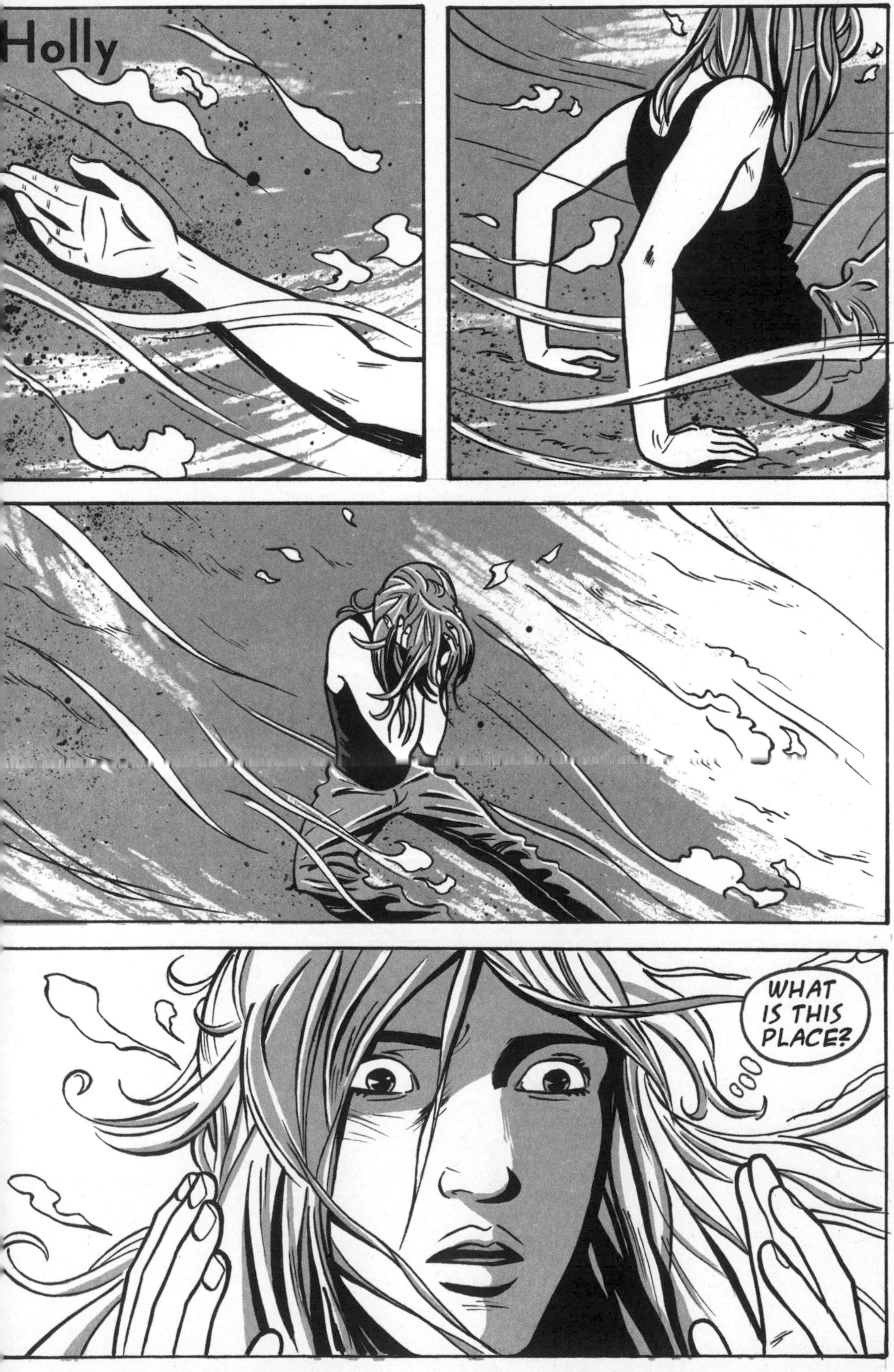
Holly
WHAT IS THIS PLACE?

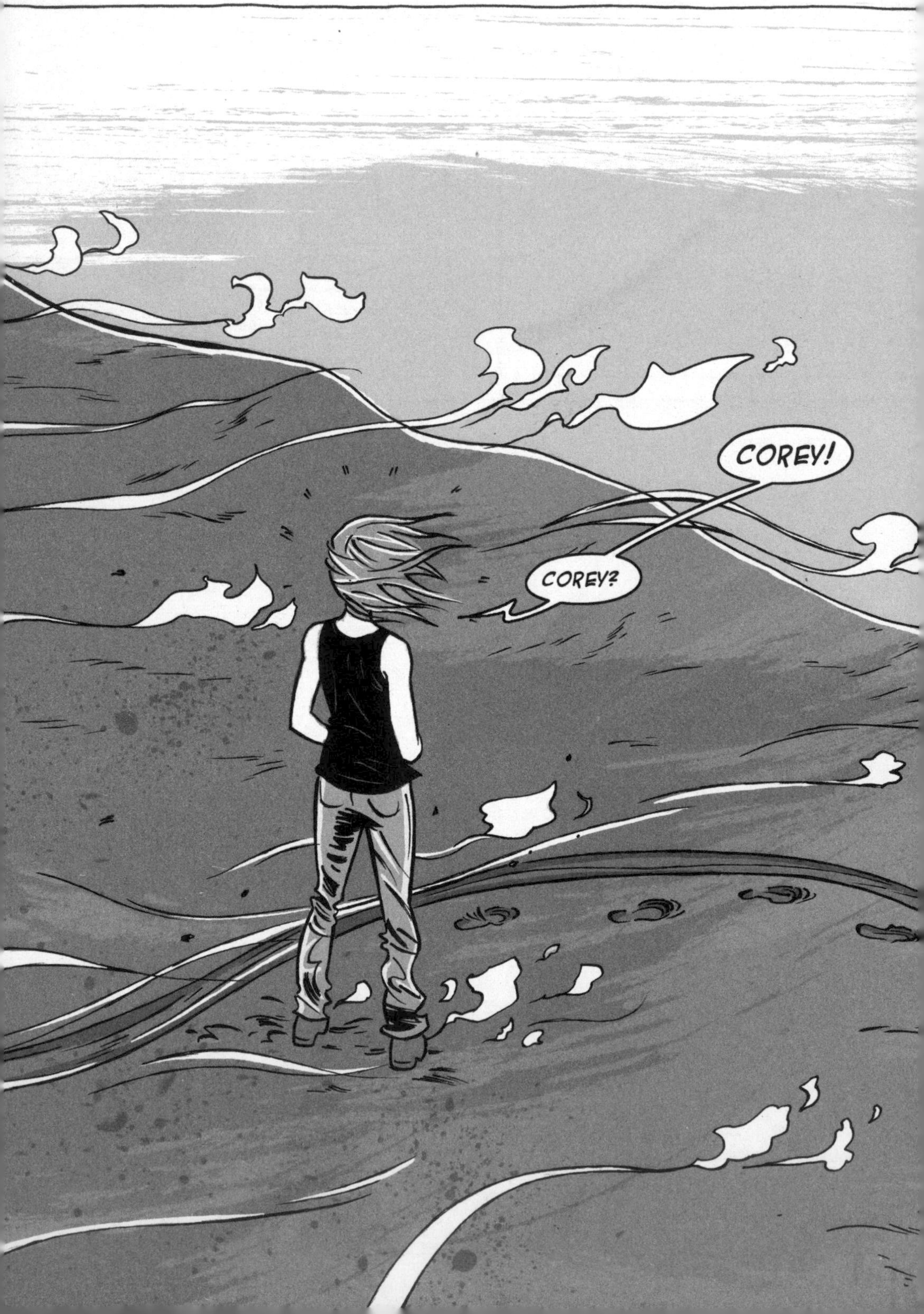
COREY!
COREY?

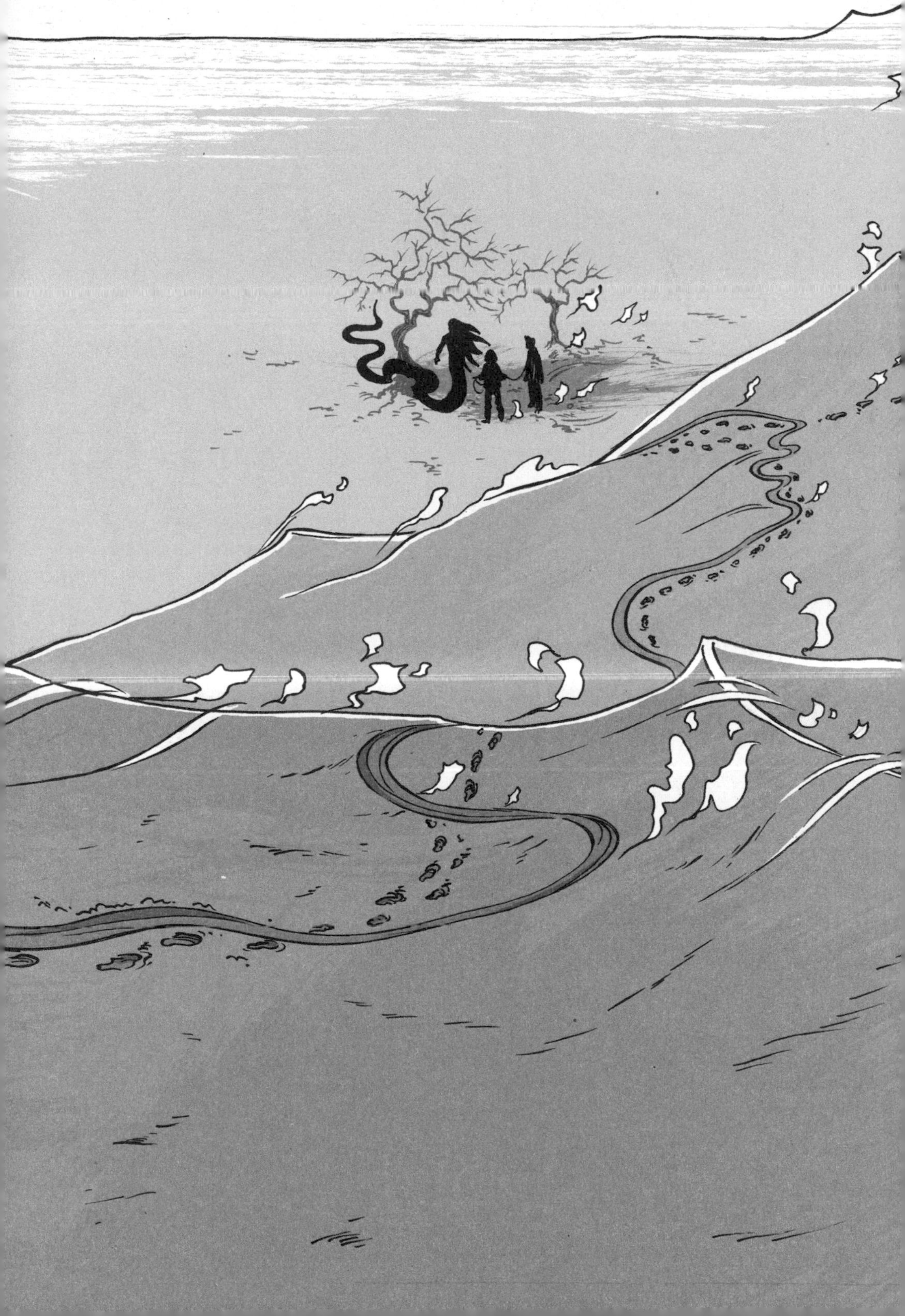

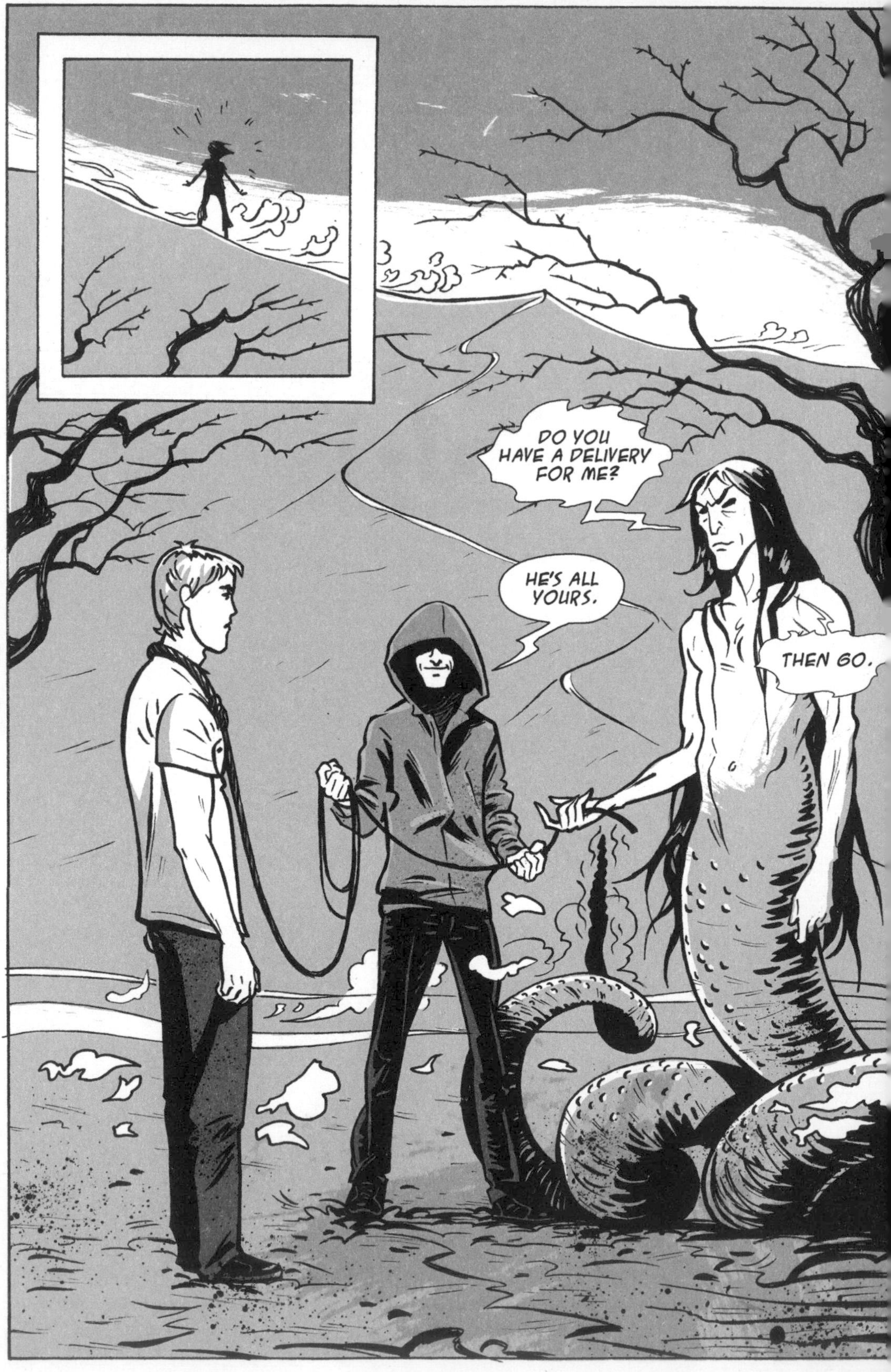
DO YOU HAVE A DELIVERY FOR ME?
HE'S ALL YOURS.
THEN GO.

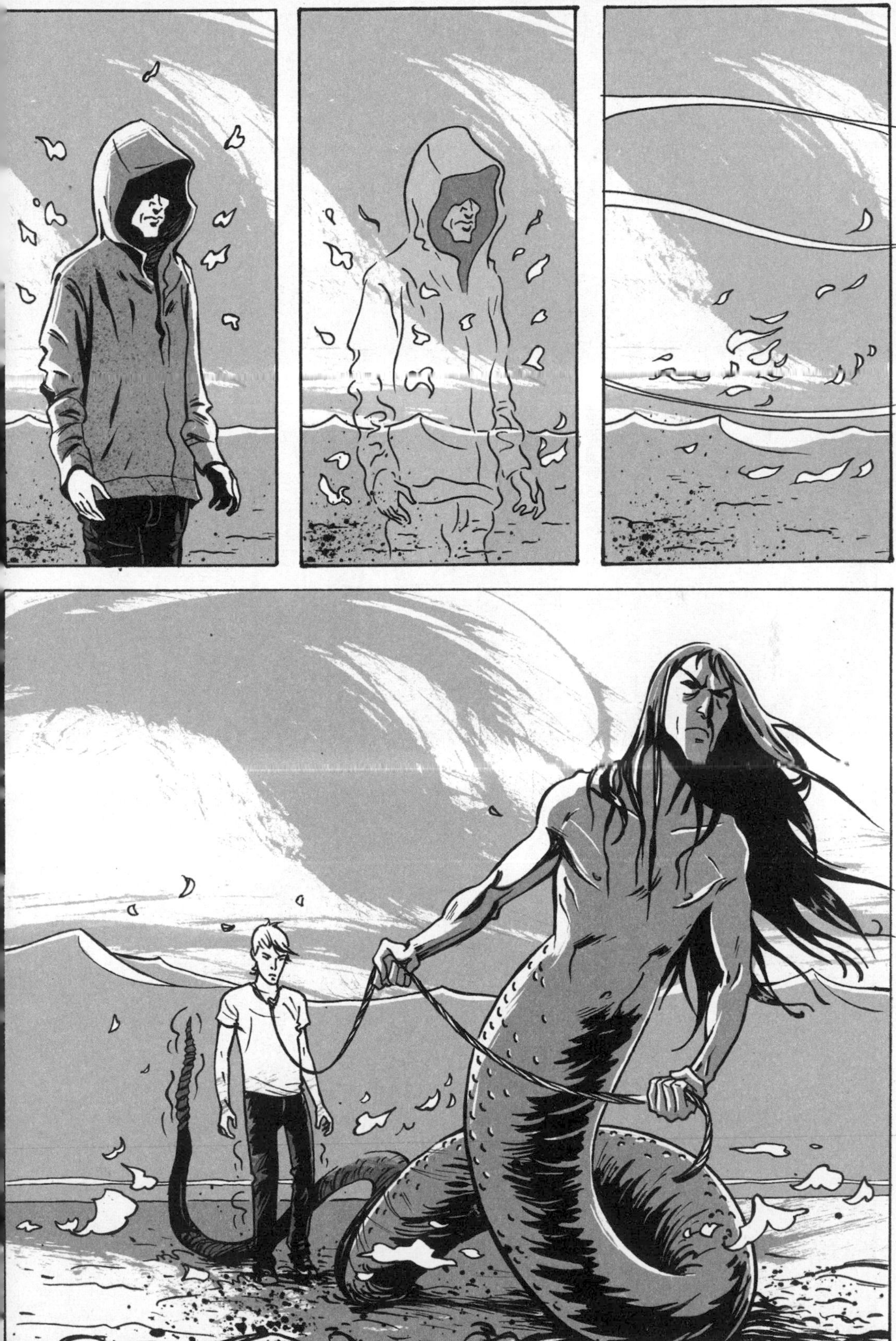

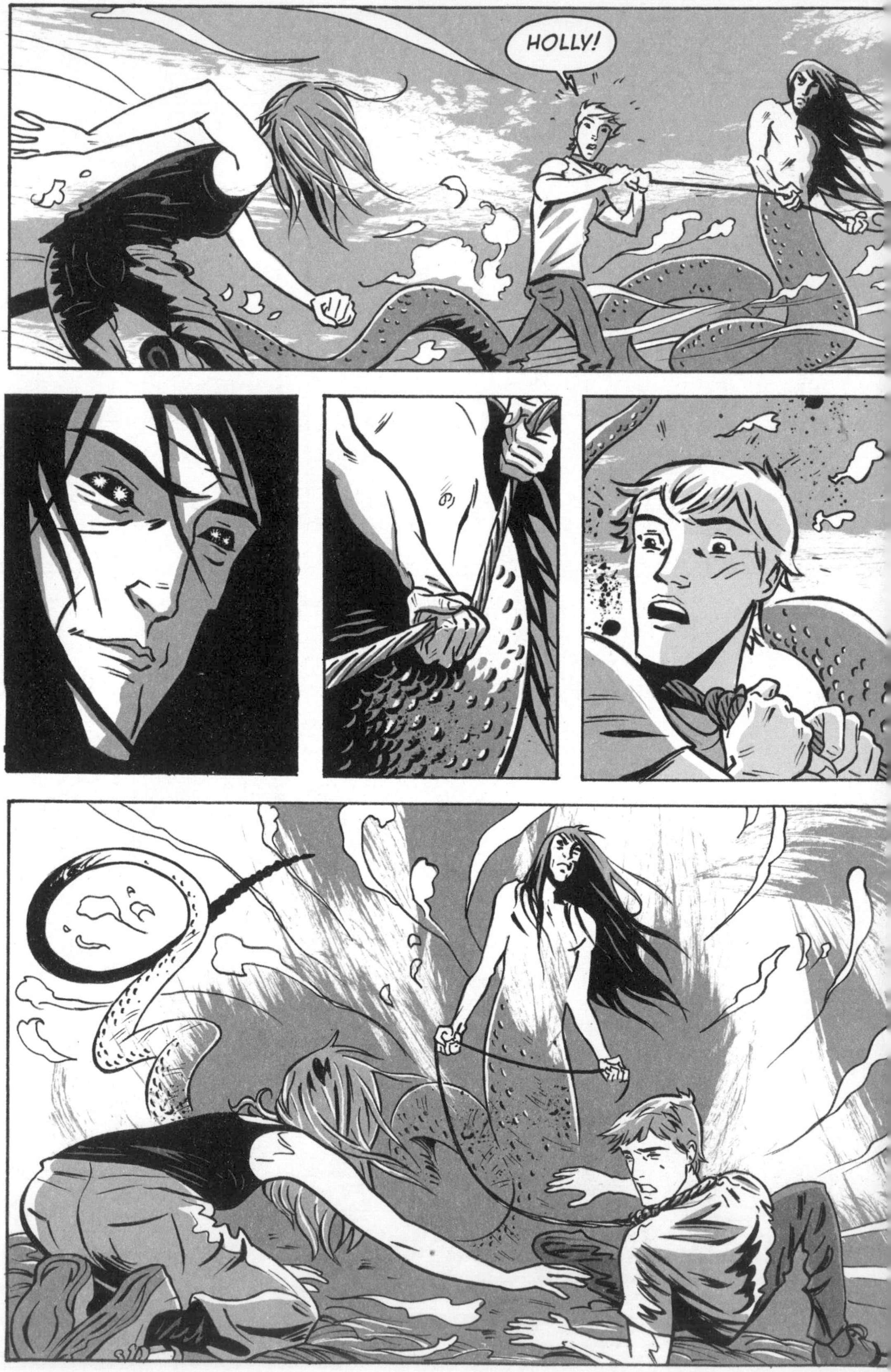
HOLLY!

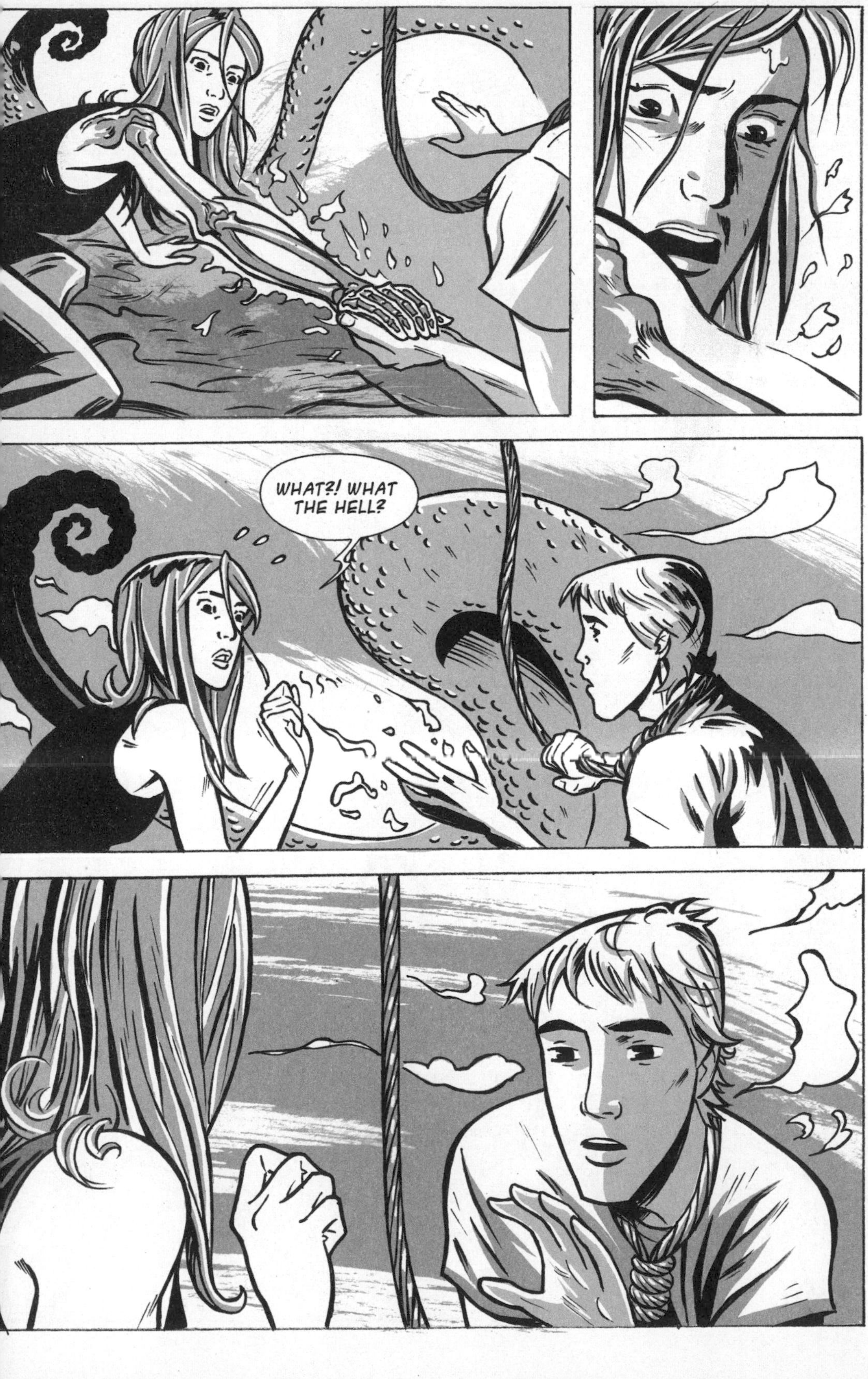
WHAT?! WHAT THE HELL?

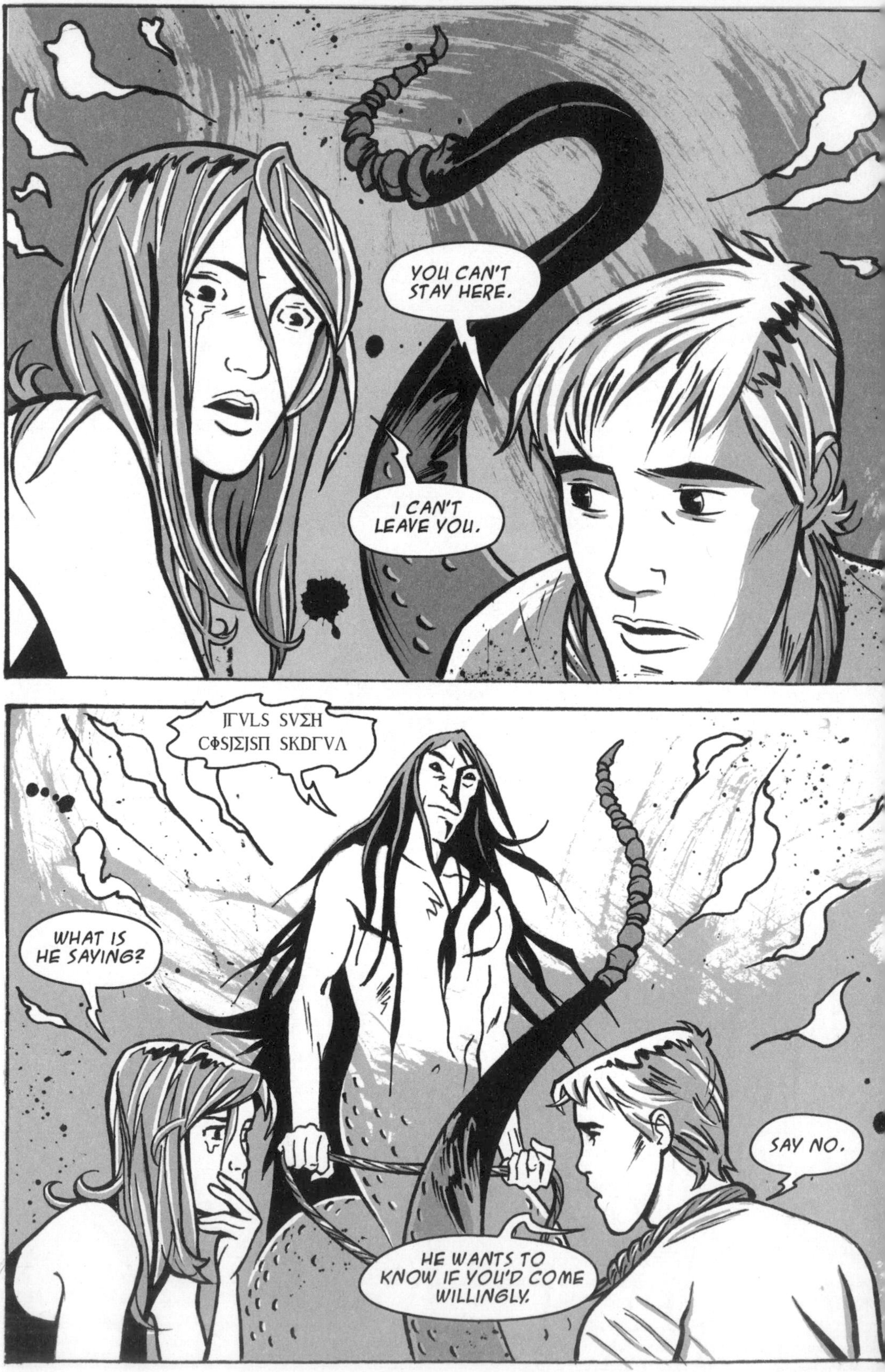
YOU CAN'T STAY HERE.
I CAN'T LEAVE YOU.
JΓVLS SVΣH CΦSJΣJSП SKDΓVΛ
WHAT IS HE SAYING?
SAY NO.
HE WANTS TO KNOW IF YOU'D COME WILLINGLY.

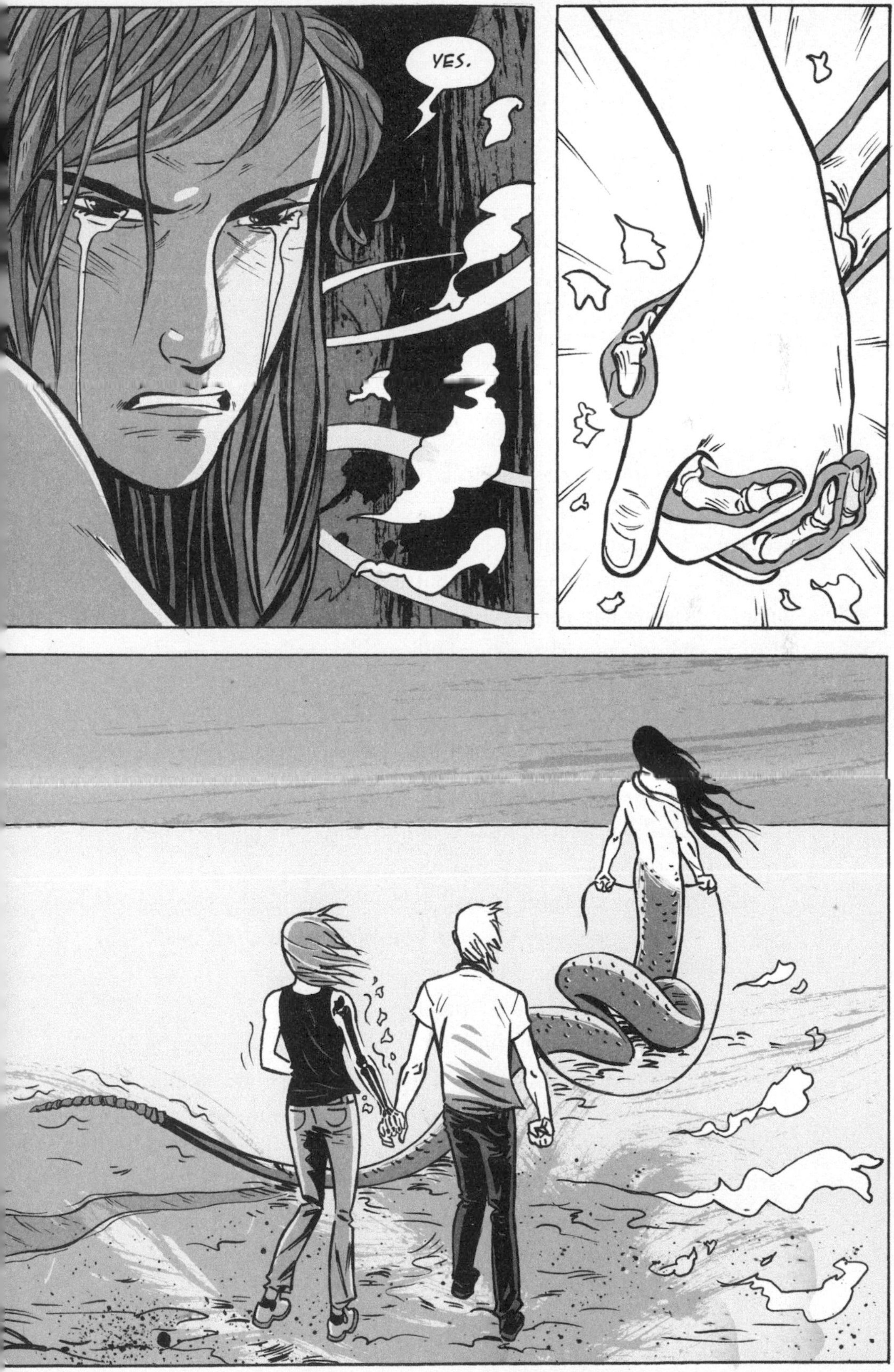
YES.

Savitri

48 minutes after

At the police station, phones shrill, tripping over each other. A line of ragged people wait in a row of chairs. One claps at something invisible while practicing arguments alone. Officers stream in and out and cluster in small groups, talking in hushed, hurried voices. In the corner, an outbreak of laughter jolts through me.

Dear World, shouldn't you stand still now? Ruined and reverent?

Time keeps moving as if nothing has changed in the forty-eight minutes since I put my hands on Corey's skull. The detective who helped me stop screaming, who turned me away from the scene and walked me down an alley to let me keen and rock, that detective now leads me to a "private room," an interrogation room, and informs me he'll be right back. He shuts the door and I close my eyes.

Contradictory thoughts pinball around in my head. *Corey can't be gone. . . . If Holly goes with him, then at least Corey won't be alone. And, God, don't let her die.*

Keep breathing, Holly. Keep breathing.

I stand up, and the chair flips out from under me, clattering against the floor. The hospital is a couple of miles from the police station. Sixteen minutes—probably less, considering the adrenaline in my system. Less than sixteen minutes of the pavement under my feet and I could be with her. I pace, getting nowhere.

The police wouldn't let me ride in the ambulance, not even after everything changed—when I told the detective that Holly and Corey are a cop's kids.

The EMTs had dragged Corey onto the asphalt and left him. No sheet, no gurney, his body reduced to a piece of evidence. Once the detective told them to "prep the scene," that "Sergeant Paxton might come," they pulled on bright purple gloves and wrestled Corey's body into a bag. I turned away before they pulled the zipper closed.

Pressing both hands against the side of a building, I crouched and vomited on the street—acid and bile erasing Corey's mint.

An EMT checked me over. He gave me a thin green shirt—hospital scrubs—wrapped in a plastic bag. I couldn't get it open. He ripped the plastic and helped me pull the shirt over my head, guiding my arms through the short sleeves. I realized how I must have looked—down to a sports bra and covered in blood. When I tried to turn around to see, he told me to look forward ("Just another second, miss"). He gestured with a towel at my cheek and then brushed my jawbone. The towel came away stained. He handed it to me and I wiped the blood off my arms, but without water, the outlines remained. Red lines snake down my arms even now. And the shirt has a Rorschach pattern of blood on it from where it touched my stomach.

Keep breathing, Holly. Keep breathing.

The door swings open and Detective What's-His-Name enters. For the first time, I look around. Grimy beige floors, cement-block walls, and a barred window that has been cracked open to let the claustrophobia escape. But I'm sixteen minutes of pavement away from Holly.

Detective What's-His-Name seems too young to be a homicide detective, with his close-cut hair and body that hasn't been ruined by coffee and doughnuts. Someone else—a woman in uniform—brings me a plastic cup filled with tap water. The minerals in the water spin before they settle. I force myself to keep still.

The woman introduces herself, and I wonder if I'm supposed to remember her name. Detective What's-His-Name and Detective What's-Her-Name. Partners. She tucks a file under her arm, rights my chair, and gestures. I sit and try to take a sip of water, but it splashes onto my upper lip. *Why can't I stop shaking?* I put the cup down.

33

"How is Holly?"

The woman says, "She's in surgery."

WHN says something else, but I ignore him. Holly is alive. I try not to think about blood loss, stroke, cardiac arrest, or the other thousands of ways life can slip away. I try not to think about the days my mother sits with shoulders slumped when a birth goes wrong. So many ways to lose someone.

Keep breathing, keep breathing.

WHN taps the table and the sound ricochets through me. I tune back in. "Savitri. Don't you want to help her?"

"What? Of course. How can I do that?"

"By answering my questions. Aren't you interested in finding who did this to her? Don't you think that would help her? That it would help Corey and his family get whatever relief they can find?"

Help Corey? *Help Corey.* The phrase sticks in my ears, worming its way into my mind, where it lodges. I didn't help him. Not when it mattered. Not like the Savitri in the story I was named for. Savitri-Devi saved her husband from death. And me? Well.

"Savitri," WHN says. "I need you to focus."

Okay. My mind goes blank—every thought passing through it too fast to catch. "He shot them." *Why? Why did he shoot them? What was the knife for? What was that tassel thing he came out with?*

WHN leans back and folds his hands. "Okay, what would you do if you were at the hospital?"

I shake my head. I'd send *keep breathing* vibes to Holly and sit vigil in a waiting room, avoiding the expressions of the twins' parents. Trisha will be a wreck and Sergeant Paxton will be upright, impassive, and in shock. I'd be crying, leaning against my mom. But maybe I'd stop shaking.

Truth is, I'd be as useless as I was while Wiry squared his shoulders and took aim.

"At least here you can help her."

34

Which finally gets me out of my head.

"Yes," I say. Meade, that's his name. "Okay, Detective Meade."

I take him through the afternoon step by step. He raises an eyebrow when I tell him about Holly's slip on the building top. As I'm talking through Corey's handstand, the irony hits me: we thought freerunning was perilous and glamorous; we thought we could predict where the danger was coming from. One close call, one risky move—both survived. Train enough and life bows to you. Train enough and nothing can touch you. Train enough and you can lie to yourself all you like.

When I finish telling him everything, I say, "I'd like to be at the hospital. I need to call my mom. She can—"

"I have some questions about the shooter. How tall was he?"

"Five foot five, maybe?" Judging from where the Dana's roof came to his chest.

"Weight?"

"Thin. Wiry."

"Race?"

"White."

"Hair color?"

"I couldn't see it."

"Eye color?"

"He was wearing a hoodie and jeans," I say, grasping.

"Any symbol on the hoodie?"

"I don't know."

"Scars?"

"I don't know."

"Any distinguishing marks?"

"I don't know."

I'm useless.

When we are finally done, Detective Meade closes the file and opens the door. In front of us, Sergeant Paxton is leaning against the wall, and as we come out, he stands up, perfectly straight—iron spine and a face of angles and ridges. His white T-shirt is blotched with what I assume is Trisha's mascara and eyeliner.

"Ron," Meade says. "I hoped you'd come. I'm sorry for your loss."

When Meade reaches out to shake Sergeant Paxton's hand, he gets a floppy yellow spiral notebook followed by a small black one.

Sergeant Paxton says, "Unsolved cases and open cases."

A shudder starts at the top of my head and races down my back. Oh. Oh. Wiry didn't target Holly and Corey. He targeted Sergeant Paxton's kids. A police officer must make innumerable enemies.

"This will help," Meade says. "Thanks."

Sergeant Paxton nods and then turns his heavy gaze on me. Intellectually, I understand that he doesn't know what happened, that he is here only to find out who killed his son. But still, I feel an accusation settle on my shoulders: *Milliseconds mattered and you just sat there.*

My throat tightens—too tight to ask what I need to know. And maybe I don't really even have the right to know: *Is Holly still breathing?*

Holly

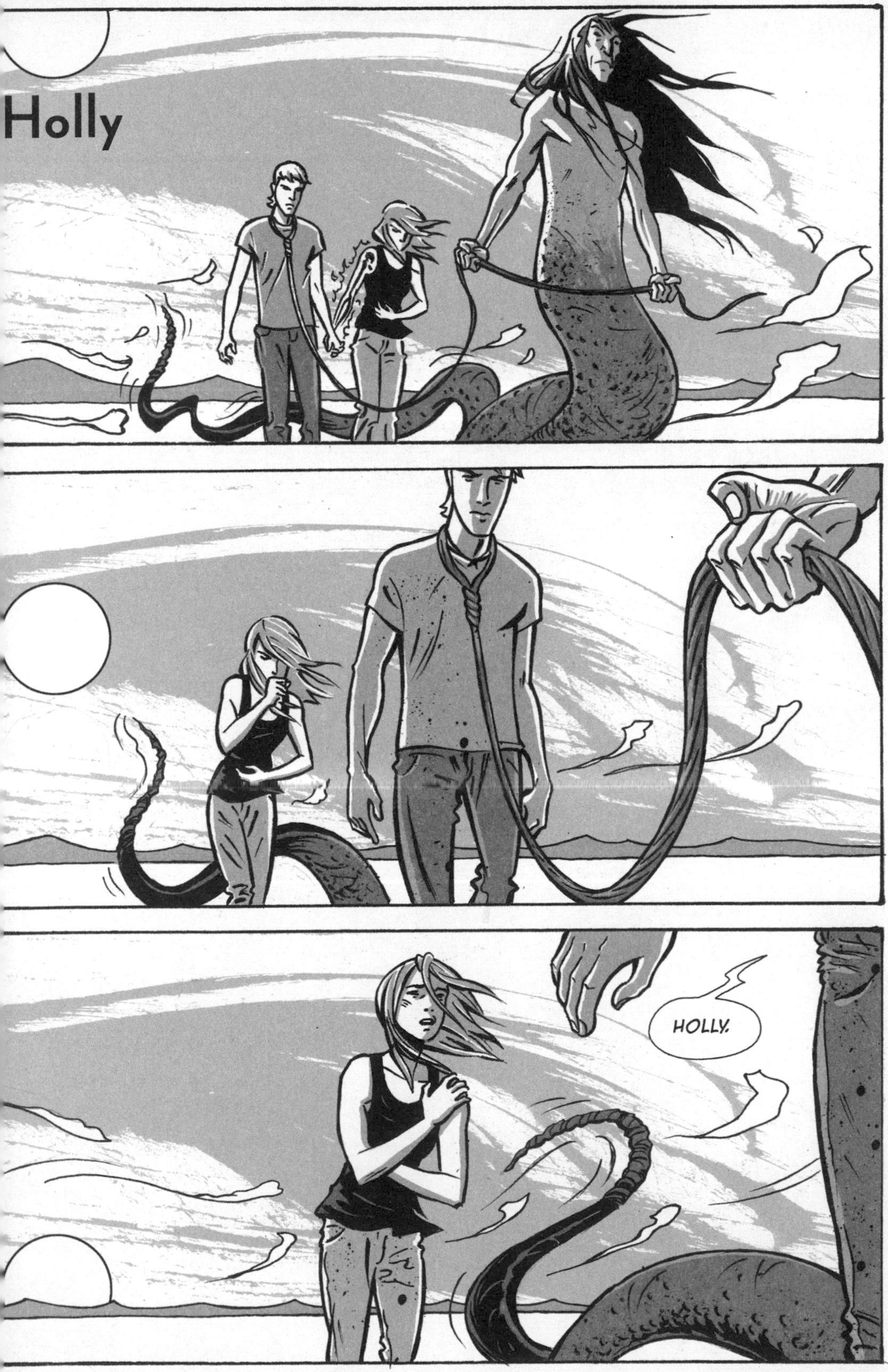
HOLLY.

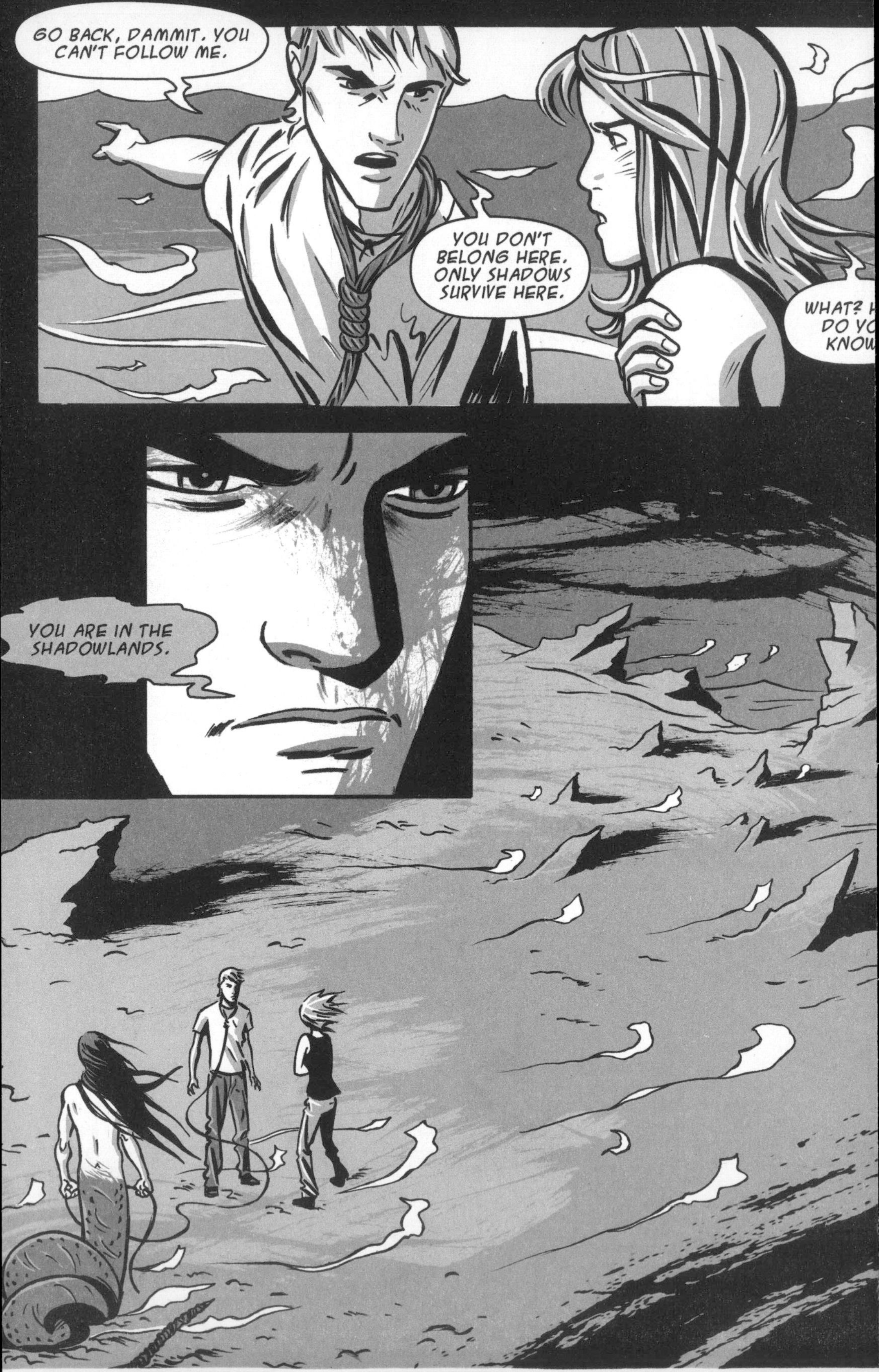
GO BACK, DAMMIT. YOU CAN'T FOLLOW ME.
YOU DON'T BELONG HERE. ONLY SHADOWS SURVIVE HERE.
YOU ARE IN THE SHADOWLANDS.

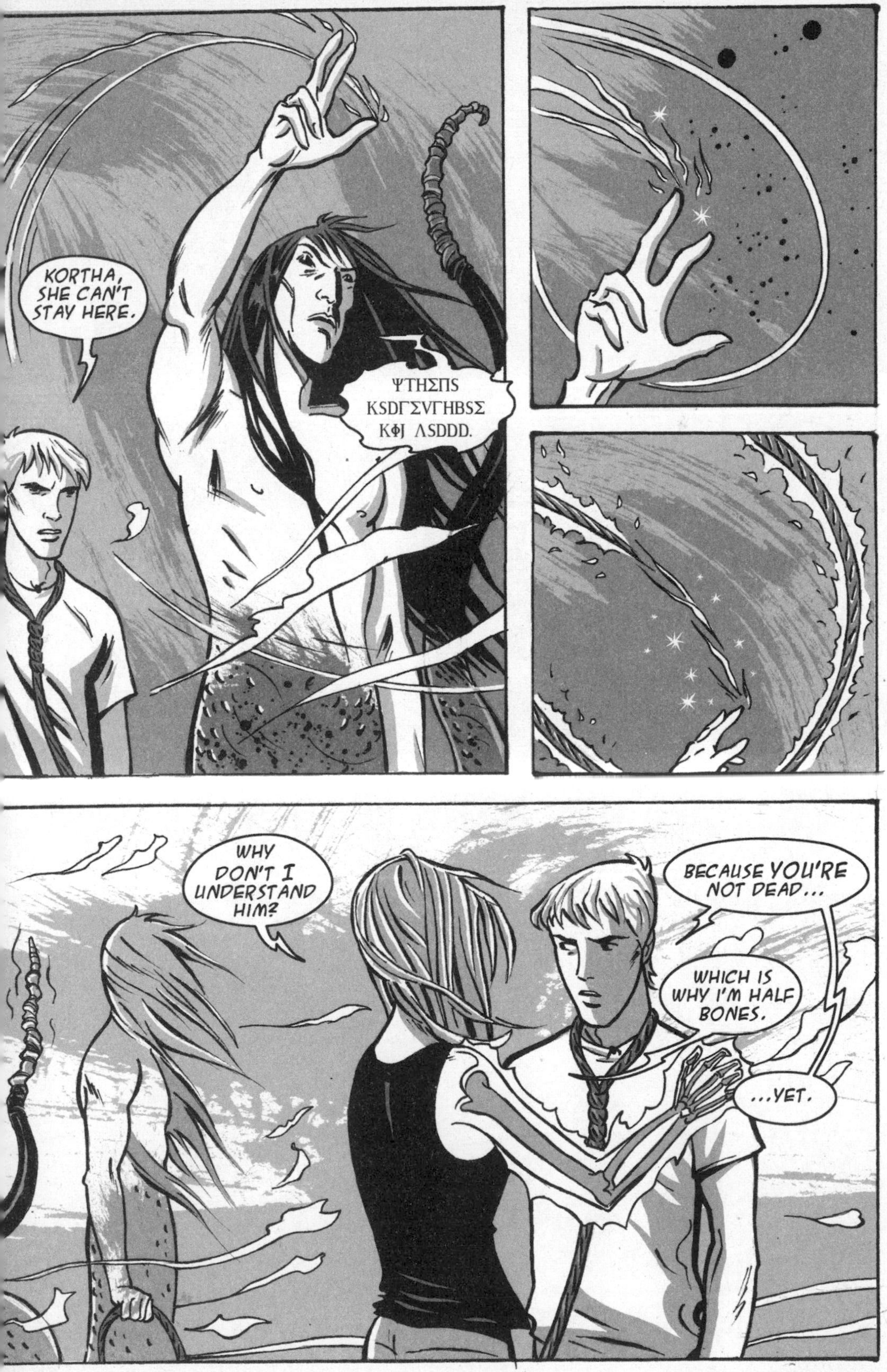
KORTHA, SHE CAN'T STAY HERE.
ΨTHΣΠS KSDΓΣVΓHBSΣ KΦJ ΛSDDD.
WHY DON'T I UNDERSTAND HIM?
BECAUSE YOU'RE NOT DEAD...
WHICH IS WHY I'M HALF BONES.
...YET.

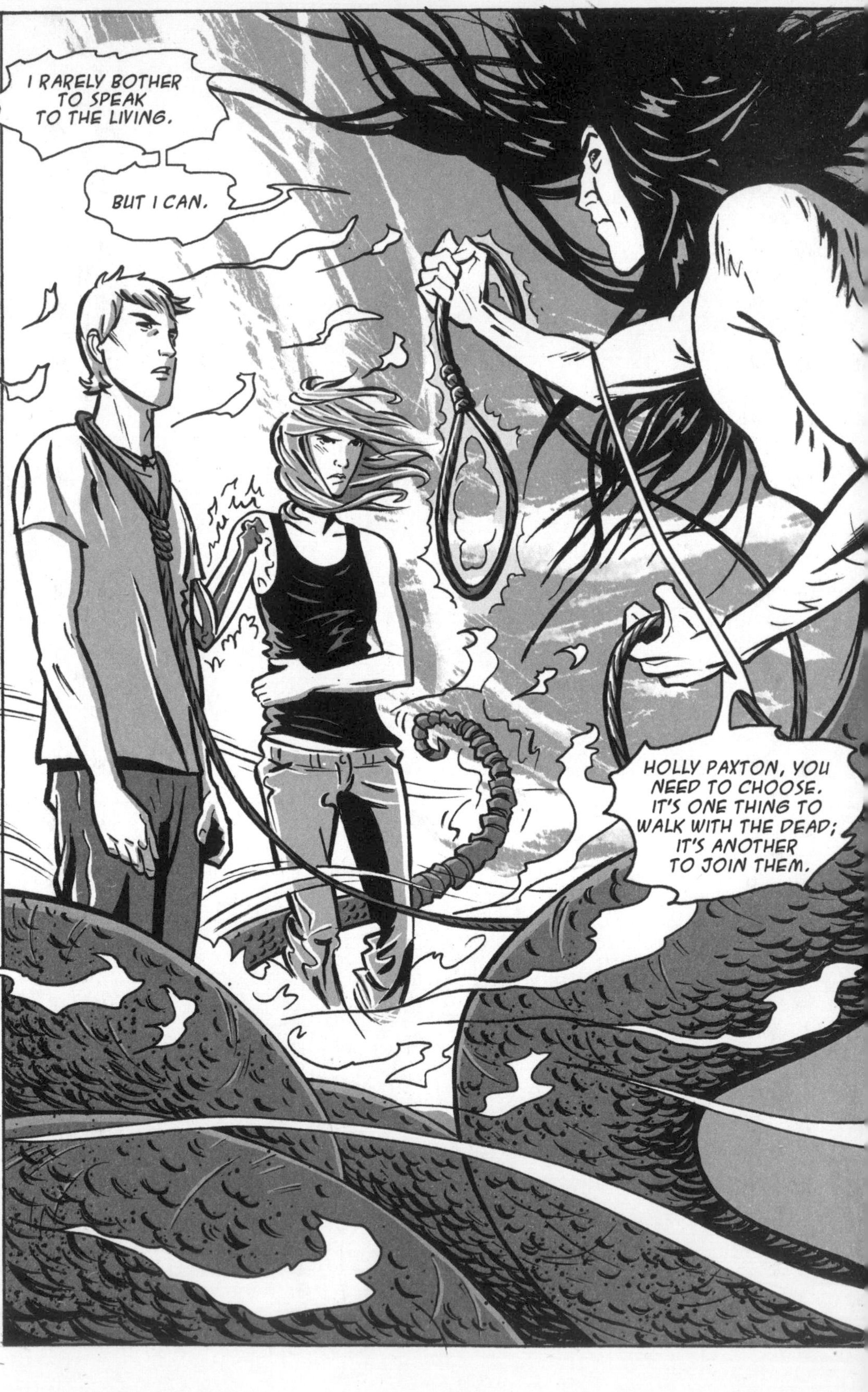
I RARELY BOTHER TO SPEAK TO THE LIVING.
BUT I CAN.
HOLLY PAXTON, YOU NEED TO CHOOSE. IT'S ONE THING TO WALK WITH THE DEAD; IT'S ANOTHER TO JOIN THEM.

Savitri

Unknown minutes after

You're told there's nothing you can do but wait and watch. So you wait. And you watch. You become an expert at watching. So good at it that you even watch yourself.

As soon as you arrive at the hospital, time starts to move erratically. The clock in your head stops. Entire days that are actually only seconds pass. Like when you are waiting to see her after surgery. While you were at the police station, during "the golden hour"—the time in which she could be saved, if the pressure in the skull was relieved—they drilled a small hole in her skull and drained the blood. You waited in post-op for seventy-five m-i-n-u-t-e-s. In those seventy-five endless minutes, you stayed in your mother's arms on a green couch in a private conference room, watching her parents flip through emotions unpredictably . . . clinging to each other, screaming at each other. When the doctor says there were no complications, Sergeant Paxton leaves Trisha's grasp, kisses the St. Christopher's medal he wears around his neck, and gets down on his knees, hands clasped.

The first time you see her, you realize that "she looks like she's sleeping" is Hollywood nonsense. Machines stand guard around her, pumping in life. Their various colored tubes and wires crawl under her blankets and hospital gown. A needle is secured to the back of her hand with three white butterfly Band-Aids. You had thought it would be in the hinge of her elbow. ·

Someone prepared you for the bald patch on her head. You can't help

41

but worry about how she will respond when she sees they shaved part of her hair. Her hair is what *Cosmo* would call her "standout feature." Long and auburn. She spent precious morning minutes on it, curling, straightening, doing up, adding silver extensions on her eighteenth birthday last week. It will take months for that patch of hair to grow back and longer to forgive the neurosurgeons.

You weren't prepared for her face. Not pale like she's sick, not flushed like after a run, but a lifeless color, as if what is keeping her alive has gone underground. The pink in her lips is buried under layers of colorless skin. Every cell in your being wants to climb into hers and wake her up. But you remain—as ever—a witness.

Full days that are actually hours crawl by.

Outside her room, you look at brain scans and see the impact of the bullet—a small chip and a long river of black where her skull split. You are told that she is lucky, that the bullet didn't touch the gray matter, that they are hopeful. One overeager intern tells you that if he had to get shot in the head, this is how he'd want it. And for a moment, you ponder a world where he gets his wish.

You search for a McDonald's a nurse told you about that is hidden somewhere in the labyrinth of basement corridors. You finally spot Ronald McDonald's sugar-charged grin. At the counter, you get stuck. How can you order fries and root beer without her cherry pie? You can't, and the cherry pie goes to waste—getting hard and cold in her room.

When it's your turn to sit with her, you haul a large leather chair across the room, scuffing the floors. Everyone else wants it on the right, but she is left-handed. During your nights on, when you're relieving her parents, you sleep on a fold-out chair and have to ask for more of those thin, waffled covers that provide no heat. Your eyes are just closing when she suddenly starts to thrash, her body torquing at the waist, her legs whirling through free space, while you press the button and scream for a nurse. She is in pain, you tell the doctors. But they say no—it is not a seizure. It means nothing. And in that instant, you suspect her doctors are incompetent. They were the ones who put her into this coma, this barbiturate-induced coma to keep the swelling down, to prevent brain damage. And now, now, they can't get her out.

For some reason, no one says her name anymore. Not her mother, whose hair has remained in the same hurry-up bun since you arrived. Not her father, who has more and more questions each time you see him and who never sits—always at the ready, even though there is nothing to be ready for.

You never say her name either. Unless you are talking to her. Then you say "Holly, Holly, Holly" in every sentence practically, as if she is simply lost and might come when called.

You plead, you beg, you comfort. When that doesn't work, you talk and talk and talk. You talk about the things you've done together. You remind her about the time you forgot your wallet and she flirted with a creepy guy until she got you a free milk shake. Or the time you brought your Indian comic books to second grade and everyone stared at your blue-skinned, multi-armed Gods with a mixture of horror and curiosity. You had tugged on your braids, praying for a good smiting, but then she yelled, "Cool!" And in that instant your neighborhood playmate morphed into your best friend. Even at that age, she understood without being told what was sacred.

You try not to cry; sometimes you succeed.

You succumb to negotiating with thin air. You tell the silence: *You already took Corey. Doesn't that meet your quota? No? Then take someone else. Take the seven-year-old next door who leapt headfirst into a shallow pool.* You know you're becoming a horrible person and take the thought back. Sort of.

You try to tell her she is strong and she should fight, but your throat gets too tight because Corey was strong too, and perhaps death isn't something you can fight. You work hard to ban all thoughts of Corey, all thoughts of death. They cannot enter or they might take hold. They are not for this hospital. Not for this room.

Just when you are ready to crawl into her bed with her and join her, wherever she is, your mother tells you it is time to go home. But if you go home, you'll be outside this bubble.

Out there, there are bullets and death and funerals. And you will not let those outside thoughts—Corey's blood and S&W 9 mm—inside this room or inside your head because you need to stay above those murky, guilty waters.

Besides, if you step outside and return, will you contaminate this place with the no-hope vibes that wait out there? No-hope vibes you just know are clustering in school hallways, gathering around water fountains, and proliferating beside lockers. No-hope vibes that are implied in Channel Nine's coverage, where reporters become actuaries, tabulating the probability of recovery.

Your mother persists. What about school? You protest—you talk about how you've been very efficient from the ICU, reading the books she's brought, emailing your homework. She says she's worried about *you*, but you tell her that *this* is where you need to be. She sighs; she can't say no to you, not right now. So she continues to bring you changes of clothing and food you can't taste. She finds a shower for you in her ob-gyn department. Much of the time, she stays with you.

Once, when you're back in the ICU and you're watching her again, you fish a safety pin from your bag. You unfasten it and stare at the sharp end. It doesn't gleam or twinkle. But it does draw blood when you stick it in her arm. You watch her face but nothing changes. You clean up the blood, cursing her stillness and stoicism. Why won't she come back? She needs to come back. Now.

You discover that there's a deadline for healing, a deadline for hope. She has seven more days. Seven days of hope before "temporary" becomes "permanent." Permanent comas are different. Permanent facilities have perfect carpets and no scuff marks on the floor where the position of the chair has been fought over. Life on hold is better than life after the hold is over.

And time, the thing that has been eluding you, grinds into motion. You are no longer floating outside space and time and your own body. You are no longer watching because now you have to do something. . . .

I have to reach her.

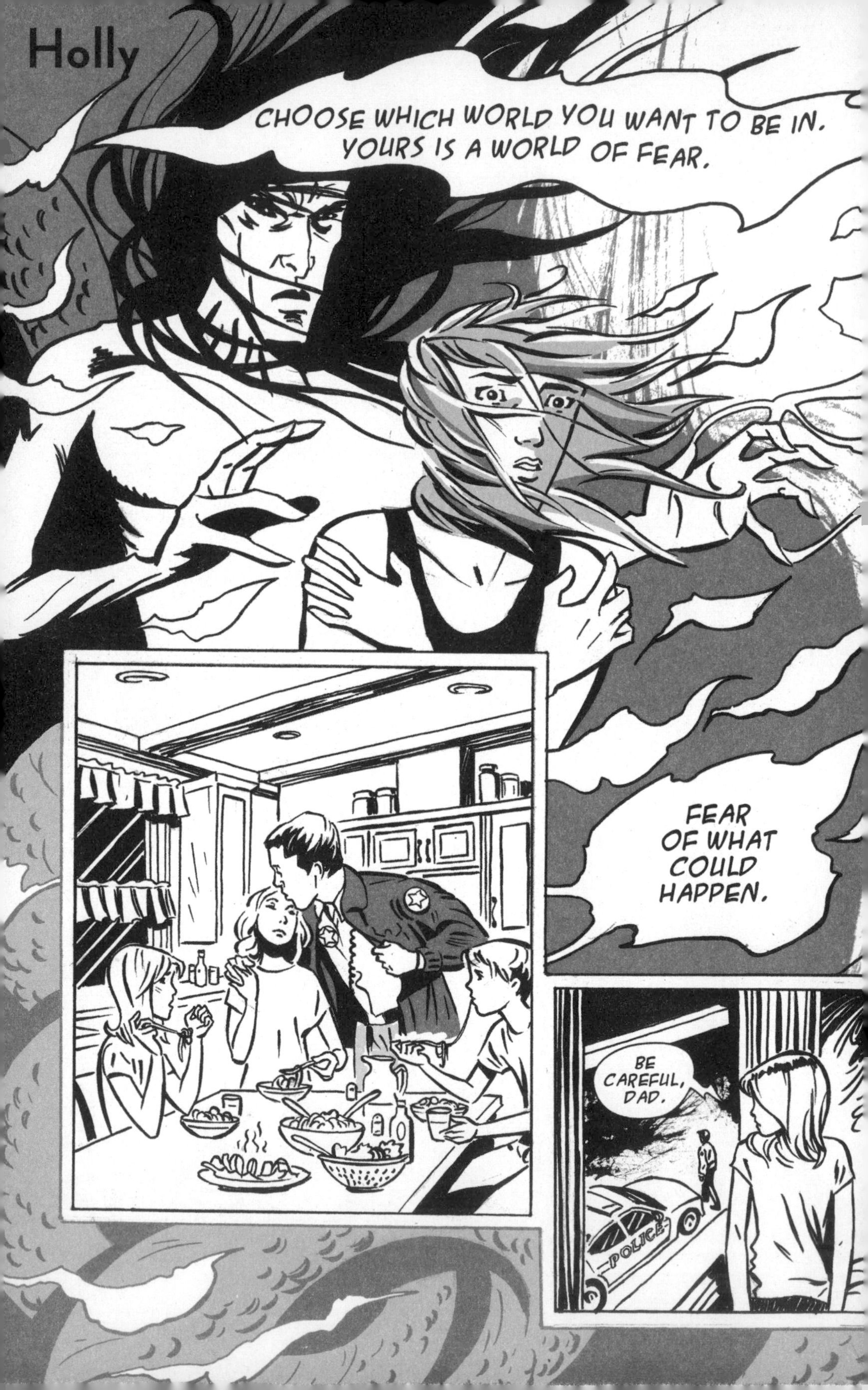
CHOOSE WHICH WORLD YOU WANT TO BE IN.
YOURS IS A WORLD OF FEAR.
FEAR OF WHAT COULD HAPPEN.
BE CAREFUL, DAD.
POLICE

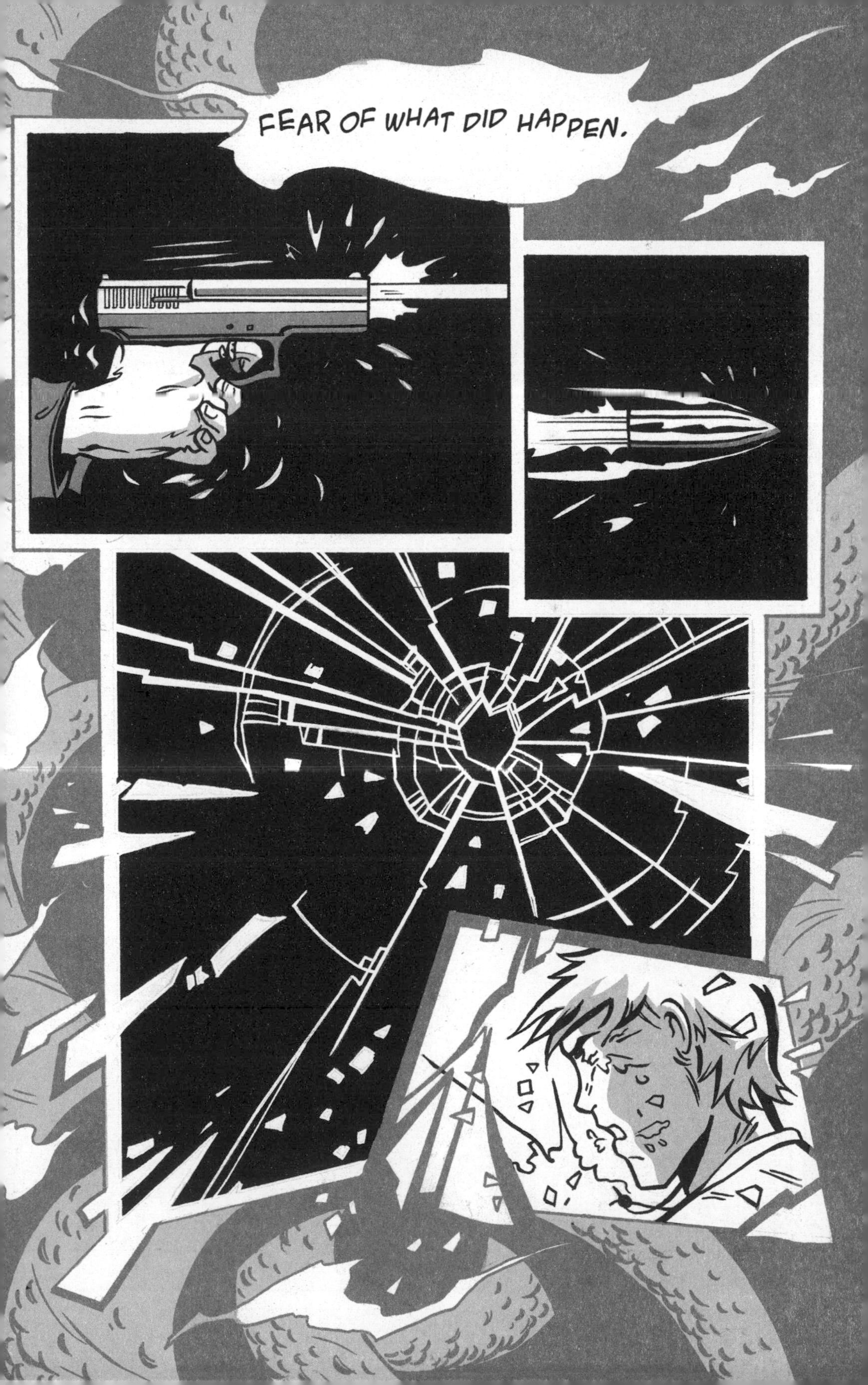
FEAR OF WHAT DID HAPPEN.

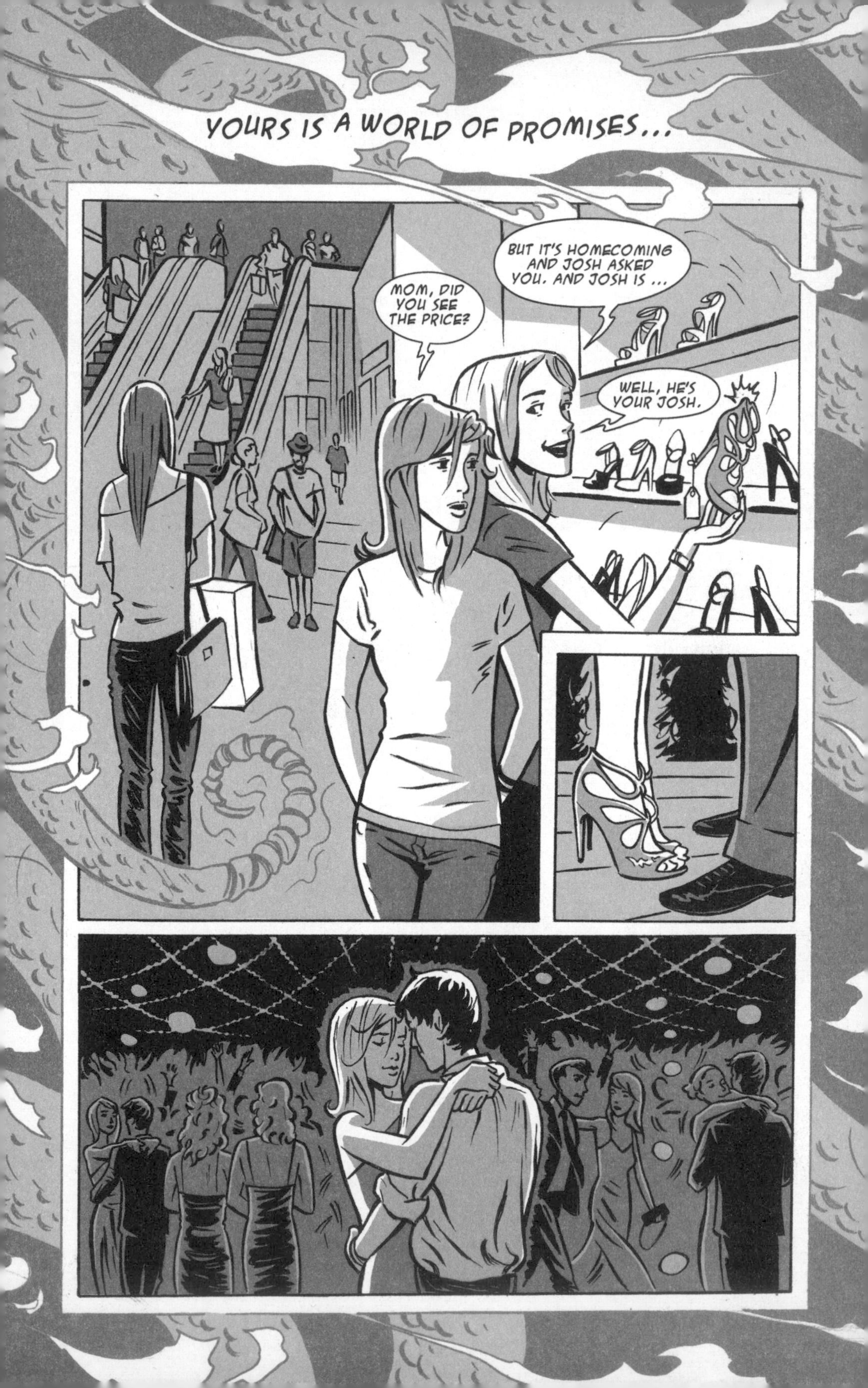
YOURS IS A WORLD OF PROMISES...
MOM, DID YOU SEE THE PRICE?
BUT IT'S HOMECOMING AND JOSH ASKED YOU. AND JOSH IS ...
WELL, HE'S YOUR JOSH.

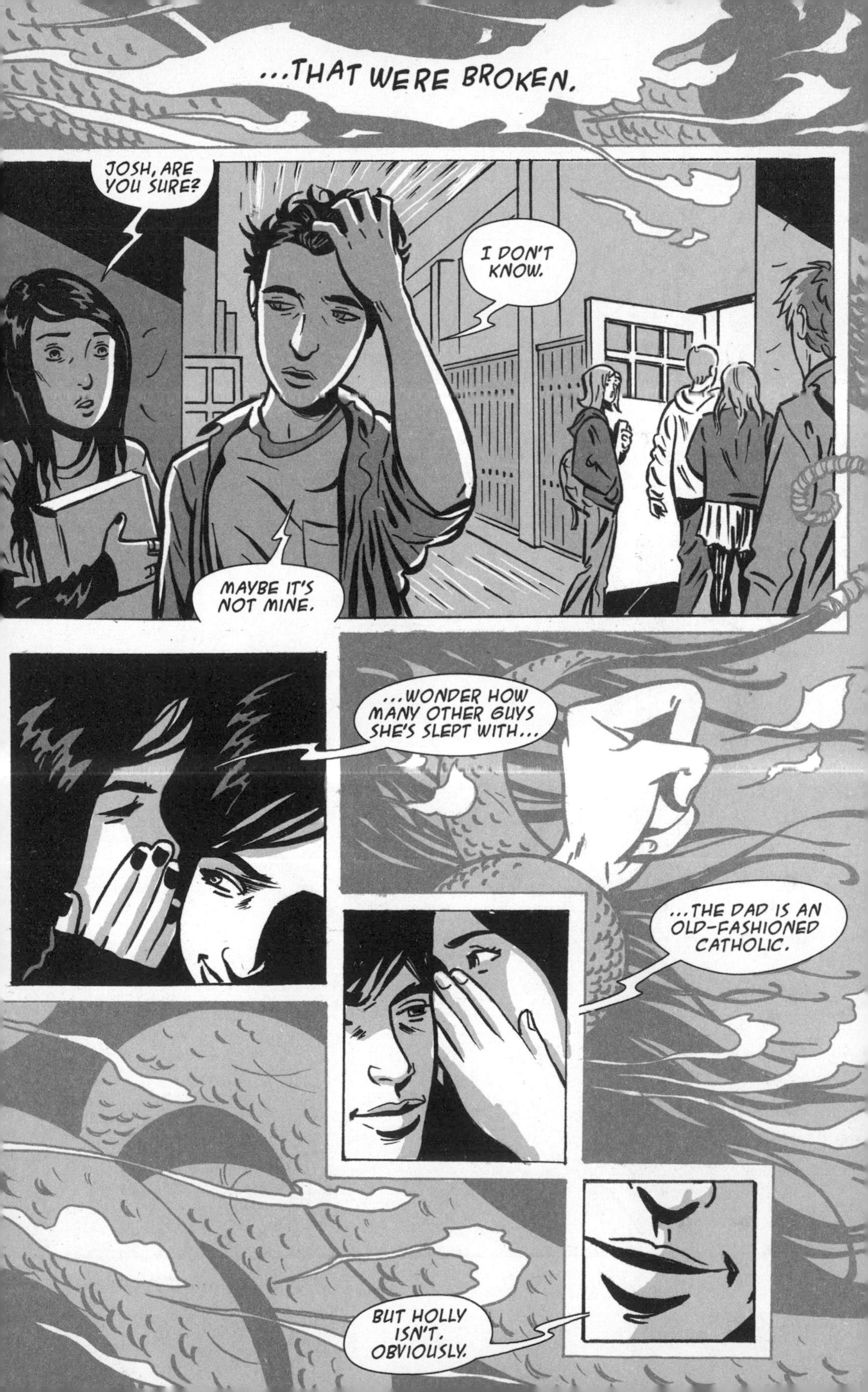
...THAT WERE BROKEN.
JOSH, ARE YOU SURE?
I DON'T KNOW.
MAYBE IT'S NOT MINE.
...WONDER HOW MANY OTHER GUYS SHE'S SLEPT WITH...
...THE DAD IS AN OLD-FASHIONED CATHOLIC.
BUT HOLLY ISN'T. OBVIOUSLY.

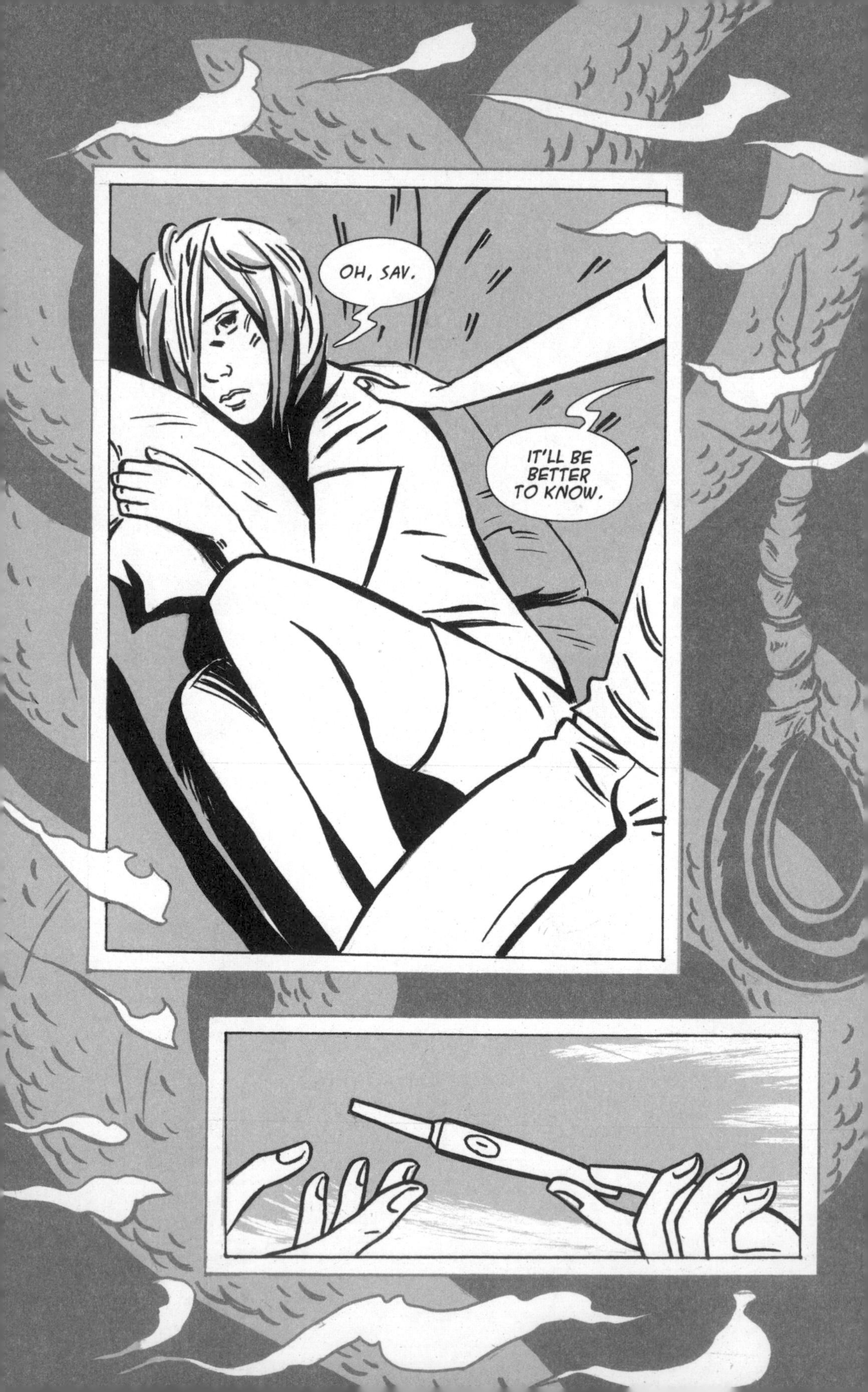
OH, SAV.
IT'LL BE BETTER TO KNOW.

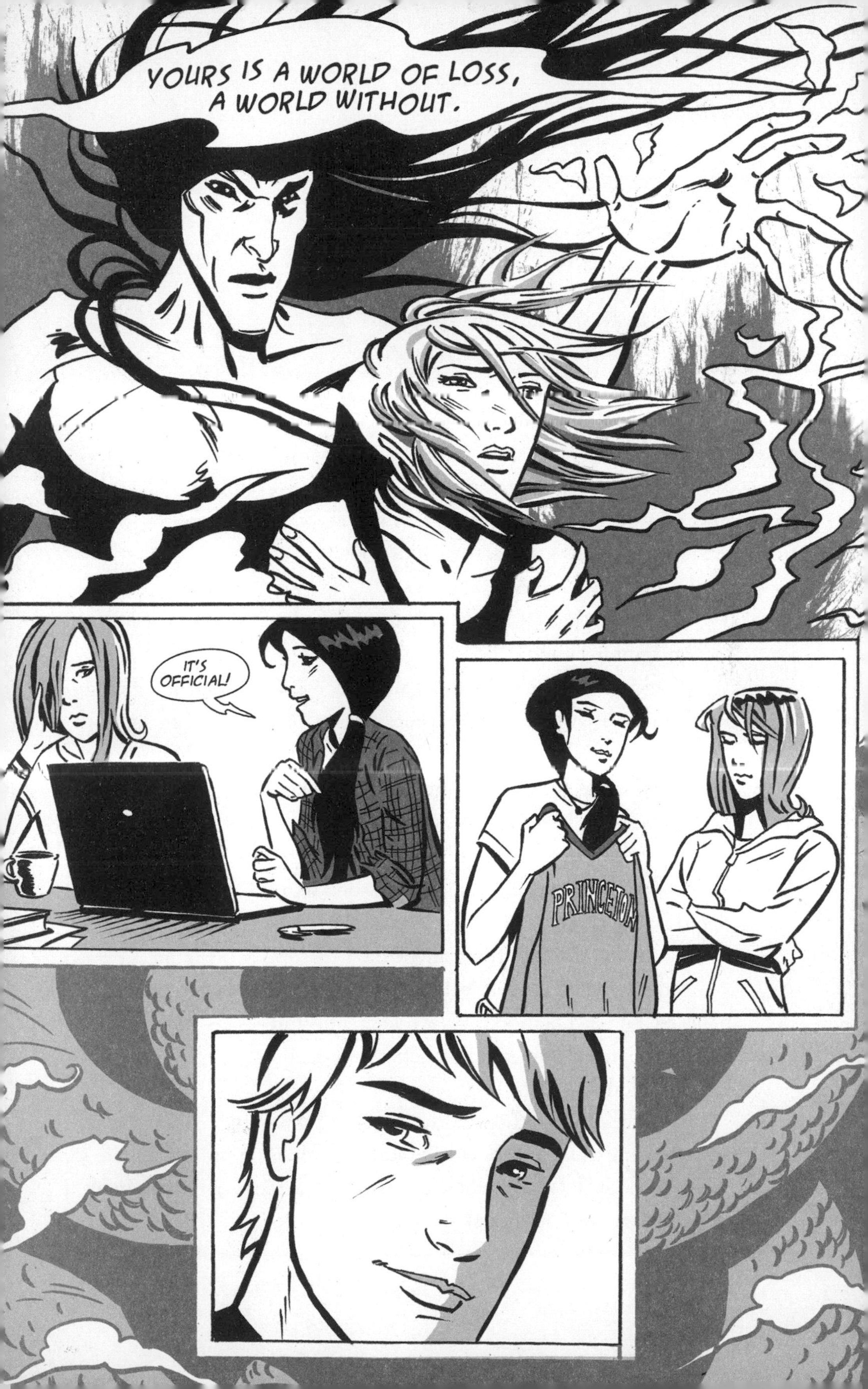
YOURS IS A WORLD OF LOSS, A WORLD WITHOUT.
IT'S OFFICIAL!
PRINCETON

Savitri

7 days and 18 hours after

When I leave the hospital, sunlight assaults me. I blink and blink, but my eyes won't adjust. My mom grabs my elbow, leading me. She hands me her keys once we are in the parking lot.

"Why don't you drive?" she asks.

She knows that I'll be better behind the wheel, with something to still my spinning mind.

I glance at her; she looks as she always does—her blunt-cut hair curls just below her jawbone, her makeup consists only of kajal to line her eyes, and her posture remains neither ramrod straight nor slumped. Her show is, I assume, for me. Keeping me calm by keeping herself calm. But her composure is belied by one telltale trait: she is mouth-breathing.

I take the keys and we get in the car.

I suppose she's one up on me; I'm beyond trying. Calm isn't the goal. Speed is: the faster I can get back to Holly, the better. I drive over the speed limit and she doesn't say anything.

After spending a week in the hospital's efficient spaces and sterile hallways, my neighborhood's old-world architecture seems oddly foreign. Even our living room—plush couches and open archways—seems too big, too colorful.

At home, I hurry through the ritual of showering, brushing teeth, and changing clothes. The letter from Princeton is on my bed. I leave it there, untouched. When I come downstairs, the scent of frying onions, garlic, and mustard seeds makes me pause.

In the kitchen, a pot of chole is sitting on the burner. Mom is spoon-ing a puri out of the hot, bubbling oil. My favorites. She knows better than to tell me to slow down, knows that if she says it, I'll bolt out of the door.

"I wasn't going to stay," I say.

"You don't have to," she says. "You can take it with you."

The sun has turned the walls a warm yellow, and even the hard wood chairs around our kitchen table look inviting. Here, I could eat off a heavy ceramic plate, not a light plastic tray. Besides, puris don't travel well.

Reading my silence, she gets out a plate and serves. I settle myself at the table, tear a piece off the puri, and watch the puffy bread deflate. I scoop up the chickpeas and eat. When the flavors hit my tongue—clean, sharp cilantro and dark, rich mustard—I have to fight back tears. I can't remember the last thing I've actually tasted.

No, wait. I can.

I fish a mint from my purse, slide it in my mouth, and suck till it's just a sliver. Then I slump in my seat.

"Maybe you should take a quick nap. You'll get better sleep here," she says.

If I head upstairs to my room now—the thick quilt on my bed, the familiar order of my bookcase—I'm not sure I'll leave.

"I've been away for forty-three minutes already."

She clicks her tongue and says, "Try not to worry, beta."

"Why can't she wake up?"

"Everyone responds differently to medicine. Maybe it's just taking longer for the barbiturates to move through her system. You need to start taking care of yourself, okay? Or you won't be able to take care of her either."

"Mom, not now. Once she wakes up."

She opens her mouth and then hesitates.

Don't say it; don't say "if she wakes up."

53

"Okay," she says, but she doesn't meet my eye.

Using the hidden key to unlock the Paxtons' door, I speed through the house to Holly's room, tearing the corner of a poster as I pull it down from the wall. I grab a stack of comics and a glue stick . . . and . . .

Corey's room beckons. I step inside and scan the walls—Diego Rivera poster, desk, and unmade bed. The last time we lay here together— could it really have been the last time? I sink onto the bed and curl his sheet and comforter over me, flannel against my skin, his scent still alive. My throat aches. No, no, no. I can't stay here. Holly needs me. No tears—stay frozen. I get scissors from his desk, clip off a corner of the sheet, and tuck it in my waistband—flannel against my skin.

On the way back to the hospital, I speed and slide around cars, making up for lost time. But when I get there, nothing has changed. The monitors beep, and the machines swish. Normal.

When I cross the threshold back to Holly's room, Trisha nods and then grabs some pamphlets from the bed and stuffs them into her purse. I catch a glimpse of a coffin.

"Can you stay with Holly? I just need to start making arrangements."

I try to say, "Okay" lightly.

How can Trisha plan Corey's funeral now? When his scent is still alive in the folds of his sheets. How can she let in any thought except Holly?

I can't think about Corey now. I focus on what I have left. When she goes, I pull the seat around to Holly's left side and thread my fingers through hers for a moment. Then I fish the glue stick out of my bag and push it a millimeter away from Holly's nostrils. The olfactory sense supposedly brings back memories.

"Remember this, Holly?"

Where do the memories of the dead go? Am I the only scrapbook of the three of us left?

Nothing changes—no fluttering of her eyelids, no twitching of her fingers. Just the whirring of machines.

Dear Coma, while we appreciate what you've done, keeping her brain from swelling, you have overstayed your welcome. It's time to leave the girl with us. You can keep the ICU.

If I had the Elmer's bottle, the kind we always used, would the sharp smell wake her? But this ridiculous purple stick was all I could find. I twist the base of the glue stick, and it emerges, like a fat, flattop lipstick.

"A new color!" she'd say. "It makes you fashionable and gives you that ultimate form of attraction—silence!" She'd pretend to smear it on and mime lips that couldn't be pried apart. I half laugh.

Holly's fingers are curled in toward her palm. I press them down against the bed and hold them there while I draw the jumbo glue stick across her palm, from wrist to the finger base five times, covering every inch of skin. When I let go, they resume their claw-like pose. I skip the fingers—too difficult to hold them open while sliding the stick.

I blow on her palm and wait.

When we were younger, we would sit at my kitchen table and spread glue over our hands. We'd chatter, poking the glue intermittently to test whether it had dried. When our patience was rewarded, we rolled the edges, creating a handle. We peeled the glue off and the second skin would carry the impressions of us—thin lines that stretched across our palms and coiled over themselves on our fingertips.

Now, in the hospital, I lean close to her ear, close to the bandage above her temple. I try to ignore the smell of blood and maybe another fluid.

"Holly," I say. "Remember this. Remember."

I try to roll the glue on her hand to find a handle. But nothing happens. I keep pushing and eventually I get a scrap of glue. I tug at it gently, but it comes free, bringing nothing with it. The glue stick spread a layer too thin, so all I can get are detached little pieces. No long, stretchy shadow of her, no second skin, just worms curling up her palm.

It's not a sign. It's not a sign of anything, I tell myself. Relying on superstition has a downside.

I switch tactics, pulling *The Leopardess: Origins* out from my bag of tricks.

I love the series because it's one of the few comic books that isn't generated by men for men. For starters, there is no Leopard—no man that the Leopardess is copying. And then there's the fact that she remains . . . well, fully dressed; she doesn't fight in costumes that show more skin than they cover. When I pointed that out, Holly smiled big and got the action figure she'd been coveting; she is all about "girl power."

I couldn't find her copy for some reason, so I open mine and read it aloud to her, hoping she'll imagine the pictures for herself.

Halfway through, the words turn to ash in my mouth. In comics, bullets seem avoidable, harmless, and fear is controlled with a snappy comeback. I once did a paper on the misrepresentation of women in comics—somehow I missed the misrepresentation of violence.

But *The Leopardess* is her favorite. For a fraction of a second her breathing changes—shallows. Am I getting through? Her eyes flutter and I say her name but . . . nothing. *Come back to me, Holly.* When I'm done, I put up her poster. It is *her* room, and no one is going to move her into a permanent care facility.

As I walk back to my chair, my foot slides on something—the comic book has hit the floor. I pick it up. My fingers brush the cover and then my forehead—an automatic gesture, ingrained by an Indian mother as a sort of apology for disrespecting the knowledge in a book. I've never understood people who dog-ear pages or desecrate the margins with notes. But now I carefully tear the pages out of the book, one by one, and tape them to the walls. Anything to reach her.

When I'm done, I return to my chair and my voice comes out strong and demanding. "You're my hero," *for teaching me how to live at full speed.* "And heroes don't leave."

I end up with her hand in mine, curled over her ear, repeating my two-word plea:

"Don't leave, don't leave, don't leave."

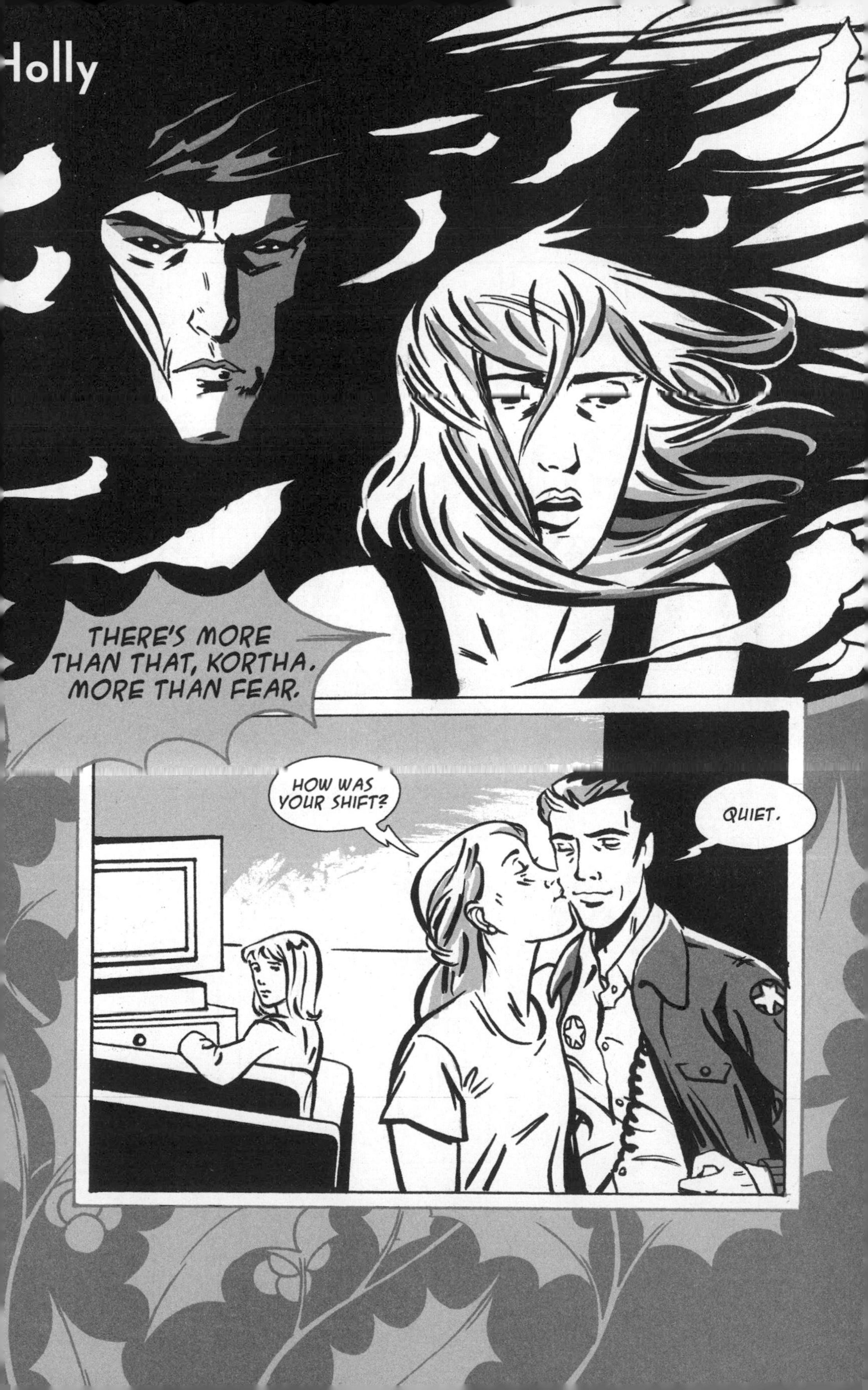
THERE'S MORE THAN THAT, KORTHA. MORE THAN FEAR.
HOW WAS YOUR SHIFT?
QUIET.

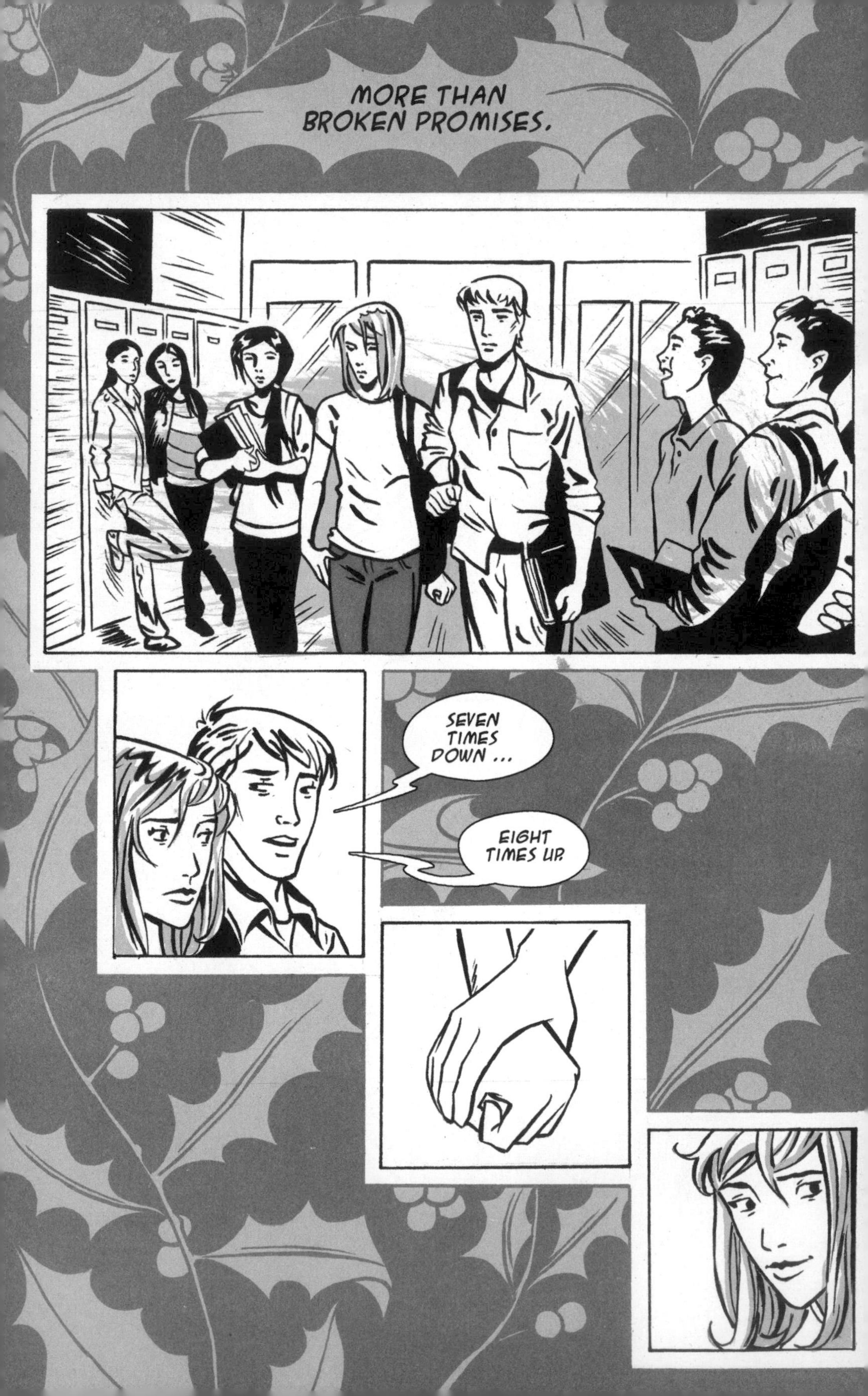
MORE THAN
BROKEN PROMISES.
SEVEN TIMES DOWN ...
EIGHT TIMES UP.

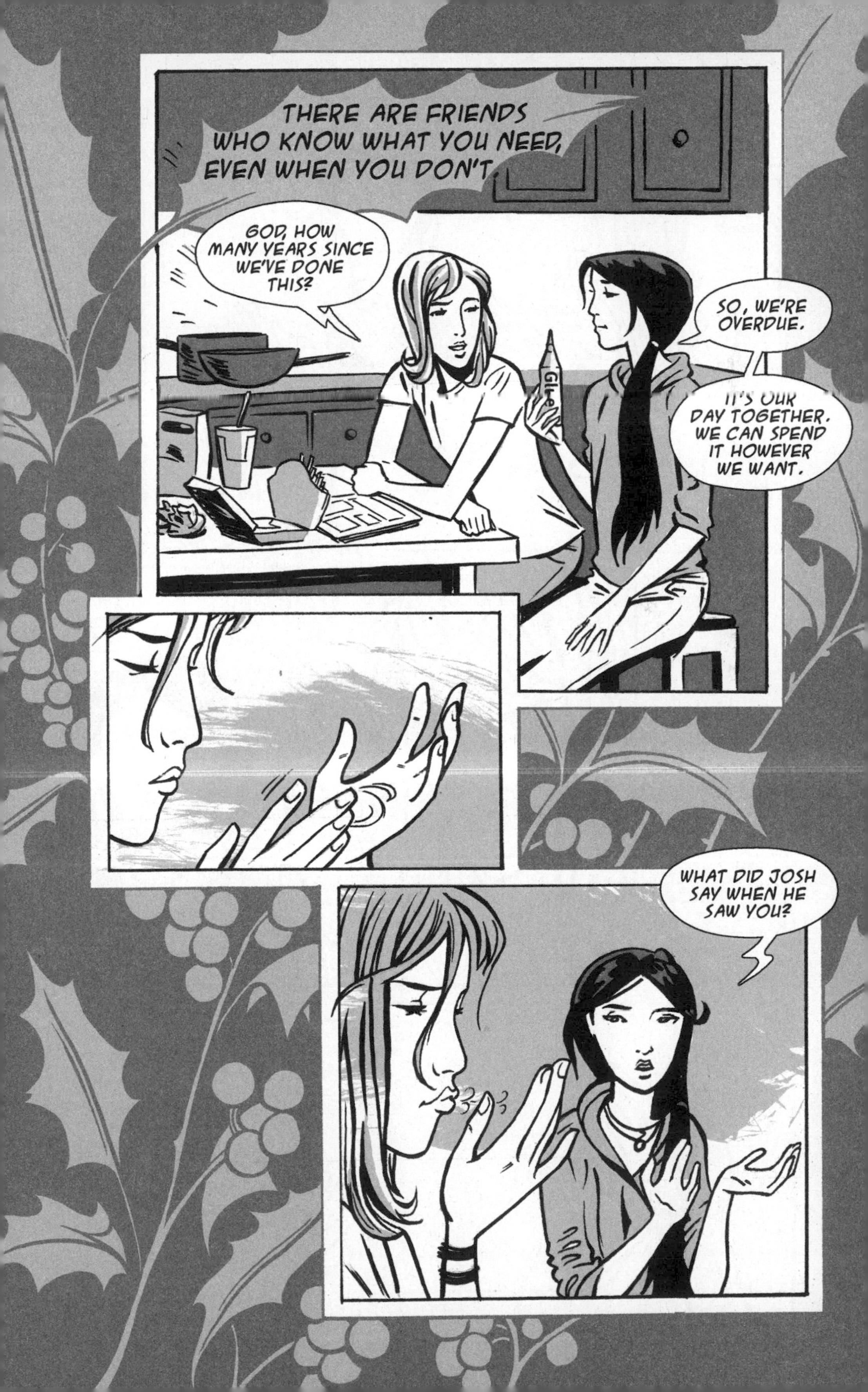
THERE ARE FRIENDS WHO KNOW WHAT YOU NEED, EVEN WHEN YOU DON'T.
GOD, HOW MANY YEARS SINCE WE'VE DONE THIS?
SO, WE'RE OVERDUE.
IT'S OUR DAY TOGETHER. WE CAN SPEND IT HOWEVER WE WANT.
WHAT DID JOSH SAY WHEN HE SAW YOU?

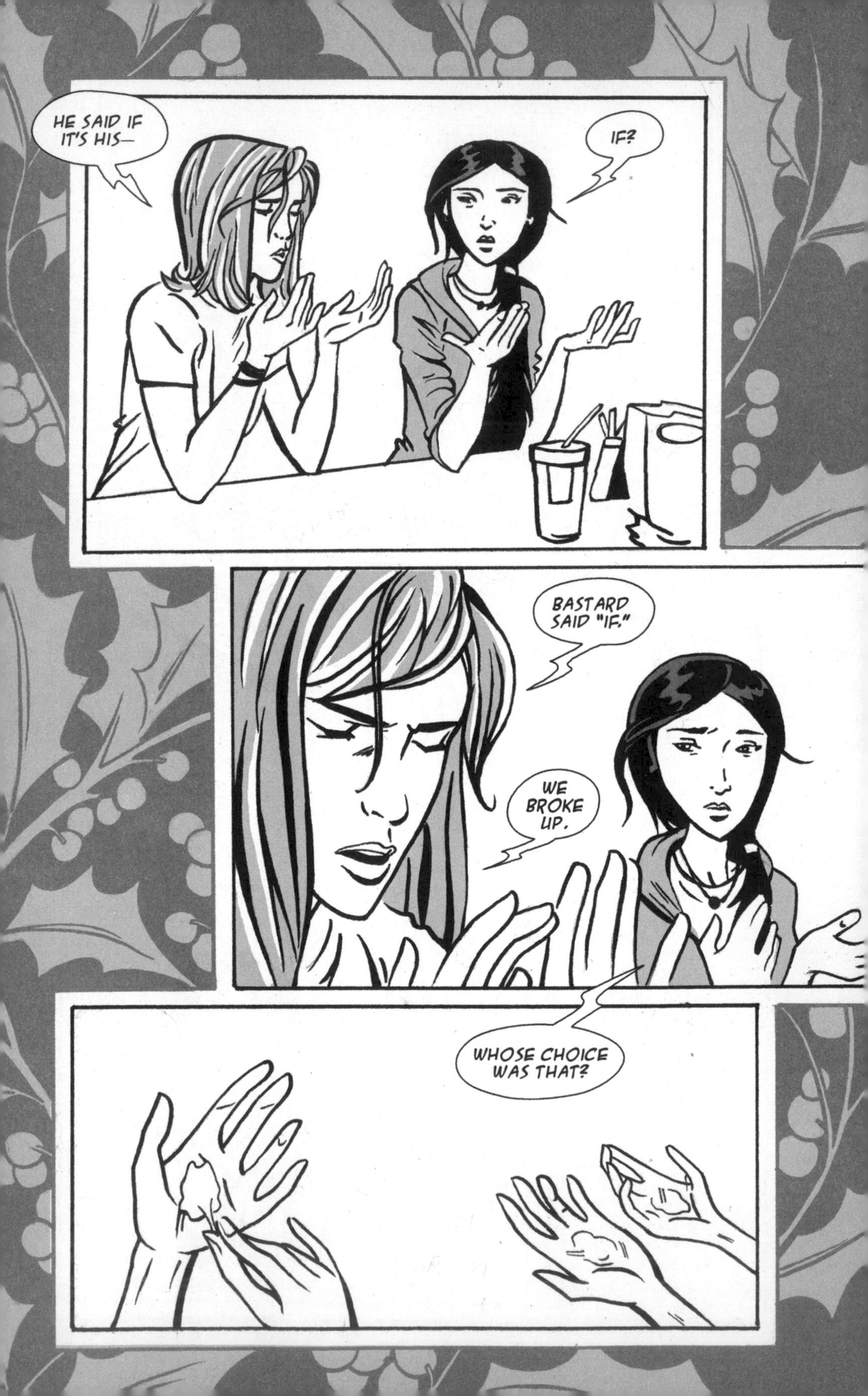
HE SAID IF IT'S HIS—
IF?
BASTARD SAID "IF."
WE BROKE UP.
WHOSE CHOICE WAS THAT?

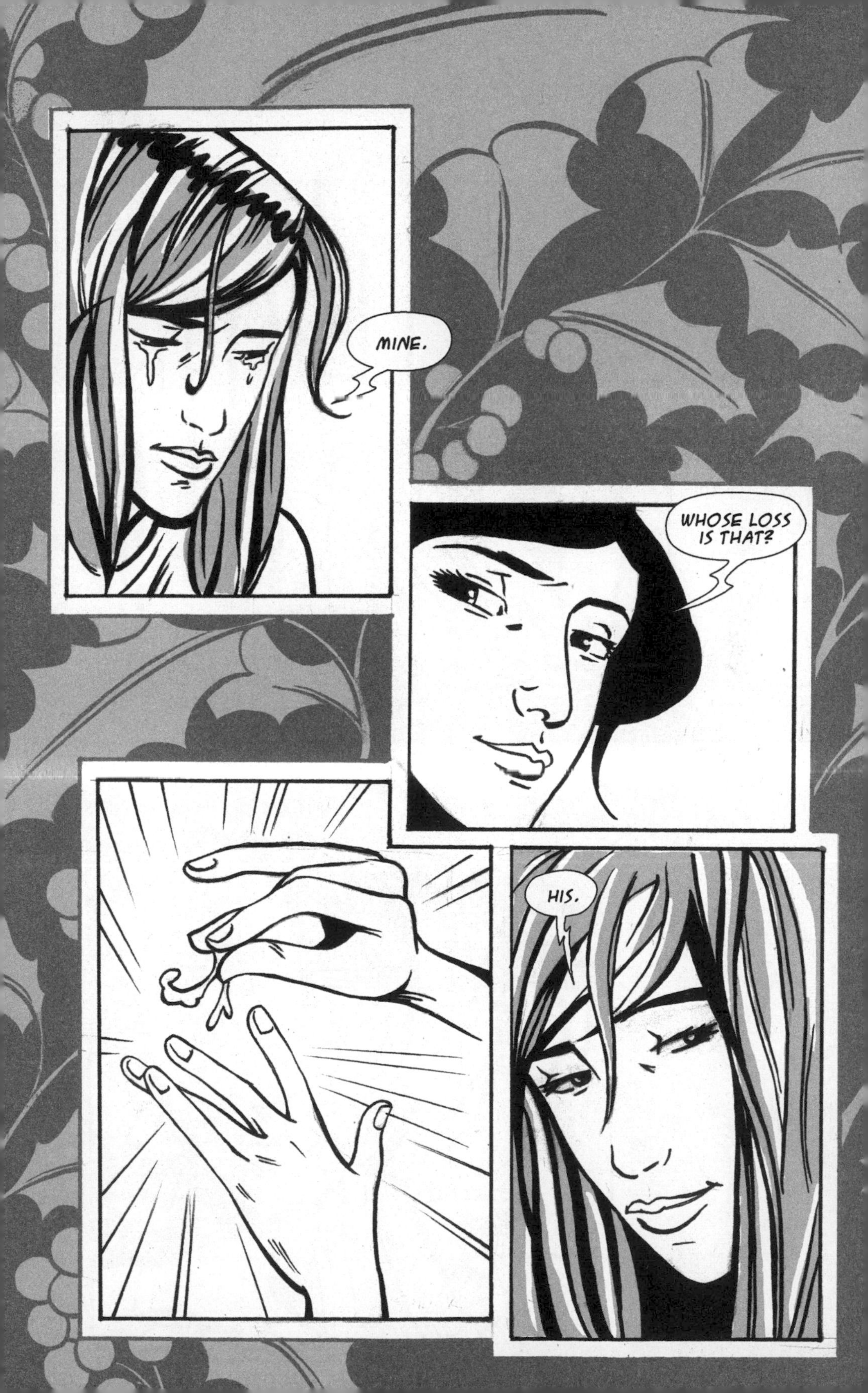
MINE.
WHOSE LOSS IS THAT?
HIS.

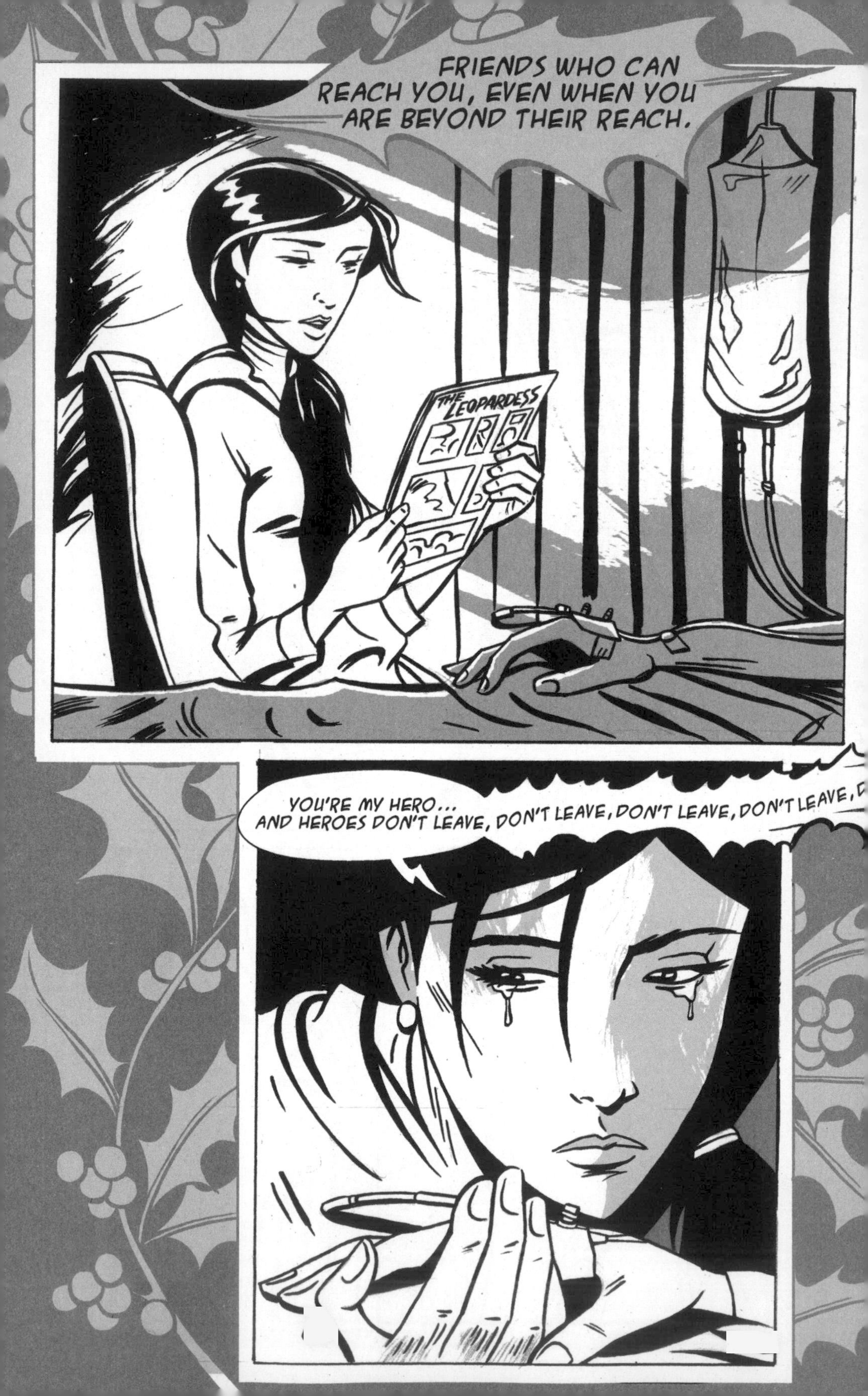
FRIENDS WHO CAN REACH YOU, EVEN WHEN YOU ARE BEYOND THEIR REACH.
THE LEOPARDESS
YOU'RE MY HERO... AND HEROES DON'T LEAVE, DON'T LEAVE, DON'T LEAVE, DON'T LEAVE,

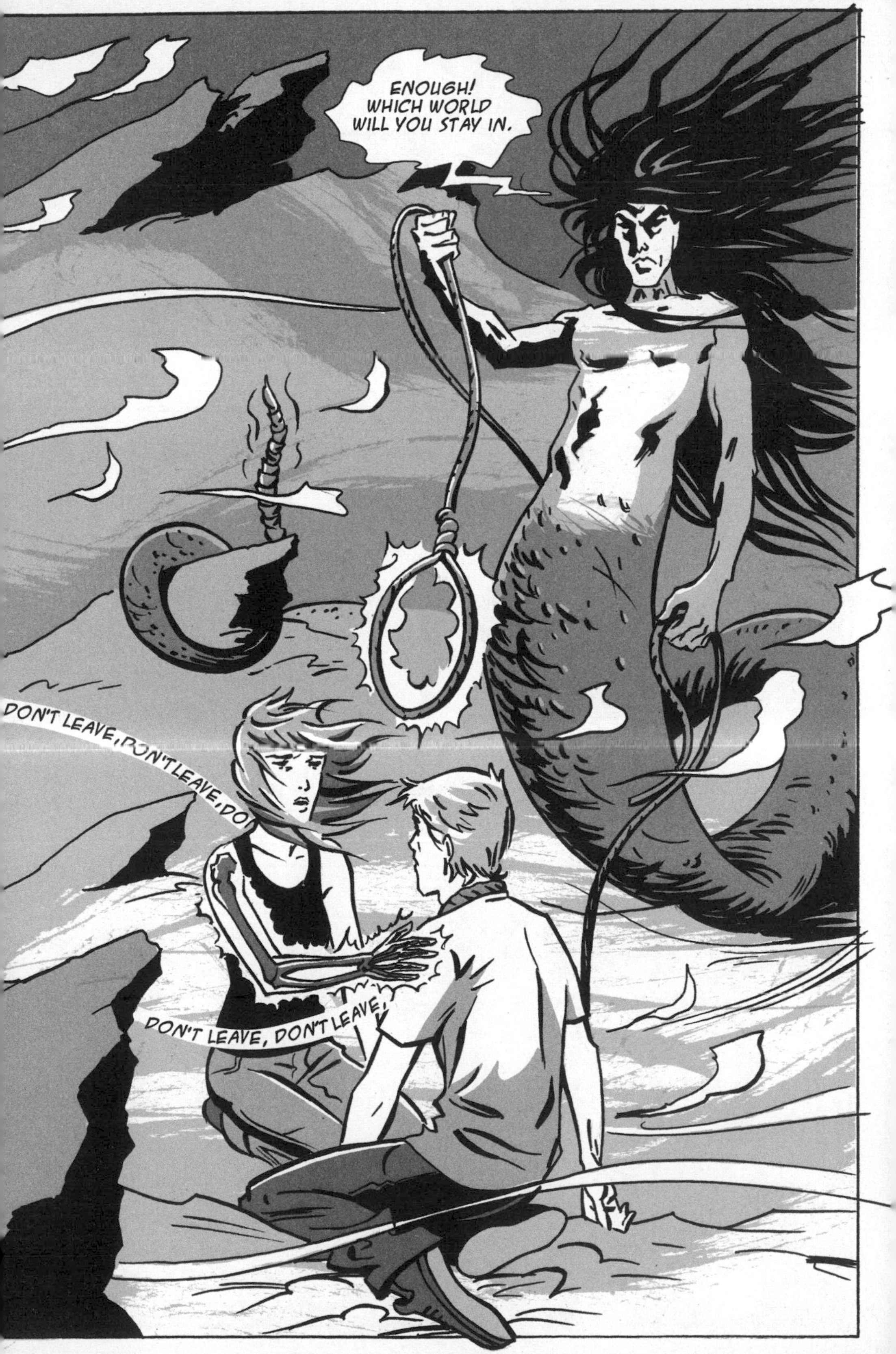
ENOUGH! WHICH WORLD WILL YOU STAY IN.
DON'T LEAVE, DON'T LEAVE, DO
DON'T LEAVE, DON'T LEAVE,

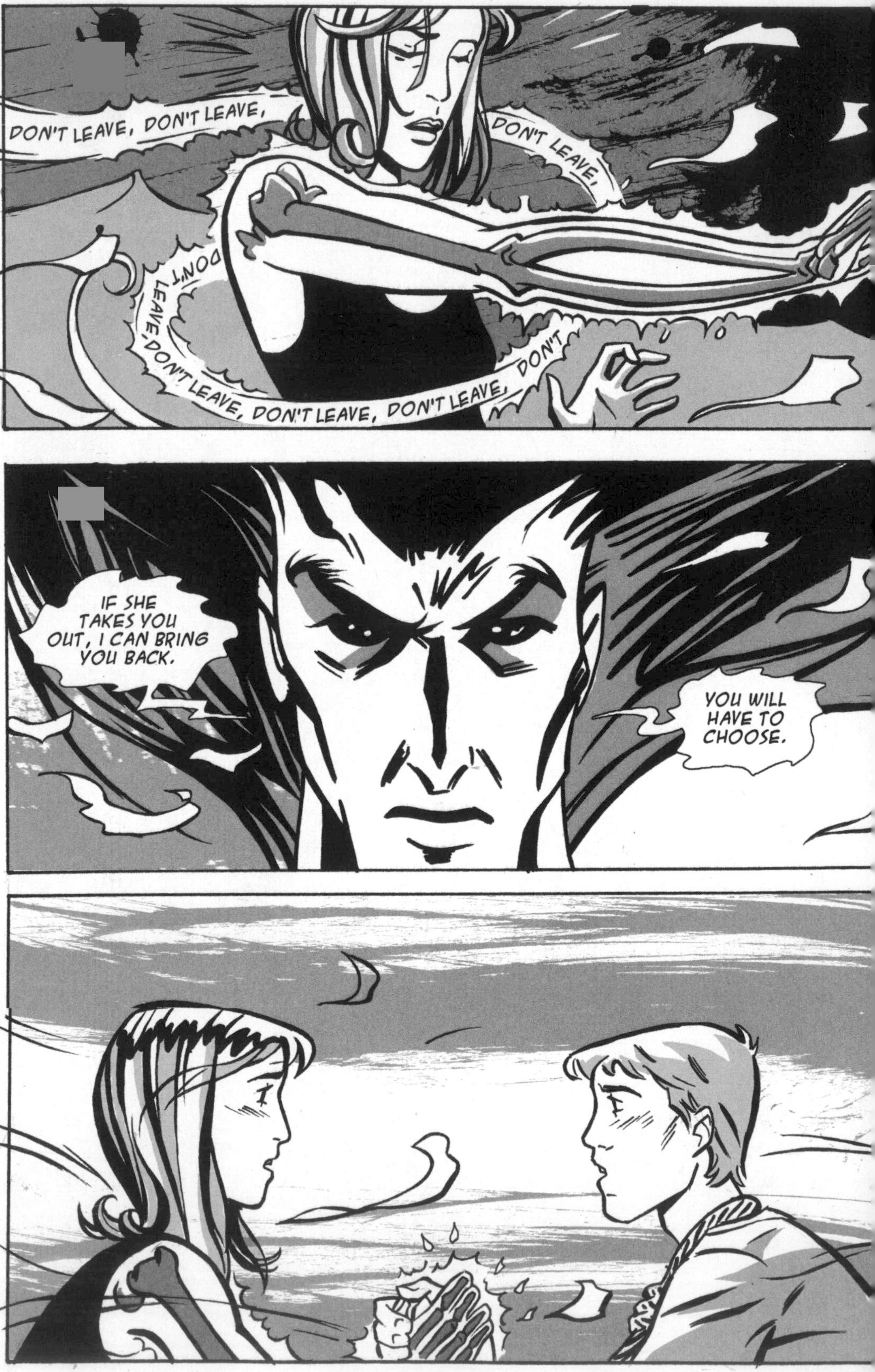
DON'T LEAVE, DON'T LEAVE,
DON'T LEAVE,
DON'T LEAVE, DON'T LEAVE, DON'T LEAVE, DON'T LEAVE, DON'T
IF SHE TAKES YOU OUT, I CAN BRING YOU BACK.
YOU WILL HAVE TO CHOOSE.

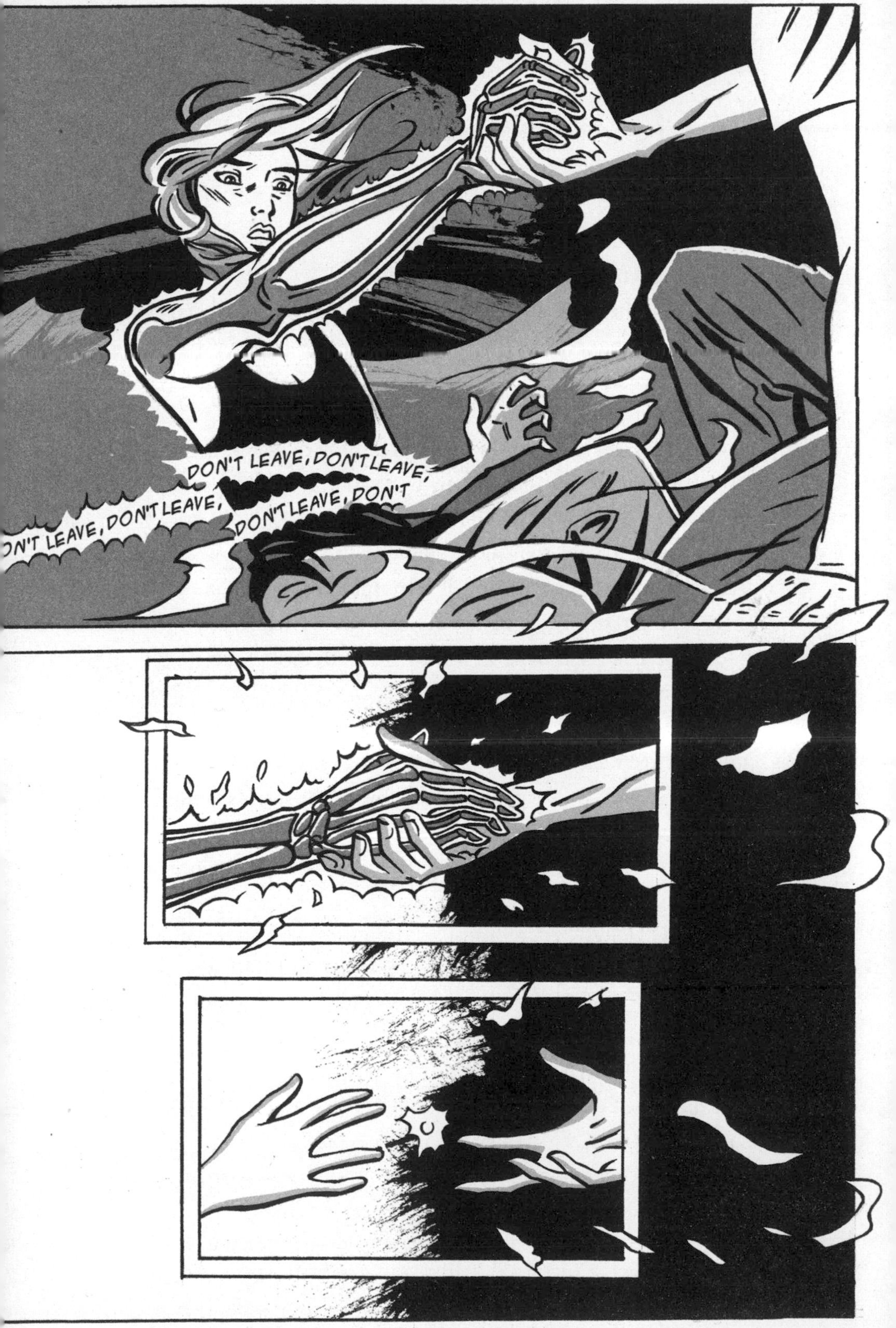
DON'T LEAVE, DON'T LEAVE,
ON'T LEAVE, DON'T LEAVE,
DON'T LEAVE, DON'T

I

    co

       me

          back, back

             in my own world.

I've been hearing sounds the whole time. Voices that raced along. As cryptic as Kortha's babble. But now Sav's words reach me. And I'm back.

"Oh, my God. Holly? Are you awake?" Her gravelly voice comes full volume now.

My lungs feel raw. As if I've been breathing too hard too long. When I suck air, a knife rips through my back and my muscles seize. I inhale shallowly, testing—will the air have edges?

I struggle for my own sound, my own voice. Nothing comes. I am desert-dry. Underneath the smell of hospital antiseptic, a darker scent lingers: gunpowder, rot, and blood. From the corner behind me, Kortha slides into view. He is here. In this room. With me.

Without Corey.

Savitri is standing up and she has ahold of my hand, her fingers curled between mine. She lets go and I try to reach for her.

"One second. Stay right here," she says as she sprints around the bed and grabs my other hand.

She gets something—some kind of wire—and then interlaces her fingers again.

"Holly? Holly?"

A woman I don't know hovers over me and tells me to squeeze Sav's hand if I can understand her. Sav's skin is warm and her flesh is springy.

"Corey?" His name scrapes over my tongue.

Kortha looks at me, and when he speaks, he uses the language of the living: "He is mine."

His body goes translucent, and I can only make out his outline. I blink and he is gone.

"I have to go back." My tongue sticks to the roof of my mouth on the *t*.

"No," Savitri says. "You have to stay here now. Stay here, Holly. Stay with me."

"Corey?" I say again.

Sav's eyes narrow and her mouth tightens around words that don't need to be said. I know where Corey is; I know where I left him.

And I slip away again. But this time, I'm alone. This time, I slip into the darkness of sleep.

*   *   *

A doctor says something about my eyes and my mother freaks: "Can she see? God, can she?"

There isn't anything but pain. Sharp. Hot. White. So intense that I don't even know where it comes from. Pain that buzzes so loudly it swarms out my consciousness.

*   *   *

My palm itches, and when I rub at it, my hand shreds—odd little bundles of skin gathering under my nails. My skin is falling off. Because I'm dead.

But no, I'm not. Because my dad appears.

*   *   *

SLEEP IS MY REFUGE. I HIDE IN DARKNESS.

*   *   *

My parents stand over me, crying. I've never seen him cry before. Water leaks out of the corners of his eyes—just like Corey. Where is Corey? Maybe I asked it.

The next time I wake up, my father is beside me murmuring, and then I catch a phrase of the Lord's Prayer. *God, please,* I pray, *make it stop hurting.*

*   *   *

Remembering has become like sifting through a box of lost puzzle pieces—not sure which puzzle they belong to.

Josh and me . . . a pair of strappy high heels and a prom dress . . . Savitri on top of the metal dome at our playground, too scared to jump . . . Corey's hand in mine . . . choking on dust and sand . . .

But finally, I start piecing together whole chunks—Pain no longer a Dictator. I am out of the ICU. At some point, I must have come here—to this new hospital room that has a curtain on a track and an empty bed beside mine.

Mom and Dad are in the corner, talking in low voices.

Mom says, "Corey can't wait any longer. It is past time."

"We can wait."

"They said three weeks if he's kept cold."

"He'd want her to be there."

I swallow, and even a movement that small throws a bone-cold blade into my skull. My head will never stop hurting.

No, that's not right. It will stop. Just not yet.

I used to never take meds, not even aspirin—something about drugs and my dad. I can't really remember. But right now I thank God for pain meds. Anything, anything, to dull the pain. Even distraction.

I try to tune back in to my parents' tight voices.

I close my eyes for a minute to keep the light out.

When I wake up again, no one is in the room. They were here, though. They were fighting. I keep thinking that Corey should stop them from fighting before I remember that I left Corey. Savitri walks in and tells me to rest.

Then—my parents are back. (Did I fall asleep? Where did Sav go?) The pain in my head has dulled. It aches rather than bites. The rest of my body feels disconnected, as if I'm floating above myself, though my stomach seems to think I'm on a boat. Probably side effects of the medicine. Why am I taking meds?

My parents rush over to me and run through a battery of questions. *Are you thirsty? Hungry? How are you feeling?* I reassure them that I'm okay.

My mother begins to cry. Were they fighting again?

Normally, they have two types of fights: You Take Too Many Chances or We Never See You. Being a cop's wife is hard, but Mom's crying is different. No tissues, no turning away, no trying to hide. Instead, with her face expressionless, the tears flow, like she doesn't even know she's crying.

"Mom?" I say.

My head throbs intensely for a moment until there is nothing but pain. I focus on it; I go into it. Only one way to conquer Pain. Go straight through it. Teeth gritted, shoulders back. I groan until it recedes at last. When I open my eyes again, Mom sighs and says, "Good, that's good."

"What, in the name of all that is holy, is good about that?" Dad says.

"Pain is a gift. Where there is pain, there is life," she says.

Mom and Dad stare at each other for a moment—a look between strangers. Eighteen years of marriage—Poof.

In the Shadowlands, Corey was pained, thirsty, desperate. Those are Sensations for the Living. Or was I the one who was thirsty and coughing?

"You should bury the body," I say. He might need it.

Dad's eyes snap toward me. "How did you know about Corey?"

"Because I left him in the Shadowlands," I say.

They look at each other again, finding Common Ground—worry.

My dad comes over to the bedside and puts his hand on my head, stroking my hair. But I wince and he pulls back, his hand finding the headboard instead.

"What are you talking about, SP?"

As a baby, I had a onesie that said *Sweet Pea.* He liked it so much it became his nickname for me, but somehow it got shortened.

I look from him to Mom and back again. I scooch down deeper into the bed.

"Where do you think Corey is?" Mom asks. She leans back a fraction of an inch, assessing me through slit eyes.

In the Shadowlands, where I left him, I think, but I don't say it because their worry makes sense. I couldn't have been with Corey. Right? Actually, there are no Shadowlands. Everything I saw—the snake-man, the wasteland, Corey fading—was just the coma, right? Which means I'm thinking like a fucking lunatic. Or like a brain-damaged lunatic?

The pain seizes me again until I can't think. This is good, I remember. Pain and life. This is good. When it eases, I say, "I know what happened to him."

HE'S TRAPPED IN THE SHADOWLANDS. I REMEMBER EVERYTHING.

Oh, God, what the hell am I hearing? Because I'm not thinking it; I'm hearing it, like someone's whispering to me, hissing at me. Not brain-damaged but crazy? Is one better than the other? Mom and Dad don't react to the voice; they don't hear it.

BUT IT WAS REAL, says the lunatic in my brain. Her voice crashes around inside my skull. I want to put my hands to my ears, but I know I can't touch my head.

Dad takes his hand off the bed, drawing away, his back stiffening from Father to Cop. "Did you see what happened to Corey?"

"Ron, she's not ready."

"She is a witness," he says, looking at her over me. The ball at his jawbone moves under his skin while his eyes narrow. Which means he's barely keeping it together. Which means that they haven't found the guy—the bastard—who did this.

"She is also a victim."

I wince at the label. Victim. Brain-damaged. Lunatic.

"Exactly. Her memory is fresh."

"No, no, it isn't. Where have you been?"

"Right. Here. Trisha."

My mom's upper lip crinkles with disapproval and she tells him that they should talk outside. She grabs his arm and he pulls away from her as they walk into the hallway.

Why am I hearing someone? Who is she? A voice from the Shadowlands?

My jaw is so tight that I practically expect the hinge to creak as I open it to stretch, but moving my jaw is Bad. Pain bounds and rebounds. Yawning is not for the Recently Resurrected.

My parents' voices get louder and I can make out what they are saying.

"... keep out of it, dammit."

I blink. My mother is cursing at my dad now? This world I've woken up to makes less and less sense by the minute.

"Right, Trisha. I'm going to become a rogue cop now. I'm going to track down the guy outside of the law that I've spent my entire life defending and kill him in cold blood. Is that what you think, Trisha? I meant that Meade can use anything she remembers."

"Then let Meade question her. In the meantime, don't interrogate our daughter. She deserves to recover."

"What about what Corey deserves?"

Her voice drops, and even though I can't hear what she says, I know that it is the kind of cruel remark that only my mother could think of. She's got an imagination on her and a sharp tongue when she wants it—how else do you survive as a cop's wife?

My dad comes back in alone. He sits beside me.

71

"Do you remember what happened? Only if you're ready," he says, but he leans in, his eyes wide—a starving man, hands pressed against the window of a five-star restaurant.

Dad used to tell me I'd make an Ideal Witness because I think visually, because I remember in images. But his Ideal Witness Didn't See Anything.

"Think hard. What's the last thing you remember?"

I tell him that my last moment with Corey was when I tried to grab his shirt, yank him out of the line of fire, that I didn't see Corey get shot. *Too slow to save Corey in the car. Too weak to hold on, to take him with me when Sav dragged me out of the Shadowlands. Wait, no, I tell myself. The Shadowlands were an illusion. Not real.*

REAL. THE STENCH OF GUNPOWDER SAND AND THE CRUNCH OF GRIT IN BETWEEN YOUR TEETH AFTER A GUST OF WIND. UNDENIABLY REAL.

I swallow and taste metal. I ask for water and suck it down, erasing the taste. I want to pull the covers over my head, stuff earplugs in, anything to quiet this hissing.

Mom uses a Shakespeare quote as code for when we've "failed to use our imaginations." She says, "There are more things in heaven and earth." She likes to remind us that imaginations connect us to all that is possible but unseen. So what are the Shadowlands? Real and unseen? Or in my head?

"Tell me what you remember," Dad says. "Start at the beginning."

I tell him everything I saw. At least, everything in his version of heaven and earth.

Savitri

14 days and 16 hours after

School means order. Steady, reliable order. I will go from one predictable moment to another. Nothing unexpected. Nothing random. Safe. And yet all the muscles along my spine have contracted into tight balls— a line of walnuts lodged between my vertebrae.

When I pull open the door, silence ripples away from me. Blood thrums in my ears, its rhythm quickening. People part before me. I try to take in faces—kids I've been in school with for four long years—but they blur into a sea of onlookers. Or gapers, Corey would say.

I pull the cuffs of my jacket into my palms and my fingers work the ribbing. For a moment, I'm not in school. I'm on the street, my hands pressed against his skull.

His blood is hot, and slippery, sliding under my hands. Alive.

Before I left for school today, my mom took me by the shoulders and reminded me, "The first day back will be the hardest. It will get easier." One day—six hours and thirty minutes—until easier.

I make it all the way down the hall, passing rows of blue lockers and a patch of chalk dust caught in the sunlight. When I get to my locker, the sea closes behind me and the hallway comes back to life. A locker slams, and I flinch, and another batters my eardrums, and the third rattles my ribs. The cacophony builds—lockers, voices, laughter—so loud it blinds me. And then the bell.

Sirens crack into my consciousness.

"Savitri?" I startle and turn. Kessa from Speech reaches for my forearm, but I can't feel her touch through my jacket. "How are you?"

"Holding up." *Saying it will make it true.*

After I assure her I'm okay, and she tells me to come to her if I need anything, she gives my arm a squeeze before she goes.

Bodies slide by me, hurrying. I should hurry too. I need to get to class and the bell has already rung. *Hurry.* But my muscles are stiff. Another locker slams and then the last set of footsteps peters out.

Nothing but the sound of my own ragged breathing.

If I can't handle sounds and I can't handle silence . . .

Well.

I want to stay here—in the intersection between horizontal and vertical lines. But I head to class. When I walk in, Mr. Truerer's eyebrows rise and then he nods at me and my seat. Bunsen burners are shoved against the wall. Glass beakers imprinted with their consistent marks sit empty and transparent.

Glass shatters onto the street.

No, no. Forty minutes—for the next forty minutes, all I have to concentrate on are vectors and momentum. Parabolic trajectories that can be calculated, that have predictable formulas. A random spray of bullets has no place here.

As the class ends, I prepare for the bell. *Loud, but predictable,* I tell myself, but I still jump. Three-ring binders snap shut. Chairs scrape and sneakers squeak across the floor. I flinch at each sound, at each movement, as though each were an electric shock.

I close my eyes and try to pop my neck, but the walnuts in my spine don't dislodge. When I open my eyes, Ellie Bennett stands at the corner of my desk, staring down at me. My hands work on the cuffs of my jacket again.

I glance around—anyone but Ellie Bennett. Ellie Bennett—the girl who used to date Corey, who spread rumors about Holly. Ellie, who was on the news last week, sandwiched between a gang killing and a fire.

With perfectly glossed lips that had a just-applied glow, she talked about how everyone loved Corey. Ellie Bennett—rumor mill queen and spotlight seeker.

That Ellie Bennett stands over me now, running her fingers over my desktop. She waits until her friends flock to her—a wake of vultures, wings beating the cold classroom air.

"How are you holding up?"

"How is Holly?"

"I heard you stayed in the hospital this whole time?"

"Would you tell Holly we're thinking of her?"

"What happened?" Ellie Bennett asks. "You were the witness the cops are talking about, right? You saw the whole thing, right?"

Detective Meade swung by the house last night, leaned against the doorframe, one leg crossed behind the other. "Any news?" I asked, my mouth dry. "No, no. I hear you're heading back to school tomorrow." "Yes." "Lots of questions." "I imagine so." "So I wanted to remind you not to talk to anyone about what you saw. It could influence a trial or, worse, your memory. And if it got into the press . . ." He doesn't even want me to admit I was there. "For your own protection," he said.

Now Ellie says, "Sit with us at lunch, okay?"

They finally pause long enough for me to answer. I turn into Bartleby the Scrivener, borrowing his polite but irrefutable protest.

"I would prefer not to." I sound so calm and quiet I can barely hear my voice over my own heart. They try to laugh, furrow their brows, and—all aflutter—take off.

Corey would appreciate the cool cover. The day we had to peel a lewd arrangement of condoms off Holly's locker, he put his hands on her shoulders and said, "Laugh. Now. So they don't get a piece of you." *Yes, Corey. No pieces of you either. Something I can do for you.*

I stand up, yank my sleeves all the way over my hands, fold my arms, and walk to my next class through the clutter of bodies in the freezing hallway. I overhear "spring break," "Florida," and "never too old for Disney World." Beside me, a group of kids burst out laughing. I watch their alien mouths, watch how smiles slide easily on and off their faces. I don't even have a map to that place anymore.

Teachers ask gently after Holly. Tell me they are sorry for my loss. Mrs. Richardson—who has taken a special interest in me since the Princeton letter—nearly cries, doe eyes welling up, when she stops me in the hallway. Irrationally, I hate her. And Princeton.

The bell fractures my day. I do not, will not, think about the shooting for forty-minute blocks. Vectors and momentum—forty minutes. *Don Quixote*—forty minutes. King George II—forty minutes. This works, for the most part. And when it doesn't—when I think of the momentum of a bullet and the angle of ricochets, when my eyes flick over to his empty seat in history and my chest cavity hollows out—I dig my nails into my palms until I can concentrate again.

Halfway through the day, the lunch bell rings.

Dear Bell, I propose a pact: don't scream and I won't wrench you from the wall and throw you out the window.

Lunch means forty minutes of unstructured time, without a distraction, and with so, so much noise and movement—everything letting that night in.

On my way to the cafeteria, I notice that Dan Morgan's hands swing just off rhythm while he walks, that Justin Winters keeps his weight on his toes, heels unscuffed. I've seen that before. My brain won't stop profiling and can't shut the Pandora's box of questions.

Who is Wiry? Where is he? Did Corey need help? God, did he need me? And worst: Why? Why, why, why? A three-year-old searching for answers that will not come, a reason that will soothe all I cannot change.

The cavernous cafeteria is colder and louder than any place I've ever been in my life. Sounds ricochet, amplify. Sirens.

Lights and motion everywhere. A small piece of metal. S&W.

I stand at the threshold looking at the empty corner of our table, my arms folded over my chest for warmth. People pass me in fluid motion and I'm a boulder in the stream. Kessa is setting down her lunch bag when she catches my eye. She smiles, walks over, slowing as she nears me. Her eyes search my face and she puts out a hand, reaching for me like I'm an animal she doesn't want to startle.

Comfort is a Trojan horse; it will take me apart from the inside.

I can't. . . . I sprint past Josh, can feel his gaze on me as I slam through the door. Outside, I find a place, a hidden set of steps to the basement of the science building. I sit down and the cold seeps into my jeans. I shiver. Soon Holly will be out of the hospital and here with me and then . . . we'll get a group rate on difficult days.

Better out here.

Better frozen.

After a few minutes, Josh finds me. He doesn't say anything; he just sits next to me. And whether I want to admit it or not, having him here, beside me and silent, keeps me from losing it, keeps the noises away. His silence is a sort of strange acknowledgment that words won't help.

Not today.

He takes off his jacket and puts it over my shoulders, but I keep shivering. He shifts back to his spot, sitting on the top step with the soccer fields behind him.

The day Ellie Bennett and the gossip mill started to grind out slut stories about Holly, I was in the gym after school with her, lifting weights to muscle up for freerunning. We saw a stream of people run by, so we hopped off the machines and followed the crowd to the soccer fields. When we heard Corey yelling, "Come on," Holly grabbed my hand and shoved us through the crowd.

Corey knocked Josh to the ground, straddled his chest, and slammed his fist into Josh's face. Josh grunted, and Corey screamed, "Fuck!" while he shook his hand out. I ran behind him and grabbed both his arms and, with Holly's help, hauled him to his feet. He kept screaming at Josh, who had rolled over onto his side. We learned later that Corey had broken his hand and dislocated Josh's jaw.

Some of Josh's friends dragged him up, and Corey nearly went after him again while Ellie Bennett shrieked in the background.

"Stop," I told him. "Stop it. This isn't helping."

"It's helping me."

He cradled his hand in his elbow. Mud and grass stained his cheek.

I looked him over and frowned. "I'm not convinced."

After the teachers and nurses intervened, Holly drove Corey to the hospital, the three of us in the car, Holly racing at ninety miles per hour.

"Once in a while you could try showing some restraint," I said to Corey from the backseat, hitting the consonants hard.

He turned, looked at me, and said, "Believe me, this is restraint."

When we hit a bump, he curled over his hand and started alternating between swearing and promising to learn how to punch.

"That's the way to learn restraint? Learn to punch? Smart," I said.

"What do you expect from him?" Holly said, flicking her gaze to the rearview mirror and meeting mine. "He's a cop's kid."

"Then he should know better than anyone that justice and revenge aren't the same thing."

"Hey, I'm sitting right here," Corey said. "And because *he's* a cop's kid, *he* knows better than anyone that they are the same things—one is just dressed up in better-looking clothes." He turned around in his seat to look at me. "You know what my dad always says? He joined the biggest gang in Chicago. Only the pay ain't as good if your colors are blue and white."

And yet, the biggest gang in Chicago can't find their target.

When the bell rings, Josh and I go our separate ways, neither of us having eaten, neither of us having spoken.

The day passes and I stay rooted in my forty-minute periods that start and end with sirens—or, rather, bells—until my mom picks me up. She asks me how it went. I say the only thing I can think of to make the day feel normal: I tell her it was easy.

* * *

The hospital has started to feel like a home away from home—better than school, at any rate. The muscles in my back begin to release and the walnuts between my vertebrae shrink to peanuts. My mom gives me a quick hug before she gets off the elevator at her department, and I keep riding up to see Holly. I take quick steps until Sergeant Paxton's voice fills the corridor. Then I slow down and step quietly past the open door of a meeting room he's in.

I am about to exhale when I hear footsteps in the hallway behind me, following me. Holly's room is two turns away.

Every time I see him, he has another question for me: "Tell me again about the knife." "What about the thing he took? A silver tassel? Describe it for me." He wants to reach into my brain and suck out every last scrap of information. *Please, take it! Take these memories. And use them. Find Wiry, find him.*

When I left the hospital last night, he told me to think about Wiry as I was falling asleep and see if I could remember more in the morning. I nodded silently, the most polite response I could muster. Does he think I can sleep if I'm thinking of Wiry? As it is, I've taken to blaring music in my earbuds to block out dreams. It almost works, but I still wake with unaccountable scents lingering—mint, gunpowder, and melting snow.

When Sergeant Paxton calls my name, I'm far enough away that I could pretend not to hear him—I could pretend I was lost in my own world.

But he's Corey's father. I roll my shoulders until I hear them pop, and then I turn around. I wait for him in the corridor and make a plan. When he catches up, I pivot on my heel and set a quick pace toward Holly's room. *I can control the conversation until we get there.*

"How is Ho—"

"Did that trick work? Did you remember anything new this morning?"

79

Okay, bad plan. "I'm sorry."

Sergeant Paxton sighs. "Savitri, this is important."

I stop and stare at him. "I know that."

He puts his hands on my shoulders, as if his gaze wasn't pinning me to the spot by itself. "Look, the physical evidence isn't enough. They got a print off the door handle. Forensics got a fingerprint."

"But . . . isn't that good? Shouldn't that make it easier to find him?"

"Not when there are no matches in the system."

I step back and his hands fall off my shoulders.

"Are you telling me that . . ." I can't finish the sentence. "Are you telling me that he's going to get away with this?"

"I'm telling you that you're our best link to him. You can't give up."

"I wasn't about to," I say.

He nods and I turn, walking to Holly's room. Corey broke his hand and a three-year friendship with Josh over mere cruel gossip. I know what Corey would want for his murderer. I know what I owe Corey.

Dear Wiry, pray for invisibility.

Holly

Mom is fussing with my Brand-New Helmet, given to me by my Brand-New Therapists in this Brand-New Rehab Wing. With their private rooms and cushy visitors' chairs, they try to disguise that we're in a hospital, but the starched walls, starched sheets, and starched smiles give it away.

Mom pushes my wheelchair toward the mirror that hangs on the back of the bathroom door and resettles the helmet on my head. *Fuss all you want; I still look like a shrunken-head voodoo victim.*

"See?" she says. "It's like a bike helmet. Not so bad. You could come."

"Are you insane?"

Her eyes narrow and she crosses her arms. "How you look isn't that important. No one will say anything. Everyone is on their best behavior at a funeral."

I sigh. I'm not a Fashion Diva, but I'm still not going to be paraded around in a Helmet and a Wheelchair. Hospital Policy for any trip outside. Apparently, surgery plus two weeks in bed equals serious weakness. They tell me I've lost somewhere around thirty percent of my muscle mass. Nice. On the bright side, the helmet covers up my bald spot.

Mom tries to logic me: you'll be fine, no medical worries. The doctors said it would be all right, that I've aced all the tests—cognitive, physical, blood work, scans. All that's left is for a hairline fracture in my skull to heal. And even that will happen before my hair grows in.

Bastards.

And the voice that slams around in my head? The docs don't need to listen in. That would bring me back to square one. No thanks, I'll just leave the voice here, where it belongs, when I get out.

I notice Savitri, hovering in the doorway. Long, Boring, and Tedious excuse themselves as she comes in. *Nice to have you back, Sav.*

She hoists her pack off her shoulders, puts it down, and straightens up. But her shoulders stay slumped. "So?" she says.

A Day of Defeat for her, but she's still All About Me.

"Will you please tell my mother why I don't want to look like this at—"

"It won't be so bad," Mom says.

"Have you forgotten high school, Mom? I'll be the Main Attraction at the Freak Show."

"Don't call it that. It's your brother's funeral, for God's sake." Mom slams the brush against the basin top, and Sav jumps.

"I know what it is. Didn't you hear the doctors: no brain damage." Mom and I have been at it for at least twenty minutes and my patience is eighteen minutes gone. "Sav, tell her."

Savitri steps in the room. She lets the silence stretch out and Mom watches her. Then Mom crosses her arms and cocks her head. Smug, sure of what Sav's Silence means.

"Well, Savitri, what do you think?" Mom says.

"Do you really want my opinion?" she asks.

"Don't you think—don't you know he'd want his sister there so she could say goodbye, pay her respects?"

"Actually, I think Corey would protect his sister. I just came from— Trust me, after the . . . shooting . . . it's harder than you'd think to be among so many people." Sav's hand flutters by her ears and her voice breaks. "Even their sympathy is too much. . . ."

"Oh," says Mom. Mom folds her into a hug and, after a moment, releases her. Then she rubs Sav's arms up and down, up and down, as if Sav is cold—no, because Sav is shaking.

"I'm okay. Thanks." Sav clears her throat and says, "If you want my opinion, it would be too much. I could barely manage school, and I wasn't shot."

"Besides, Sav can go for me," I say.

When Mom looks back at me, her eyebrows are raised—ready to

resume the fight. Sav widens her eyes and tightens her lips—a clear "shut up" written on her face. I shut up. Sav's the one with the Silver Tongue when it comes to Authority Figures. Speaks their language. I handle all the things outside those lines—Perfect Team. Unstoppable.

"Holly," Sav says, her tone borrowing the reprimand I'm about to get from Mom. "It's not about what you want or what I want or even what your parents want." She turns to Mom. "I can't see Corey putting his sister into a situation that might hurt her."

Mom shifts her feet and looks at me in the mirror. "I just don't want you to regret it someday. I know it's hard right now, but you have to say goodbye. It's the first step toward moving on."

MOVING ON WITHOUT HIM IS NOT AN OPTION.

I drop my face into my hands. "Please. Please. Not like this. Not with this—" *Voice in my head.* I tap the helmet and the sound pings so loudly that my head hurts. Again.

When I look up, Mom is watching Sav, who is watching me. Mom sighs. She leans down and tries to kiss my head, but the stupid helmet interferes. So she turns my wheelchair around and kisses my nose.

"Okay, we'll come up with something else, then." She straightens up and says, "I'll go talk to your father."

She walks out, leaving just me and Sav. Sav leans backward, looking down the hallway for a couple of seconds, counting down to privacy.

When she returns, I shake my head and then say, "You, my friend, have a gift."

"I don't know, Holly. I think maybe she's right. You might regret not being there."

"No, I won't. She wants me to say goodbye? I don't know how to do that. I can barely think about Corey, much less talk about him. He isn't missing for me yet and I don't want . . . not yet. Trust me, Sav. I shouldn't go."

"Okay," she says. She reaches into her backpack and digs out a wide headband decorated with a leopard print. "Speaking of gifts . . . the helmet won't be for forever, but the hair, Holly. The hair . . ."

"Nice. Now I can look psycho *and* outdated."

We're both laughing as I take off the helmet and put the headband on—cool and soft against my scalp. I glance in the mirror. At least the surgeons left my extensions. Well, most of them. She sits down on the bed, folds her hands in her lap, and stares at them.

"So?" I say.

"So." She organizes her hair in a ponytail and holds it for a moment—a signature Sav Move. "It was horrible. Everyone wanted the story. And they're asking about you."

"Yeah, I noticed." I gesture to all the flowers in my room. Their heads loll and the petals sprawl. "Could they be more clichéd?"

Sav scans them and I see them through her eyes—she'd be counting them.

"Twenty-two? That's a lot of best friends. You must be popular."

"And some are from groups. Winner of the Most Surprising category: Josh's freerunners." I point to a bunch of wildflowers. "Runner-up: school paper." Yellow roses. "And dead last: teachers." Calla lilies.

"*Flores por los muertos,*" Sav says. When I wrinkle my eyebrows at her, she explains, "*Streetcar Named Desire.* Means 'flowers for the dead.'"

"What's the Spanish for 'Back from the Dead'?" I say. "What do you call that?"

"Lucky," she says. "Strong."

"Saved." When I reach out, she grabs my hand and I swing her arm back and forth, back and forth. "Do you know what the golden hour is?"

She nods.

"Good thing you're quick," I say.

Sav shakes her head. "Not quick enough."

I squeeze her hand.

"Yeah, well. Me neither."

"We're going to get through this, Holly. And you know how?"

"Together?" I say.

"Together."

Savitri

20 days and 17 hours after

The new black dress that my mother bought me dominates my room. I haven't touched it yet, but I can see that its fabric is stiff—smothering.

In thirty-five minutes, half a mile from here, Corey's funeral will start. And I'm sitting on my bed in my bathrobe with a towel wrapped around my still-wet hair, surrounded by Hindi texts, looking for some comfort before I go.

Three different versions of *Savitri: The Perfect Wife* are splayed open on my bed. I pick up one of the comic books and rest it on my lap. I stare at Yama, the God of death—crown on his head, noose in his hands, compassion on his face. I turn the yellowing pages, reading and rereading.

Savitri is determined to marry Satyavan. When a soothsayer tells her his past—that Satyavan's father, a former raja, was blinded and his family banished—she says his family will be hers. When the soothsayer reminds her of his present—that he is poor and makes his home in an isolated forest—Savitri says she will live in poverty. And when the soothsayer tells her his future—that he is destined to die in one year—she says, no matter how long or short his life, she will share it with him. So she follows Satyavan around the fire seven times, marrying him.

One year later, when Satyavan collapses and is dying for reasons unknowable, she stays with him, cradling his head in her lap until Yama appears. Yama gently draws out Satyavan's soul, a white silhouette of Satyavan's form. Yama loops a golden noose around his neck and guides him away. To a place the living cannot follow.

But Savitri does follow Yama through the forest, mile after mile, rough road after rough road, disregarding her exhausted limbs and bleeding feet. Impressed by her devotion, Yama offers her a boon—anything, he says, except the life of her husband.

"I wish for my father-in-law to watch his grandson eat from a golden cup with a silver spoon," she says.

She recovers her father-in-law's sight and his wealth. And she salvages Satyavan's life, by her wits and grit, with her words and devotion. She follows a God.

I sat in a car fifteen yards away.

My finger is tracing Yama's noose around Satyavan's neck when my mom calls upstairs to remind me that it is getting late. I dress slowly, letting the fabric scratch my skin. Promise fulfilled.

In the church parking lot, two news vans are waiting. The camera operators and perfectly coiffed reporters are poised on the street to capture a glimpse of the Paxtons. Footage for the six o'clock news.

The church steeple's shadow darkens the walkway, and next to it are a number of strange, unidentifiable shapes. A group of boys stands on the roof—the freerunning team Corey and Josh created. Holly would know how to react, what Corey's response would be. She might flip them off for their too-little, too-late display of loyalty or she might climb up there with them.

I place my hand on my chest and then point to one of them—though with the sun behind them, I can't really distinguish which one. He returns the gesture and then they all do. My eyes are already stinging.

Holly should be here, should see this. I don't understand why she didn't want to come. It's not like her to avoid things. When the world charges her, she charges back—head-on. It's even less like her to admit she couldn't manage it and volunteer me up. And make me do this alone.

My mom and I pass familiar faces from school, and some not so familiar. Two girls are huddled together, giggling. When they see me, they stop laughing and stand straight, putting on shamed expressions. Boys I know from Speech stand around with their hands shoved deep in their pockets—awkward hands, awkward feet. Novices to funerals, novices to death.

As I approach the church, Sergeant Paxton leans down toward me and stares intently. I shrink back.

"Ron," my mother says, inserting herself between us. "Let's think about laying him to rest now."

Sergeant Paxton puts a lot into a look: *Corey won't rest until his killer does.*

I nod; I know; I agree. But I can't seem to help.

Mom and I slide through the door. I haven't been inside a church often, since my mom and I worship at our mandir at home. The way the air changes—temperature drops and people quiet—stops me. Calla lilies stand up tall at the aisles and a massive flower arrangement decorates the coffin. As we're escorted to the front, we pass pew after pew of officers, dressed in blue. Experienced at funerals, experts at death.

We sit in the second row, right behind his family, right in front of Meade and Magruder. I feel their gazes on my back.

Everyone knows the longer it takes to find Wiry, the colder the case gets. Everyone knows that if they don't find him soon, they might not find him at all.

Maybe this isn't the time or place, but I turn around and say, "Anything?"

Meade shakes his head. "Don't worry. The department isn't sleeping until we have him."

I regard the wall of blue. Sturdy and overwhelming. Faces hard and bodies tensed. I nod. Maybe there's some comfort in that.

An organ plays and whispers quickly peter out. The ceremony begins, eulogy after eulogy.

I stare at the hymnals and Bibles crowded into the pew back. I focus on them, trying to keep everything comfortably remote, comfortably surreal— better frozen than falling apart. Holly said that his murder wasn't real for

87

her yet. *Me neither, Holly.* But this . . . these flowers, these requiems, these eulogies . . . I need them to stop; they will take him away.

He lifted the gun and took aim.

I pull out a hymnal, and run my fingers over the typeface on fragile pages, trying to find words to replace what I hear, but the priest's voice worms its way in. He tells us murder is cruel and death seems random. I find the word *plan.*

The priest tells us to measure life not by its length in years, but by the depth of its moments. I find the word *patience.*

A few months ago, Corey and I started to fight about sex. I wanted to wait. After a long negotiation, he said it wouldn't be much fun if I weren't happy. When I said that didn't sound like the single-track mind of a seventeen-year-old boy, he paused momentarily and then said, "Wait, did you say something? I was looking at your boobs."

I fold my arms and knead my elbows.

Did Corey live deep? Did I shallow out his life whenever I grimaced at his risks, at his handstands four stories up? When I said wait, think, careful . . .

Corey is dead, I tell myself, and the word *dead* remains flat because he's not gone for me; he could be here with me. I could be holding his hand. Fingers in the hollows between his knuckles.

A screen is lowered and the sound system starts a song he loved. Religion in high-tech. The movie rolls: Trisha in nineties grunge flannel with Corey and Holly in her arms and a tired smile on her young face. Mr. Paxton in his uniform while Corey holds his CPD star in the air. Corey ages into kindergarten and first grade—the last of the years I didn't know him. And then I recognize him, recognize the birthday parties and the Ping-Pong tournament that we set up in their backyard, the days of knights and swords, the superhero phase. A picture of him making a face behind Holly elicits murmurs and a light laughter that makes me jump.

Pictures of the three of us are spread throughout the montage— playing with light sabers during his rattail years; hanging upside down off the crossbar of a light post, his teeth crosshatched in junior high braces; holding a lit lamp during Diwali; his hand around my waist when we posed at our junior prom. I swallow hard, remembering the texture of his tux against my bare shoulder, the warmth of his breath against my neck.

Every moment is being memorialized and then laid to rest. Memorialized and then erased.

My lungs shrink and each breath requires more effort, each breath is smaller, shallower. *You can't erase a life in a two-minute picture show. Not gone. Please, please, not gone.*

I find the word *spirit.*

The video cuts to a freerunning session Josh filmed of us last year. Once we're done practicing, Corey walks off—his transition from step to step is fluid, his balance perfect. People used to ask Corey if he was a dancer because of his walk. But the camera isn't good enough to capture his agility. His flow is gone.

It was his flow that made me start freerunning, so I could watch his lithe movement, his muscles popping in and out of relief while he flew over, slid around, glided past one barrier after another. So we could be moving together.

Inside our cells we have some kind of liquid and it drains out of me.

Corey is gone.

To a place where the living cannot follow.

I remain empty on the way to the cemetery. Empty as I stand on perfectly manicured grass, watching his coffin slide into the earth. Empty as we fill his grave.

*   *   *

I don't stay for the reception. My mom makes my apologies. I need to see Holly. As I drive to the hospital, three words dog me: *Corey is gone.* Three words that carve out the contours of the word *dead.*

As I cross the parking lot, a car's engine growls behind me. I turn and see an SUV.

My muscles lock.

The door opens slowly and Josh slides out of the passenger side. I grimace—I can't panic every time I see an SUV. Especially one that's white and the wrong model. He waves to the driver with one hand, carrying flowers in the other.

Yellow roses and sprigs of grass and baby's breath.

Corey is gone.

I'm frozen still, except for my gaze, which follows Josh as he hops onto the sidewalk. He sees me and stops.

"Hiya," he says.

"Flowers?" I say, and my voice comes out harsh as I hurry onto the sidewalk, reaching him at the entrance. "You brought her flowers?"

Anyone who knows anything about Holly knows she thinks flowers are trite and stupid. Anyone who knows anything about anything knows flowers don't help. But here stands Josh, knowing nothing. He knows nothing and he thinks he has the right to see Holly?

"What's wrong with flowers?"

"You're such an idiot, Josh." I scream it, surprising myself. My voice breaks. "His funeral was today. Did you know that?"

"Well, ye-ah, I was there. On the roof."

Of course he was. He was probably the one who organized it; I can't even make the simplest connections right now. *What is wrong with me?*

Corey wouldn't have wanted Josh at the funeral or here now, would he?

The truth is, I don't know the answer. For years it was Josh and Corey, me and Holly. Does old history trump recent history?

No pulse under my fingers. Blood cooling on my skin. He is dead.

Josh continues, "I thought she could use some comfort today, you know?"

"You're going to comfort her? You?" I shout. "No one wants you here."

Josh grabs my elbow. "Savi," he says, using my old nickname. "Calm down, okay? Come here."

He steers me over to the side of the building, where I pull away from him. I drop my voice, but I'm still spitting out my words.

"Corey hated you. Do you understand—do you even have a clue how much he hated you?"

"Yeah, I picked up on that when he dislocated my jaw." He looks at his shoes. "From trusted buddy to the fricking Antichrist in three seconds flat. A world record, probably."

"Then show some respect for the . . ." I can't get out the word *dead*. It has gotten so heavy and thick that I can't push it through my throat. "Then show respect for the living and leave her alone."

I turn and walk through the hospital door, but I can hear Josh behind me.

As soon as the sterilized scent and the recycled air of the hospital hit me, a pain in the hollow of my chest balloons so hard and fast that I have to lean against the wall.

No more sliding notes between the vents in each other's lockers, no more spotting each other on flips, no more slipping into his bedroom at night—something not even Holly knew about—and lying together in the darkness, my head against his shoulder and one leg hooked over his knees. No more skin against skin, hip against hip, mouth against mouth.

No more.

I push myself off the wall, try to will myself to walk down the corridor. One foot in front of the other. *Keep it together,* I yell at myself silently. *For Holly.*

"Savitri," Josh says, his voice softening. "You can't go see her right now. Not like this."

I grit my teeth. "I'm fine. Holly needs—"

"You're not. Everyone, and I mean everyone, knows how much you loved him."

Except that I was ready to leave him.

I stare at Josh. *Frozen is manageable. Frozen is manageable.* But the ice is fracturing. If I fall to pieces, who's going to take care of Holly?

Corey and I—we made the leap from friends to more based on an unspoken rule: stand by Holly, keep her afloat after Josh. After years of watching Corey spiral from one girlfriend to another, years of holding my breath between his breakups while Holly campaigned for me, begging him to date "someone who deserved him," he finally asked.

The first time he kissed me, I pulled back and asked him why now. He said that watching me stand up for Holly was a beautiful sight.

I tucked my lip inside my teeth and pulled out of his reach.

"What's wrong?" Corey asked.

"Gratitude doesn't last."

"It isn't gratitude," he told me. He reached for me and dipped his fingers in my hair at the base of my skull and I tilted my face up to him. "It's how damn sexy your loyalty is."

Now Josh touches my arm and I flinch away from him.

"Don't," I say.

"Can I just say this? You've gotta give yourself some room. It's your loss too."

I've hated Josh for a solid year now, but when he puts his arms around me, I collapse against his chest, grip his shirt, and hang on. I'm sobbing so hard that I'm not sure whether I'm screaming or crying. Foreign sounds break out of me, long as my breath. Again and again.

"Hey, hey," he says.

"I didn't do anything, Josh. I just sat there."

"What could you have done?"

I've trained to react. I've spent countless hours on angel drops and wall runs, on dash vaults and backflips. See a wall, find a hundred ways to get over it, bounce off it. We react to our environment, adjust our movement to our surroundings, respond to what is coming. When milliseconds mattered, I didn't move.

"Something. Anything. What was I waiting for?"

"You were waiting for it to stop, Savitri. It's okay."

"How can you say that? It's not okay. He is dead."

Savitri Devi walked until her feet bled. Where was my loyalty when Wiry raised the gun? All I have left to give Corey now are my tears. But to the dead, tears are just water.

Holly

While I'm stuck in a hospital bed, my brother is stuck in another kind of bed, half of Chicago away.

Mom told me that when Corey and I were babies, we held hands while we slept. I didn't believe her until she showed me a photo. Once she found it, she mosaicked a frame for it and hung it in the hallway between our rooms. In the picture, we are two lumps, curled toward each other. Little ovals sleeping underneath a single white blanket. Our hands, above the blanket, remain in a funny clutch. One inside the other. No one can tell who is who in the picture, which one is hanging on to the other.

They say twins are connected. That sharing the same womb somehow unites us. All I'm sure of is the same blood that was pumped into him was pumped into me, and that shared blood is still moving.

HE IS NOT GONE, NOT REALLY.

I try to picture a coffin lid closing and being encased in black. I try to picture his hand around mine. But what I see is me reaching out to grab him and getting only a scrap of his shirt—not enough to hang on to.

You can't follow me. Not where I'm going, Corey said.

I open my eyes and The Leopardess stares back at me from the wallpaper job Sav redid in my rehab room. I can't read the words from here, and my muscles are still shaky from running a pathetic eight-tenths of a mile on a treadmill, so I rely on my memory.

The night after the funeral when Larissa Powell buries her mother, she climbs to the top of the Imperial Tower and looks out over Hamilton

City. Something in her breaks and hardens into a new shape—jagged, serrated, powerful. Her epiphany floats in a banner above her head: *Pain Transforms Us All.*

Mom and Dad argue sometimes about whether cops (i.e., heroes) are born or built. My dad says stress reveals character and my mom says it builds character.

If I were The Leopardess . . . If only I were her . . .

I let images wash over me; I welcome them.

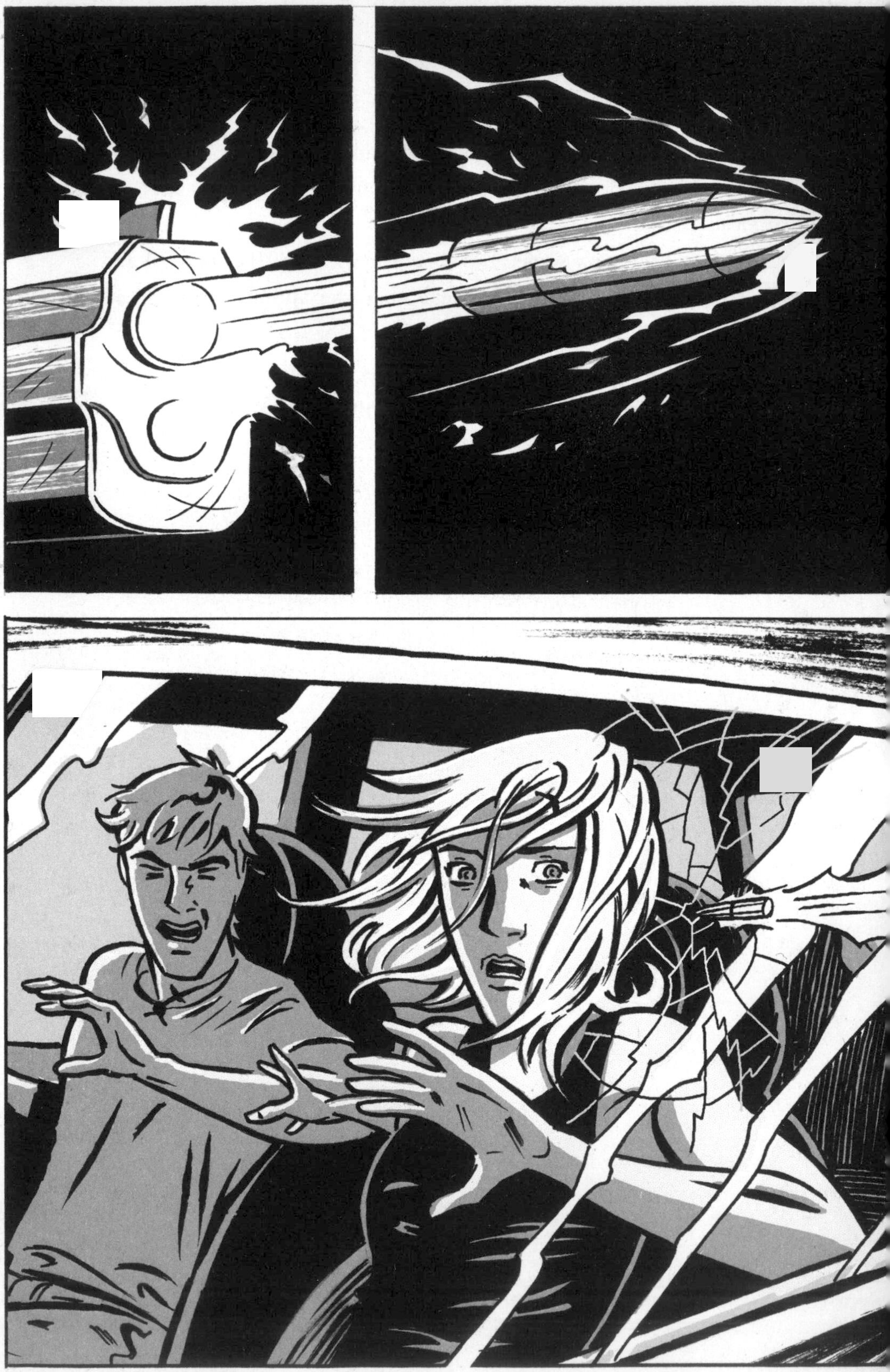

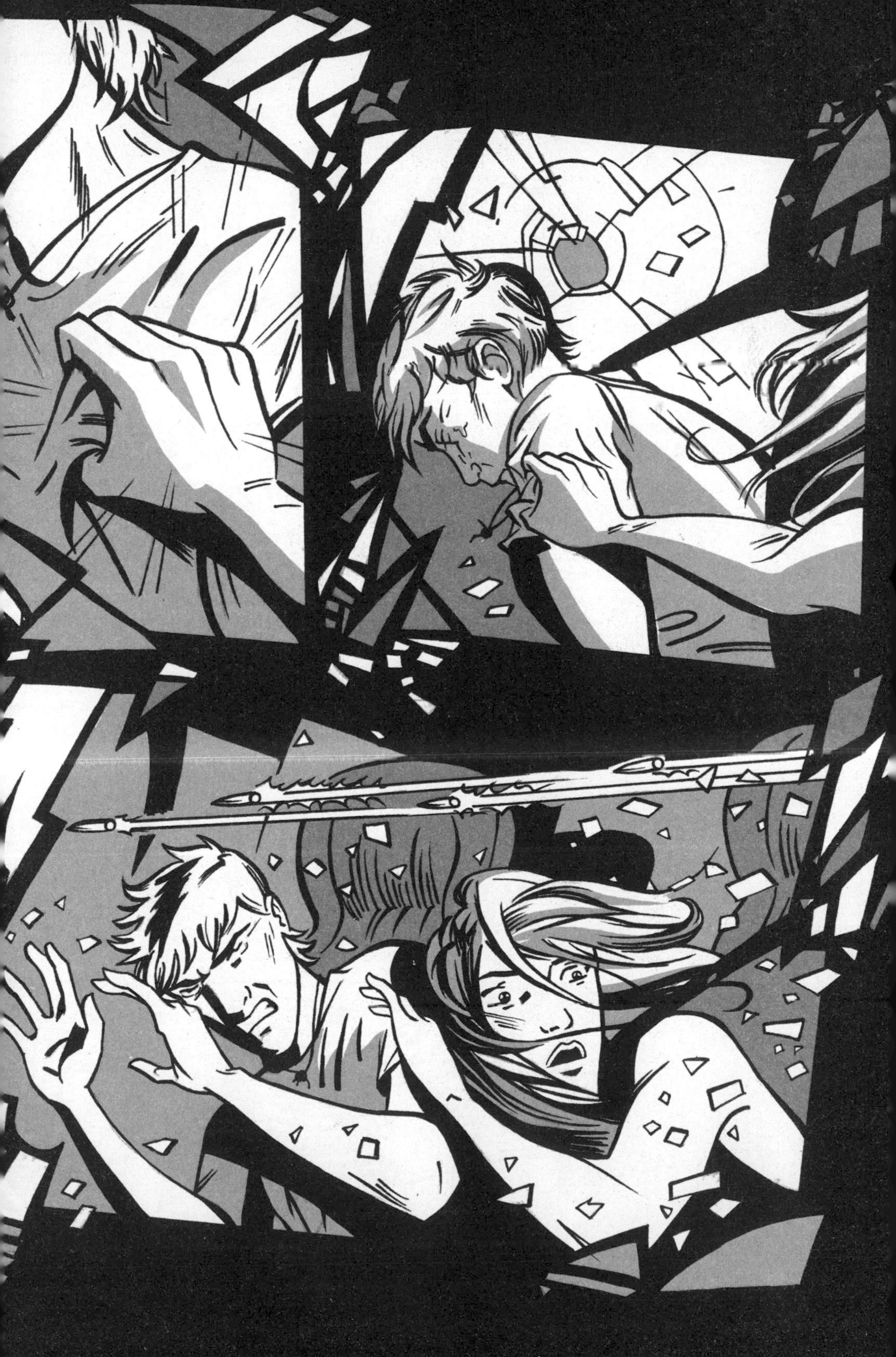

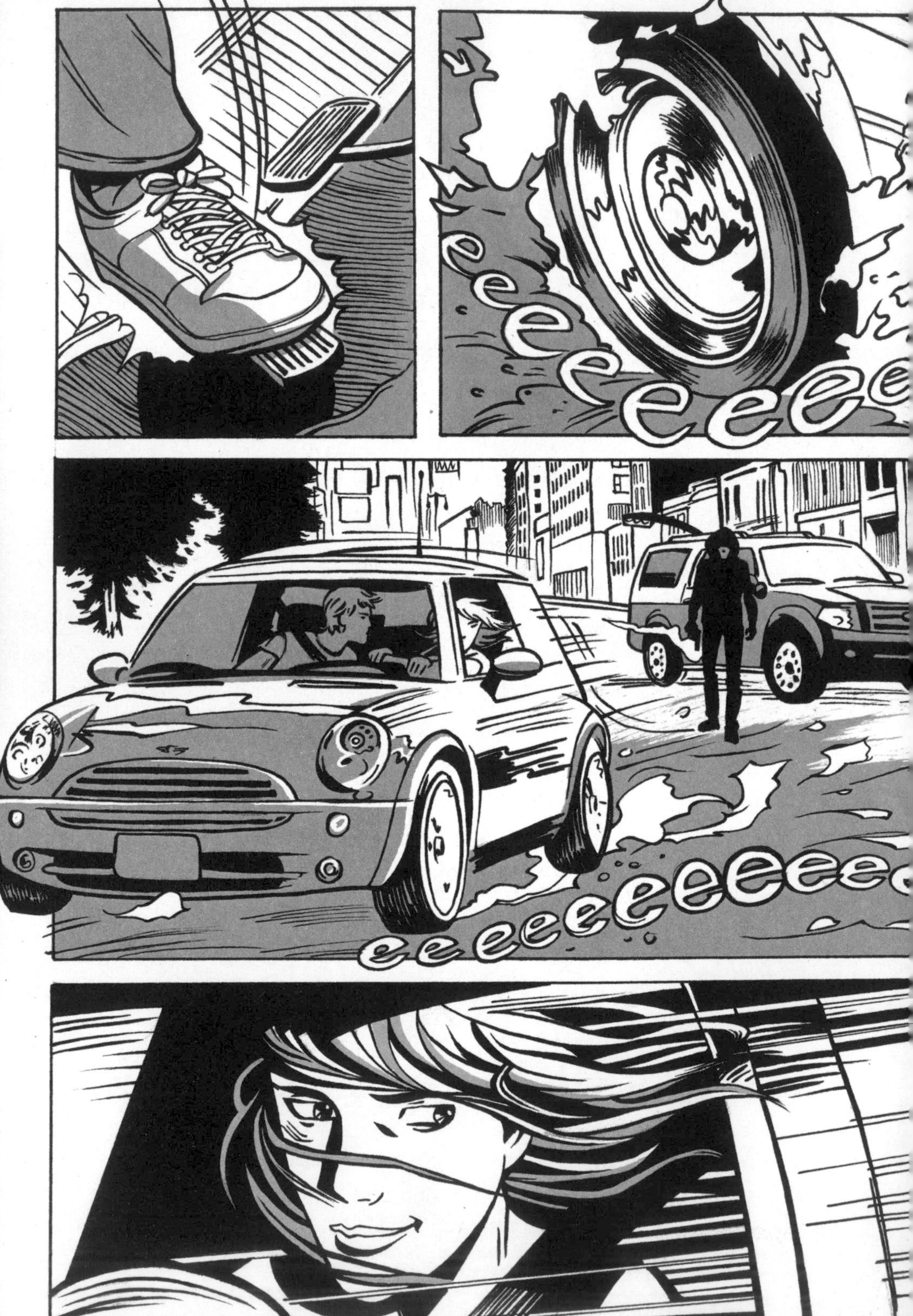

But I am not The Leopardess.

I push myself out of bed, my feet on the cold tile floor, pacing from square to square, making patterns. Hurts to move. Hurts more to lie still.

Corey didn't just wind up in that coffin. I didn't just end up in this bed. It wasn't an act of God. Some evil son of a bitch did this. He put me in a hospital, where my muscles have shrunk so badly that running a mile is a goddamn challenge. I used to leap off roofs.

Jesus, where is Savitri? She'd talk about Patience and Justice, not Revenge. Or whatever. She'd talk and that would be enough. We'd be getting through this together.

I press the call button since any words will be a distraction, and soon a young girl appears—no older than me. When she sees me standing, she says, "Oh," and then, more slowly, glancing at the door to the bathroom, "Do you need help?"

I look her over, taking stock: a small gold cross rests on her breastbone. It is overshadowed by a gaudy larger cross, made heavy with turquoise and red stones. Her tag says VOLUNTEER. She has the face of an Overeager Kindergartner—Scrubbed Clean and Hopeful. What is she hoping for? Miracles? Confirmation of God and all His Glory?

"No, I just . . ." This was a mistake; I should have tried texting Sav, but I don't have my cell phone. Impounded by the cops. Evidence. The Dana—shot up and shattered. Corey's body—gone.

"Should we go for a walk?" she asks.

I glare at her. Hospital policy dictates that I need to be in a wheelchair unless I'm on a treadmill. Fricking Lawyer Logic.

"I'll bring a chair, and we can get you out of this room."

Out of this room. Yes. After she returns with a wheelchair and settles me in it, she pushes me out of the room. The scenery finally changes.

I glance in the rooms as we pass. A woman sits knitting with her ball of yarn on the floor while she waits for a kid to wake up. A man sleeps, his toes out of the blankets. Something about it feels typical . . . staged.

Maybe I'm not out of the coma. Maybe the Shadowlands live outside and this hospital is an illusion.

Once a thought like that gets into your head, you just have to disprove it.

COREY IS A PRISONER ON A LEAD. KORTHA WILL NEVER LET HIM GO.

I grip the armrests. An exit sign hangs from the ceiling.

"What's it like outside?" I ask. My voice comes out strained.

She stops the wheelchair and walks around to look at me. "You want to go outside? I think that might be against policy."

Her cross hangs at my eye level and I resist a smile as I figure out just what to say. "My brother is being buried right now."

"Oh, no. Oh, that's terrible."

"I can't be there, but I need to say goodbye to him in my own way," I say. "Under God's own sun."

When she says she can't think of a way to get me out there without anyone seeing, I say the roof. She ducks her head to hide a smile. She can help the victim. She glances down the hall one way and then the other before she wheels me to the elevator. I need to see my city—alive, electric. My City by the Lake.

Once we are on the roof, the sun stings my eyes. I slowly open one eye and then the other. The air has dulled while I was in the Shadowlands. Volun-Twit wheels me closer to the edge so I can see the lake.

I stand and take unsteady steps and Volun-Twit is suddenly beside me, her hand on my wrist.

"Careful."

"I'm not going to throw myself off," I say.

Her laugh—a nervous titter—is high and light. She releases my wrist and steps back. And it is just Me and My City. But the concrete sleeps and I can no longer Wake. It. Up.

My legs tremble. Some bastard somewhere has made them tremble. Has let time eat my muscles.

If I were The Leopardess, I would look like this:

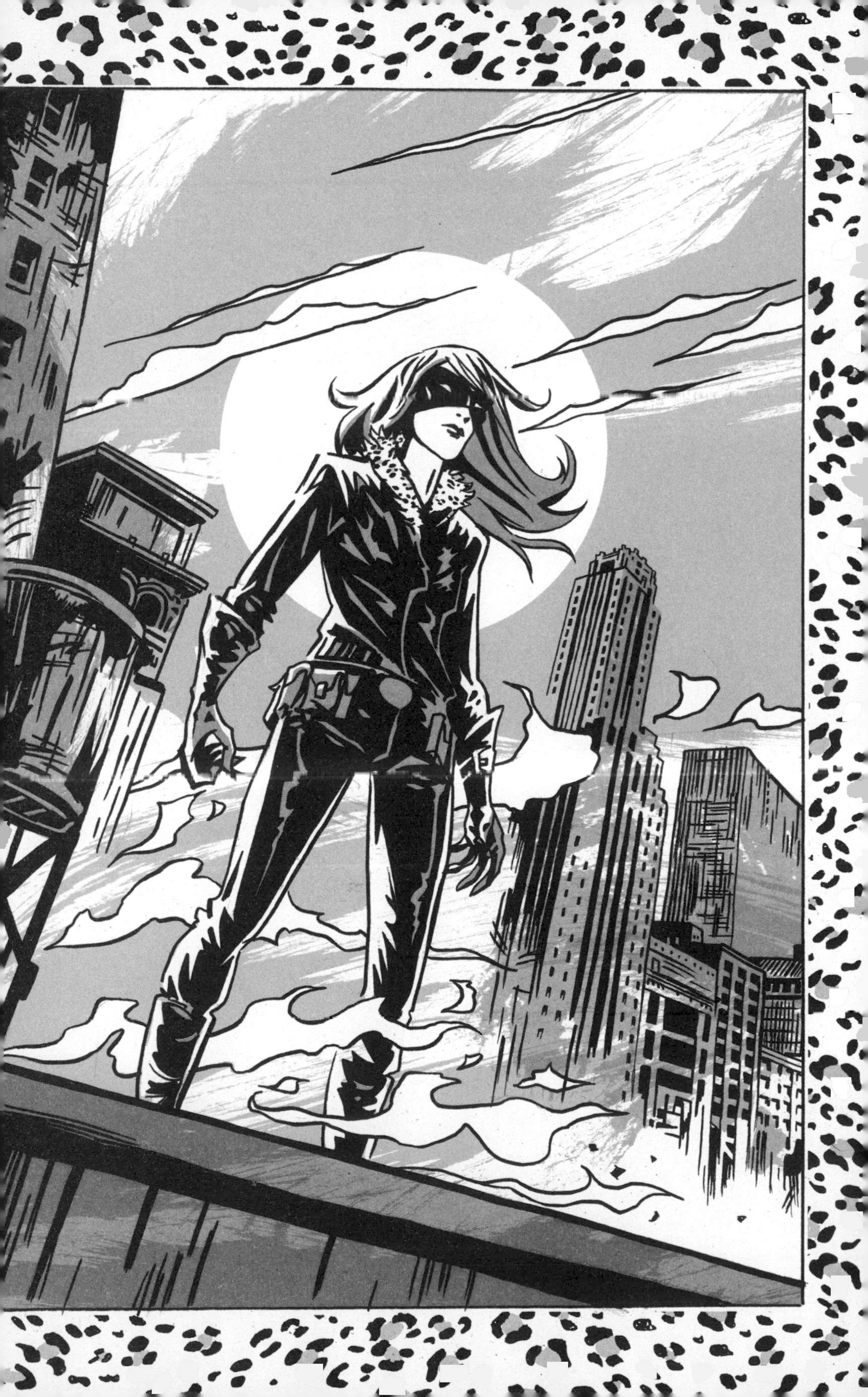

I am not The Leopardess.
But pain transforms us all.

PART II

Savitri

29 days and 8 hours after

I'm watching the clock on my night table, waiting for midnight. Seniors nationwide are sitting up right now, refreshing their email again and again.

But Holly isn't one of them. She's asleep on my trundle bed, breathing regularly and deeply, with her red hair and silver extensions splayed against the pillow. She looks so much healthier now: warmth in her cheeks, limbs that have been reconditioned, flow that is returning to her movement. It's hard to believe she couldn't wake up before. She rehabbed her muscle power at a pace that had the doctors congratulating themselves and the therapists calling her a model patient. She lifted her eyebrows and said, "I've never been a model anything," and then went back to her treadmill. All she did was sleep, eat, and exercise, like something was driving her out of that hospital.

But then she got home.

And now, one week later, she prefers to sleep here.

Maybe I just overworry. Maybe all the little things I've been noticing—that her former dog-with-a-bone focus seems to elude her, that she loses track of conversations as though a third person is speaking, that she never asked me about the funeral—maybe all those are just little things. Truth is, I don't know what recovering from the murder of your twin brother is supposed to look like. Maybe this is normal.

My phone dings—email. I hop off the edge of the bed, landing softly. I sneak to the desk and grab the phone.

And there they sit—my college-admissions letters, my future.

Princeton's at the top, but I save it for last. Northwestern: *Thank you for your application; we regret to* . . . University of Chicago: . . . *overwhelming number of qualified candidates and so we chose to extend you an offer on the wait list* . . . Loyola: *We are pleased to inform you* . . . So, at least I'm going somewhere, I suppose. Princeton. I hesitate; I brace; I read.

   . . . *pleased to invite you* . . .

My stomach flutters and electricity pumps, heartbeat by heartbeat, through my limbs into my fingertips and toes.

I did it.

Me, Savitri Mathur, heading to an Ivy League college. *Dear Northwestern, Eat my dust. Dear University of Chicago, Wait list, schmait list.*

I creep out of my room, down the hall, to the top of the steps. I rest one hand on our oak banister and call. But Mom's with a patient and will call me right back so I call Corey. Before I hear a ring, his voice mail kicks on and I realize what I've done. "I missed you. Leave a message and I'll catch you later."

My stomach cramps and folds me in half. I sink to the floor.

I am hunted by memories. They lurk silently, stealthily. Striking at random, swallowing me whole. I was once undone by a burrito. The smell from the cafeteria wafted into the hall, reminding me of Corey gutting it through hot salsa. I had to bolt to the bathroom and sob in a stall. Who cries over a burrito?

Dear Death, Trying to move on is like building a sand castle while the waves keep coming in.

I don't have any idea how to start over, but sobbing on the floor probably isn't it. I push myself up and tiptoe back into my room.

My cell phone rings—not my mom's number. *Who could be calling me this late?* Holly sits up, the accumulation of noises getting to her at last.

I look over at her while I listen, hardly hearing the words but absorbing the meaning: the Chicago Police Department wants us to come in for a lineup. To see if we can identify Wiry.

Yes. Find Wiry. Start over.

I wave my hands at Holly: *Get up, get ready.*

"What?" she mouths.

"Hurry up," I whisper. "Get dressed."

I start yanking my clothes out of the dresser while I'm talking.

"Right away," I tell Meade. "We're on our way."

After we work out the logistics (my mom has our car), we jump into Holly's dad's car—taking corners fast and speeding through yellows. I keep glancing at her out of the corner of my eye. Is she up for this?

"This is a good sign, Holly," I say. "It'll be better once Wiry is locked up."

She sighs. "I know you're all about the Future and What Happens Next, and I know you've got him all Confessed and Convicted in your head, but it's just a lineup. It might not even be him."

"But they must think they have him if they're calling us at midnight, right?"

Holly shrugs and I pinch the back of my hand, and when I release it, two crescents from my nails imprint the skin. Maybe I'm the one who isn't ready for this.

I put out my fist and she meets it with hers.

"Together," she says.

When we arrive at the station, Meade looks at me and then at Holly. He slides some papers inside a thick file with a CPD shield on the cover and a tab at the top: PAXTON, COREY. A whole bevy of answers lies in between those manila covers. *Who? Why?* Meade slides the file under his arm.

"Holly, it was good of you to come with her, but you don't have to be here."

Holly's eyes widen and her hands clench. "What are you talking about?"

I realize that Meade didn't call Holly; he called me.

107

"The state's attorney said . . . Listen, you didn't get a good look at him anyway."

"Well, shit. Well, dammit. Well, fuck."

Then I get it. If she and I pick out different people, then a jury won't believe either of us.

"So . . . ?" I say to stall. Only one word, but my voice shakes.

I try to crack the spine walnuts. Holly bangs her fist against a desk. Neither of us is enjoying our newly ascribed roles: me—only witness; her—victim only.

What if he's there but I don't recognize him? When Sergeant Paxton said I was their best link, he meant I was their *only* link.

After I sit down with a state's attorney, who gives me too many in- structions to keep straight, Meade puts his hand on the doorknob and I watch him twist it. Slow motion. Wiry steadied his aim before deliber- ately pulling a trigger. Why would someone do that? Who does that?

I'm about to find out. Nothing but glass and a wall between us.

I step into the darkened room and my eyes slowly adjust. Meade's voice drops to a whisper.

"Remember to breathe."

When I exhale, my breath shakes. I open my eyes wide and stare through a window, searching for Wiry among the five men who face me. They have roughly the right build and height, but their features—blond, brunet, salt-and-pepper, blue eyes, brown eyes—are varied. One man wipes the back of his hand against his cheek.

My throat tightens painfully. There is no way—no way—I could identify Wiry like this.

I don't know what he looks like. I only know how he moves.

As a freerunner, I'm attuned to movement. People walk in all sorts of different ways. We all have unique gaits. Our feet meet the ground in specific places (heel, mid-foot, toes). And we carry our balance in differ- ent spots (hips, spine, chest). There are an infinite number of combina- tions. The police have their fingerprint and I have mine.

I picture Wiry and his walk: his foot-strike on the balls of his feet, his center of gravity mid-hip, his weight slung back, short stride. But none of that knowledge will help while the men before me stand still.

"Take your time," the state's attorney says.

"Can I . . . can they move?"

"What?" asks Meade.

"I have to see them move. Can they walk?"

"How far?" he asks, his voice steady. "Toward you, away from you?"

"In profile? The length of the room?"

After he gives the instructions into a radio that hangs on the wall, number one strides to the end, makes a sharp turn—too sharp, too military—and strides back.

Number two shuffles—too old and uncertain.

Number three has his weight in his heels; number four swings his arms like a gorilla. The possibilities are dwindling. *Please let him be here.* I open my eyes as wide as I can, trying to take in every detail. Every moment.

Number four, no.

Last chance, last chance. When he walks, he kicks ever so slightly. Could it be him?

"Do you see him?" Meade puts his hand on my arm. "Savitri."

When I blink, my eyelashes get wet. I shake my head and swallow. No one like Wiry.

We step back into the brightness of the police station.

"I'm sorry," I say, but I'm not sure who I'm saying it to.

No, wait. I am, but he can't hear me.

They try to reassure me as they lead me back into the bright hallway. "You did good—no, great." "The fact that you are looking at more than just the face makes you a better witness," they say. *A better witness is someone who might, you know, help.*

When Meade walks me out, Holly is sitting at someone's desk. She reads a *Leopardess* comic and tugs the headband I got her, pulling it over the shaved short hair above her temple. Then she sees us. She stands up and reads my face.

"So?" she says.

My throat is so tight I can't answer. She hugs me, and instead of "I told you so," she says, "Okay."

When she lets me go, I spot Magruder in the corner and catch her eye, but she dives into a file. She's just one of the cops who promised they would find him, who claimed that they wouldn't rest until Wiry was in jail. And I don't see bags under her eyes.

I swear I can hear the seconds passing. Seconds that add up to minutes, to days, to weeks. And still nothing.

"This feels like a step backward," I say to Meade, and put my hands on my hips.

"No, it isn't. We've just eliminated another suspect." He puts Corey's file on the desk's edge, where it teeters. How much do they actually know?

"I know it's hard to wait, but finding a guy like this requires a sort of . . ." He turns to Holly. "What did your dad call it? A sort of 'ruthless patience.' We'll keep at it."

He puts his hand on Holly's shoulder; she hugs him and she thanks him. All I can manage is a terse goodbye.

As we walk down the hallway, my eyes trace cracks in the plaster.

"I thought CPD was supposed to be this powerful brotherhood—"

"They are."

"Then why can't they find him?" I ask.

She frowns and calls the elevator. "Not here and not so loud."

"No one in that lineup was even close to Wiry."

"At least you get to go in and try," she says. "At least you could recognize him if he were in front of you."

"Did I mention that I hate this?"

We get in the elevator and ride it down, and just as we step off, she grabs my arm, turns, and looks at me.

"Wait a minute. I've got it. I know what to do," she says, and her lips curve into a real smile—the first one I've seen since the shooting.

"What?"

"Trust me," she says, and laughs. "This is perfect."

She races out to her dad's car and I follow, trying to dodge the raindrops. She throws open the door and waits while I jump in. When she speeds off, I clutch the dashboard and glance at her. She drives directly west and takes a few turns, deeper into the neighborhood where Corey was killed. Two turns later, we speed past the last building we stood on together—perched on that false podium, believing ourselves invincible. My stomach tightens with every yard. I can't be here.

S&W 9 mm. A scrap of metal in my fingers.

"Look, CPD is full of good cops. And you're right, they have a bunch of resources. What they don't have is— Our descriptions suck. 'Weight backward when he walks' doesn't work for an APB. But you—you can recognize him, if only you can see him."

She pulls over on the street where Corey was killed. I fold my arms across my body, kneading my elbows. Every night I pump my ears full of sound just to sleep. I push images out: paint spilling—out; splattered cell phone—out; this street, that night—out, out, out. Now, I close my eyes.

"I can't," I say.

"Sav, I need you to look for him. You're the only one who can find him. Don't you owe Corey that much?"

Her words are like a blow to my back, knocking out my breath. I grip the edges of my seat and slowly lift my eyelids.

No yellow tape; no chalk outlines; no sign of a crime at all. The diamonds of glass and the blood have been cleaned up. On one side of the street, an open lot with nothing but scrub brush and broken bottles. A lone tree stands with a plastic bag tied to it randomly. On the other side, chain-link fences guard the backyards of houses. There is more dirt than grass in most of these yards. In one, an old TV—the kind with an

111

antenna—sits with its broken face toward us. It has been tagged by a gang: 12SS.

Acid and bile flood my mouth and I swallow them down. She watches me intently.

"How can you stand to be here?" *Why isn't she reacting? What is going through her head?* I'm overworrying again.

"Because I need you to find him. I need to see him for what he is. Flesh and Bone."

"Flesh and bone?" I say, startled by her near poetry.

"Flesh and Bone."

"You want us to sit here and hope he walks by?"

"We're going to do more than that." She digs in her messenger bag and pulls up her phone. "We get his picture. We get his picture and then . . ."

". . . and then the cops can find him? And if they can't, they can release the picture to the media. His face on every TV screen, every front page . . ." I continue her thought. Turn the vultures into scouts.

". . . He won't have any place to hide anymore."

She crosses her arms over her chest and sits back, waiting for my praise. Holly might not be able to ace her classes, but she has an inherited sense of strategy. A smile starts to creep on my face, but practicality chases it off.

"But what if this isn't his routine?"

She grabs my arm and gives me a little shake. "But what if it *is*? Sav, you said you wanted to do something for Corey. Well, this is something."

Her smile is big and broad and she looks better than I've seen her since the shooting. Which is enough for me to stay and look. More than enough.

Holly

I try to hide in sleep, but then the nightmares start.

By the time I'm fully awake, Dad is sitting on my bed beside me, and I've been folded into his arms. I open my breathing deep into my lungs while the Shadowlands disappear and my room takes shape around me.

My bureau with comics stacked high. My walls with my mom's mosaic of a rainstorm. My covers. My bed. Here. Real.

Coming Home was supposed to Make It Easier. But as soon as I walked in, I knew something was wrong. The air in the house was Thin and Still without him. The Voice started shrieking. Wordlessly. Endlessly. The floor came out from under me and I ended up in a ball, covering my ears. Once my parents got me into my room and into my bed, Mom assured me, "It'll be better tomorrow. I know this is hard, but still, you're home and that's already better."

But it isn't. His absence has only gotten worse in the ten days I've been home. The fridge, packed full with casseroles, doesn't have his favorite orange juice; his jacket isn't slung sloppily across a dining room chair; his stereo doesn't lull me to sleep. Even being rooted in my room—right here, right now—only means that I'm out of the Shadowlands. Which means he isn't here.

DID YOU THINK PICKING YOUR POISON WOULD BE PLEASANT? THE SHADOWLANDS WITH HIM OR HOME WITHOUT HIM.

Tears leak from my eyes and my sobbing quiets her voice. Then Dad's voice echoes through his chest when he says, "Tell me, SP."

We figured out our Post-nightmare Fix when I was eleven and my bad dreams became a fixture. Dad, Mom, no one knew I overheard a blow-by-blow about how Dad had stopped a convenience-store robbery. While Mom tried to figure out what had set the nightmares off, Dad said the dreams were nothing to worry about, that I'd inherited Mom's imagination. "You imagined your way into the dream. You can imagine your way out," he'd say, and together we'd rewrite the scenes. Together we'd see my way to safety.

Now I tuck my hair behind an ear.

"Sav, Corey, and I are freerunning and I'm in that midair, out-of-control moment when I . . ."

How can I tell him that the voice is infiltrating my dreams? How can . . . Wait a second. Yes, I *can* talk about the Shadowlands without getting stuffed into the loony bin. If I pretend everything I saw in the coma was a dream, Dad can help me find a way out. I can shake the Shadowlands at last.

Inside my head, the voice chuckles, low and confident. Thunder rolling between Spine and Ribs.

YOU CAN'T LEAVE THE SHADOWLANDS BEHIND. NOT WITHOUT COREY.

I stand up and brace myself—feet slightly apart, like I'm setting up for a risky jump. "When I was in the coma, I had a dream too. A different one. I was stuck in the . . . a shadowy place and a guy in the dream had Corey in a noose and was—"

"This is what you remember from the coma?"

I nod. "He had Corey in a noose and was leading him across—"

My dad stands up, grabs me by my shoulders, and leans down to me. His Midnight Breath reeks of meat loaf and sleep.

"Holly, what did he look like, Holly?"

He used my name twice in a single sentence—a sure sign of Anger Management in Action. *Why is he mad at me?*

I back up, pulling myself out of his grasp. "It doesn't matter."

"It does matter, Holly. Describe him for me."

The chuckle comes again. UNBELIEVER.

Shut up shut up! Please, shut up!

114

"Holly?"

"He looked like . . . a snake. He was a snake. Part snake, part human."

"Uh-huh," he says, and grabs a pencil and *The Leopardess* off my night table. He scribbles it down on an open page, the graphite scratching deep into a gutter. "What kind of snake?"

"What difference does that make, Dad? The coma—"

"Maybe the shooter had a tattoo that you're thinking of . . . or . . . or . . . a . . ."

"Dad!" I shout. I grab *The Leopardess* away from him. "I'm not talking about the shooter right now; I'm talking about a dream so I can leave it behind. You're supposed to help me leave it behind."

NOT A DREAM. A REALITY. STOP RUNNING FROM WHAT YOU KNOW IS TRUE.

I look from the floor to my desk, my desk to my bed, my bed to my father. He breathes heavily and watches me. He rests a hand on my shoulder—no tight embrace. After a long pause, he offers to get me water. Interrogation room tactics.

Nothing is the same. Nothing makes sense.

When he comes back, I get him out at speed, swearing I don't remember anything, swearing that I'm all right, and just plain swearing— "so damn tired." He goes and I dial Sav. When she doesn't pick up, I check the clock: 11:32. Yeah, she'd be asleep by now. I turn off the phone, roll over, and put my pillow over my head. Listening. Waiting. But no Lunatic Voice now. Minute after minute ticks by while I stay Restless but Frozen. A thump comes from Corey's room.

COREY?

Just the room settling.

But I go into Corey's now-cleaned-out room (thanks, Mom) and check. Through the shade, I see a shape. Someone is planted outside the window, trying to open it.

COREY?

I rush to the window, ID the shadow, and stop. It's only Savitri. I unlock the window and slide it open. The backyard is lit up by the alley's streetlamps and the pinkish haze that reflects My City's restless life. I reverse-engineer her path up to this window: from the fence, she could make the leap to the low roof over the porch, then walk the incline to his window.

"You called?" she says.

I chuckle. "That's some service."

She smooths her hair. "I figured if you were calling me this late . . . so I thought I'd just . . ."

"Just what? Break into a cop's house?"

"Corey never locked the window." She stops, as if she's realized what she just said.

My chuckle turns into a full-fledged laugh.

"Shut up," she says.

Which only makes me laugh harder. Then I say, "Shhh, shhhh," as if she was the one making noise. Her lips tug into a smile and her eyes crinkle.

I step back and she climbs in the window. Her smile collapses as her eyes read the Naked Walls. She turns a full circle slowly, and I just know she's taking inventory—stripped mattress, bare bureau, dustless desk. Finally, she sits on the floor.

"Why would she do this? It hasn't been that long."

"The Mourning Period is now Officially Over."

From his closet, I drag out an overstuffed plastic hamper.

"Rescued from the Great Purge," I say, and we both try to laugh. "You can keep whatever you want."

She hefts a couple of his fave books out: Dr. Seuss. *Peter Pan.* I tilt my head and stare at it—the boy who lost his shadow and stayed forever young. Books and Truth.

She flips open a cover and reads, "'Baby, oh, baby, the places you'll go, the worlds you will visit, the friends you will know.'"

Her voice breaks and she puts it on the floor. One by one, she places his things in a semicircle around her: his Flites, an ivory-handled pocket-knife, a few shirts. She puts one of the three shirts—one she gave him—to her nose. She looks at me, wincing.

"I thought it was supposed to get easier. People keep saying it gets easier, but time just eats away everything. Even his scent . . ."

Yes. Exactly. She always gets it; she always gets me.

"Everyone wants us to move on, but how can we when . . ."

"Corey can't?" I finish her thought.

"Until we have Wiry."

UNTIL WE HAVE COREY.

The Lunatic Voice has not left the building. She has set up shop. I can't talk to Mom, not to Dad, and not to Corey, but this is Sav.

"Savitri?" I proceed slowly. No Rushing In, like I did with Dad. "What do you think happens when you die? I mean, something happens, right?"

"Karma, reincarnation, no heaven, no hell—typical Hindu stuff."

Oh, there's a hell; I've found it.

She continues, "But lately—maybe it's just what we tell ourselves to get through the night." She pauses. "Why? What do you think?"

"When I was in the coma, I was . . . somewhere else."

She waits while I try to think of a way to explain the Shadowlands. Not under or over our world, but through it. With us. Inside our world.

YES.

"I was in a . . . place I've never been and Corey was . . ." *captured by a giant snake-man who led him through a desert of gunpowder?* Okay, I can't say *that*.

"Corey was what?"

"Corey was with me."

She nods as if she gets it, but then she says, "The doctors said that your brain was firing low electrical impulses. Like dreaming."

Right. Not real. But . . .

When I say nothing, she cocks her head and looks steadily at me. "Talk to me. What else, Holly? What's going on with you?"

I want to tell her so she can do what she does best—fix me. I open my mouth. But what if I do tell her and I'm unfixable? Where am I then? Humpty Dumpty on her way down? If she says I'm crazy, I probably am.

I shake my head. "I don't want to think about him there. I just want him back. Is that so wrong?"

"Of course not. Me too."

Silence falls. I guess if I can't tell her . . .

"It's late," I say.

"Do you want to talk—"

"No." It comes out sharper than I mean.

She nods and repacks the hamper, keeping the shirt. Sliding her arms in the sleeves, she wrestles it over her head. I notice that she is dressed in sweats and a workout top.

"Hey," I say. "You weren't asleep?"

She shakes her head and then gathers her hair into a ponytail. "Can't."

"So you run at night, alone?"

"What?"

When I ask about her clothes, she tells me she didn't change after her self-defense class—something that she started, ironically, the day after she went back to school. Then again, maybe that's why she did. I don't know how she is making it through that shark tank day by day.

"Will you be okay?" she asks.

I nod. She grabs the top of the window ledge and, using it as the handhold for an underbar, jumps her feet through. At the edge of the porch roof, she puts out her arms to prep for a trick. I haven't been free-running since the shooting. Haven't thrown one flip. Haven't Pushed the Edges. Maybe training will get rid of this voice in my head.

The chuckle comes again. GO AHEAD, TRY IT. I'M UNDEFEATABLE.

"Wait. Sav? Hang on a sec."

I run back to my room, change into workout clothes, tie on my Flites,

118

and pop out of the window behind her. She looks me over, her eyes resting on my shoes.

"What?" I say. "It'll help you sleep."

"You're sure? You're ready?"

"So past ready."

While she considers, I stare her down.

"I've been okayed by all the doctors. So stop treating me like I'm damaged. I'm fine."

She sighs. "But let me lead. I route the path."

She repositions herself at the edge of the roof, lining up her heels to the gutter for one of her favorite flips—a back layout, straight body arcing through the air. She puts her arms out and her eyes empty as she conquers whatever fear lives inside her. But then her eyebrows come together, and she turns to me. She steps away from the edge and scans the roof for another path. An easier path.

Her fear for me comes only in the Unconquerable Variety. She races to the side of the roof and hops down onto the fence. She takes the four-foot jump to the ground. So simple she doesn't even need to roll.

Options: Play by the Rules or Take the Leap.

I walk to the edge and look down. She stands there, waiting for me.

FEAR CANNOT LEASH YOU ANYMORE. YOU'VE SEEN DEATH, ELUDED HIS GRASP.

"No, Holly, take a safer way, okay?"

No, Sav. Fear isn't conquered by safety.

I leap and tuck. Humpty Dumpty stood on a roof; Humpty Dumpty had a great fall. I control the landing: feet to hands to shoulder roll. Perfect. A night off for all the King's horses and all His medics.

When I get up, a jolt of hot lightning sears through my skull and my brain spins off-kilter. I want to put my hands on my head as the world shifts back into place. But if I let on, Sav will only baby me.

Pain can be good for you, I remind myself.

THAT WHICH DOESN'T KILL YOU HAD BETTER WATCH IT NEXT TIME.

Sav puts her hand on my arm, steadying me.

I pull away and smile. Big. "If you're going to make a mistake, make it at full speed."

Sav narrows her eyes and draws her lips into an *I'm-not-amused* line.

"'Take a safer way'? Just who'd you think you were talking to?" I start to laugh.

Savitri's smile comes slower, cautiously.

This is what I need, Sav. Keep up.

I hold out my fist and she balls her hand. We bump knuckles and hiss: *ssshaww.*

Grief can't keep up as we speed through the night.

Savitri

31 days and 20 hours after

When the noon bell rings, I walk the long way around the building rather than pass by Corey's locker. Someone—no, lots of people—turned it into a shrine: his senior picture center, fresh flowers in the vents, cards taped open so we can all compare, see who is the most devastated. School may be filled with land mines, but after three weeks back, I'm learning where they lie.

It's too cold to eat outside again, and so I find Josh in the corner of the library where we've been eating lunch together. After that first time, he came back to the staircase where I was hiding and we repeated our routine, saying nothing, neither of us eating. Both of us shivering. Day by day, he coaxed me inside, first bringing lunch, then getting me to eat, and finally finding a spot in the library—behind the stacks, with a small table and two big chairs—where no one else was. We made it through a whole forty minutes once, talking. He keeps me there with anecdotes about Corey.

I am sinking into the soft purple chair when he starts.

"Did Corey ever tell you about the streetlamp and the fire truck?"

I lie and say no. I open my yogurt and spoon some into my mouth while Josh talks. I wish I was swapping stories with Holly, but she does not reminisce about Corey. Not ever.

"You know how stoplights hang out into the street, right? Well, we wanted to get on top of one of those."

They leapt off the roof of a parked armored truck and clung to the

121

crossbar. Then, daring each other to touch the light itself, they swung out there and propped themselves up. They were still laughing and congratulating themselves when the armored truck pulled away. Free-runners are improv artists, adjusting our movement to our surroundings, but when the surroundings change . . .

Well.

Stranded twenty-five feet aloft, like two wingless birds on a wire.

When the fire department arrived, they jumped to its truck bed and off that onto the asphalt, rolled their landings, and ran—one west, one east, so only one of them would get caught. Of course, Josh was the one who ended up stabbing roadside trash in an orange vest.

"Corey always had luck on his side," Josh says, finishing the story.

A knot of bodies. Dear Luck, you are wasted on the wrong things.

Josh gets his first bite of his sandwich and pops open his Coke can. He takes a long pull.

"Listen," he says, "I know Holly's at home now and I still haven't seen her. Do you think she'd be up for a visitor?" When I hesitate, he hurries to make his case. "Fact is, Savi, I'm still in love with her. I'm not going to do anything to hurt her. Not again. And especially not now."

I press my lips together. It's something I've known all along, and part of why hanging out with Josh makes sense to me now. He was one of us and has a piece of Corey that is beyond the flowers-in-the-locker bor-rowed grief of the other seniors.

"You're a loaded topic for her. If she wants to, she'll come to you."

I finish my yogurt and slide a mint into my mouth.

"Okay. But you do believe me about wanting to help her, right? So can I ask you to . . . just don't stand in her way."

Somehow he has missed the most fundamental dynamic between Holly and me.

"You say that as if I could," I say.

"You kind of are."

"What?" My mouth dries out as I try to parse what he's saying—or, rather, what he's not saying. If he sees me as an obstacle, then why did he leave his lunch buddies to sit here with me?

"Did Corey . . . did he stand in her way before? I mean, he was so pissed and maybe . . ."

I shake my head. "Breaking up with you was her decision."

"Okay." Josh's eyebrows lower and he looks down. He swallows loudly. "Well, can you tell her I want to talk to her? It's not her choice unless you tell her. . . ."

I clench my jaw. Why didn't I see Josh's sudden kindness for the agenda it is? Corey would have. Corey would be livid that I let him in at all.

The least you can do for the dead is protect the ones they have left behind.

"I'm not your way back to her, Josh. Guess you wasted your time."

I get up and walk off, throwing the rest of my lunch in the trash. I don't respond when he calls my name.

Holly

Being early—or even on time—is for people who have nothing better to do than wait, people who would let time tick-tock-stop. But here I am, sitting on my bed, waiting for Sav so we can train and then look for Wiry—our new routine, established circa one week and four nightmares ago.

Mom's three-beat knock sounds from my door before she opens it and sits down on my bed. Her face cracks obscenely when she tries on her New Smile. Warning: contains Artificial Flavoring.

We go through a quick "how are you today?" and other such crap. Then she looks me over and says, "Maybe you could change and we can go visit Corey's grave."

NO. For once, the voice is small—almost vulnerable.

"No."

"Holly, you missed the funeral and I want you to . . . say goodbye."

"Did you get that from a book or your shrink?"

Her mouth returns to a flat line. Which is better. Anything is better than that dishonest smile. Anything is better than the Move On mantra she spouts. Last week, she cleaned out Corey's room. Next week, I'm supposed to Return to My Routine. But first I must visit Corey's grave. The moves for her three-step dance to the theme music of Closure. Screw Closure.

WE'RE NOT GOING TO LEAVE COREY BEHIND.

Options: Feed the Lunatic Voice with responses or ignore it. It will go away. Somehow. *It's not a voice from the Shadowlands, not Kortha's way to drag me back, because it is Not Real.*

NOT FROM THE SHADOWLANDS. FROM WITHIN YOU; BORN OF YOUR PAIN.

I'm not listening.

THAT'S NOT POSSIBLE.

Mom takes my hand. "I know you're afraid, Holly."

"I am not—"

"You look like you're . . . Let's not argue about that. You can't let fear stop you."

"Original," I say.

I've heard it before: Embrace your Fears, Conquer your Fears, Be One with your Fears. The Paxton family glue. But without Corey, glue ain't gonna cut it. Corey's absence has gutted my parents. All they have left for me are Fake Smiles and Loud Fights—ones I hear through doors, through walls, through floors. I had thought they'd cling to each other, but instead it's like watching a building implode in slow motion, as if the foundation has been ripped out from under it. This Corey-less World makes as little sense to them as it does to me.

"We're all hurting, but being rude to me won't make it easier."

Mom crosses her arms over her chest—prepping for Lecture the Kids Mode. But then I hear Sav's voice downstairs. When I turn to leave, Mom sighs.

"I already have other plans," I say. "My therapy comes first."

"Maybe afterward?"

"It'll be dark by then," I say, glancing at the clock again. We ended up with a late start since Sav had homework. "Besides, the whole point of the training is to push myself as much as is . . . safe. I come back exhausted. Another day."

"Soon," she says.

I bolt down the steps and, catching Sav by her sleeve, pull her outside.

Even though it's April, I wouldn't call it spring yet—there's too much muck, a coat of wet snow lies on the lawns, and the air still has Teeth—but I'm down to short sleeves. I'll be generating my own heat soon enough.

"Let's run," I say.

Sav lets me set the pace. Because of the Baby Steps I'm supposed to take, we've returned to the playground where we first started free-running. We jog, slowly, just warming up, past the park with the tennis courts, past Josh's house—the block in Slo-Mo.

Mom and Dad moved to the Morgan Park neighborhood when Mom was pregnant with us, right after they got married—a compromise. Dad wanted to stay in the city, not only because CPD required it but also because he's a true South Sider: a Big Shoulders, Blue-Collar, the City that Works South Sider. Mom—a suburban native—was soothed by Morgan Park's big lawns and old houses ("Original woodwork!"). Barely the city, she calls it, far enough south of the notorious South Side to be safe, she says. Now, I'll bet she wishes she'd built six-foot-tall perimeter walls around Morgan Park and kept track of the keys.

Three blocks into the run, we crunch down on clumps of sidewalk salt, left over since everything is melting. Sav changes course, hopping onto the lawn. I give her a funny look.

"I can't . . . something about the sound." She waves a hand by her ear. I'm about to crack a joke about her princess-and-the-pea-sensitive ears when she looks down and away from me. She nearly whispers, "The sound bothers me now."

I don't know how crunching on sidewalk salt and the shooting are related, but I join her on the lawn.

"You know what really pisses me off?" I say. "Wiry is out there some-where, and for him, nothing has changed. And here we are . . ." As-saulted by sounds. Sav can't even run down a sidewalk and I'm battling a Voice in my head. If I'd seen Wiry—like any Ideal Witness should have—then I'll bet I could convince the Lunatic Voice that he is Flesh and Bone, not of the Shadowlands at all.

Our playground sits in the middle of a park—an Oasis in Reverse. We have random wooden posts, monkey bars, a red dome, swings. Every-thing. I start on monkey bars, crossing back and forth twice. Hand over hand, my body flies cleanly through the air. I walk over to the two metal bars at different heights—four and five feet. A long time ago, I had to climb to the taller one. Now I have to tuck my legs. Hanging upside down, I hook my knees over the bar, ask Sav to hold my feet. Clenching my core, I do inverted sit-ups.

The blood crawls down into my skull, and my head becomes an overripe melon. Already split once. After four, I grab onto the bar with my hands and swing myself down. The world tilts again and my head aches. No more upside down, not for a while.

The voice chuckles.

At least she's in a good mood.

GET STRONGER.

I spot Sav, who passes my four without hesitation. A corner of her shirt slips out of the grip of her waistband and I watch her six-pack abs contract and release. No thirty percent muscle mass loss for her. She only gets twenty-five, though—not her usual thirty. Sitting beside me week after week without training took its toll on her too.

At least I can outdo her on pull-ups. Or I used to. Twenty to her fifteen. She gets on the short bar and I grab onto the taller one, our feet hugged close to our bodies. After a measly twelve, the strain across my collarbone begins to sting and I'm slower on my rise.

Sav looks at me sidelong. Watching me Fail. Again.

WEAK AND SLOW. DO ANOTHER.

I yank hard; my biceps clench and hold but can't overcome Gravity.

COREY NEEDS YOU STRONGER AND FASTER.

I rise. Gravity be damned.

STRONGER.

Two more. Matching her fifteen.

BETTER.

When Mom found out that I was training again, she put a call into my physical therapist, who reassured her that training is good for

127

me as long as I'm keeping the goal simple—get me back to where I was before, get back to one hundred percent. I don't know what the Lunatic's goal is.

Sav climbs to the top of the dome and stands there. I wait. Usually I'd goad her, but today I'm silent. *Let her be limited by fear long enough that I can catch up.*

I'm horrible. I know. I don't really care.

She swings to her hands and drops to the ground. Still too freaked to try the back layout from the top.

"Precision jumps?" she says, pointing to a set of picnic tables.

We make a circuit, playing that the ground is lava as we leap from tabletop to bench to tabletop. There's no Thrill in Picnic Tables, but even I know that rooftops are Off-Limits.

FOR NOW.

The sun has melted into the horizon by the time we are finished. My arms, neck, legs, and—God—my head aches, but I push myself to walk alongside Sav on our way back, our slow cooldown.

PAIN TRANSFORMS US ALL. MAKES US STRONGER. COURT IT.

The quiet is broken by the occasional car a couple of blocks away on Western Ave. We turn a corner and I can't describe how I know it, but something is wrong.

BEING WATCHED.

Come on, I dare the world, *throw something else at me. I can handle it. In-fucking-vulnerable. Survived a bullet to the head. What else you got?*

COME OUT, COME OUT, WHEREVER YOU ARE.

I look behind us and scan the parked cars on the street. Nothing. But I inhale a familiar smell—gunpowder, rot, and blood—the Shadowlands.

I rely on what I see. My eyes can see beyond darkness and into the Shadowlands.

YES.

Which is when the world flashes halftone—

128

And then the world returns to normal.

Savitri is still keeping her pace, her expression unfazed.

She didn't see it.

BUT YOU CAN'T DENY WHAT YOU SEE.

I'm just tired. Just exhausted. Oh, God, don't let this be real.

Sav stops walking and points up the street. Small eyes, low to the ground, are staring at us.

I KNEW WE WERE BEING WATCHED.

Then she tilts her head, curious, and walks toward them. I charge it—whatever it is. *Bring. It. On.*

A CREATURE OF THE SHADOWLANDS?

The eyes turn and the shape moves, light on dark, until it slides into the beam of a streetlight. Its tail skitters out of the edge of the light.

"An opossum," she says, delighted.

NO, NO, NO. SOMETHING ELSE. ANOTHER KIND OF TAIL ENTIRELY. A CREATURE OF THE NIGHT.

"Leopards are nocturnal," I say.

"Are you okay?" she asks.

As we approach my house, Dad's voice breaks through the walls, through the door, and greets us on the sidewalk.

". . . Trisha. Stop blaming me, Trisha," he says.

She is louder than him. "Everyone's blaming you. Meade's investigating your cases, isn't he?"

"He's investigating every—"

"Because everyone knows Corey didn't have any enemies, but you . . . you have a whole cityful. You brought this violence to our door—to our kids. Did you think 'Serve and Protect' only applied to strangers?"

I don't mean to, but I shrink closer to Sav. If we're going to hunt for Wiry, I'll need to go inside and get the keys.

"Come on," she says. "Let's just go to my house. It's late and I'm tired."

Silver-Tongued Sav gives me an Out. I nod.

We walk a couple of doors down, and she pulls the hide-a-key from under a big planter. When the planter meets the cement steps, the noise slices through me. *God, God, Goddammit. My head hurts.* Sharp and brutal.

AND TEMPORARY.

Once we're inside, the banister greets us with a pink Post-it. She glances at it, but we both know it means that another birth has taken her mom out.

Sav's front room is set up for comfort. Two big sofas sit at the edge of an area rug. Block-printed pillows, which Sav has told me are native to some region of India, are piled along the backs. They are the not-too-soft, not-too-hard, just-right kind.

"Oh, hey," she says, "I have something for you."

She goes upstairs and I get ibuprofen from the bathroom. I fish out three capsules. Normally, I wouldn't take the meds, but screw it. I'm too tired. In the kitchen, I pull down two short green glasses.

130

Sav stops in the doorway and looks from me to her laptop, which is sitting open on the counter next to a pile of thin Indian comic books. She hurries over and closes the computer, even though the screen saver is on.

"What was that?"

"I was just . . . surfing." Her voice sounds deliberately casual. She hands me a comic book—the latest *Leopardess*. "Came out today," she says.

Nice try, Sav.

"Surfing for?"

She looks away and is silent.

So I say, "Porn?"

She smiles and shakes her head. Then she says, "Is there such a thing as academic porn?"

"Professors in their underwear? A ruler in one hand and handcuffs in the other?"

"Ewww," she says, and laughs, but when she is done, she still doesn't answer. So I stare at her.

She shrugs. "Just looking at colleges."

Oh. My. God. "Princeton."

She nods and grabs the glasses from me. She turns her back on me, walks over to the sink, and fills the glasses. "It's official. You didn't check yours, or . . . his?"

"I'd have to graduate for that."

"I'm sure the teachers will help you catch up when you're ready to come back."

I snatch the glass from her and gulp down the medicine. I can't even imagine being back at school.

She regards me and her lips twist to one side. "Are you okay?"

"Dandy." When she frowns, I say, "Ask a stupid question, get a useless answer."

I walk into her front room and plop down on her couch. My muscles rest heavily against the smooth fabric. I curl up and grab a pillow. She hands me my favorite throw from the other couch.

"So, where else did you get in? Northwestern?"

Sav shakes her head. "Safety schools. Loyola. DePaul. And Princeton. As if that makes any sense."

I remember the way she sighed and watched Corey climb down the podium building that night. Maybe I'm just being paranoid. She wouldn't leave us. Can't leave us. Not now. I float a test balloon.

"So when do you leave?"

"I have to commit on May first, but I won't go until August," she says quickly.

Corey is gone, Mom has become a tearless automaton, Dad wears his badge even when he doesn't, and Sav . . . she's probably drawing big Xs through each day on her calendar.

YOU HAVE ME.

Oh, yeah, that's a consolation.

THEN LET'S GET COREY BACK. NO NEED TO BE ALONE. I WON'T LET GO OF HIM.

I pull the throw over me and curl up even tighter.

"Do you want to sleep over?"

"I don't want to sleep at all."

When she sits next to me, I exchange the pillow for her legs. But all I want, all I really want, is her voice—her rough voice that can lock words together into links and chains and has a logic of its own. I want to make sure I'm Here, that sleep or the Voice won't suck me back to the Shadowlands.

TOO MUCH HAS BEEN LEFT BEHIND TO ESCAPE.

Nothing will stop the Voice. She paces inside the cage of this reality, rattling the bars. If she has this much power caged, then what will happen if I let her win?

Sav reaches for the other throw and pulls it over her.

"Just keep talking to me," I say.

"Sure." Her eyebrows come together in the silence. Nothing to say On Demand. So I point at the comic book that rests on the table. "Would you . . . would you read this to me?" I ask.

She hesitates, giving me a funny look, and reaches for it slowly.

"You don't have to."

"No, of course. It's just that . . . when you were in the hospital, I read *Origins* to you."

She reads it aloud while I stare at the pictures. Even though The Leopardess is kicking some gangbanger ass, I have to work to keep my eyes open through the whole thing. When we get to the end, I'm barely awake, but I say, "What did you do when you finished reading it when we were in the hospital?"

She tells me that she taped up the pages on the wall.

"And then you said 'Don't leave,' right?"

"How did you know that?"

Because those are the words I saw, the words you pulled me out with. But I can't say *that.* Not without sounding insane.

I can't help it; I'm just so tired that I start to cry. She strokes my hair from root to tip. Root to tip. A steady pace that promises more to come, that promises she'll stay here.

I say quietly between sobs, "Sav, I know Princeton is important to you, but . . . please . . ."

Root to tip.

". . . don't leave."

Her hand stops mid-stroke. Her body tenses and it takes a full beat before she starts to stroke my hair again.

She doesn't say *I wouldn't leave you.* She doesn't say *How could I think of Princeton now?*

She doesn't say anything at all.

Savitri

38 days and 16 minutes after

I stand and wait for my turn to be attacked. A large padded arm comes over my neck.

If an attacker comes at you from behind . . .

I slam my heel against his foot. As his head comes forward, I throw mine back and my skull knocks into his protective face mask. As faceless as Wiry. We can't find Wiry, no matter how long we wait in a car. But right here, right now, I have this body to fight. *What would I do if I had Wiry's body?*

And suddenly I'm out of my head—into a teeth-baring animalistic rage I didn't know I had. My breath grows into growls, my nails morph into claws, and every time I make contact, one word comes out of my mouth. Again and again, I yell, "Why?"

I throw my elbow into his ribs, and even though I hear something snap, the contact feels minimal. "Why?"

I slide out of his grasp. I put my hand on his padded shoulder—in control of his body now—and throw my knee into his nuts. "Why?"

As he crumples, I fire it again into his faceless face, and he flops to the ground.

I'm supposed to run. But I need more. I need to make him understand what it means to hurt, to lose. My kicks become my translator. I launch my foot into his side again and again and again. But then he grabs my foot and pulls. The world blurs and my throat tightens.

When I hit the floor, reverberations echo up my spine. He grabs for me and I start screaming wordlessly and kicking until I'm free. Then I

134

shoulder-roll backward and am up on my feet. I race down to the end of the training center and lean against the wall, trying to regain my composure, to overcome my ragged breathing. The silence that I've left at the other end of this big, open room is broken and I hear the teacher say, "Leave her alone. Give her space. This happens sometimes."

I sit down, put my head in my hands, and stare at the thin carpeting.

Before Corey and I were dating, we spent a day in a gym spotting each other on wall flips—our hands intertwined in a freerunners' hold. I was midair, with my rotation too slow to land on my feet, when his grip tightened. He tried to speed me up, pushing my back. I landed on my knees, and he lost his balance, catching himself with one hand on the wall mat. He pulled on my arm to get me standing and said, "Seven times down, eight times up."

I stood up and stared at him—too long and with too much longing. He let go of my hand fast and my cheeks flared hot while I stared at the fading impression of his hand on the mat. "Old Japanese proverb," he said, prattling on about how he learned it in his martial arts class, relieving the awkwardness.

Seven times down . . . I push myself off the floor.

But my hands stay in fists for the remainder of the class, even as everyone asks me if I'm okay. My fingers stay clenched on the half-mile walk—which I take at a sprint—to Holly's house. The world blurs—speed and tears—but when I arrive, I can finally roll my fingers open.

Flat-handed, I bang on the door.

This will be better.

Even though Holly's been colder since she asked me to stay in Chicago, this will be better.

Through the door, I hear Sergeant Paxton's heavy tread. I lean far back and clear my throat, preparing. Every time he sees me, he still asks about some detail of my story, but I have nothing new to give. *When will he stop?* But I get it. Stopping is tantamount to giving up—something neither of us knows how to do.

When the door opens, he's sipping coffee from a stone mug. His gaze slides off me.

"I can't remember. Do you drink coffee?"

I shake my head.

He tilts the cup toward me—empty.

"Refill required," he says, and leaves me un-interrogated. "Holly's in her room."

His shoelace drags on the hardwood floor, and even though I should, I don't call him back. I climb the stairs, pass Corey's closed door, and knock on Holly's.

She lets me in but doesn't sit, doesn't notice that I'm a mess any more than her father did. She just does circuits around the room. She says I'm late and we should hurry up to look for Wiry again. Am I coming or not?

* * *

The street hasn't been empty—a string of unrelated people pass by us in the course of an hour: a mom with a wobbly toddler, clumps of boys, and a man who trails a good distance after them.

I glance at Holly, who is sitting back, looking tired. We've never had a subject to avoid, and Princeton sits like a pit between us. And while it is a silence I could do without, it has given me time to mull over Sergeant Paxton's sudden indifference.

I reach across the console separating me from Holly and she jumps, her hands tightening on the steering wheel. When she sees that I'm just turning up the heat, she puts another chip in her mouth.

"So?" I say.

"So," she says, "Mom's insisting on tomorrow to see Corey's grave."

"I'll come if you want."

She nods, and then nudges me with her elbow and points to a guy who is coming around the corner.

"Him?" she asks.

136

We both lean forward, looking through the windshield as he crosses the street. She lifts her camera phone, getting him in her sights.

The man is a medium-height, slight-build white guy, but the way he clips the sidewalk, heels striking hard on the cement, means he's too old—a stride of a mid-twenty-year-old. Which means Wiry must be closer to our age.

I shake my head and Holly puts her phone down. She crunches on another chip and then shakes the bag, as if testing its weight.

"I see how my Cop-Uncles end up with surveillance stomachs."

She throws the bag in my backseat and brushes her fingers on the upholstery, leaving four trails of orange in her wake. I look back at the street and sigh.

"This isn't working."

"We're doing what hunters do, Sav. We're waiting along a well-trodden path to see if he'll wander by."

"It's not very efficient," I say.

"But you don't have a better suggestion, do you?"

When I'm silent, she turns in her seat and inspects me. "Do you?"

I shrug.

"Okay, out with it."

She leans in and looks at me the way her father used to—like she wants every scrap of information from my brain right this second. At the lineup, Meade quoted Sergeant Paxton, talking about a ruthless patience. Which means they've been discussing the case, and since Sergeant Paxton won't ever be satisfied with bits and pieces . . .

"I think your dad has a copy of the police file."

She purses her lips and twists back into her seat. "No, Dad decided a long time ago what kind of cop he was and what rules he'd break. And that would be solidly against policy."

"Do you honestly think that policies matter to him now? This is about his son, his kids."

She doesn't appreciate all she has. My dad chose his career over his

137

family. Her dad married Trisha when she got pregnant, withdrew his application to the FBI so they wouldn't be bopped around the country, and applied to CPD instead.

I explain how he's stopped grilling me, stopped caring.

"I've been under his bare bulb since the shooting. You can't imagine what that's like—"

"Actually, I can," she says, her voice quiet.

Another reason she can't stand being in her house anymore? For a fraction of a second, I wonder if she could come to New Jersey with me, but what would she do there?

"But so what if he does have it?" she asks.

"Well . . ." It seems too obvious to say. With the file, we might learn what Wiry was doing with that knife and what that tassel was that he took from them. We might learn why. "We need it."

"You want me to steal a police file?"

I shift in my seat. "Would it be stealing if you're taking it from your father? From your own house?"

"I'm pretty sure Dad would see it that way."

She sits back and crosses her arms, looking strangely smug. I squint at her.

"If you're going to start something like this," she says, "you might need to stick around to see it through."

This has nothing to do with stealing or her dad or the file. It has everything to do with Princeton.

"I thought you said you needed this. 'Flesh and Bone,' you said."

She uncrosses her arms and then laughs, caught. "You know, you're pretty good at calling me out on my shit."

I know I'm supposed to laugh with her, but I don't. Asking me to stay is one thing; trying to use our hunt for Wiry as leverage is something else altogether.

There's no humor in my voice when I say, "What are friends for?"

138

Holly

After insisting that it was time for me to "say my goodbyes" graveside, Mom wormed her way out. "A headache"? Right. But since she's the Grieving Mother, Dad doesn't push her. As for me—a Silent Car, with the Lunatic Voice in fine form. Dad stares, eyes front, hands at ten and two and jaw locked. I turn and gaze out the window while Sav sits quietly in the backseat.

WE CAN'T LEAVE COREY THERE—NOOSE CHAFING HIS NECK, GUNPOWDER SAND UNDER HIS FEET.

Not real, not real.

YOU CAN'T DENY WHAT YOU'VE SEEN. YOU CAN'T DENY WHAT YOU'VE HEARD.

That's right, and when I see Corey's grave, maybe you'll shut up.

BUT THEN, says the logical lunatic, HOW DID YOU KNOW HE WAS GONE WHEN YOU WOKE UP? NO ONE HAD TO SAY IT.

Maybe I was conscious after I was shot and my brain is doing the trauma block, or maybe I overheard my parents talking while I was in the coma. Or I could just tell by the look on Sav's face.

The lunatic's reality is so much easier than my own. If only she were right, if only there were some other reality that I could rescue Corey from, if only I could bring him back.

Sav taps my shoulder and offers me a mint. She shrugs when I refuse, popping two in her mouth. She sucks on so many of those now, she smells like a toothpaste factory.

We drive along the side of the graveyard. The spiked iron fence reminds me of a prison. As if they need to lock the dead away. Once we've parked and gotten out, we pass grave after grave on our walk up a broad path. Then Dad and Sav stop.

He lifts his hand and points. "Up that row. Fourth from the end."

When Sav starts to come with me, he puts his hand on her arm, but she shakes him off in an Un-Sav-like Move. I guess Defying Authority is an Act of Loyalty she can manage. Unlike Princeton. I wave her away.

I take unsteady steps on the sloping grass. The sun is warm overhead and the grass looks like it has been clipped one blade at a time. Birds chirp out a three-note tune. This is how "serene" is supposed to look.

THIS MOMENT IS TOO PERFECT. TOO STAGED.

As I walk, I scan names on headstones—Nameless Names. Corey is five headstones away. *Corey is there. Underground. Under that ground.*

YOU AND I—WE BOTH KNOW WHERE HE IS.

Corey is three, two . . .

I press the heels of my palms against my eyes. A headstone edged in purple appears in the blackness. When I pull my hands away and open my eyes, a familiar figure is waiting at a gravestone in the distance.

Who is that?

HAS COREY SLIPPED HIS NOOSE AND FOUND HIS WAY BACK?

There is no way back from dead, Lunatic.

YOU WALKED THERE, SMELLED THE DUST, FELT THE HEAT. AND THEN YOU RETURNED. TWINS ARE CONNECTED BY BLOOD. WHERE YOUR HEART BEATS, HIS ECHOES.

Corey?

I'm trying to force myself to look to Corey's gravestone when it clicks. That's not even a man.

My eyes find him again. He raises his head. Recognition comes into his face and I'm caught in his headlight eyes. I am here in this cemetery; I am not dreaming; I am not in a coma. And I am not dead.

And yet:

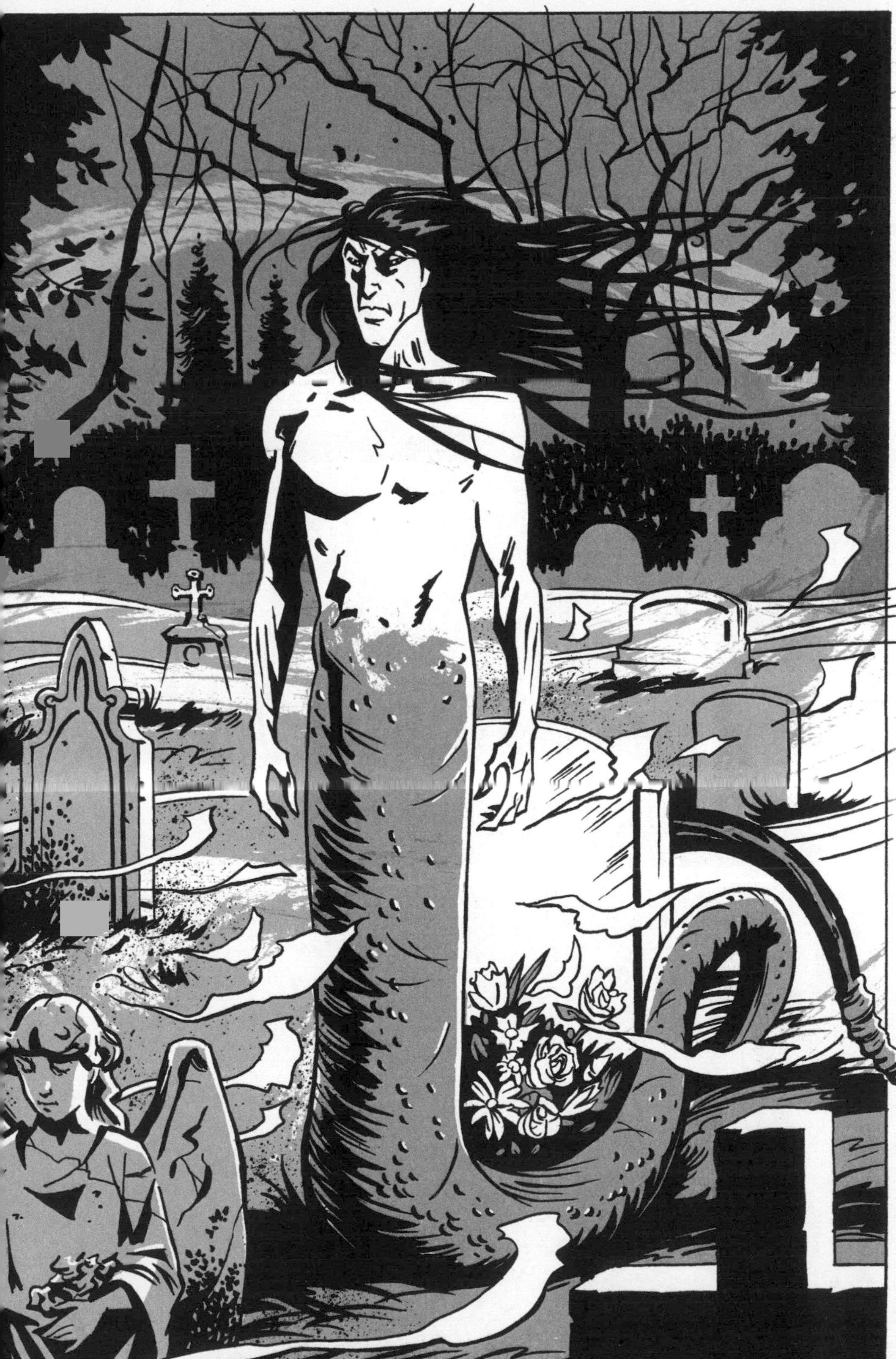

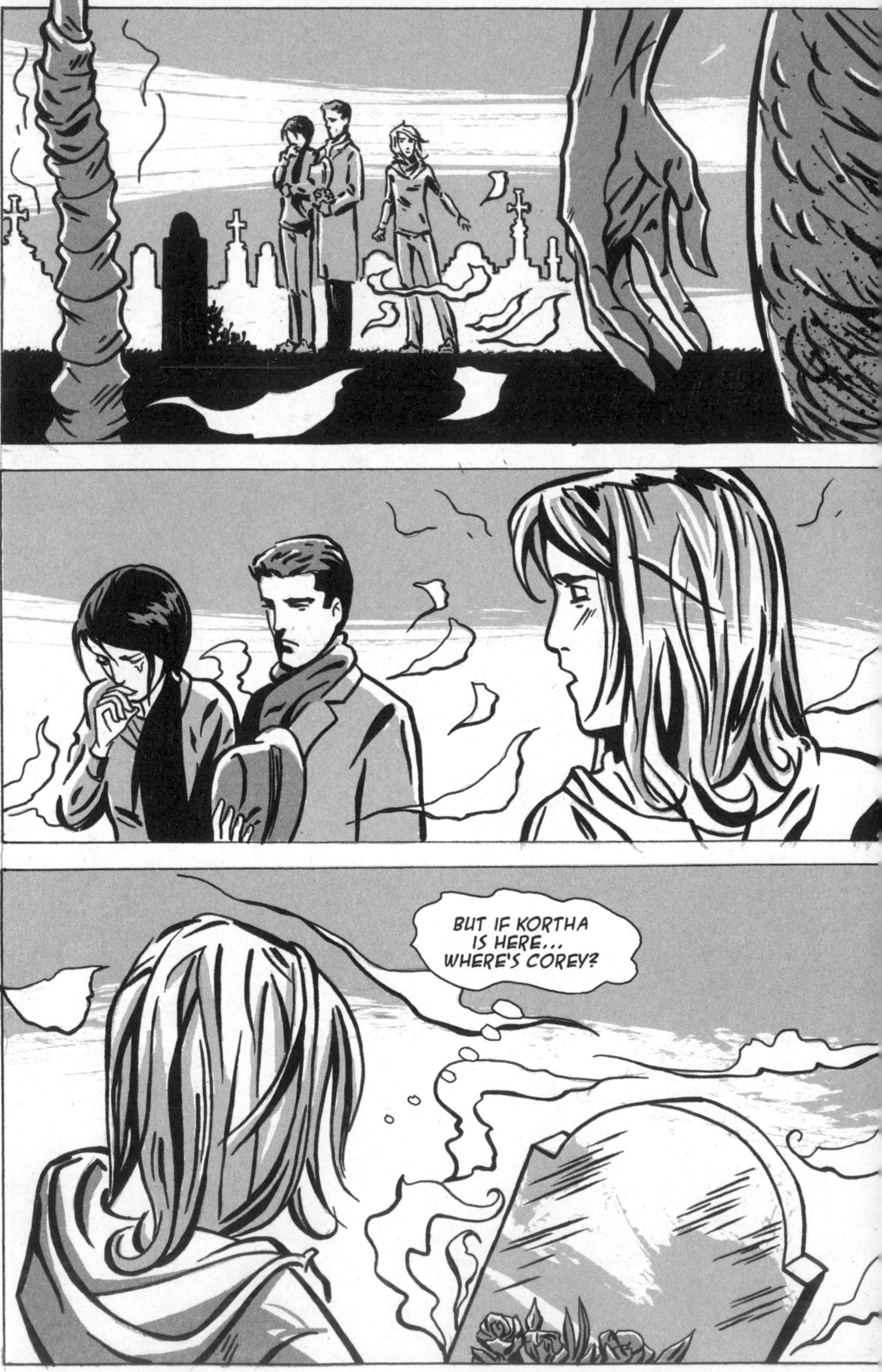
BUT IF KORTHA IS HERE... WHERE'S COREY?

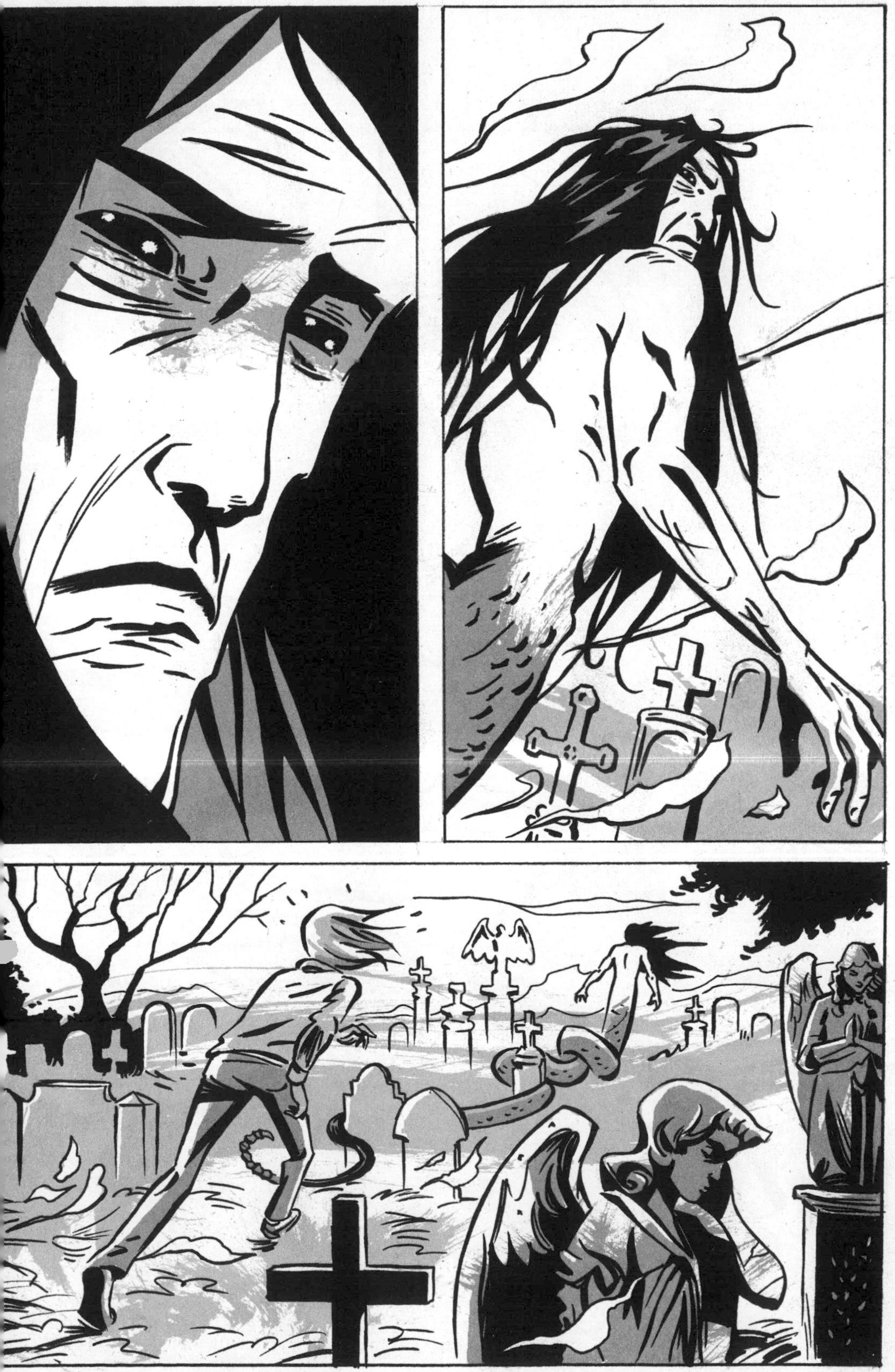

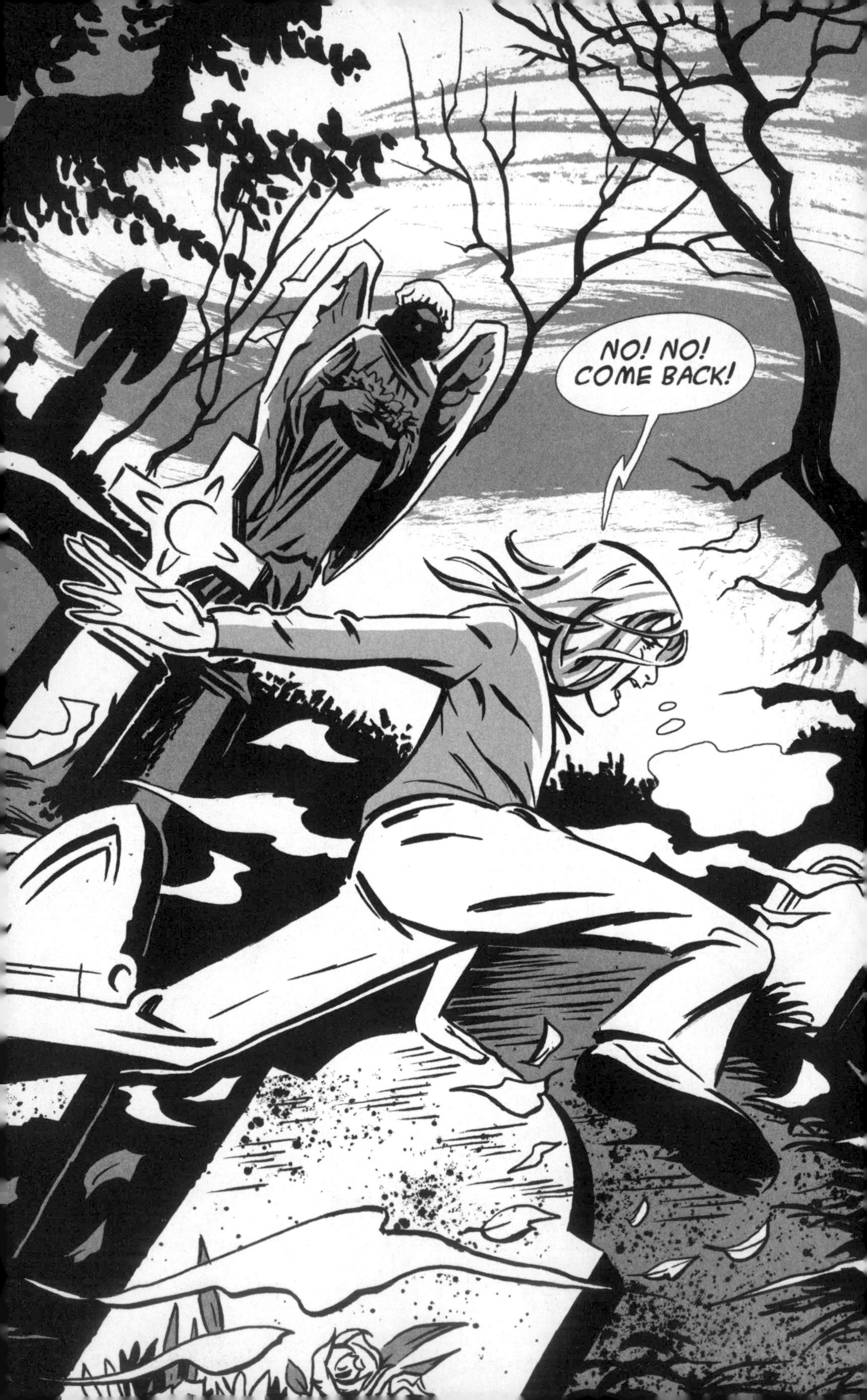
NO! NO! COME BACK!

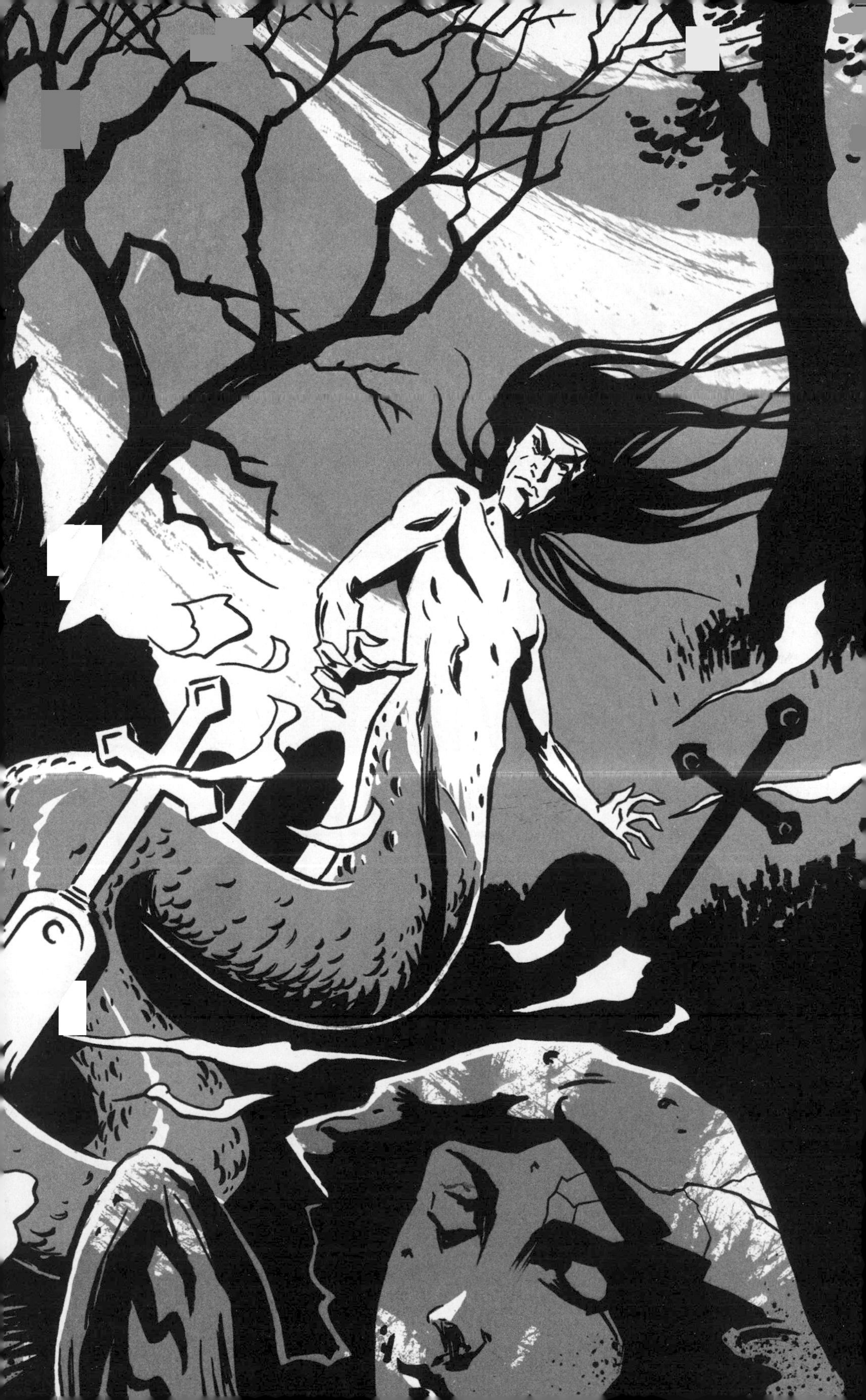

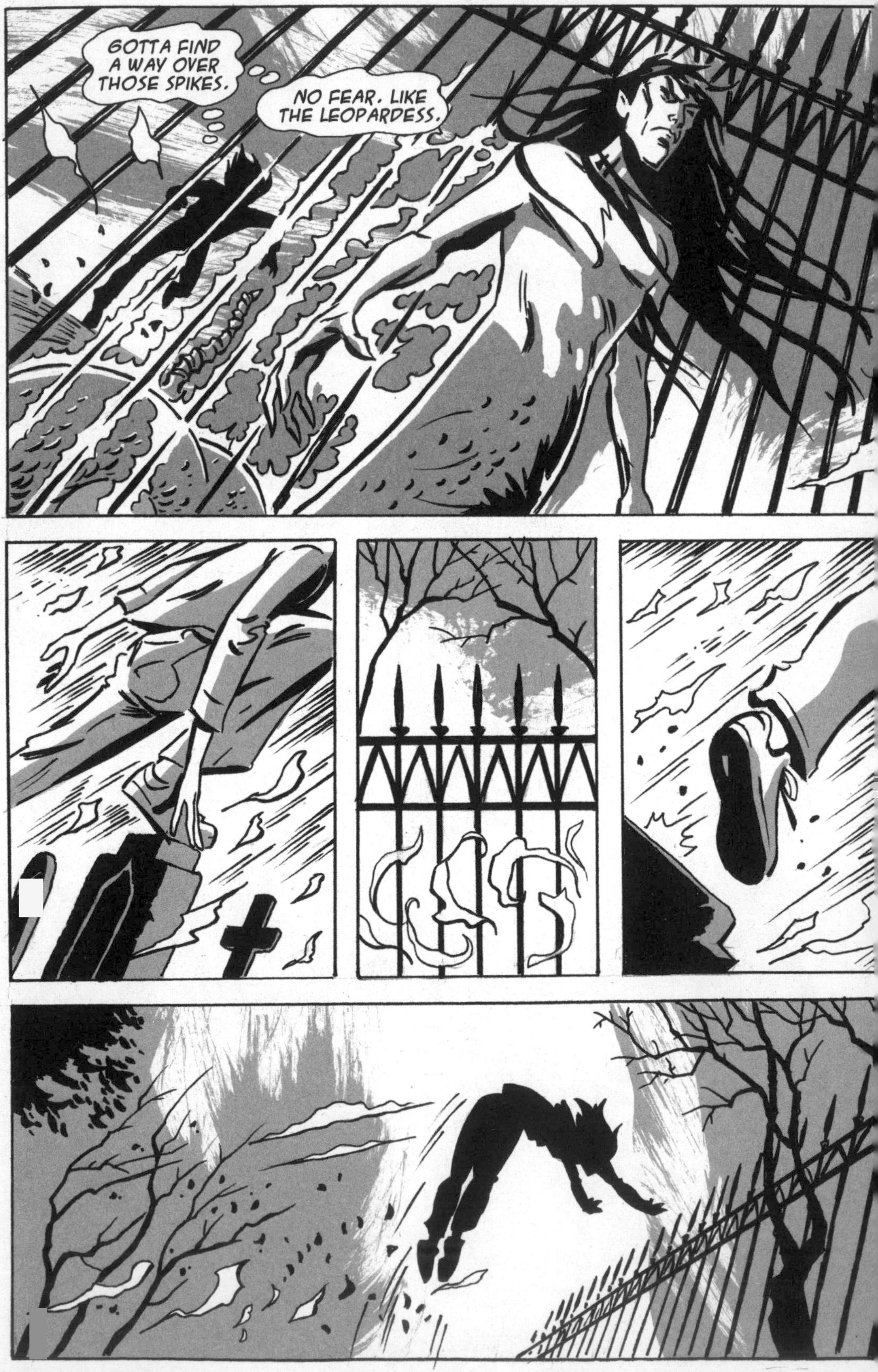
GOTTA FIND A WAY OVER THOSE SPIKES.
NO FEAR. LIKE THE LEOPARDESS.

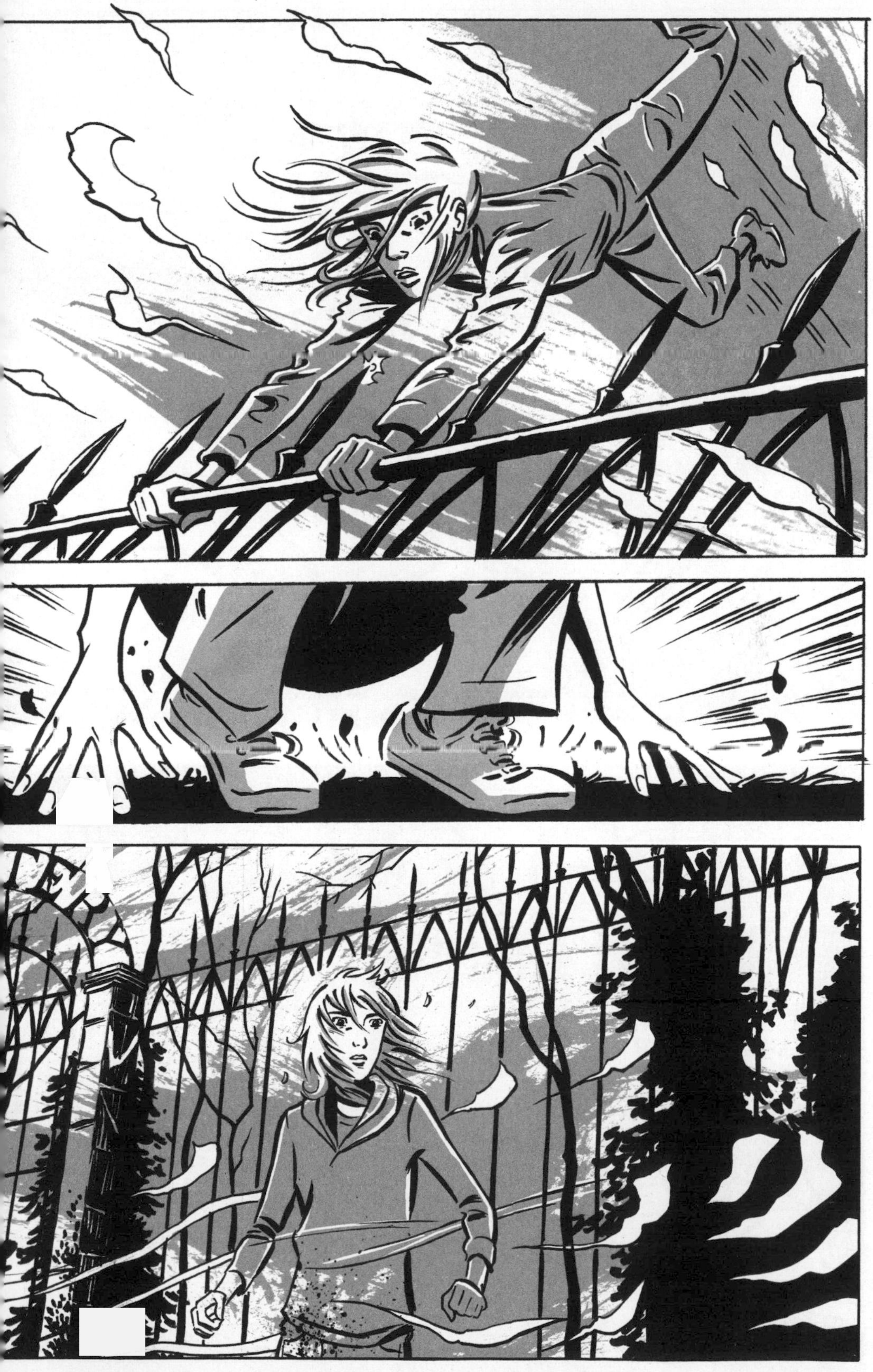

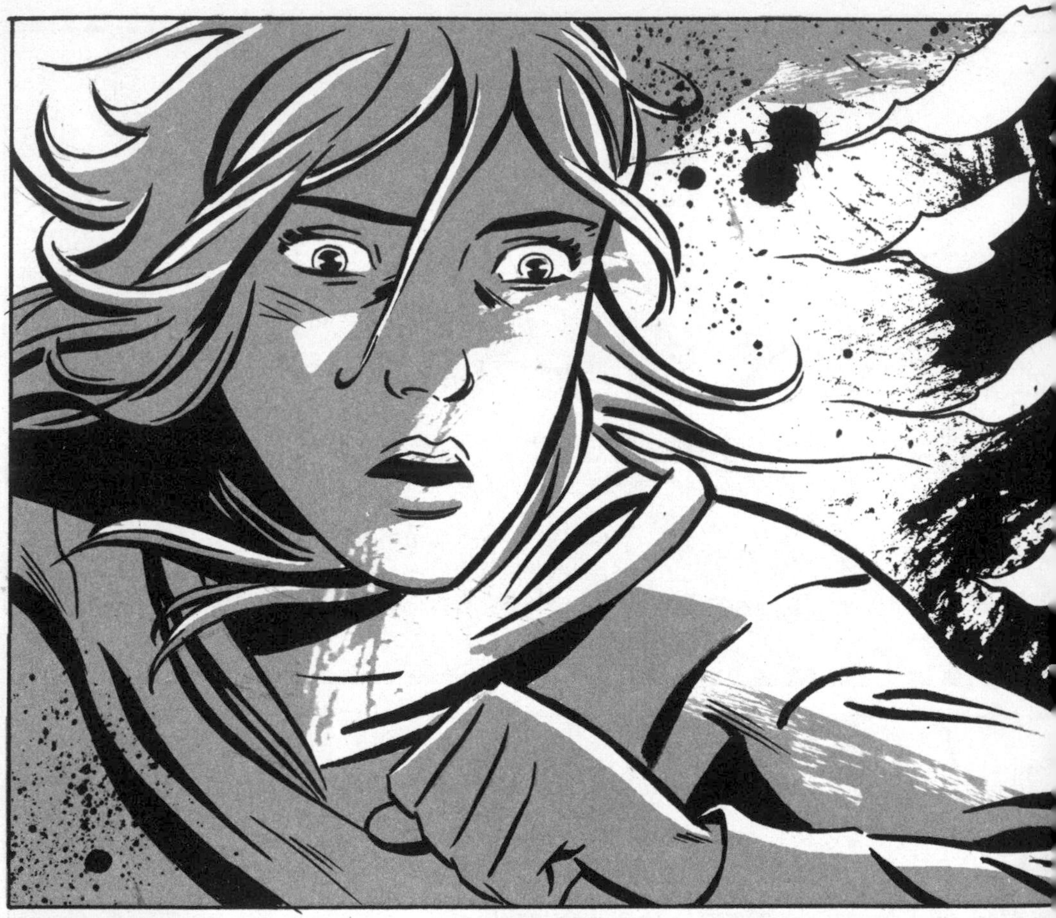
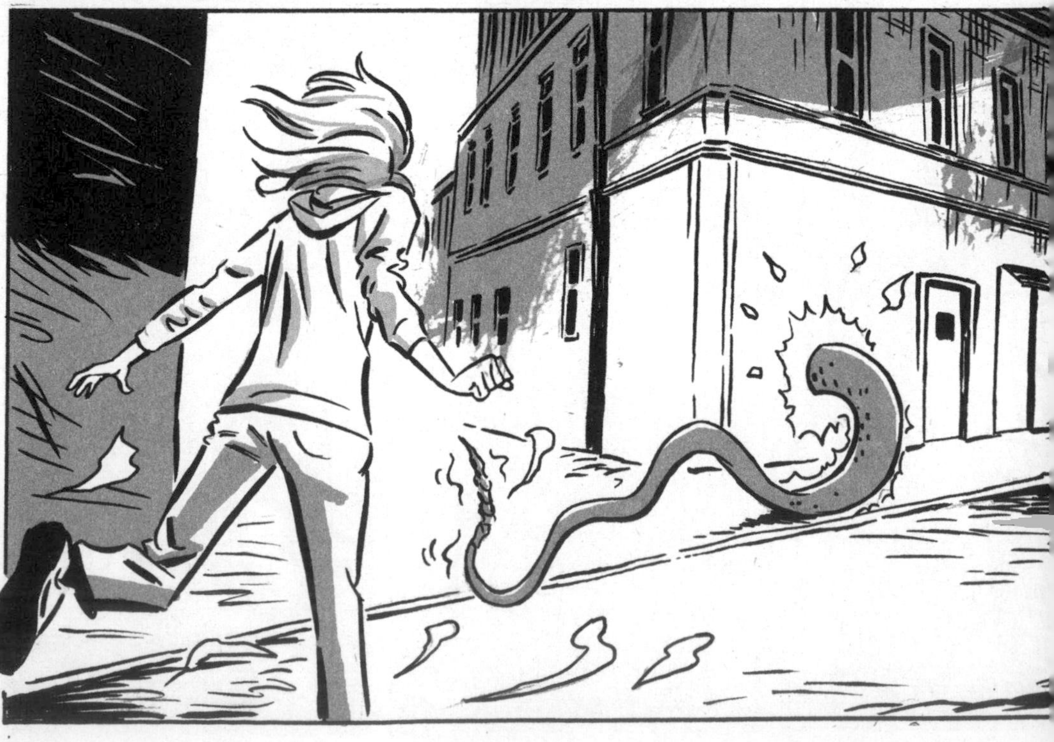

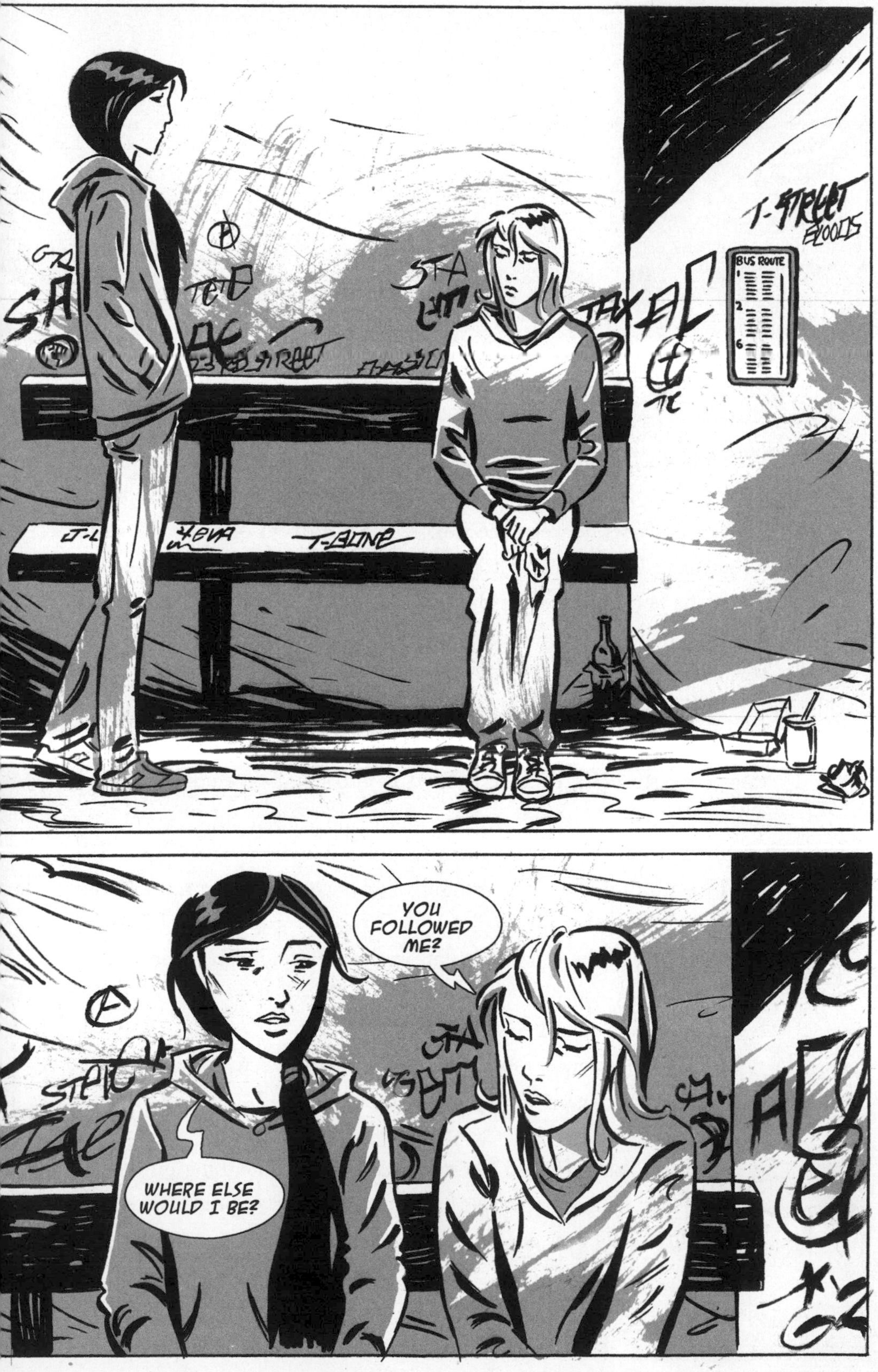
T-STREET BLOODS
BUS ROUTE
T-BONE
YOU FOLLOWED ME?
WHERE ELSE WOULD I BE?

Savitri

39 days and 1 hour after

When Holly takes off, I sprint after her. She vaults one headstone, then springboards from another. Midair, she twists and grabs the top rail of the fence, wrists between the spikes. For a fraction of a second, she is poised in a handstand on top of the fence before gravity claims her. Then she is on her feet on the other side. I've never seen her do that move—I don't even know what it's called. A tic-tsuk with a handstand thrown in?

My lungs shrink as I approach the fence. Before I'd do a move in this setting, I'd practice it in pieces, making sure I had the height, the distance, the strength; I'd have trained it into muscle memory. And normally, Holly would have too.

But the fence is fast approaching and either I chase her or I lose her.

I leap off one foot and cat-grab, hands clutching the top rail, feet trying to keep purchase on the bars. I flip my grip on my left hand, safety-vault over the spikes to a cat on the other side, and then drop to the concrete.

Holly is half a block away.

Mr. Paxton stands, pinned behind the fence, screaming for Holly. For a moment our gazes meet. And then we break—him back to the car, me directly to Holly.

Chasing someone and freerunning are fundamentally different. I abandon flair. I am relying on luck and need and all the speed I can muster.

"Holly, stop!" I cry out.

Holly whips past an old woman who is dragging an oxygen tank behind her. She swears at Holly, so when I dash past the old lady, I apologize for Holly, apologize for me.

I know it's useless; Holly has always been faster than me. Her small frame flying in front of me, she turns the corner.

"Holly!" I shout. *How do I bring her back?* "Holly, please!"

The block stretches out before me. I turn the corner, expecting to see nothing but empty space. But Holly is sitting on a bench, her knees pressed together, her hands folded in her lap. Proper and contained. The only sign of her desperate sprint is her breathing.

Dear Panic, we've been seeing too much of each other lately. I need some time apart.

"Holly?" I approach her slowly, like she's an injured animal I might scare off.

She turns and looks at me. Her lips, which were pinched together, relax.

One of her knees is bleeding and the skin on her forearm has been textured by cement. *See,* I tell myself, *nothing to be afraid of. Just a skinned knee.* But my hands are shaking when I squat in front of her and use my shirt hem to clean a line of blood that is oozing down her leg.

She leans over me and puts her lips to my ear. "Did you see him too?" she whispers.

I stand up and take a step back. "You saw Corey?"

"Oh, God, did you? Did you see Corey?" Her voice comes out loud and urgent.

"Of course not."

Holly covers her face with her hands, and tears slide down the curve of her cheek before they drop, splattering the pavement. I sit next to her and put my arms around her.

"Savitri," she says. "What's happening to me? What am I turning into?"

She leans against me and cries.

Dear Panic, weren't you listening?

I stroke her hair while she sobs. I rock her back and forth, telling her that she'll be all right. She'll be all right. Finally, I take her by her shoulders and straighten her up.

"Honey," I say at last, sounding like my mother. "What did you see?"

She puts her hands in her hair. "Nothing. A shadow."

She looks at me as if I am her life preserver. *Corey, damn you. We need you. Right here, right now.*

She clutches my arm and says, "You told me to stay here. Say something, Sav. Keep me here."

Did I tell her to stay when she took off running? I'm pretty sure I didn't. I try to chase down other memories, but none are coming.

"We'll get through this, Holly, I promise you. It's okay. It will be okay."

I revert to platitudes: time will help; wounds will heal. It's the natural state of the world. We go from stability to crisis to resolution. We all find a way through.

But what if we don't?

Holly

After we've dropped off Sav, my father still won't speak to me. He hasn't said a word since he reamed me out in the middle of the street, shouting, "What were you thinking? Where were you going? What was that, over the fence? You get in that car."

He pulls into the garage. When the wheels stop, I jump out of the car, burst into the house, and race up the stairs to my room. On the way, I pass Mom, who asks what's wrong. I slam the door.

WE HAVE TO GET COREY BACK. HE'D COME FOR US.

It wasn't Real. I'm seeing things. I'm Under Stress. This will get better. This is grieving. That's all. That's all it is. I'm not going crazy. I'm not going crazy. I'm not going crazy.

NOT CRAZY. POWERFUL. WE CAN SEE THE TRUTH. IT'S TIME TO STOP RUNNING FROM THE POWER THE PAIN HAS GIVEN US.

The Crazy don't know they are going crazy, right? They just believe the delusions they come up with. But if it's not crazy, then what is it?

REAL.

I pace my room, a caged animal. How do you convince yourself that you aren't seeing what is right in front of you? How do you decide what is Flesh and what is Shadow?

SHADOWS ARE REAL.

Shadows are nothing, just an Absence of Light.

REAL, REAL, REAL, REAL.

I shake my head, trying to get the voice, the visions, out of it. I close my eyes. See no evil. I blast music from my speaker. Hear no evil. But the voice continues. When I glance up, Dad is framed in my doorway, a cup of coffee in his hands. He tells me to turn down the music.

When I can hear, he says, "What are you doing?"

"I'm . . . upset, okay?"

"Calm down, SP."

He sits on the bed and pats it. When I join him, he says, "What am I going to do with you, kiddo?"

"Fire me."

"Holly, I need to know what happened at the graveyard, Holly."

My name twice in a sentence. The In-Trouble Quotient has doubled.

"And I'm likely to confide in you because you're so warm and fuzzy with me?"

He puts down his coffee cup on my night table and leans in. His voice is softer. "Am I grounding you? Am I yelling at you?"

"You already did that."

"I'm sorry about that; I'm not even mad at you. I'm just so— Your mother and I are—"

"What? Worried about me?" *Well, you should be. After all, I'm seeing things that no one else can see.*

WHAT YOU ARE SEEING IS A GIFT—A GIFT THAT WILL LET US FIND COREY.

"I'm doing the best I can, Dad. What else do you want from me? Maybe, instead of making me listen to you, you should try listening to me."

"I'm trying to, Holly. I'm here and I'm asking you. What is going on?"

"I told you both I didn't want to go to the graveyard. But you ignored me."

"So that stunt was . . . payback?"

I won't look at him; if I let him believe his Little Theory, then he'll stop asking.

"I wasn't ready. You need to stop pushing me," I say.

"Okay, SP. You set the pace." He pauses. "But then you need to do something for us. Mom and I think you should see a grief counselor."

No, no, no, no.

154

NO, NO, NO, NO.

"Like a psychiatrist?"

"Just someone you can talk to."

I get up and walk to the mirror. What if I tell the therapist too much? Tell her about what I'm seeing, what I'm hearing. Daily Sanity Cocktails and Weekly Headshrinkers.

And no more voice?

NO MORE POWER TO GET HIM BACK. I—WE CAN BRING HIM BACK.

I turn around and face Dad.

"I don't want to talk to a stranger. I mean, come on, Dad. Would you do something like that?"

"Holly." Dad says something that I can't hear over her.

LISTEN TO ME. THERE IS A WAY.

Not now. I'm trying to appear sane here.

She is quiet at last.

"What?" I ask.

"I am."

"You are what?"

He narrows his eyes at me, as if I'm being small, making him repeat it. "I am seeing a psychiatrist."

Dad—Macho Cop Extraordinaire—crying with a stranger? I can't picture it.

"Whose idea was that? Mom's?"

"Required by the department."

"Now *that* makes sense. How's it working for you?"

His mouth twitches, and I know he hates it.

"Right. So why do you think it will help me?" I ask.

"You ran out of the cemetery like you were being chased, screaming for Corey to come back. What was that about?"

He finally nails me down. A direct question. But me, I'm a Slippery Fish. For the best lies, add Elements of Truth. Subtract the Unexplainable.

"Dad, I . . . There was a date for Corey."

"You mean a—"

"I mean on the gravestone, and I couldn't look at that. Too final. Too permanent. No one was chasing me; I was just running blind."

I realize how bad a lie that is. How can someone vault a four-foot fence if they are running blind? But Dad buys it. He needs to buy it. He puts his arms around me and says how much he wishes it weren't true too. How much he misses Corey. I stay there, as if his Thin Comfort helps.

OF COURSE HE CAN'T HELP. HE IS AN UNBELIEVER. HE THINKS COREY IS DEAD, LOST FOREVER. BUT I KNOW THE TRUTH. I KNOW HOW TO REACH COREY.

"I was just upset, Dad. Can you really blame me?"

"No one's blaming you, SP. We're just trying to find a . . . Do you think it will help to get back to school next week? Go back to a routine? Your mom, she hangs on to routines."

I snort. "No. No school. Dad, please."

"Holly, you have to finish high school."

"I know that. But does it have to be right now? You took the GED and you're fine."

He hesitates; I've got a shot at this.

"Look, I'll make you a deal. Let me withdraw from school and I'll see any therapist you want."

DON'T. DON'T . . .

"You'll see a therapist?"

"I promise."

She starts shrieking. So Loud. So Hard. I ball my hands into fists to keep them from covering my ears.

He pauses, picks up his coffee, and sips while I wait for his Verdict.

"That sounds reasonable. So, if your mom agrees, okay?"

Mom is downstairs in her mosaic studio right now, reassembling shattered glass into new shapes, telling herself that what was broken can be salvaged. She's all about Second Chances. She won't fight him.

I grab ahold of his middle and hug. "Thank you, Daddy," I say.

He laughs and says he hasn't been called "Daddy" in a long time.

When he leaves, the Lunatic Voice begins pleading, telling me what I want to hear: that the Shadowlands are real, that I can have Corey back.

Oh God, if only she were right. If only . . . maybe. I walk into Corey's room, sit down on the bare floor, fold my legs, and close my eyes. If Savitri pulled me out of the Shadowlands, I should be able to tether my voice to Corey and lifeline him back to me.

YES.

Corey, don't leave, don't leave.

COREY, DON'T LEAVE, DON'T LEAVE.

I picture myself and groan. This is so stupid. It's nothing but madness. Utter Fucking Madness.

NO.

I can't stay in this room, in this house, this House Without Corey.

A flip later, I'm on the ground and sprinting through our backyard. This time, my head doesn't swirl afterward.

GETTING STRONGER.

I can escape the house, if not the Voice.

The streetlights shine brighter and brighter as night comes on. I pause at Sav's house but don't knock. I know we said we'd get through this together, but today, Savitri Mathur, the Girl whose Voice can Revive the Nearly Dead, had nothing to offer me but Meaningless Clichés.

I weave my way through the blocks, throwing in a string of back handsprings, a wall flip off a tree, anything I can think of, and then I find myself in front of Josh's house.

Josh's room is on the second story, and I can see his outline, a dark shape on the shade. When my period was a week late, I stood right in this spot, watching him the way I am now. I wanted to get his attention.

I had no way to get up to his room without his parents seeing. But another year of freerunning opens the world.

YES. MOVE LIKE A HERO.

Beneath his bedroom, a bay window juts from the house. It gets its own little roof, which is about ten feet off the ground. My goal. I take stock: a prickly shrub sits under the window—nothing to climb up. But it's not too far from the roofed pediment over the front door. Pillars on either side. Pressing my left hand-foot combination against the side of brick and my right hand-foot duo against the pillars, I scale the distance. And then grab the roof ridges and pull. I scramble up to standing. Got it.

FEAR WILL NOT BE YOUR MASTER.

One softly landed jump later and I'm in front of Josh's window. Inside, Josh is a silhouette, sitting on his bed, bent over his laptop. For some reason, his head looks Giant-Sized. I'm knocking on the window of an alien while trying to rid my head of voices: not good.

Options: Walk Away or Walk Toward.

When my knuckles strike the glass, his head turns. I knock again, and he comes over, pulling up the shade. I half smile and raise an eyebrow. His eyes widen, and then he works to wipe his expression clean. When he opens the window, his shirt rises. I want to trace the dip between his stomach muscles and his hip bones.

Yes, this is what I want. To stop the shit that is coursing through my head.

The window and then the screen slide open and I stick my hand through the gap. "You haven't come by, you haven't sent flowers, and you haven't shaken my hand."

"I thought you . . . needed space. I'm sorry. What are you doing here?"

"Shake my hand," I say.

He reaches out and grabs my hand. His palm is hot and his fingertips rest on my skin. I yank on his arm to pull myself in. His room looks completely different. A new brown carpet covers the hardwood. Behind posters of various bands and supermodels, dark green walls make his room feel smaller, like we're trapped in a forest. With light stands for trees and camera tripods for bushes. His computer screen is lit with moviemaking software.

The first time we hooked up, I pretended to be interested in videos, though I wasn't yet. In fact, I wonder now how much I ever was and how much was just an excuse; I've only made one vid since we split up last year.

A knock raps on the door, and I drop to the floor, hiding behind his bed. I have to cover my mouth to keep from laughing. Déjà vu.

"Yeah, Mom?"

"Did you hear that?"

"Hear what?"

"That . . . thump."

"What? Yeah. That was me."

She opens the door.

"I was sitting on the roof." He gestures.

I hear her tread across the carpeted floor. Could I slide under his bed? I glance at the dust bunnies that have colonized the carpet. *Blech.*

"That's pretty high," she says, and I hear the window screen lower. If she glances over the bed, she'll find me. And then tell me to go home.

"I'm inside now. Don't worry so much, Mom," he says, and laughs.

She says something I can't hear and he makes an excuse about homework before closing the door.

I sit up, knees bent and a little apart.

When he comes around the bed, he apologizes for his mom.

"Like old times," I say.

"They weren't bad times, Holly."

His pale green eyes look earnest, but I've fallen for that before. He sits down in front of me and nudges close to my feet.

"Well," I say, and let my knees fall a little farther apart.

"I'm glad you're here." He pauses. "What are you doing here?"

"I told you. You haven't offered your respects."

He looks at me sidelong and pulls on an unusually long thread in the carpet. "Then I offer you—"

"That's not the line. You say, 'I'm sorry for your loss.'"

He repeats it and then says, "I came by the hospital once with flowers but . . . Holly, how are you?"

"God, don't ask me that."

He pulls on the thread until it is even longer; it comes off in his fingers. He looks at it, lying dead in his palm.

"Funny, I've been wanting to see you, see how you are, and now that you're here, I don't know what to say. Except that I'm sorry about everything, sorry I couldn't ever make it right with Co—"

I put my finger against his lips. Like I want to hear about how hard Corey's absence is on him.

"You've always been better with your hands anyway."

He wears the Concerned Mask that I see on everyone. I want to rip it off. I move in closer and slide my hand along his chest.

"I've missed you, Josh."

I grab the back of his head and taste his lips. When I kiss him, my mind starts to quiet.

That's better.

His tongue is real. His fingers are real. My mind might be everywhere, but this—my body—won't let me down. I take off my shirt. When his eyes widen, I grin and slip out of my bra too.

"Holly," he says, "are you sure this is what you want? That this is what you need right now?"

I kiss him hard, fast, while I unzip his jeans. *Quiet the mind, quiet the voice.* I push Josh's head down toward my neck. He goes slowly over my collarbone and works lower. Corey would hate this. *Good. He can just come back and lecture me about it then.*

HE CANNOT COME TO YOU. YOU MUST GO TO HIM.

Once Josh is low enough, I tell him to bite. But he stops. I open my eyes.

"I'm not your razor blade, Holly."

My face flares hot. Josh has become a wimp.

160

OR PERHAPS YOU'VE BECOME TOO STRONG FOR HIM.

I push him off me. "Is it better for you if you pretend to care?"

"I don't have to pretend."

"Really? 'Cause, as I recall, your talent was saying whatever made things easiest."

"God, both you and Savi . . . It was a long time ago. People change, you know."

As if *that's* what I want to hear. *That's* what I'm worried about.

"Not that much. You're a heartless dick. Don't try to be anything else. You'll just embarrass yourself." I hook my bra and grab my shirt.

"Sure, Holly. Sure. That's why I'm not laying you down right now. Because I'm heartless."

The screen screams when I yank it up, and I hear a tread on the steps. What was his mother doing? Waiting at the bottom of the stairs? Probably.

"Don't go," he says. "I could be a friend at least, if you'd let me."

When I slide out of the window, I try to clue him in. I look down at his opened jeans and let my eyes linger there while I speak.

"Josh." I say his name as if it's an insult. "You're not qualified to be my anything."

161

Savitri

39 days and 3 hours after

When I get home after chasing Holly, mint perfumes the air. In the kitchen, a small bunch sits on the counter and the cutting board is stained green. I tear off a leaf and hold it to my nose. I slide it onto my tongue, pin it against my palate, and suck on it. It is so strong it burns, but I keep it there.

My mom, who is rolling out circles of atta for roti, has her back to me. I watch her as she puts one on the open flame from our stovetop. The dough puffs into a balloon and then falls when she takes it off the heat. I pick up the rolling pin and press my palms into a little mound of flour that my mother has poured out. She glances at me and smiles. The flour is cold and silky under my fingers.

Corey loved watching me cook and helping me prep. Last year, when I improvised a subzi using broccoli, carrots, and mushrooms and spiced it on the fly, he said only people who were truly comfortable in their skin could whip up a new recipe. He loved the oddest things about me—my cooking, my loyalty, my vocabulary, of all things.

Before the SAT, he asked me to quiz him and he handed me an alphabetized vocabulary list. I looked at the paper—250 words, none with a definition attached.

"Okay," I said, a little confused, and started. "'Abjure.'"

He missed a plethora of words as I filled in definitions. When we got to *pellucid*, we got stuck. I said, "I'm not sure either. I'll have to look it up."

162

"What are you talking about?"

I showed him the sheet of words and he realized that he had given me the wrong paper.

He looked at me, puzzled, and then said, "We got all the way to the *P*s."

He came over to my chair and tipped my chin so I was looking up into his eyes. He traced my lips with his finger and said that he loved all the words that were in my brain that could just slide out of my mouth.

My chest hollows out; it doesn't seem possible, but I physically ache. He loved those parts of me I kept hidden; he saw them and brought them out. And now . . .

Well.

Time to pack them away again.

How could I think about leaving him behind?

"Mom?" I say.

"What's wrong? Wait, just a minute." She tilts her head toward me as she pulls a roti off.

"I don't think I can . . . go to Princeton," I say, and peel the dough off the counter.

"What? Why not? Is there a problem with—"

I shake my head and tears drop onto the counter, splatter in the flour.

I give the dough a quarter turn and then roll it again. She sighs and then leads me over to the table and sits me down. I rub my fingers on its smooth top and then put them to my cheek.

"I know you miss him. It's okay to miss him, but you can't let that grief make your decisions for you."

I shake my head. "I can't lose anything else."

"What else would you be losing? Going away won't change that. You'll always be connected to him. When you think of it like that, you can't really lose him. Not altogether."

"I can't leave, Mom. I just can't."

"Savitri, you just came from your boyfriend's grave. This might not be the day to make that decision."

"I've been thinking about it for a while now. I'm not ready to go. Plus, you'd be all alone."

And so would Holly. Corey would never willingly leave her side, leave her alone. So how can I?

"Oh ho, beta," she says, using Hindi to tie us together, reminding me that I'm always her daughter—here or miles away. She clicks her tongue at me affectionately. "Don't stay for me. I've worked this hard so you can do what you want, okay?" She cups my cheek with her palm.

"Maybe this is what I want," I say.

"Savitri, what is this really about?"

My eyelashes wet and the edges of her face start to blur. "I really do have obligations here."

"Holly," she says, and the name sounds like a weight.

"Today, at the graveyard . . . it was too much for her."

She sighs. "Honey, what did you expect from her today?"

"I'm not sure if . . ." *if she'll make it,* but I don't say it, as if giving voice to the thought might give it power, might turn my worry into a prediction and a prediction into a truth. "I think she is seeing things that aren't there."

"What do you mean 'things'?"

"People."

She sits back. "Well, that's not unusual with deep grief."

I slide my fingers back and forth on the counter. "It's not?"

"People think they see their loved ones all the time."

But she didn't see Corey.

"Do they see . . . other things?"

"Like what?"

"I don't know," I say.

"Holly will be all right. She has her family to see her through. They can—"

"She *is* family, Mom. And she's falling apart."

"And why are you the one to pick up the pieces?"

"Because . . . well, for one thing, her parents are unraveling, which is baffling but—"

"Most marriages don't survive the loss of a child. The parents punish each other to punish themselves. But if they can help Holly together, then I think they have a chance. Let them help her."

"Look, I know that you had your cousins and aunts and uncles when you were growing up in India. But for me, Holly and Corey . . ."

My mom sits back and frowns. "Maybe we should have kept in better touch with the families on the North Side."

My mom has never liked how my friendships shrank when we moved out of our Indian neighborhood to Morgan Park. Divorces, official or not, aren't *verboten* technically, but even at age eight, I noticed how my mom stood alone amidst couples, how silence interrupted more often than laughter. Still, she did everything she could to keep me in touch with the Indian girls I liked—Pratima and Purnima, Radhika and Rajni. We had sleepovers and she drove them both ways, long as it was.

"If we'd kept in better touch, maybe you wouldn't be so alone now," my mom says.

"I stopped getting along with them," I say. "It wasn't because of you or Dad."

I don't tell her how I ran over to Holly's, sobbing because they called each other good Hindustanis and me "Hindu-stupid." After all, I never went to India and my Hindi was slipping. I may not have been able to articulate it then, but I felt their frosty judgment: too assimilated for them. Not assimilated enough for Morgan Park Elementary, where I was pegged as "weird." Which morphed into "exotic" in high school, which meant the same thing. So I learned to keep certain things hidden.

Except with Holly and Corey. We even celebrated Diwali together. We'd pull cotton balls until they extended into long strings, stretching like cotton candy, and roll them into makeshift wicks. We slid them into

165

small lamps, followed by oil, and then—match to wick—grew a steady flame. We'd put a lamp in each window and celebrate the new year.

And now . . .

Well.

Our lamps will not be lit this year, our windows darkened for Corey, and my extended family . . . it begins and ends with Holly.

"It doesn't matter. What matters is that I need to help her, and if I go to Princeton . . ."

"Friendships can't be all one-way. She isn't being your friend if she's not supporting you too. What about what you want?"

No walks under the cherry trees, no late-night talks, no gulping down knowledge so fast that excess streams down my chin. No new place to discover, no new awakening.

"Honey, I know that, right now, it seems you need to be her anchor, but you're more than that."

What does that mean? I'm more than that? I'm barely even that. I cross my arms on the table and put my head down.

"No decisions today, okay? Not yet. Just give yourself some time."

I promise her, but so far, time has only made things worse.

Holly

The day after the Josh Debacle Redux, I'm reading in bed when I discover that The Leopardess is dead. Dr. D. Lusion killed her.

A shiver starts from my feet and crawls all the way up my body as I put the last book of the series down and sit up. My head throbs. I grab my hair and hang on, pulling it for a sensation to keep me here in this world. The Leopardess cannot be dead.

HEROES DON'T DIE. SIDEKICKS DIE, VILLAINS DIE. HEROES DON'T LEAVE.

Yes, yes. I shouldn't listen to the Lunatic Voice, especially since my therapy appointment is in a few days, but she is finally making sense. Robin dies, not Batman. Batgirl is confined to a wheelchair before her newest iteration takes over. I think of Jane Grey and the Phoenix. Larissa Powell might be dead, but The Leopardess will live on. Someone will pick up her mantle.

THE LEOPARDESS WILL BE RESURRECTED, REBORN IN . . . ANOTHER.

I stand up. Gotta be moving. When I walk to my door, Savitri's voice breaks into my hearing. I turn toward her gravelly sound and realize it is coming from Dad's room down the hall.

What's Sav talking to Dad for?

There's something artificial to the sound, something canned. The voice has all the signatures . . . her sandpaper and silk, but . . .

NO, SAVITRI ISN'T HERE. THAT IS A RECORDING.

Why would Dad have a recording of Sav, Lunatic?

Now I'm arguing with the Lunatic Voice? Really? As if that's a way to stay sane. I pull my door open.

"How is Holly?" comes Sav's voice.

Another woman's voice—I can barely make it out, but she says, "She's in surgery."

Score one for the Lunatic Voice.

I start putting two and two together while the voices drone on. When I was in surgery, where was Sav? At the police station, of course—giving her statement. And if this is her statement, then Dad has the file. A chance to get all the information we need. He wouldn't keep it out in the open—too risky. So, where? I creep down the hall to his closed door.

SEE FOR YOURSELF.

How do I do that? X-ray vision?

The voice chuckles again and then she says:

YOU HAVE TO STOP UNDERESTIMATING YOUR POWER. MOVE LIKE A LEOPARDESS. MOVE IN THE NIGHT.

Dad's window is blocked by a maple out front. Which . . . I could climb.

I use Corey's window, precision-jump to the fence, and then land on the ground. The night air still bites. I hurry around to the other side of the house and look up. The maple branches are too high, even with a jump.

I look around. The fence.

I scramble onto it, balance.

Phase 1: control the takeoff.

Phase 2: I leap and let the air rush under me.

Phase 3: the landing.

My hands grab the branch, chafing on the bark. I use my momentum to swing my legs up and hook one knee over the branch. From there it's easy. I get on top of the branch and start to climb. Fast now. Catlike.

YES, PUSH HARDER.

When I'm high enough, I climb out on the branch by his window. The light is on and Dad's inside. Alone. Mom's got to be asleep in her studio. Their constant fighting has landed them in different bedrooms. Dad is at his computer, his side to me. I try to stay out of his peripheral vision and gaze in the window. I see a corner of his unmade bed, the desk, and a large computer monitor.

On the screen, Sav is wearing a green scrubs shirt, blood is smeared on her cheek, and she is rocking slightly as she talks. I watch Dad watching her. When he is done for the night, he grabs what's got to be the file and puts it in his closet, under the lockbox for his old .38, the one he taught Corey and me with. Easy.

BUT THERE'S HARDER WORK TO COME. FIND WIRY, KORTHA'S MINION. HE WAS IN THE SHADOWLANDS, HANDING THE ROPE TO KORTHA, WASN'T HE? WIRY WILL LEAD US TO KORTHA AND THE SHADOWLANDS. HE KNOWS THE WAY IN.

Yes. The best reason so far to find this bastard.

YES, YES. TIME TO HUNT AGAIN.

Savitri

40 days and 17 hours after

The thin pages of *Savitri* are beneath my fingers again. Satyavan's head rests in her lap. When Yama comes, my chest tightens and I can't turn the page.

I know she follows him; I know she gets him back. What I don't know is why I keep torturing myself with this book. I close it and shove it on my shelf.

Face it, I tell myself: Corey got it wrong. Mom got it wrong. I'm not that loyal, not when it counts.

The doorbell rings. I go downstairs, open the door, and find Josh. Which I don't need. He'll only ask me about Holly and I hardly know how to answer him. He shifts from one foot to the other and looks at the ground as though he's a kid selling cookies.

"Holly's fine," I say.

"You think so?" he asks. "Can I come in? I have something to tell you."

I open the door wider. He steps over the threshold and looks at the row of hooks for jackets and the shoe cubbies. One of my Flites has fallen on the floor.

"Okay," I say, and rest my eyes closed for a second before opening them again. It's been a challenge to keep up with Holly, schoolwork, and Speech. I'm relieved my self-defense class will be over next week. Maybe I should start drinking coffee. I stretch my neck and tilt it from one side to the next, letting it pop. Finally, I say, "So, tell."

He inspects me from one angle and then another. "You look awful."

"That's what you came to tell me? You look tall. Done now?"

"No, how have you been holding up?" he asks.

I shrug a shoulder.

He hesitates and then says, "Well, listen . . . there's a meet-up today. And I thought that you . . ."

"What?"

I'd expected some kind of big announcement with all that buildup. Then again, inviting us back into the freerunning group we abandoned is sort of a big deal, I guess.

"I'll ask Holly if—"

"No," he says fast. And then says, "I meant just you, actually. Look, I've been wanting to ask you to come back—everyone misses you and you seem so . . . alone. And it's kind of my fault in a weird way." He shifts his weight again. "You want to come or not?"

I stare at my shoes. I remember Corey telling the group to cast out Josh. "Us or him," he said. When no one agreed with the binary, we quit. And I was never lonely, never regretted it. Until now. I have two months until graduation and school has become a place of silence and isolation. Self-created, sure. But still.

"Savi, I'm taking that as a yes. Come on," Josh says. He kicks my Flite. "Get dressed. Let's go."

* * *

When we arrive at the UIC campus, I look it over. College campuses are the perfect place for a freerunner. They are adorned with benches, low walls, stairways down into buildings—multilevels everywhere. Josh's group is lounging around on top of a three-foot brick wall that is capped with a smooth cement slab. When we walk up, they hop down and surround me. Josh stays right beside me as old friends tell me how they are sorry for my loss, and from these guys, I believe it. The tallest one, Hector, reminds me that Corey taught him how to roll. And when he quotes Corey's instructions—"Grab the concrete, and put the world on your shoulder"—I know we're both hearing his voice.

Once the hellos are over, we start with a familiar warm-up: dash vaults, speed vaults, kong vaults, finding our way over. Then, with heat in our muscles, we start to play. Josh speeds toward the wall, tictacs off the tree, clears the wall, and lands on the grass. Nice. I wait for my turn and rehearse in my mind's eye. Tunnel vision: the bark, the wall, the grass.

When it is my turn, my head clears—no more Holly, no more Wiry, no more fruitless stakeouts—just a tree and a jump.

I push hard against the ground, my muscles firing fast as I get up to speed. Except for the tree, the rest of the world blurs.

Spot the bark.

I leap, plant my shoe on the tree, spring off it, my torso finding mid-air balance. The wall is under me and I sight the landing—green grass. The world spins as I roll. The impact of the landing on the ground— softened by the spring melt—is textbook, spread out from my shoulder over my spine to my hip. And I'm up on my feet. Yes, this is freerunning at its best. My muscles hum and I want to go again.

I jog out of the way and, while I'm waiting for the next guy, throw a flip, rolling out of it.

We wander over to a seven-foot wall that has three steps, each one about a foot higher than the last. Everyone wants to show me something— new moves, variations. Then Hector scrambles to the top and looks down. "No, no," he says.

No one objects; no one pushes him. As a freerunner, you have to learn to recognize the difference between fear that is holding you back and fear that is keeping you safe. You have to trust that instinct, trust your muscles, trust your sense.

"Adjust your movement to your surroundings, not the other way around," I say, repeating one of the freerunning mantras.

Hector puts his palms on top of the wall and lowers himself until he's comfortable, and then he jumps the rest of the way. In increments, he jumps to the ground, from a one-step up, from a two-foot drop, four foot. Until he finds his limit.

This is what I loved about freerunning—not the risk, but the concentration, the sharing. Somehow I've gotten away from all of that.

Before we leave, I have three new moves, and for the first time since the shooting, I've gone whole hours without thinking about Holly.

When we get off the train, we walk back through our neighborhood and arrive at Josh's house first. "We meet up every Saturday. So, same time next week?"

My phone buzzes.

"Just a sec," I say, and read the incoming text. "It's from Holly."

She wants to know if I'm home. I sigh, feeling the weight return to my blood. I brace myself; we need to talk about what happened in the graveyard. I tap in, *Almost.*

Josh is leaning in as if he wants to read the phone.

"What? Oh, um, sure," I say. "We'll do it again sometime."

I say thanks and hurry to my house, where Holly sits on my front steps, her head down while she plays some game on her phone.

When she looks up and sees me, she stands and waves an envelope. She bounces and her grin is so big that I feel my own creeping up.

"Have I got a present for you," she says.

I cock my head and wait for her to explain.

"You wanted information. Well, we've got it. Lots of it."

"You got the file?"

Answers. Answers. Finally.

* * *

42 days and 3 hours after

When we first got the file, we ran up to my room, locked the door even though my mother wasn't home, and started reading page after page after

173

page. After two hours, my room was cluttered with papers. After four, we added a pizza box and two Cokes to the clutter. At six, Holly fell asleep. Sergeant Paxton's words—"a ruthless patience"—kept me glued to the file for a full eleven hours. This file must have answers. Something we can use.

Now, one day later, with answers still eluding us, I'm sitting on Holly's bed, with my laptop warming my legs and looking at my Known-Unknown table. Holly is reading through our copy of the medical examiner's report again. We're surrounded by charts, timelines, reports, and maps—our attempts to make sense of the crush of information in the file: suspect videos, endless interview notes, ballistics reports. They even had a tape from a security camera that caught the shooting, but the angle was wrong and the SUV blocked the lens.

We watched it, and I couldn't look at Holly during the long lag between the squealing-tires departure and my on-foot arrival at the Dana. Forty-nine seconds.

When you're waiting for help to arrive, a minute can string out, each second longer than the one before it. How much longer would those seconds seem if you were on your last breath? I dove back into the file: Answers. Answers. There must be answers.

If I thought the cops were remiss, I was wrong. "Obsessed" is an understatement. As soon as the police learned they didn't have a match with Wiry's fingerprints, they started on Sergeant Paxton's logbooks—name after name. From traffic stops to domestic disturbances to unsolved murder cases—everyone *without* a fingerprint on file.

When they got nowhere with that, they brought in anyone with even a whiff of a motive, followed by anyone who might know anyone with a whiff of a motive. I recognize a guy from the lineup—he had no alibi and was suspected because he's a member of the Twelfth Street Serpents, a long-established Chicago gang. Arrest after arrest for minor infractions; one for jaywalking.

The interviews make it clear. Jail time unless they can cough up

174

some info on the shooter. A lot of Serpents are in jail. Corey was right—CPD is the biggest gang in Chicago. And it is at war.

"Why do they think it's the Serpents?" I ask Holly.

Holly shakes her head. "A gang doesn't make any sense."

"Because?"

She ticks off the reasons: (1) Wiry's white and white gangs don't exist in Chicago anymore. Mafia, yes; gangs, no. It's all very race-based, she says. (2) The shooting doesn't feel like a gang's. Wiry wasn't wearing any gang colors—just a black hoodie and jeans. And gangs don't do lone-gunman-like killings; usually they operate in a group. (3) Most of all, Sergeant Paxton has never worked gangs, so there's no motive.

"There's no motive anywhere in this file. It's like it was just random," she says.

"Random? It can't be random. Random is just . . . not a good reason," I say stupidly.

Wiry must have had a plan. You don't kill someone at random. Could he have chosen his victims the way you decide what to eat for breakfast? *I'm in the mood for eggs and toast—or, hey, maybe some target practice. Those kids look as good as any.*

Could that really be right? That nothing stands between any of us and a bullet except a whim and a window?

My throat spasms open and I gag on nothing. Holly puts her hand on my back while I dry-heave, tears squeezing out of my eyes.

When I can speak again, I say, "It can't be random."

There must be a reason for all this misery. There must be a reason Corey is dead and Holly is drifting farther and farther away from me.

If I could just get this organized, I'd find the pattern. And I'd stop shaking.

Holly grabs the file.

"Not random," Holly says, and she shakes her head. "No, because . . ." She pauses and her gaze becomes vacant.

"Holly?" I say. She doesn't respond, so I grab her arm and shake her. "Holly?"

"What?"

"What were you saying? Why can't it be random?"

"Because they'll never find him. This is how cops solve cases—evidence and motive, right?"

Our gazes lock. But neither of us has any comfort for the other. She breaks away first and returns to the file.

"Look at this," she says, and shoves the medical examiner's report at me. "What do you think this means?"

I read carefully but can't make sense of it.

"What's 'stippling'?" I ask, handing it back to her.

She rolls her eyes and says, "Don't you watch any TV? When a gun goes off, it releases gunpowder. You know that much, right? If the gun is close enough, the powder gets embedded in the skin."

"So that means the muzzle—"

"Up close and personal, yeah."

"Which means that . . ." Corey was already over Holly when he was shot. He must have unhooked his seatbelt and crawled over her, using his body as a shield. "Oh, Holly."

"Yeah," she says. "Pretty damn heroic, huh?"

I thought the file would have answers and that answers would be better. But now, looking at how hard her face is working, how her eyes can't stay on me, I wonder if the truth is any help at all. I grab her arm. "I'm glad he did. He wouldn't be able to live with himself if he hadn't tried."

"He didn't just try, Sav." She pulls her arm away.

Why can't we talk about Corey? She looks at the report in her hand. "But that wasn't what I was asking you to read. I was asking you about this: '1.25 inches behind the bullet hole, a 0.05-inch section of hair was cut away from the victim's head. The clean edge suggests the use of a knife.'"

I remember how Wiry snicked out a blade and leaned in the car. "He cut off Corey's hair."

"Why would he do that?"

"Wait a minute," I say. "There's something in Meade's notes about that too."

I scan and skip through pages until I find a notation: *Det. LaShawn Jackson in Gangs: MO for Serpents' initiation = hair/trophy.*

"That's why they think it's a Serpent," she says. "Because he took Corey's hair."

"He killed Corey to get into a gang?"

But Holly shakes her head and says, "No, gang initiations aren't shootings, or else our graveyards would be a lot bigger. They're usually beatdowns, and if the guy stands up while his buddies beat him for—like a minute or two—he's in," she says, as though it's common knowledge. I always knew that Sergeant Paxton was the kind of cop who came home and told his kids what happened on the job. I just didn't know how much information he gave them.

"So Wiry's not in a gang?"

"We're going in circles," she says.

"Just like the police. What's the good in following their leads when they don't know where they are going?"

Dear File, you promised answers.

I close my eyes and return to that night and what I saw to try to piece it together. Wiry used the knife to take Corey's hair. And the tassel he was carrying . . .

It didn't look like Corey's hair. It was long . . . and . . . Oh, God.

Holly

The Lunatic Voice has started screaming. Since I figured out that Corey leaned over me, saved me.

WE NEED TO SAVE COREY. PROVE THAT OUR LOYALTY IS TWIN TO HIS.

I'm staring at the file, trying to stay here, when Savitri jumps up—eyes wide, flurried motion—in Full Panic Mode. She grabs me by the shoulders and turns me around, muttering—no, counting. My extensions.

And it clicks.

"You said he had a silver tassel? Silver?" I scream.

I jerk away from her and run to the mirror, where I count them too. I figured that when the surgeons shaved off my hair, they cut one of the silver extensions out, but what if . . . ?

Thousands of cockroaches crawl across my scalp.

He touched my hair. He must have leaned over Corey, grabbed a fistful of my hair after he shot us. I've washed my hair, done it up, tried to hide the shaved spot. I've touched it every day.

He cannot have a piece of Corey, cannot have a piece of me.

I get my scissors from my desk and hold them out to her.

"Cut it off."

"What? No, I couldn't do that."

"I can't have it anymore. Cut it off, cut it off." When I scream, it sounds just like the Lunatic's Voice.

"But you love—"

I walk toward her and keep coming and she backs up, backs up until I've hemmed her in against the wall. I put my face close to hers.

"Cut. It. OFF!"

178

"Quit it," she says, her voice calm, nearly bored.

I should have known better. If anyone can defuse a situation, it's Sav. Silver-Tongued Sav, whose Voice can bring me back when I'm Off the Rails. *That's it, Sav, reassure me.*

She takes the scissors from me.

"Scared you into it?" I ask.

"You're going to wish a real hairdresser was in on this," she says, and avoids looking at me. I realize that I actually did scare her.

How can I scare her? Doesn't she know me better than that?

She pulls my desk chair over and sits me in front of the mirror.

"I imagine it should be wet, right?"

I tell her I can't wash it out; I can't even touch it. She frowns, Unimpressed by my Drama. She gets a spray bottle from the bathroom, squirts my hair, and starts to snip. Which is taking for-ev-er. His Hands in my Hair. His Hands on Me. Corey's body over me.

"Hold still, Holly," she says, and keeps cutting.

The cold water makes me hunker down, lower and lower. I grip the seat. I want those scissors back—I'd be faster. How long can she possibly take?

"Holly," she says. "What do you think Corey . . . God, he must have been terrified, seeing that gun. And then . . ."

She stops cutting for a moment and covers her eyes with a hand.

In the Shadowlands, I reached for him too. Missed again.

"We've got to find him," Sav says.

Tears start to rise. "Do you think we can?"

Does she want to go to the Shadowlands with me and find Corey?

"I don't know how, but he's out there, somewhere, and Corey would want . . ."

Wait, what? Oh, Wiry. Of course, she means we've got to find Wiry.

Sav says something but it's hard to hear her over the thoughts that are screaming in my head. I put my hands over my face for a moment, trying to block out everything. When I pull my hands down, I am changed. I have a strange bob that shows my earlobes—my seven-year-old haircut revamped.

NOT ENOUGH. TRANSFORM.

I grab the scissors out of her hand, open them, and slide the cold blades against my scalp. I snip out a chunk. She snatches the scissors.

"Holly, stop it. I can't fix that."

"Shave It Off. Get Corey's razor. Just get it off me."

"Okay, okay," she says. "Let me help you, all right?"

I start to laugh, even though I'm pretty sure it's mixed with tears. "Help me? Just how are you going to do that? By telling me it will be all right, like you did in the graveyard?" My voice is rising. "How will it be all right?"

She backs off and stares at me. For a second, I think she might walk out. Shit. I'm being a bitch. Again.

And Sav is standing by me. Again.

I get my voice under control and say, "I know you want to help me, but you've gotta stop judging what I'm doing to get from one minute to the next. I mean, unless you have some magical cure, stop questioning me and just help me. The way I ask you to. Trust me, all right?"

She swallows a few times; I can hear her throat working. Finally, she just nods.

"Then shave it off. I need this."

She walks into the bathroom and comes out with Corey's fat black electric razor. She runs it over my scalp, from the nape of my neck to my forehead, in long buzzing passes.

When she's done, when my hair is in chunks on the floor, she regards the mess and then gets a broom. I should help her, I guess, but I watch her sweep the remnants of my hair up while tears slide down my cheeks. She tells me she's sorry, so sorry, and I tell her it's all right.

"It's the New Look," I say, reaching for a laugh.

"Why won't you talk to me anymore? I've been here every day and I miss him too."

I shake my head. Her problems are so simple, so ordinary. I tell her that I just need to be alone.

She winces. She packs up every single scrap of paper, organizing her charts and maps in Slow Motion. But I still don't take it back; I just stare at the mirror. There's no way to hide how much I've changed.

PAIN TRANSFORMS US ALL.

I close my eyes, and when I open them again, the world has gone halftone, and I can't fight it anymore.

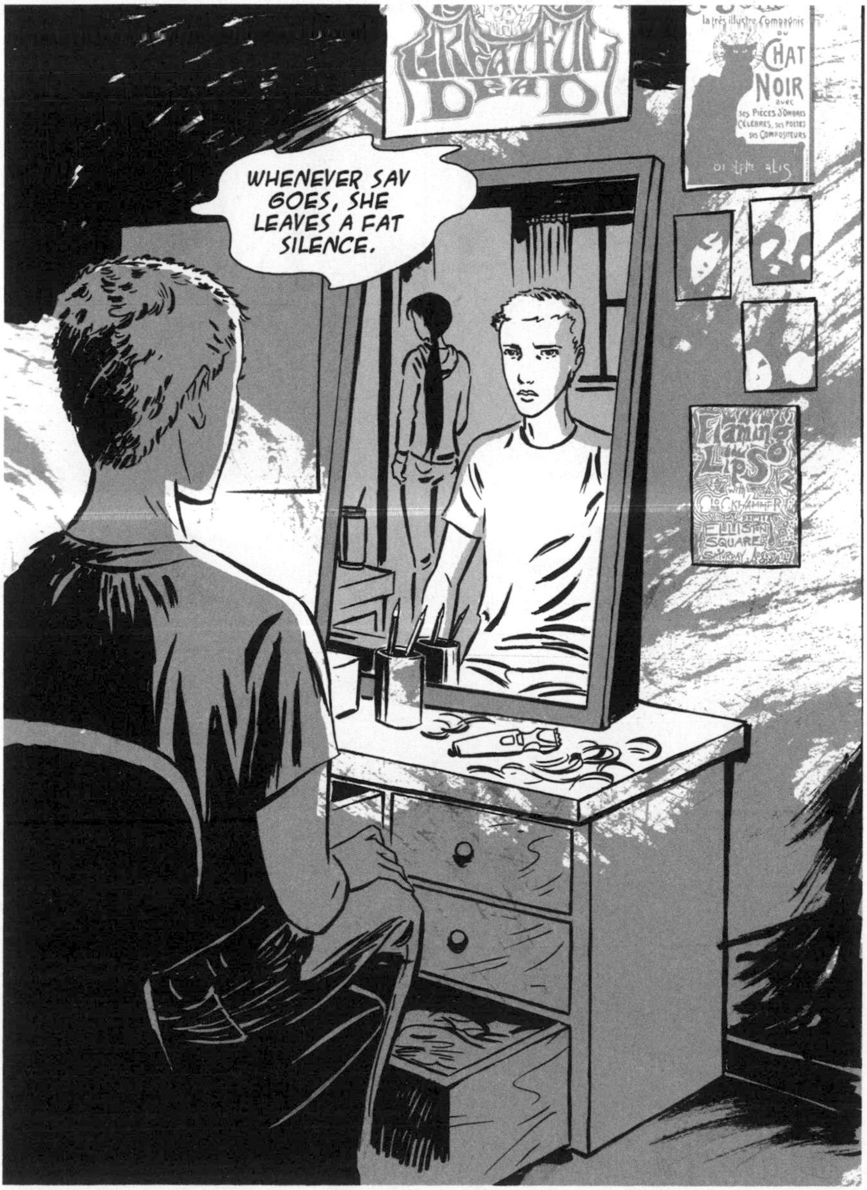
GREATFUL DEAD
la très illustre Compagnie du
CHAT NOIR
avec ses Pièces d'Ombres Célèbres, ses Poètes ses Compositeurs
WHENEVER SAV GOES, SHE LEAVES A FAT SILENCE.
Flaming Lips
SQUARE

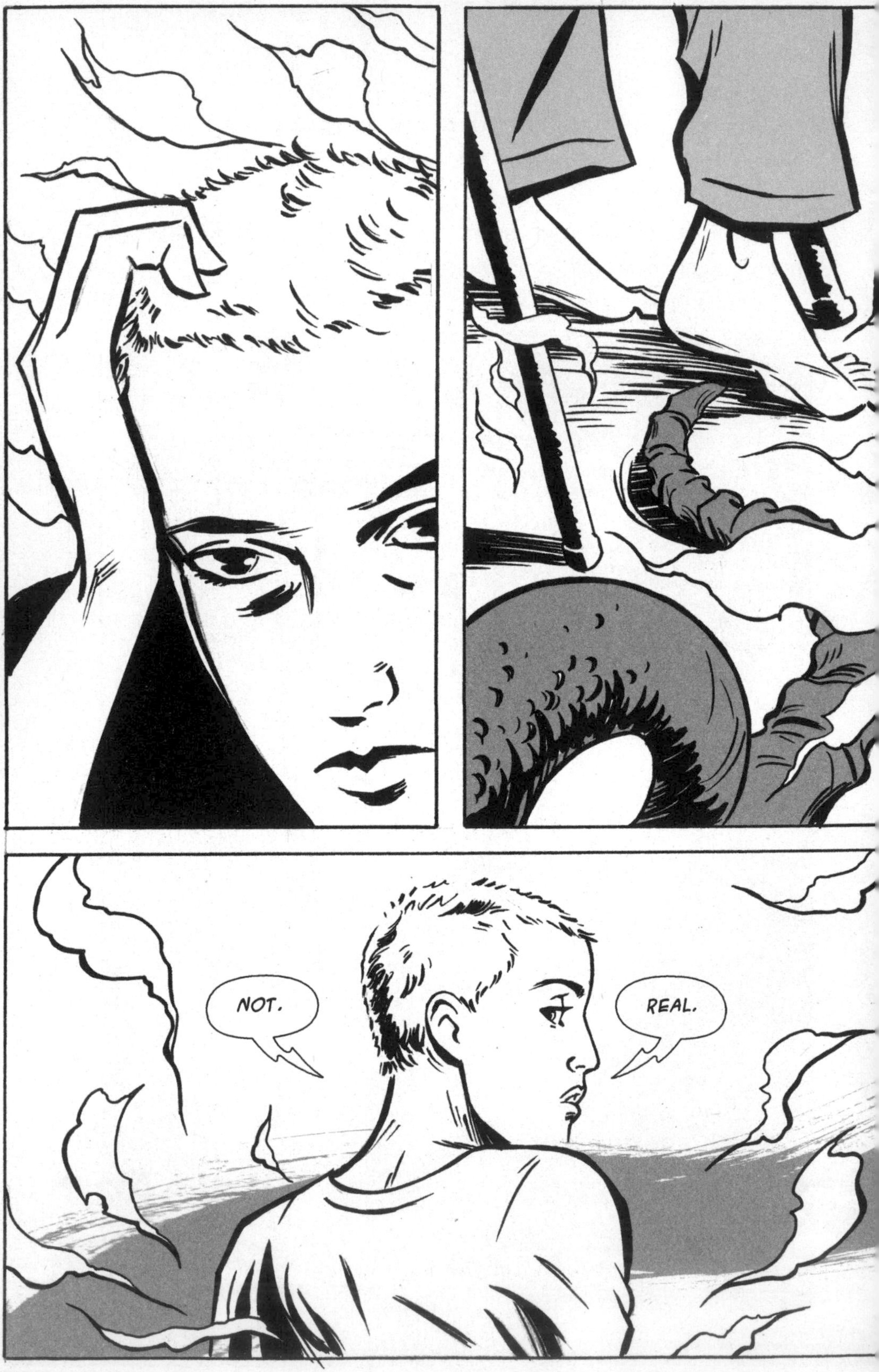
NOT.
REAL.

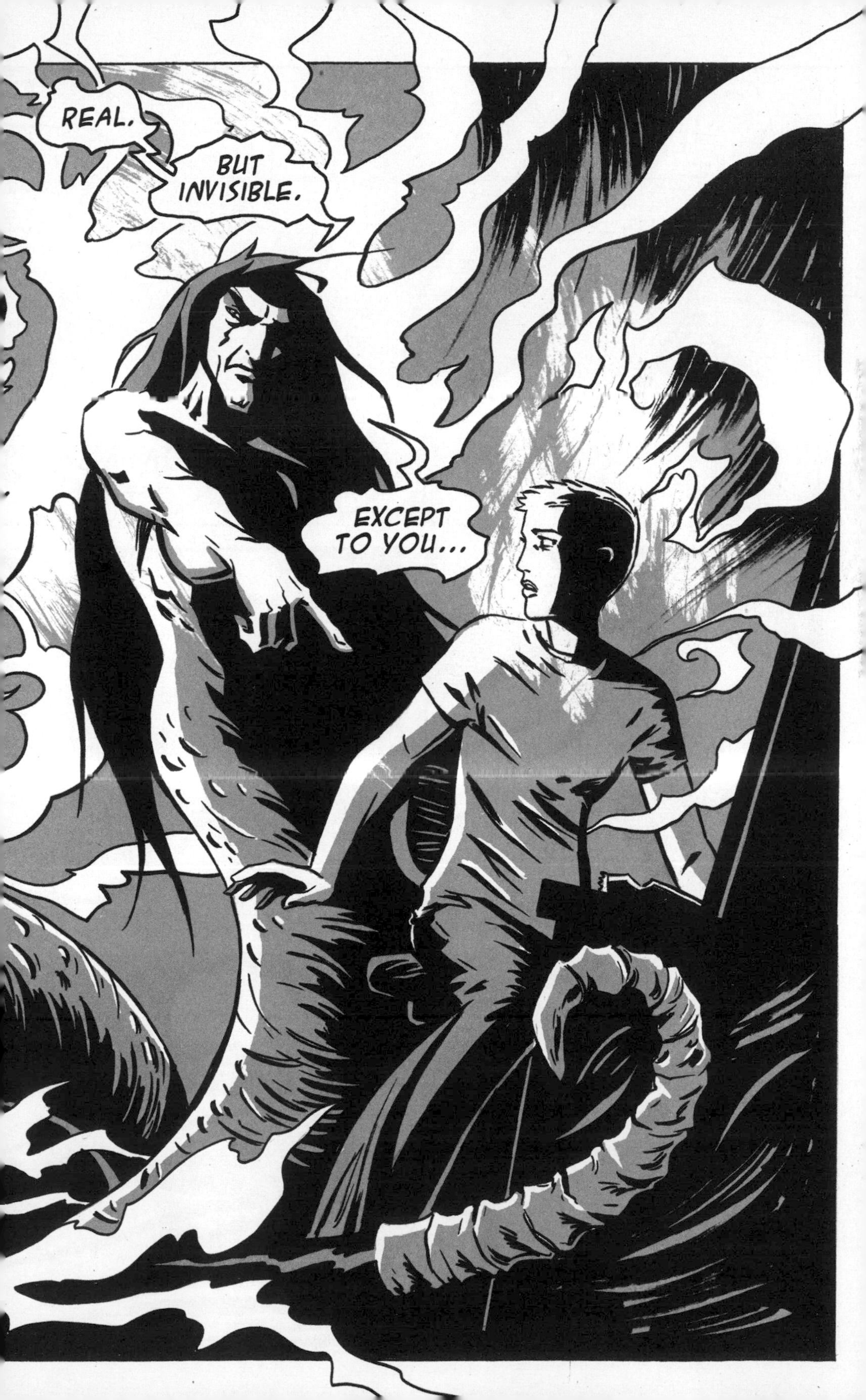
REAL.
BUT INVISIBLE.
EXCEPT TO YOU...

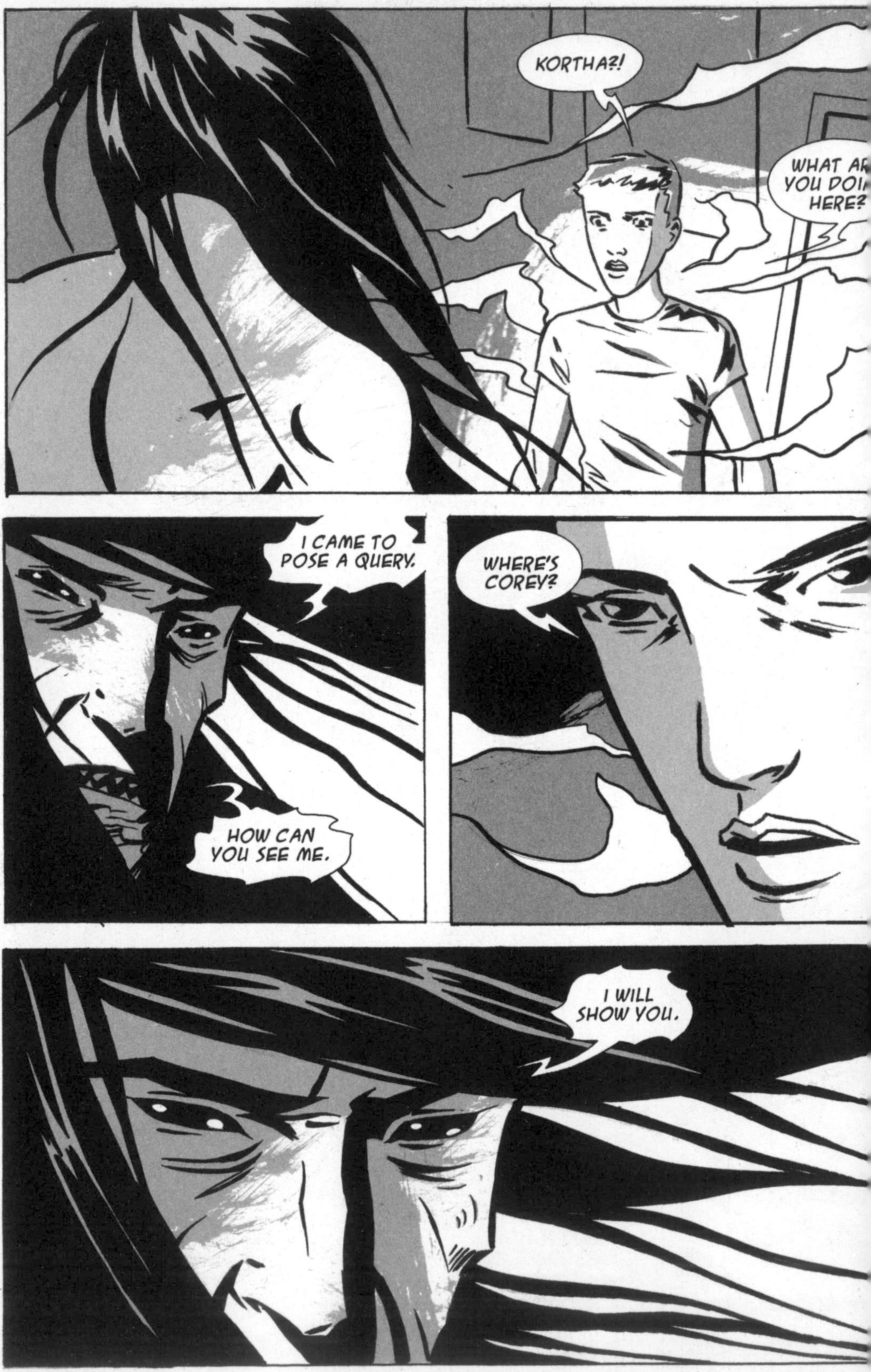
KORTHA?!
WHAT AR
YOU DOI
HERE?
I CAME TO POSE A QUERY.
HOW CAN YOU SEE ME.
WHERE'S COREY?
I WILL SHOW YOU.

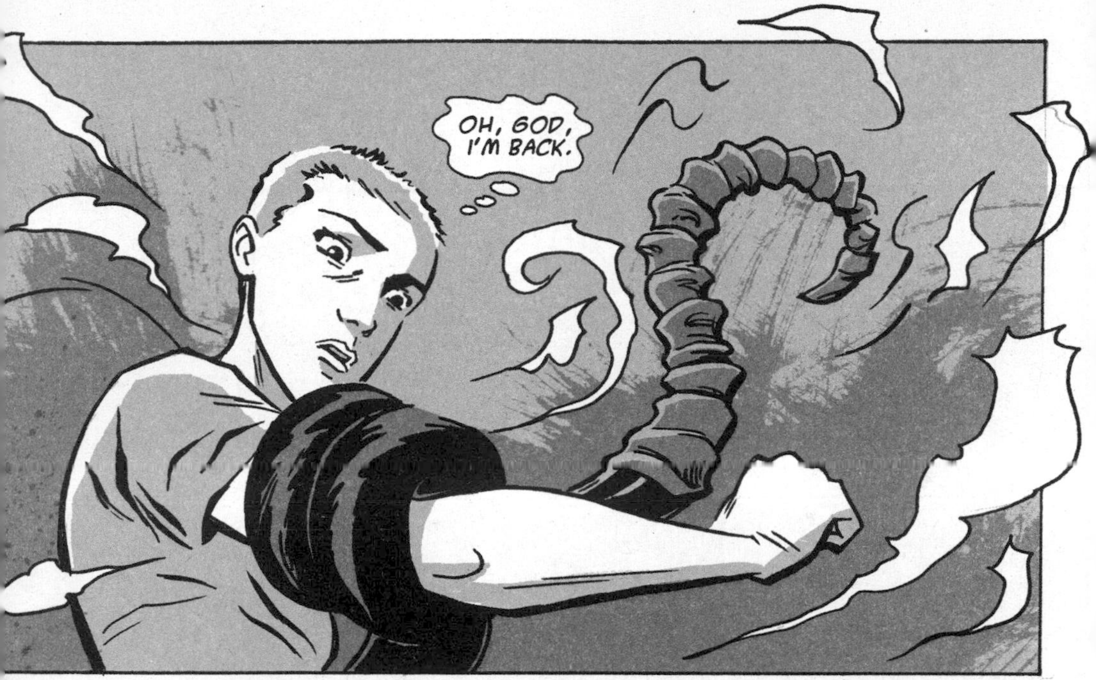
OH, GOD, I'M BACK.

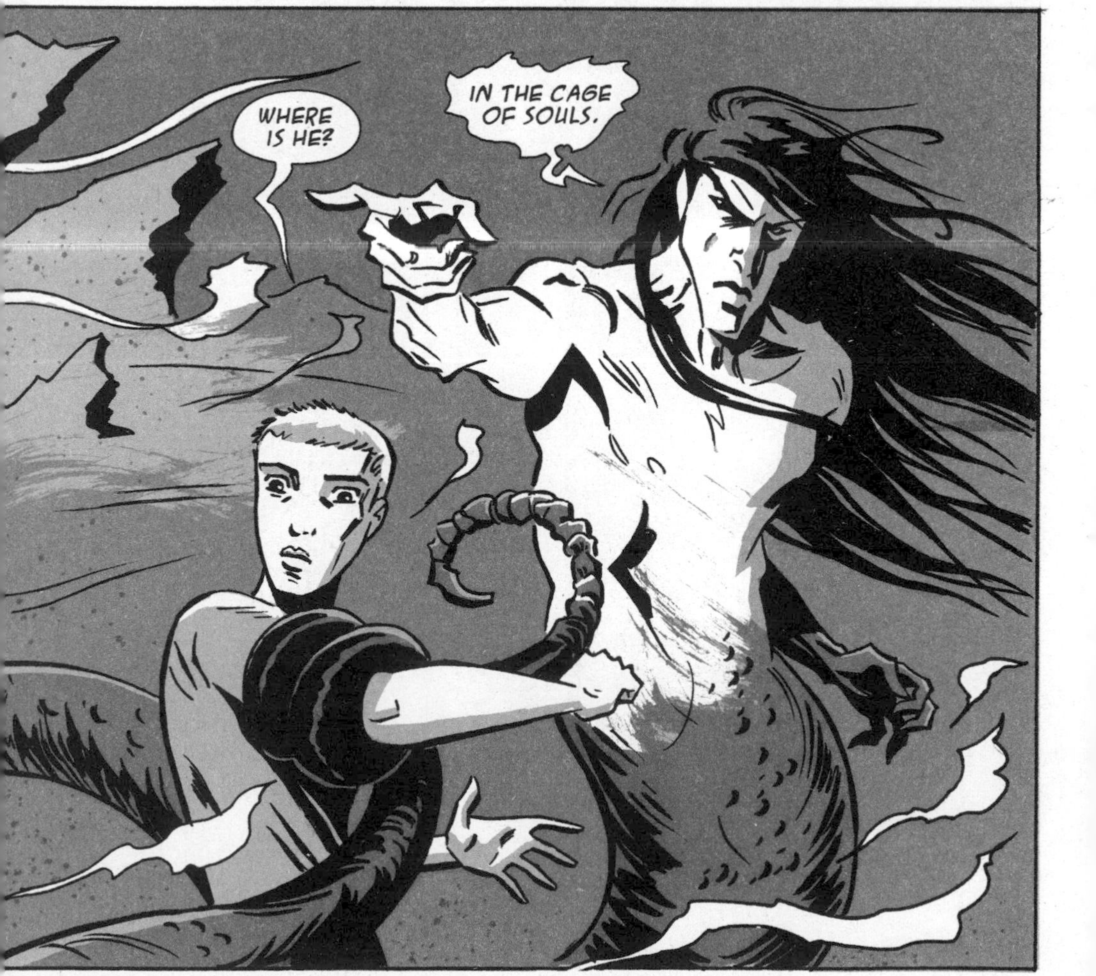
WHERE IS HE?
IN THE CAGE OF SOULS.

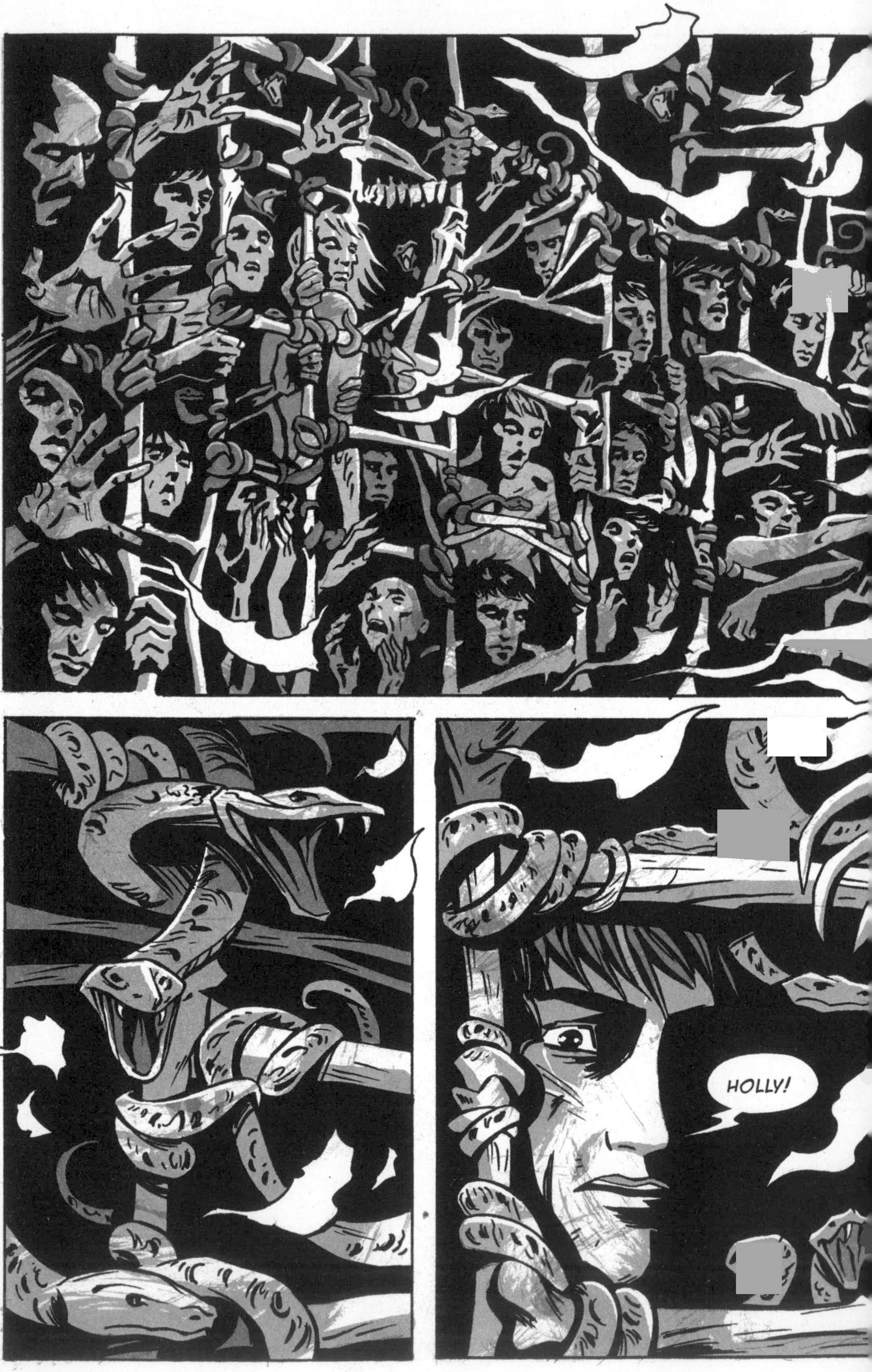
HOLLY!

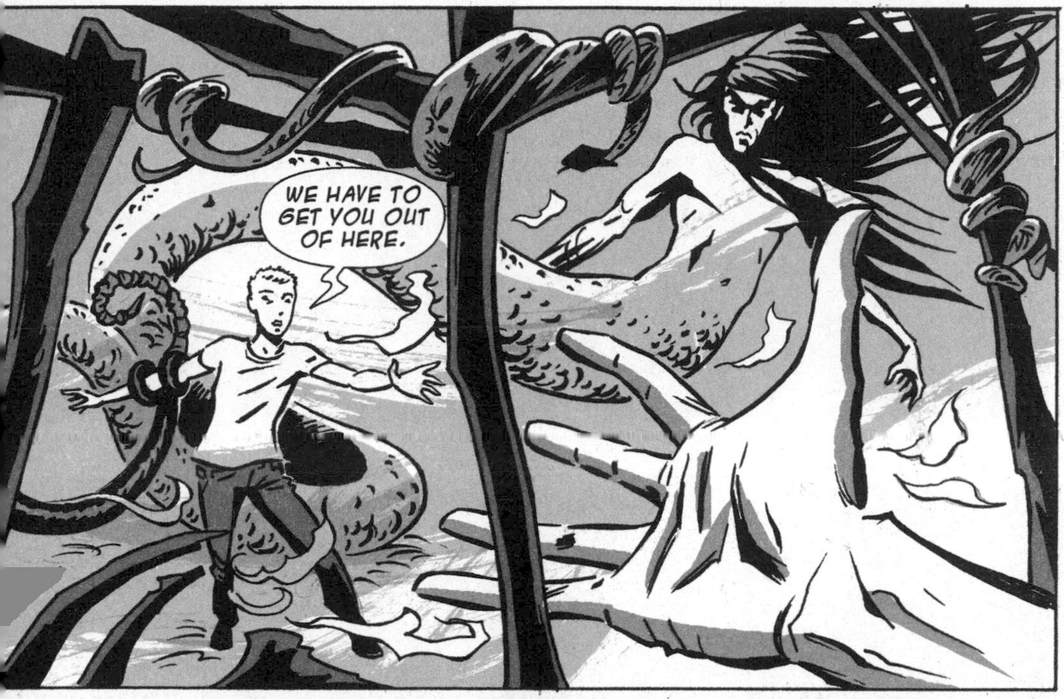
WE HAVE TO GET YOU OUT OF HERE.

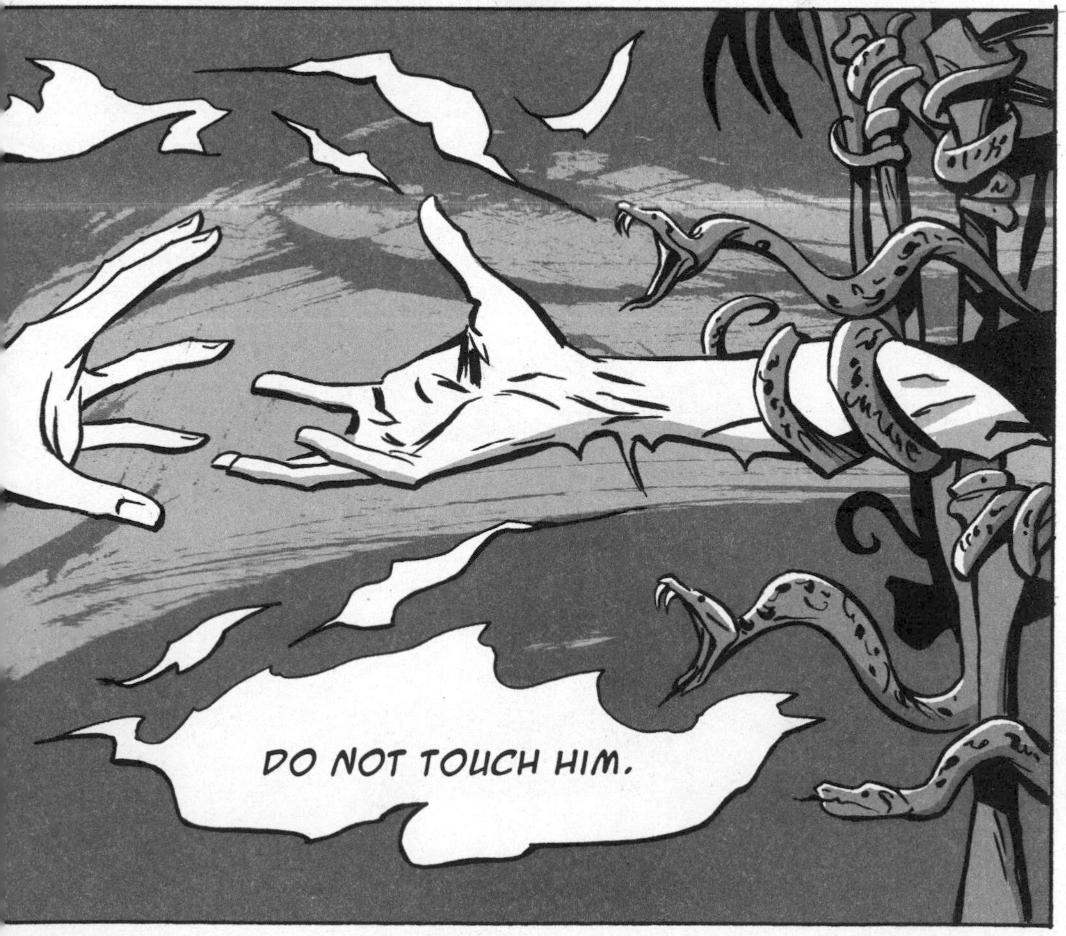
DO NOT TOUCH HIM.

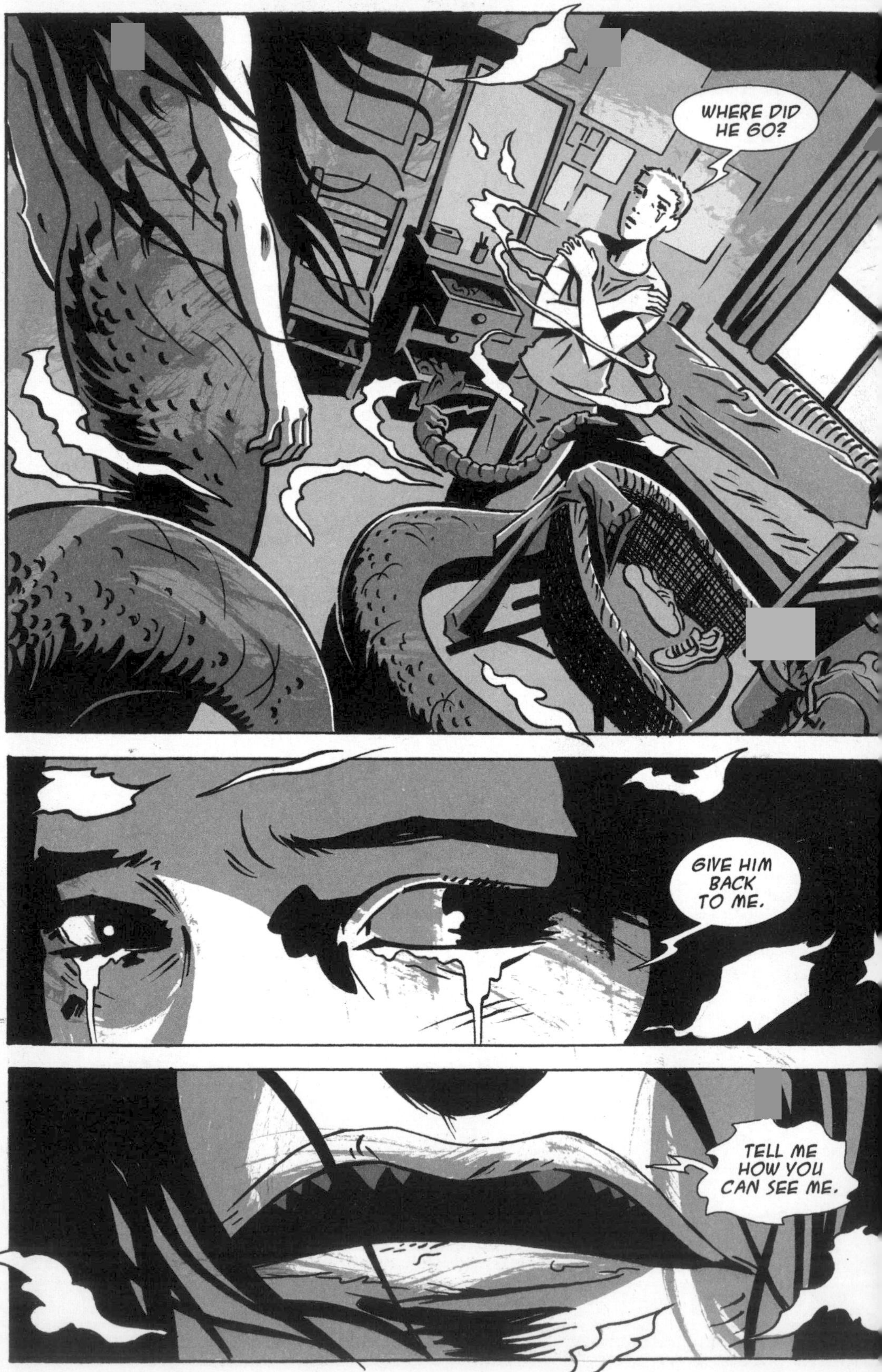
WHERE DID HE GO?
GIVE HIM BACK TO ME.
TELL ME HOW YOU CAN SEE ME.

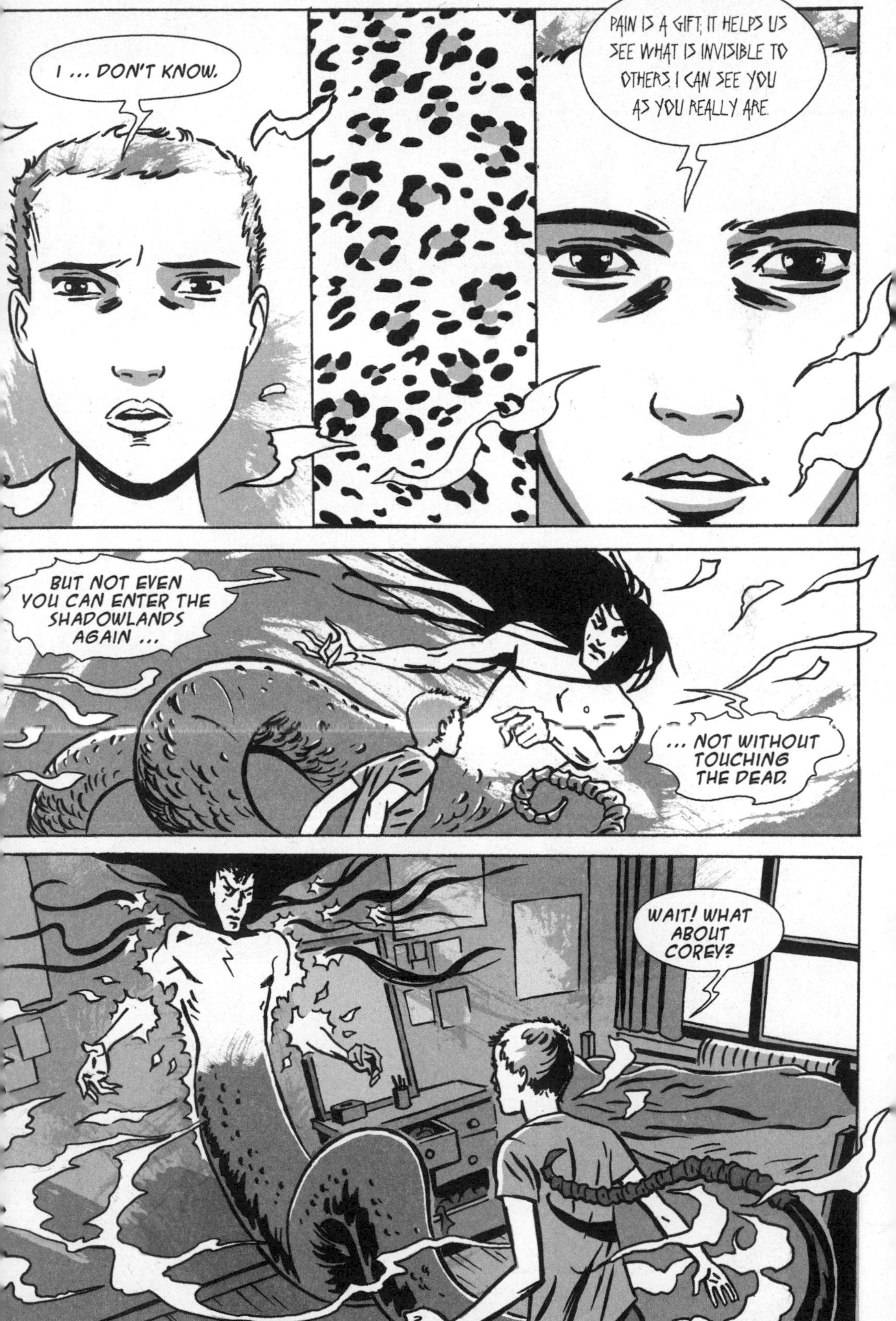
I ... DON'T KNOW.
PAIN IS A GIFT; IT HELPS US SEE WHAT IS INVISIBLE TO OTHERS. I CAN SEE YOU AS YOU REALLY ARE.
BUT NOT EVEN YOU CAN ENTER THE SHADOWLANDS AGAIN ...
... NOT WITHOUT TOUCHING THE DEAD.
WAIT! WHAT ABOUT COREY?

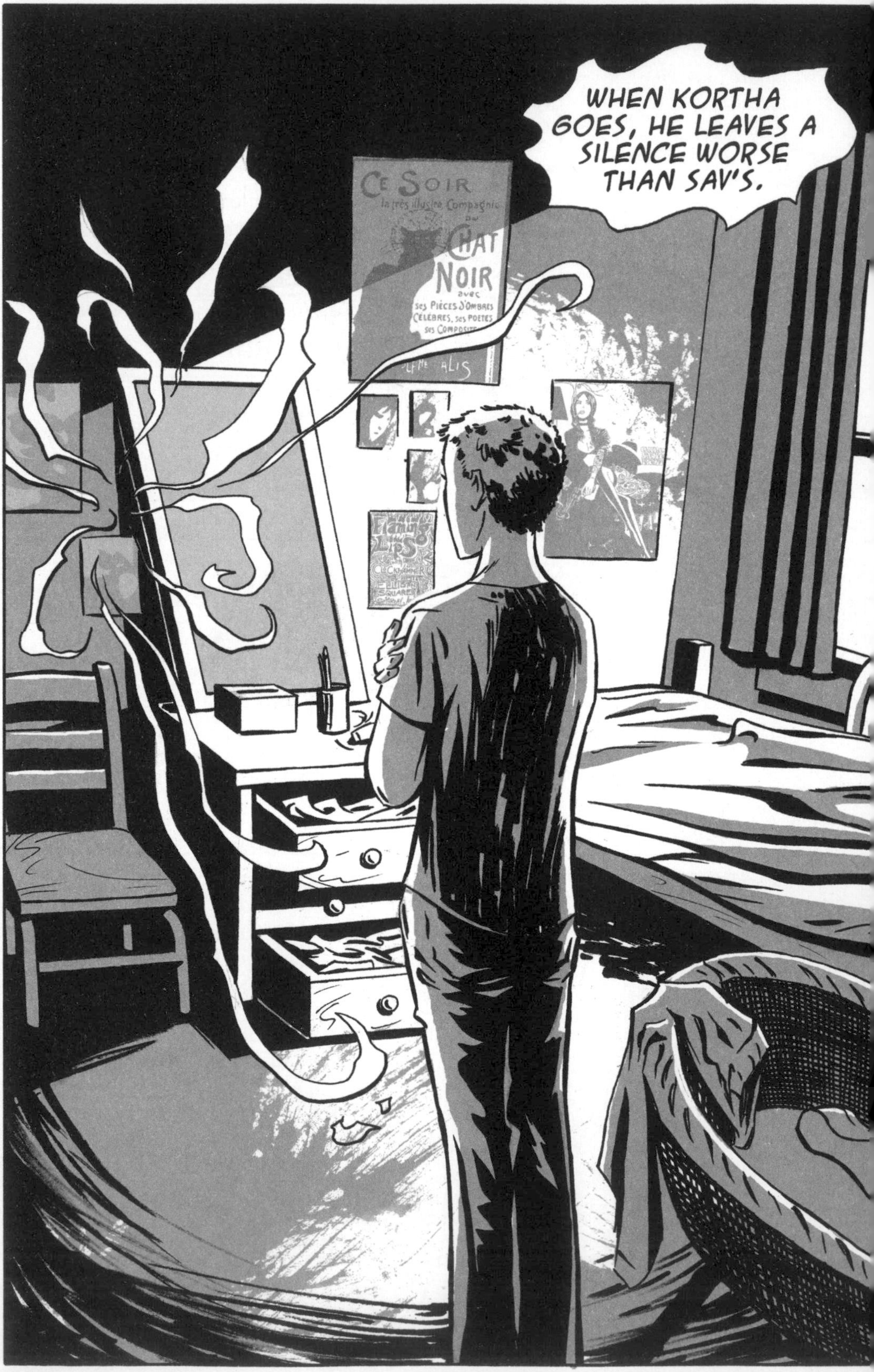
WHEN KORTHA GOES, HE LEAVES A SILENCE WORSE THAN SAV'S.
CE SOIR
CHAT NOIR
avec
ses PIÈCES D'OMBRES
CELEBRES, ses POETES

From my backyard, I can see Sav's light shining in the darkness. Eighty feet to her front door. Five seconds away. She would open it and fold me in her arms while I collapsed against her. She would do it for me, in spite of what a bitch I've been. Her voice would root me with her, on solid ground, in this world. But that would drag me away from what I know is true.

IN THIS WORLD, WE ONLY BELIEVE WHAT WE CAN PROVE. FAITH WAS FOR ANOTHER AGE.

We believe what We Can Touch. I rub my wrist where Kortha's scales slid across my skin, wrapping around to my elbow, the rattle on his tail rough and hard.

The Voice was right all this time. I strain my ears for her, invite her to me. I listen for what I know is true.

TWINS SHOULD NEVER BE SEPARATED. BORN TOGETHER. BORN AS ONE.

What I know is real . . .

COREY IS TRAPPED IN A PRISON OF BONES AND SNAKES. IN A LAND THAT EXISTS HERE ALONGSIDE OUR OWN. WE CAN GET HIM BACK. JUST NEED TO TOUCH THE DEAD   OR KORTHA.

Corey saved my life, using his body like Kevlar when Wiry fired the gun.

MY TURN.

Savitri

42 days and 5 hours after

After I leave Holly's—or, rather, after Holly tells me to leave—I head to my house. The moon backlights a circle in the clouds on my short walk. *Holly would never shave her head. Holly would never kick me out when I tried to help. She is drowning.*

The first time Corey and I saved Holly, we were thirteen. I tagged along as the twins visited their aunt. On her property, we found a half-finished pool she was having installed. The concrete had hardened and it had been left unfilled. About five feet of rainwater had collected in the deep end and frozen, but the ice didn't reach the pool's walls. At the time, I didn't understand why there was a half-foot gap of murky water between the concrete and the floating ice, didn't understand that the cement retains heat and would melt the ice at the edges. All I knew then—all the twins knew then—was that it looked like the start of a good game.

We jumped down into the pool and raced in long loops, our momentum fast enough to keep us from falling, even though the walls sloped sharply in the deep end. The blood pumped rhythmically, loudly, in my ears. Which is why I didn't hear Holly fall. She had slipped and slid down into the gap between the concrete and the ice, her legs trapped and the slope too steep to scramble out on. Corey was already on his way to her. I sprinted to him and we braced ourselves against each other to haul her out, inch by inch.

The second time we saved Holly, it required an ambulance and Corey's life. And this time . . .

192

Well.

This time, I'll have to do it alone. But this time, I don't know what she needs to be saved from.

When I reach my house, I flip on a light, dump my armful of stuff on our low table, and find a note on the banister: *At the hospital. Dinner in fridge. Letter for you in kitchen. Call if you need. Love you, Mom.*

I pass through the living room, leaving my coat on the couch. A big white envelope rests on the kitchen table. From Princeton. When I open it, a slick, shiny folder with Princeton's emblem embossed on it slides out and clunks on the table. I sit down and trace the black and gold shield, the tiny ridges guiding my fingers.

For a moment, I close my eyes and pretend. I erase that night: the shooting, Wiry, everything. I pretend instead that Corey and I went out and celebrated—a single piece of chocolate cake with two forks. That later, I slipped out the door and climbed into his room and we lay together, my hand on his chest rising and falling with his breath. I pretend that on April first, Corey showed up at my door at midnight, a bag of Danishes in his hand, telling me bakery was required for this. That he put his hand on top of mine and we clicked the mouse together. That when Princeton's offer became official, he pressed his lips to mine again and promised me that we would survive the distance. I pretend that I would have believed him.

I open my eyes and find my fingers resting on my lips.

The reality is that Corey is dead. The reality is that I watched Wiry line up a shot that shattered his skull, sped through his gray matter, and killed him. The reality is that I watched it and did nothing.

But there is something even less than watching. There is walking away.

I text Holly:

Princeton's out and I'm all in.

Holly

I don't even bother to sleep after I get Sav's text. I write a quick reply: *Together we'll take this City by Storm.*

I AM A CREATURE OF THE NIGHT.

I get the car keys, slip out of the house, and speed over to the lake. I park and jog through a tunnel that runs under Lake Shore Drive, dragging my fingertips against the graffitied walls. When I step out of the tunnel, I hear the lake breaking on the man-made shore. The Point—the place where the shore curves out into the lake—takes a beating on windy days when the waves slam into it. So the city planners built a shield. Big rocky steps lead to a concrete platform. There the planners' aesthetics must have deserted them, because they put up these coffin-sized concrete blocks. Not pretty, but they sit close enough together for jumps, even flips, between them.

I work. Up the steps, down the steps, push-ups, practice rolls. My City is behind me, and the busy waves of Lake Michigan are in front of me. And me—I Am Movement. I am raw power wrapped in feline grace.

When the sky over the water turns silver and then gold, I perch on a block, one leg swinging free while the hot red sun pierces my eyes. But I watch it rise over the lake, changing slowly from red to orange. It only takes minutes more before its reflection shines yellow and turns the water into a blinding mirror.

After a quick trip to McDonald's, I show up at Sav's house and at six-thirty on the dot ring her phone.

"Holly?" Her voice comes even scratchier than usual.

"So I'm a bitch and you're amazing, but I've got something for you. Open your door."

"My front door?"

I laugh at her disorientation and tell her, yes, her front door.

Centuries later, the locks click, the door opens, and Sav is dressed in purple pj's, the top with an innocent frill lining it. I shake the McDonald's bag and Sav attempts a smile.

"Is everything all right?" she asks.

"Better than all right. I love this city," I say.

Her eyes struggle to stay open and we start up the stairs. I bounce past her and then wait at her door. When we get into her room, she hits the off button on her alarm. I plop down on her bed and open the bag. A French fry scent fills the room.

"I need a shower before I can keep up with you," she says as she pulls her hair into a ponytail, holds it for a second, and then lets it fall.

I wave both hands at her and she disappears into the bathroom. I pace around the room, a leopardess, waiting. And bored.

Lying on top of the perfectly stacked books is one of the old Indian comics that Sav showed me when we were little. She brought in an Indian comic book for an *All About Me* assignment. When Alyssa Krenshaw said, "Ewww, that's weird," and Kelly Pratchett said the blue skin made her gods look dead, Sav pulled on the plastic balls that held her tight braids. I told Kelly she was being stupid, that the Skin was Beautiful and the story was better. After that, Sav and I shared a bunch of these. I had practically forgotten about reading them.

It was how we got into comics in the first place.

I pick up the comic. The paper has yellowed and it's in Hindi, but I flip through it anyway. From the art alone, I can understand what is happening: a woman's husband dies and Death comes for him. I stare at Death, with his blue and oddly familiar face. He carries a noose, lifts her

195

husband's soul out of his body, and drags a featureless white shape, like a bleached shadow, behind him. Déjà familiar. When I flip the page, the world changes.

There on the page lie the Shadowlands—the windswept desert, the endless black sand, everything.

THE SHADOWLANDS.

The door opens and Sav's mom stands framed in the doorway. Her hair lies down perfectly, her clothes pressed—it's like she's been up for hours. I sit a little straighter.

"Holly," she says, her voice high and surprised. "Your hair. What happened? Did the doctors—"

"Oh," I say, and touch the fuzz that the razor left behind. "Yeah, I shaved it last night . . . so it could grow out evenly. But I think it looks good, right?"

Being around Sav's mom is funny sometimes—the same expressions, only older. I can read her, even though I don't know her all that well. So when her lips pucker just before she speaks, I know that means she has gone into Diplomatic Mode. "I'm sure it's 'in' right now."

I shrug. Parents and Hairstyles never Get Along. "Well, it isn't unheard of anyway."

IT IS BEAUTIFUL. THE SCAR REVEALS OUR SOURCE OF POWER.

When she asks, I explain that I came over early this morning. The shower turns off and we both look down the hall, waiting for Sav.

"Do you want some French toast?"

"No, I brought breakfast." I wave the McDonald's bag.

Her lips tighten. "Hmm."

She's never really liked me, and I guess my fast-food breakfast isn't helping.

"So," I say, "you know Hindi, right?"

She laughs and nods.

"I mean, of course you do. Anyway, I was looking through this and wondered what it's about."

She smiles when I show her the cover.

"That," she says, and points, "is Savitri's name in Hindi."

I study the letters—how a sturdy bar on top connects them, how they flow in unfamiliar shapes.

"It's her story, the legend we named her after. Of course, we didn't know . . . Do you know the story?"

"I did once, but I can't remember the details anymore."

She sits next to me, and page by page, she takes me through it—how hard it was for the couple to conceive, how the baby Savitri was a gift from a goddess because of the father's devotion. When Savitri chose her husband, she gave that same intensity of devotion to her fiancé. So, even when they heard a prophecy that her husband would die one year from their wedding, she decided to marry him, decided to follow him into the forest on the day he was prophesized to die.

Sav and Corey celebrated their first anniversary two months ago.

"When the prophecy comes true and he falls, the God of Death, Yama, comes to ferry his soul. Savitri follows Yama on and on; she will not go back, saying her place is by her husband's side. Her loyalty to her husband earns her a boon—one wish, anything except the life of her husband."

"What does this say?" I ask her, pointing to the words.

"That's Savitri's wish: she asks Yama to let her father-in-law, who was blind and penniless, see his grandson, who has not been conceived yet, eat with a silver spoon. She's very clever."

SAVITRI CAN BARGAIN WITH DEATH. SHE HAS A VOICE OF POWER.

Somehow here, in a comic book that is about my best friend, the Shadowlands Are Real.

YES. REAL AND WITHIN OUR REACH. COREY CAN BE RESURRECTED.

"Are you okay, Holly? Did I say something to upset you?"

I realize that I'm clenching my hands so tight that my fingers are white. I have to breathe deeply and try to find my voice before I can answer. She hands me the book. "No. It's just—"

197

"Ironic? Yes. We named her Savitri because we waited a long time to have a daughter too. Now I hope this story can bring her comfort, but I'm afraid it's just the opposite."

Sav comes in, wearing a long robe and drying her hair.

"Your mom and I were looking through your story."

Her eyes dart from the book to my face and then back again. She tightens her robe.

"I'd forgotten it," I say.

She tugs on her sleeves. "It's just a story."

Her mom tells us she'll have breakfast ready in a few minutes and closes the door on her way out. Her mom is cool, even if she doesn't like me—understanding Boundaries and Borders better than mine. Sav sits on the edge of the bed, crosses her legs, and looks at the comic.

"Do you believe in myths?" I ask.

"How do you mean?"

"I mean, do you think they're real, that they carry Truth?"

"Yes. I'm not sure I'd call Savitri a 'myth,' though, any more than you'd call, say, Jesus rising from the dead a myth."

"You'd call it real?"

"What are you asking me, Holly?"

I exhale hard, like I'm lifting a weight, and then I say, "When I was in the coma . . ."

"Yes?"

"I saw something like this, you know?"

"You saw . . ." She leans forward.

"Remember when I woke up, how I told you I needed to go back and you said to stay with you?" She nods. "I was here and I saw him."

"You saw Yama?"

"Well, not him exactly. He was part snake—all evil—and his name was Kortha."

"That doesn't sound anything like Yama."

"Kortha!"

"Holly, trust me, that is Yama and he isn't evil. This is the story I was named after—I think I know it better than you do."

She snatches the comic book up and puts it back on her bookcase. Somehow I've offended her, but I can't quite figure it out. For a moment, I see a look cross her face—one I recognize from a long time ago. She might as well be pulling on her braids.

She says, "I don't want to argue about this; we've been arguing too much."

I don't know how to make her understand. How do I jump across this gap between worlds? I shake my head.

"But I'm telling you what I saw. Why would I see this?"

"You read it a lot when we were younger. It was why we started reading comics in the first place," she says. "Memory is a funny thing."

"I have never seen this before," I say, taking the comic down and waving it in the air. "I'd remember this. It's not even in English."

"I have a bunch of versions." She goes to the bookcase, pulls out another book, and hands it to me. "You read this one, I think."

On the front cover, a blue God is riding an animal—a bull, I think and a woman is cradling the head of her dead lover. I do remember this story now. Vividly. And there were no Shadowlands in it. I flip through it to make sure.

"I like the art best in the one you were looking at first," she says.

"So do I," I mutter.

"I used to think I was like her, that because we shared a name, we shared the same devotion to the people we love." Her voice has adopted the Quiet Confession Tone.

My head snaps up. "You are like her. You *are* Savitri. You reached in and saved me. Who else could do that?"

"Modern medicine." She picks up the books and starts to reshelve them. "If I were her . . . I didn't do anything for Corey, did I?" When she's done, she turns to me. "We should be talking about you, though. Between the graveyard and last night . . . What is happening with you?"

I want to shove the comic book at her and shout that I'm *trying* to tell her. But she needs Proof and Logic. Which I can't give. So I change the subject.

"We'll find out soon enough what's in this head o' mine; I'm getting it shrunk today."

She cocks her head, questioning me.

I tell her I get to start therapy—lucky me! And she's got school—lucky her! Which gets a laugh out of her before I go.

As I walk home, I try to think of how to convince her. I wouldn't have believed it either if I hadn't been to the Shadowlands and felt Kortha's scales on my wrist. If only she could see the Shadowlands herself. Proof, if not Logic.

*   *   *

Mom insists on driving me to my first therapy appointment.

"I'll take the train," I tell her, and munch the rest of my Pop-Tart.

"It's no problem; it's on my way." She puts my plate in the sink.

"To what?"

"To . . . your therapy appointment," she says, and laughs. "There are some things I want to talk to you about."

When we're in the car, the city slides by us sl-ow-ly. Mom drives like she's eighty-five all of a sudden. But it's not just her. Everyone is in slow motion.

"So, talk."

"I think it's great that you're starting therapy," she says, and looks at my scalp.

"Joy."

"Look, I don't want to fight."

Why is everyone saying that to me?

Silence falls while we both try to think of something toothless to say. Maybe the weather?

"What did you want to tell me?" I say at last.

"Therapy might be hard sometimes, but be patient."

Yeah, that'll play to my strengths.

She continues, "Dad and I are here for you; we want to help."

Help me leave my brother behind. I don't want your kind of help.

"I know that this has been hard for you . . . ," she continues.

"Not hard. I wish you'd both stop saying 'hard.' It's been Impossible."

". . . but you're not the only one who lost Corey. And your father and I have been giving you a lot of space to cope in your own way—"

"Yeah, you guys have been just fabulous. Really good to each other too."

I look out the window and watch My City. We change highways, and downtown slides to our right.

"Maybe you can try to give us some slack too. We're doing our best."

"Your best is treating me like I'm some Broken Doll that you need to reconstruct and treating Dad like he's a Criminal? That's just sad."

Her eyes narrow and she lets out a snort. So much for not fighting.

"God, Holly. Why are you so angry at me? What did I do?"

"Did it ever occur to you to leave Corey's room alone, to stop asking me to say goodbye?" I shout. "Maybe I don't want to Move On according to your Timetable. Maybe I don't want to Move On at all."

She frowns. "But there is no other alternative, Holly."

She pulls in and turns off the car. Then she sighs and schools her face: Pleasant. As she moves to get out, I tell her not to come inside with me, that I don't need it.

"I'm not just going to wait in the car."

"I'll take the train." I sling my bag over my shoulder, get out of the car, and slam the door.

She rolls down the window. "I'll be back in an hour. It's time you start dealing with your family."

I throw the glass door to the building open and stomp inside, passing a ridiculous water fountain surrounded by low benches and tall artificial plants. Decorating Geniuses. In the metal elevator door, my distorted image stares back at me. When I agreed to go to therapy, I thought I needed help controlling the Lunatic Voice. She gets so quiet whenever I talk about therapy and I can't have that voice whittled down to a whisper. Not now, when I finally know it for what it is—a Voice of Power. As I ride up the elevator and walk down the hall, I strain to hear her. I get Resolute Silence.

I get to the therapist's door. Dr. Justine Krenshaw. Options: step over the threshold and get shrunk or hear the voice again.

I turn around and walk back to the elevators.

THAT'S RIGHT. TIME TO FOCUS ON FINDING HIS MINION. TIME FOR A PLAN.

I smile, hearing her. I must be on the right track if she's talking to me. I need to kill an hour, so I sit cross-legged at the seats by the fountain. From my messenger bag, I pull out *The Leopardess: Collected*, a two-volume slipcased set that was released yesterday. How do heroes track down a killer? I skim, searching for clues, stealing strategies.

After a few minutes, I rest the book against my thighs. I think through all the strategies that superheroes have to track down their nemeses: (1) a computer geek or massive computer systems in a cave, (2) patrolling the city with scanners, or (3) an investigative journalist/photographer who courts danger. Not helpful. Sav and I don't have the resources.

Or do we? We know people who know how to Hunt in Chicago, who are as committed to finding him as we are. Guardians of the City who Serve and Protect. And they have given us all the information we need.

How fucking stupid we are. It's all in the file. All we have to do is follow Meade. Or at least Meade's notes. Night after night, we've been searching for him at the scene of the crime, but the night of the shooting, we had *parked* inside Serpents' territory. What if he had spotted us there and tracked us outside of Serpents' territory?

Chicago is a city of well-defined neighborhoods with borders that mean something, and we've been searching in the wrong one. We need to move our stakeout.

Actually, I'm not far from there now. So close I can't resist . . .

I wend my way six blocks, from the office, past UIC's campus, to the podium building where Corey, Sav, and I last stood together. Where Corey last ran free. I must be on the right track because the Voice rewards me again.

OH, YES, WE'LL CATCH WIRY AND USE HIM AS BAIT. TO BRING KORTHA TO US.

Kortha said I could get in by touching the dead. What if I touch a killer?

HUNT HIS MINION. FIND WIRY AND KORTHA WILL COME.

I reach the building, do a wall run so I can grab the lowest rung of the fire escape, and yank. Climbing up, I move Leopardess Fast.

Tracking down Kortha is something The Leopardess could do. If I were her. Which is what I need to be, what I am becoming.

YES.

I can do what the police cannot.

YES.

In all pain, there are hidden gifts. And with mine, I can see the world as it is.

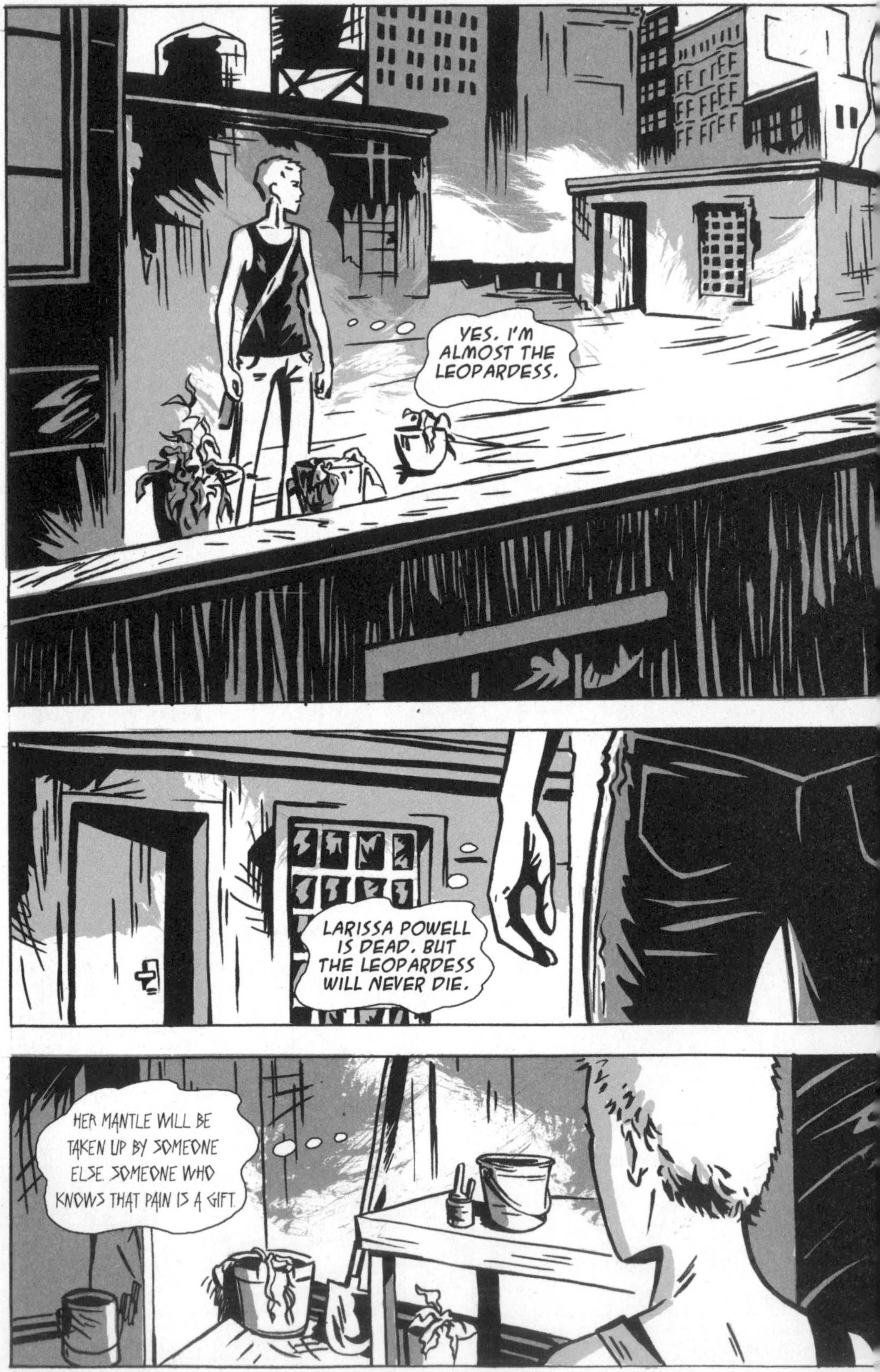
YES. I'M ALMOST THE LEOPARDESS.
LARISSA POWELL IS DEAD. BUT THE LEOPARDESS WILL NEVER DIE.
HER MANTLE WILL BE TAKEN UP BY SOMEONE ELSE. SOMEONE WHO KNOWS THAT PAIN IS A GIFT.

ALL I NEED TO DO IS BECOME FEARLESS AND I WILL BE ...
The Leopardess Resurrected

I race inside the therapist's building. No need for another fight with Mom. My heart is still thu-dumping when Mom's car pulls up. I hop in and she looks me over.

"Wow," she says. "You look happy. Did you like your therapist?"

I smile and tell her that, yes, therapy is helping. I can see my way forward now.

Savitri

42 days and 23 hours after

My English teacher keeps me late while I try to muster up the appropriately contrite tone for failing to turn in a paper. I can't believe I ever cared about any of this. How does symbolism in *The Stranger* matter? Who cares about existentialism and the futility of life? I'm trying to recompense the dead. And really, what difference does my English grade make if I'm not going to Princeton?

When she lets me go, I walk out to the parking lot to find Josh waiting for me by my car. I smile, watching him playing on his phone. I could use a break from Holly.

This morning I avoided talking to her, ignoring her message for me. Maybe it shouldn't matter, but I'm still annoyed with her for her rendition of Yama, twisting him into a snake, imbuing him with an evil he doesn't have, blithely stomping all over a sacred story. So, I'm ready to freerun with Josh's group again—to let go of all thought.

"Hey," I say as I smile and jog over.

"I just wanted to check on Holly. How is she?"

"Holly's fine, Josh," I say a little too fast, a little too sharply. "Sorry. Listen, do you want to go to the meet-up together this—"

"Holly is not fine. I've stayed away from her because you told me to, and the last thing I wanted to do was worry you more, but she's not okay. And I want to know what you're doing for her."

"I'm . . . What do you mean?"

"Holly came to see me last Thursday. She wanted to . . ."

My hand draws little circles in the air. "Spit it out."

"She wanted to hook up."

The blood drains from my face so fast that my lips tingle. That was the day we visited Corey's grave, the day she saw something she wouldn't talk to me about. A shadow, she said.

"Excuse me." I push my key into the lock right beside his hip.

"Hey," he says as I pull the door open against him, moving him away. "Where are you going? I'll go with you."

I glare at him like he's the dumbest person on earth. Which, maybe, he is. Next to Holly. *What was she thinking?*

"I'm going to talk to Holly."

"Right, as if that'll help."

"What did you just say to me?" I say, even though I heard him, and start the engine to drown him out.

"Savi, give me a lift home." He runs around to the passenger side and knocks on the window. "I have more to tell you."

I reach over, pop the door open, and wait for his seat belt to click.

I shoot out of the parking lot and head home. I don't think anyone will miss me if I skip out on self-defense today. *Why didn't she tell me?* In our whole long weekend together going through the file, why didn't she tell me? It's a three-minute ride to Holly's from school with traffic.

"So? What else?" I say.

"I turned her down. And she stomped off."

"You turned her down?"

Is that why she didn't tell me? Too embarrassed?

"I'm not the asshole you think I am."

I slow down at the red light, and once I'm stopped, I look directly at him.

"Can you turn the blower down?" Josh asks, and I realize that the car is blasting cold air at us. I spin a knob and the fan cuts off.

"What did she say? I mean, exactly what did she say?"

He slowly meets my eye.

208

"I'm not going to tell you that. Green," he says, and points at the light. "If she wants you to know, she'll tell you."

I turn back to the road and slam my foot against the accelerator so hard that Josh's head bounces off the rest. I glance at him, roll my eyes, and shake my head.

"Hey, don't I get any points?" he says.

"For what? For not telling everyone?"

"I wouldn't do that again. Listen, what happened before . . . I panicked when she told me that she thought she was pregnant, and fear makes us do some pretty stupid things, Savi."

Yes, it does. It freezes our muscles, stops our brains, and keeps our hands off horns.

"It's Sav. No one calls me Savi anymore," I say.

"Fine, listen, Savitri. Is she even seeing a therapist? She needs, like, an intervention or something. And if you need help with her . . . I could be there."

"Oh, you're just such a good guy, aren't you? Maybe you can explain why you waited until now to tell me. You could have mentioned it at the meet-up on Satur—"

Oh. *That's* what he came over to tell me. He wasn't intending to invite me at all, but then he took pity on me when he saw me, saw that I looked "awful."

I hit the brakes and turn the wheel to make it into his narrow driveway. When I stop the car, hard and fast, he jolts forward in his seat.

"I . . . I wanted to give her a chance to tell you. But it was pretty clear she didn't. Savi . . . Sav, you can't just stand by and watch her self-destruct."

"I know that. Believe me. I'm her best friend," I say, but it sounds unconvincing, even to me.

"Not a very good one. At least not right now."

I flush hot. "Get out."

"Hey, I'm just being honest," he says.

She said, "Unless you have some magical cure, stop questioning me and just help me. The way I ask you to." And I shaved off her hair, thinking that once I'd helped her the way she'd asked, she'd talk to me again.

Instead, she shoved me out the door.

Josh gets out, but then he leans back in. If I reversed right now, I'd hit him with the car door. And while that's tempting, it's a tad extreme.

"What I said before . . . it came out wrong. I only meant that sometimes being a good friend means saying the hard things. Maybe someone—maybe you need to tell her she's heading down the wrong path."

"Holly is coping. She is . . ." I don't know how to say it. "She is getting up every morning, walking through every day, with a black hole in her life. However she manages to keep herself moving, I'm going to support that."

"Yeah, that's what I mean. That may be the friend she wants, but not the one she needs."

But it's the only friend I know how to be.

* * *

When Holly answers the door, I walk in and pull her by the sleeve, turning her around.

"Where are we going?" she asks, her tone light.

"Your room. Now."

She mocks a salute and marches behind me. I take the stairs two at a time, leaving her and her joke to catch up. The spring sun has toasted her room. The place is a mess—bed not made, comic books everywhere.

I shut the door and glare at her. She smirks and crosses her arms, ready for this fight.

"So?" I say.

"So," she says back.

"You thought you wouldn't tell me and that it just wouldn't matter?"

210

"Tell you about?"

"Jo— Are you keeping a lot from me? So many secrets that you have to figure out which one I'm talking about?"

She sighs. "I thought Josh would have learned to keep his mouth shut. But I should have known he'd blab it all over the school. His latest conquest and all that." She touches her finger to her tongue and draws two hash marks in the air. "Josh two, Holly zero."

"He didn't 'blab' anything. He told me and only me because he was worried about you. And if you have such a low opinion of him, then why did you—"

"*Because* I have such a 'low opinion' of him." She makes air quotes.

"That doesn't make any sense."

She looks at the ceiling and sighs. "Forget it, Sav. You wouldn't understand."

"Explain it, then," I say through clenched teeth.

"There isn't anything to say."

"I am *sick* of this. I've done everything, everything you've asked me to. I've hunted for Wiry, I've cut off your hair, I'm turning down Prince—"

"Oh, sorry, I didn't know it was such a burden to be my best—"

"And you are *still* pushing me out the door. I can't . . ." *do this anymore*, I don't say.

There is a warning sign before the end of a friendship, a moment when one word can bring it down and you have that word ready. Of all the casualties of the shooting, it never occurred to me that our friendship might be one of them.

And now . . .

Well.

Holly sits down and looks up at me. "I'm trying too. I'm working my ass off here, Sav."

I know that's supposed to make me feel better, but why is it so hard? She is still Holly. I can still catch glimmers of her.

"I need . . . Do you ever pretend Wiry never fired that gun?"

I nod.

"This world, without him, it's unbearable. I want him back. And I know I've done things that don't make any sense to you." She touches her scalp. "But it's my way through. And it helps—God, it helps—to know you'll be with me. That you're not leaving."

"It does? Really?"

"When I went to Josh's house . . . I thought you were leaving. I'm sorry; I should have told you, but . . . Sav, I couldn't take it if you were mad at me right now. I'm not trying to push you away." She looks at me from under her lashes, her chin down, contrite.

I'm falling for something here, but the gravity is strong. She's hard to stay mad at, especially because getting a "sorry" out of Holly isn't easy. I just want a sign that she is reachable.

"So?" she says.

"So," I say. It's not perfect, but it's the best I'm getting from her.

I sit on her bed and she shoves a few books out of the way to sit next to me, but they fall back against her.

We ease out of our fight with stilted talk about my school day and her therapist.

"I did have an epiphany while I was there."

I lean in, ready, but then one side of her mouth crooks up—a classic Holly smile, the mischievous one I've grown up with—the sign I was searching for.

"I know how to find Wiry."

"You do?"

"Yes! It's all in the file and we missed it. We just need to follow in Meade's footsteps—visit all the places he has. . . ."

"Meade's been all over the city," I say.

"But he's concentrated on Serpents' territory. So that's where we look."

I groan. "More surveillance?"

She laughs. "*Targeted* surveillance."

Is going with her being the friend she wants or the friend she needs? Hours together, time to smooth out the roughening edges of our friendship.

"Maybe we can narrow down the target further," I say. "Virtual surveillance?"

"Better," she says. "Like real surveillance, only with a fridge."

We open Google Earth and start zooming in. We scroll through one block after another, checking Meade's addresses: grocery stores, gas stations, bars . . . any place from Meade's interviews.

We've been at it for over an hour and I'm losing faith when Holly sticks her finger out, pointing at the screen.

"Wait," she says. "Zoom in there."

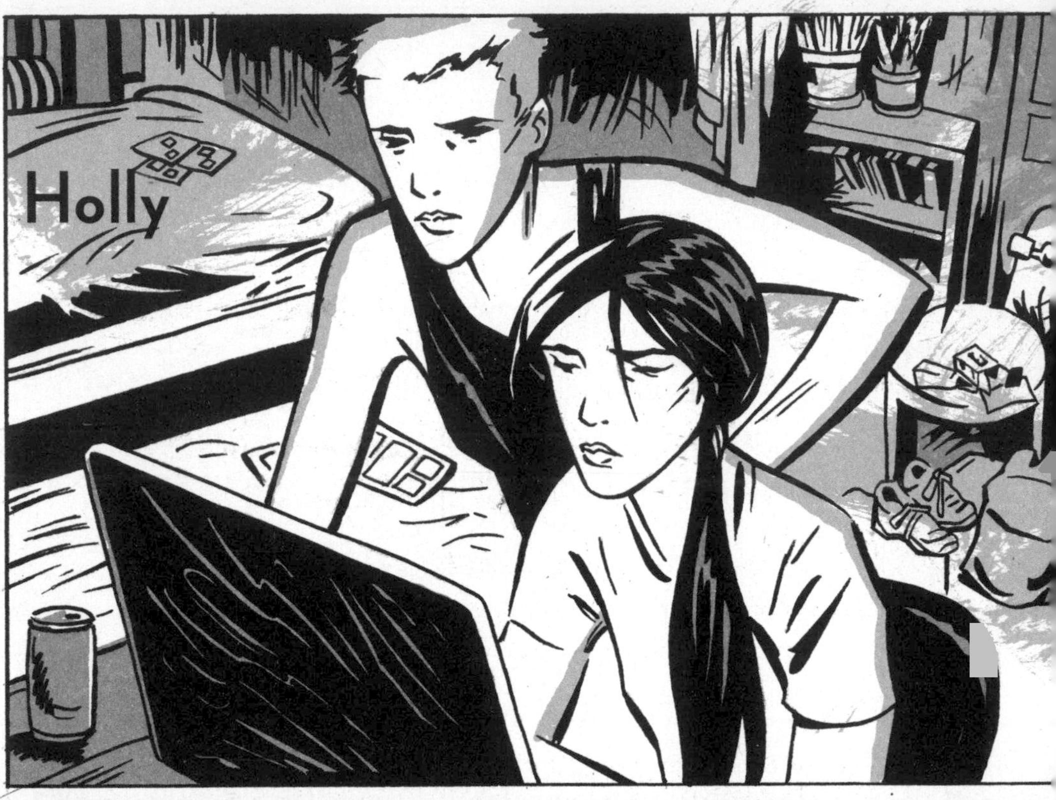
Holly

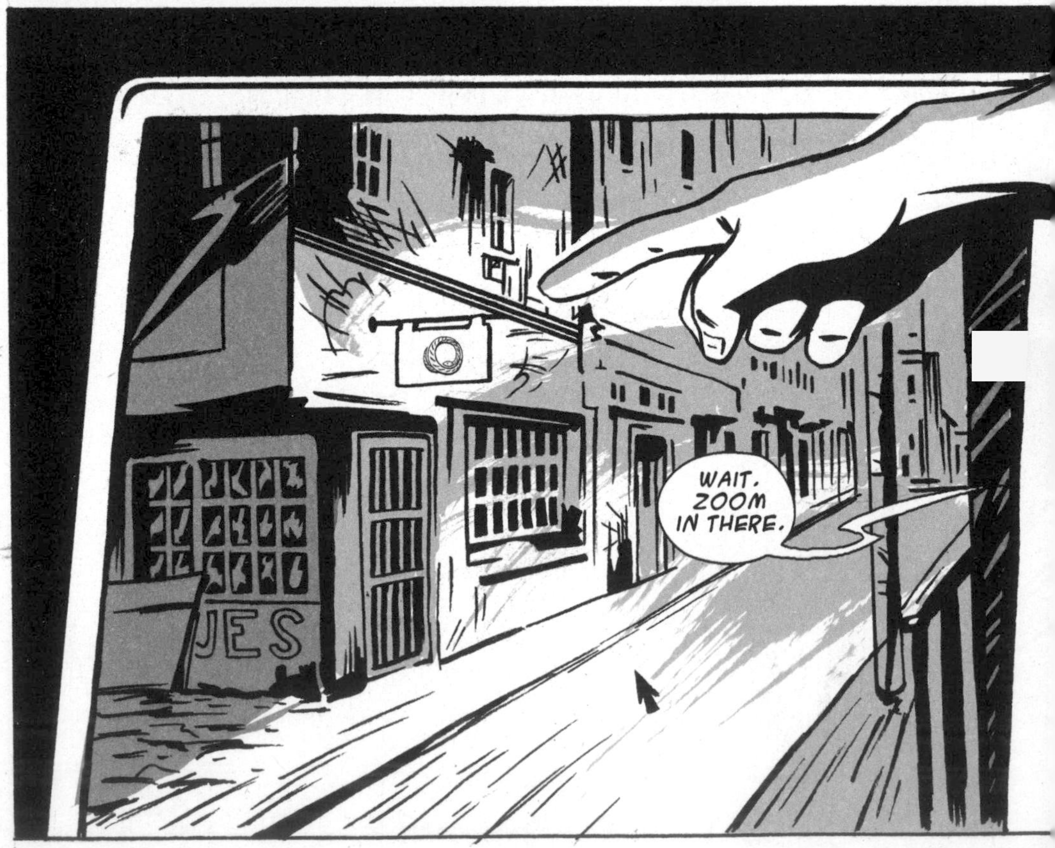
JES
WAIT. ZOOM IN THERE.

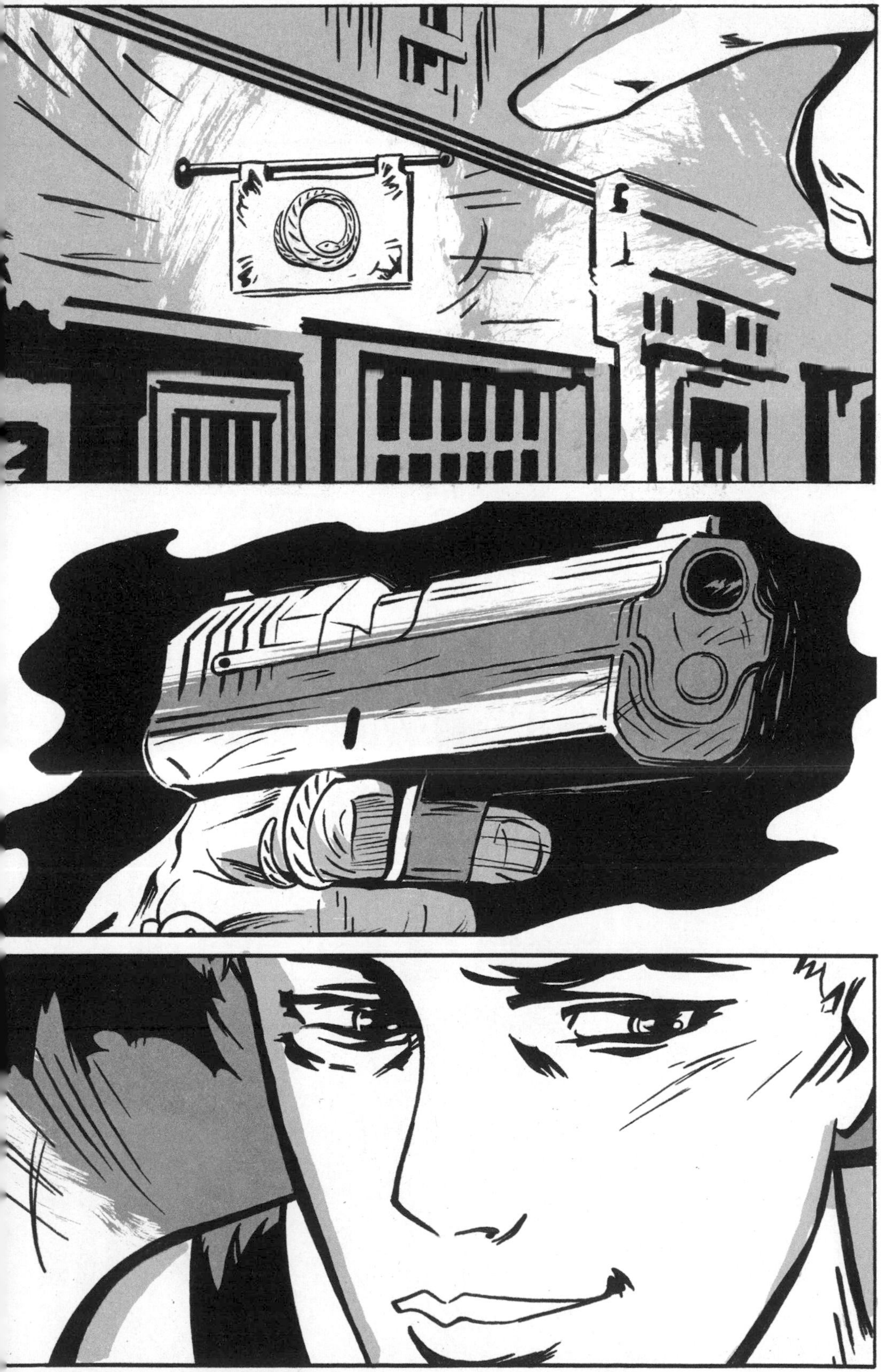

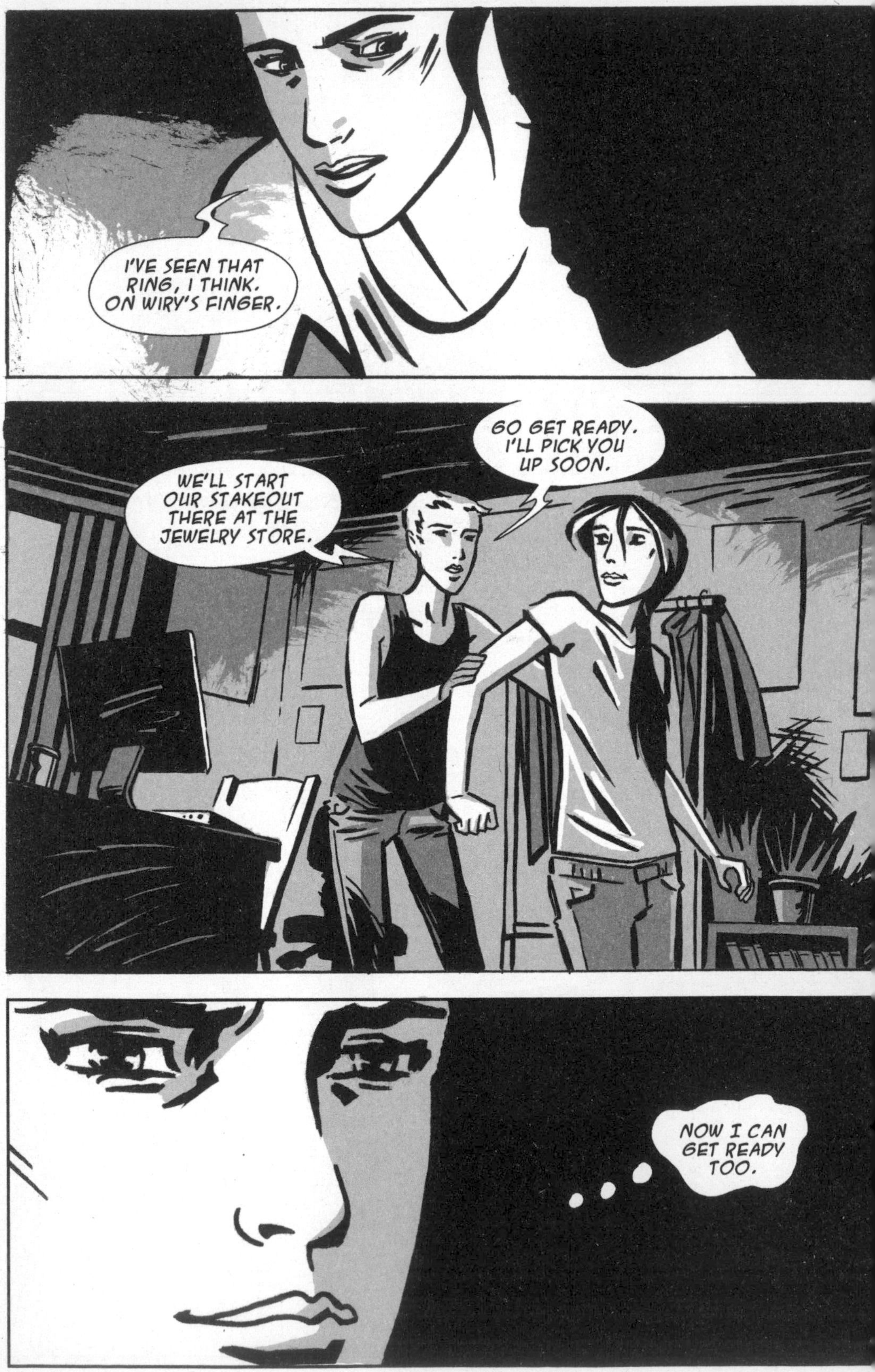
I'VE SEEN THAT RING, I THINK. ON WIRY'S FINGER.
WE'LL START OUR STAKEOUT THERE AT THE JEWELRY STORE.
GO GET READY. I'LL PICK YOU UP SOON.
NOW I CAN GET READY TOO.

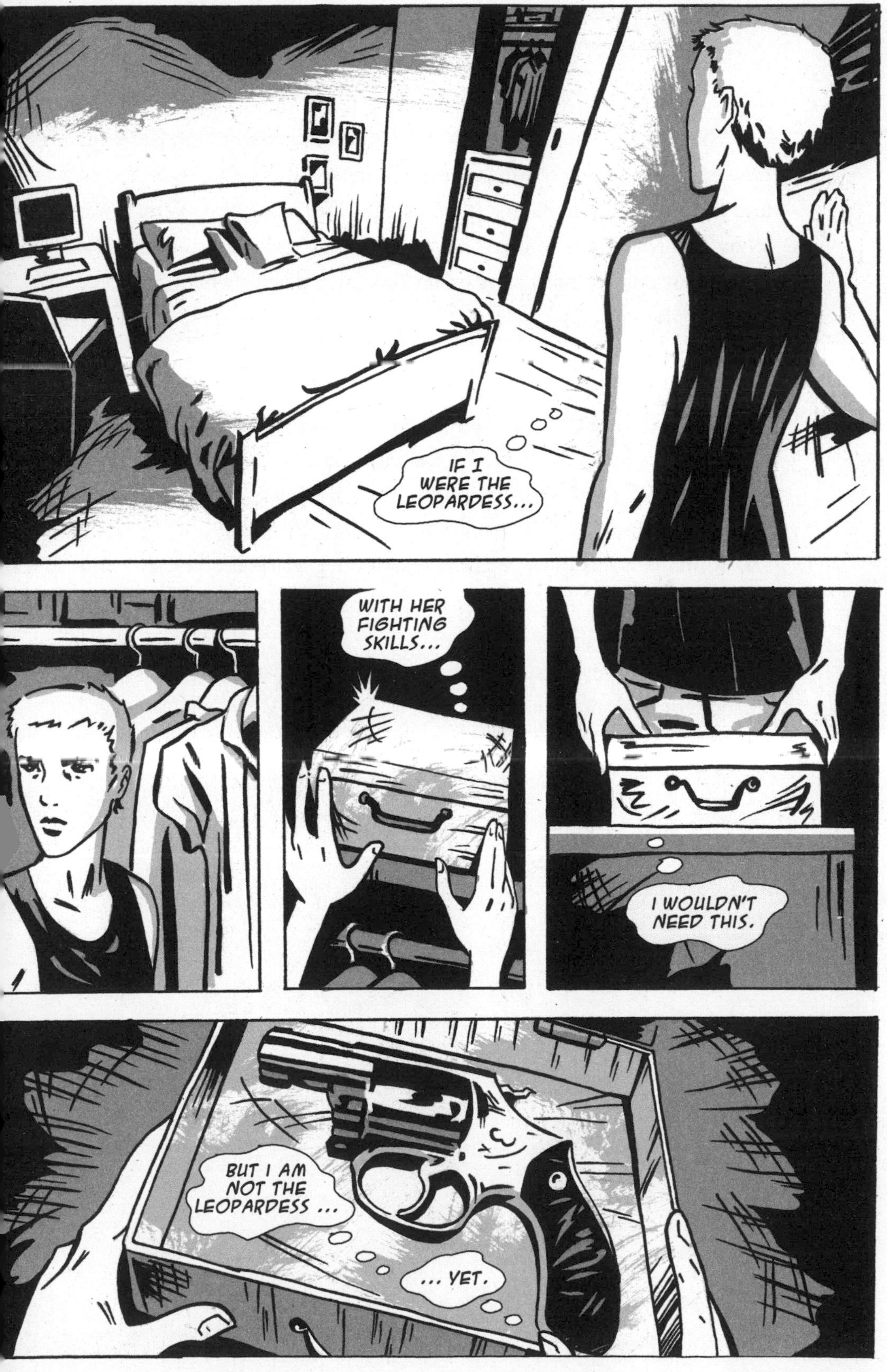
IF I WERE THE LEOPARDESS...
WITH HER FIGHTING SKILLS...
I WOULDN'T NEED THIS.
BUT I AM NOT THE LEOPARDESS ...
... YET.

I haven't fired a gun in years. Not since Dad taught Corey and me how to shoot, hoping to turn us into Hunters. After we'd mastered cans and bottles, Corey took aim at a backyard bird and got it. Which was when Dad learned he wouldn't have a Hunter. Corey kept staring at the empty nest until I finally climbed up and got it down. "There should be a reason," he said.

Well, there's a reason now.

HUNTING THE HUNTER.

Heavy and cold, the gun quivers in my hand. My body stiffens.

How does Larissa slide into her Leopardess identity?

FEAR HAS ALWAYS BEEN THE THING—THE ONLY THING—THAT HAS KEPT ME CAGED. TIME TO BREAK OUT.

When Sav gets in the car, she buckles her seat belt and then turns to me.

"Are you ready?" she asks.

I nod, open my breathing deep into my lungs, and glimpse my face in the reflection of my car window. . . . Tonight, I'll become whoever I need to be to get Corey back.

YES.

Savitri

Four days later and I've learned one thing: surveillance isn't my strong suit. Our early surveillance was nothing like this. For four days Holly has been pitched forward, her eyes roving. When I try to talk to her, she responds distractedly, looking at the street. When I suggest we look somewhere else, she deigns to give me an annoyed glance. When I pull out my phone to try to check my email, she tells me I'm remarkable—able to text and watch the street simultaneously.

I've started to drink coffee, its bitter, dark taste sliding down my throat—a sort of self-discipline to keep me focused.

Every time a guy rounds the corner, she asks me, but of course not. Wrong body type, wrong height, wrong skin color. Once or twice, I wondered. I would shrink lower and watch, but no one walked on his toes.

Now Holly nudges me with her elbow again. She lifts her chin as a group of guys and two girls come around the corner. They go by the car and I keep my eyes straight as Holly taught me, observing them in the mirror once they pass. Another no.

How do I find a wire in this haystack of passersby?

"How do you do this?" I ask her. "Aren't you tired?"

She shakes her head. "I'm beyond sleep now, Sav."

"Beyond sleep?"

She pats my hand absently.

I pull it away and stretch it across my forehead, my thumb and finger anchored against my temples. Then I wipe each tired eye.

"I have to be here," she says. "There's no other option for me anymore."

"Holly," I say. "You're kind of freaking me out. What do you mean?"

"Him?" she says, and uses her pinkie to trace his path up the street.

We must have seen over a hundred guys who are about Wiry's size. He's too far away, but the posture is familiar.

I peer through the window as he walks toward us; I sink in my seat and watch.

His heels don't quite hit the ground. He stops and peers in the window of the jewelry shop. When he knocks on the window, the streetlight bounces off a gold loop on his finger. He fishes a phone out of his pocket.

Recognition comes all at once, not in pieces, not in the swing of a hand or the step of a foot, but in one solid movement. The way he got the knife out of his pocket. The way he lifted his arms. He takes another step away from the window and down the block toward us. Only his toes touching the ground, confirming what I know.

Cold collects like an ice dam along my spine. I shudder violently.

"Him."

I lift my phone off the dashboard, frame him in it, and snap the photo. I type in our address and text the picture to Meade while Wiry walks right by our car. Holly watches him in the rearview.

"Got it, Holly," I say while I shift my weight and slide my phone into my pocket.

"Savitri," says Holly, her voice small and hard. "Are you sure?"

"I'm sure."

"One hundred percent sure?"

"It. Is. Him."

She holds my gaze for a second longer—one second too long—and it hits me: she isn't about to let Wiry walk away.

She reaches for the glove box and jolts it open, but my hand is already closing over whatever she wants from there. *Don't let it be what I think it is.* She may be quicker with her feet, but she's got nothing on my hands. My fingers close on a heavy metal cylinder. No, a heavy metal barrel.

God, no.

Her mouth crooks and she lifts her eyebrows as she stares at me with an open challenge in her eyes. I can practically hear her. Options: Help Me or Freeze. Again.

"Coming?" she asks.

Dear Friendship, where you lead, I have always followed. Where are you going now?

In response to my silence, she gives me a one-shoulder shrug, throws the door open, and bolts down the street, following Wiry.

I'll be damned if I'll let her run after a killer—headlong and unpredictable. And unarmed.

What would I do if I had Wiry in front of me? His body to fight?

I push myself out of the car and chase her, gun in hand.

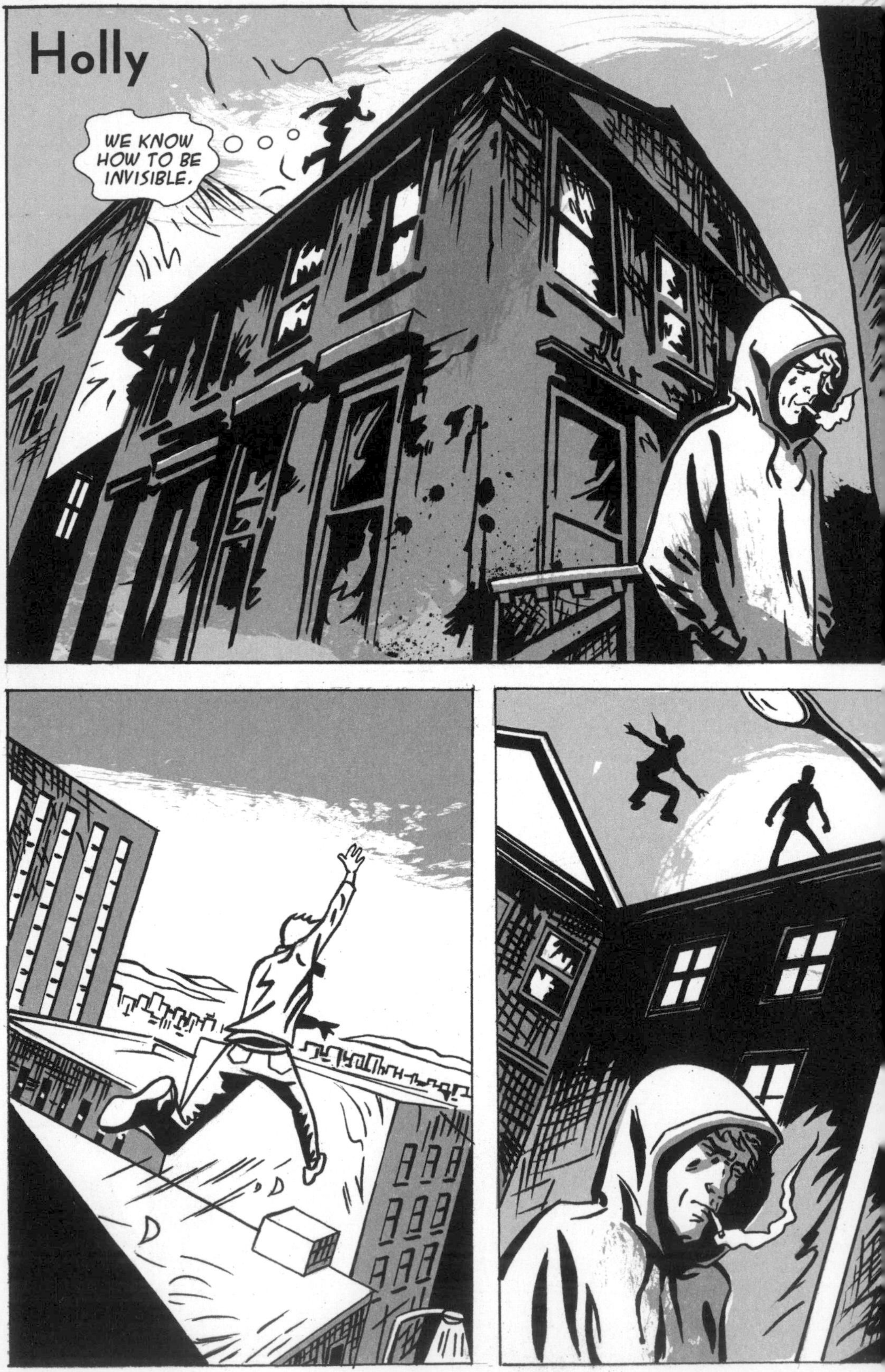
Holly
WE KNOW HOW TO BE INVISIBLE.

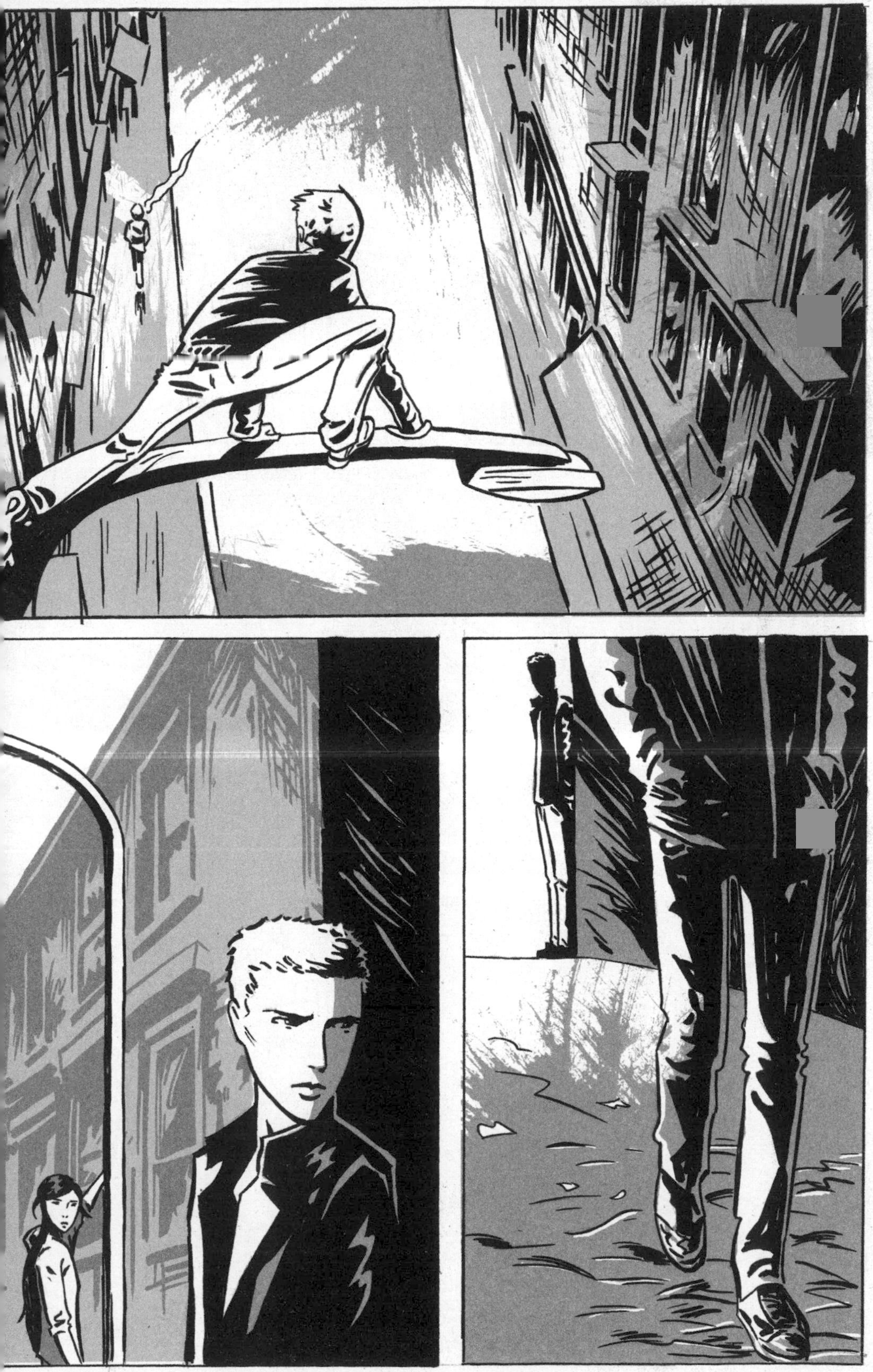

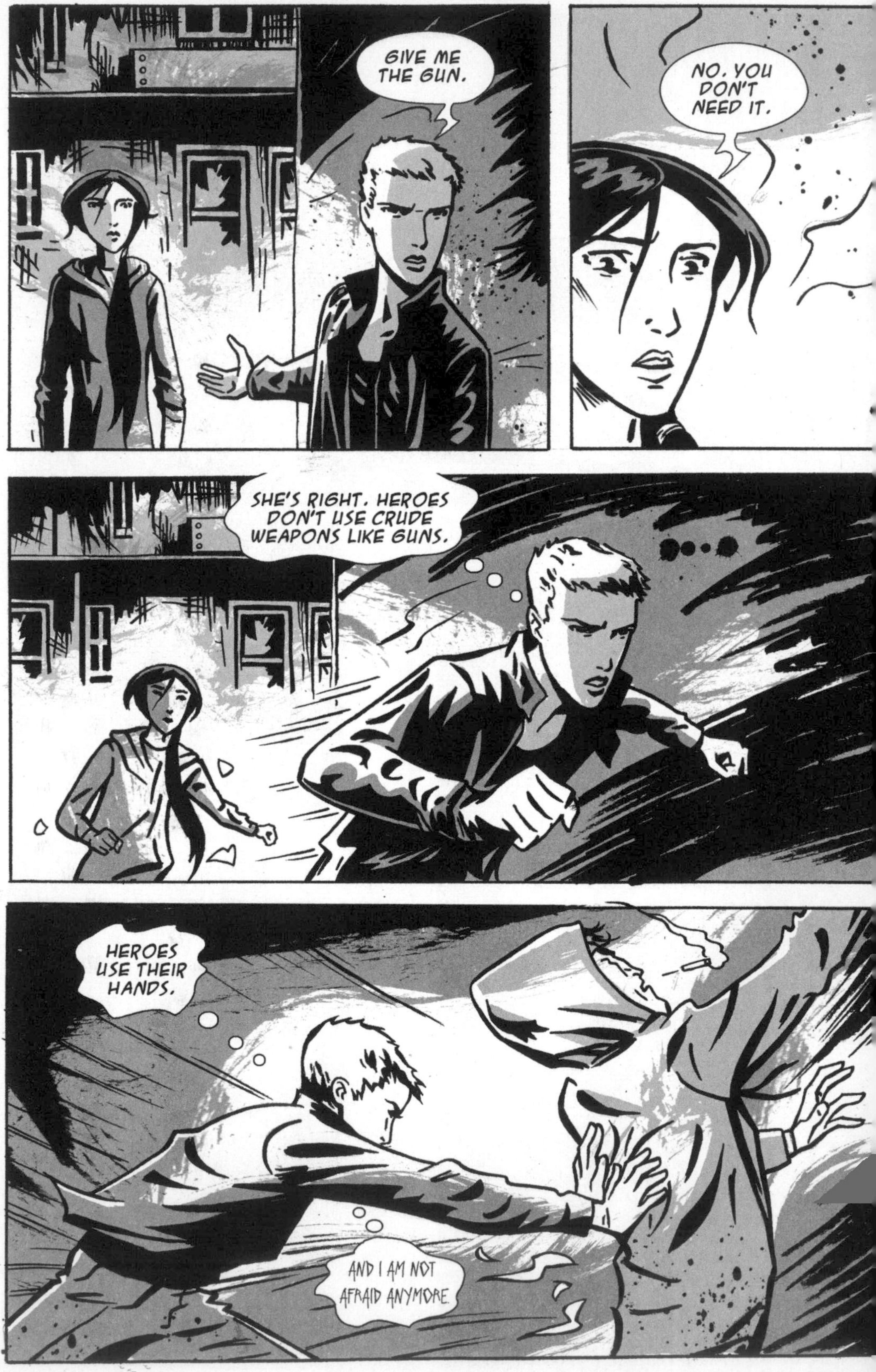
GIVE ME THE GUN.
NO. YOU DON'T NEED IT.
SHE'S RIGHT. HEROES DON'T USE CRUDE WEAPONS LIKE GUNS.
HEROES USE THEIR HANDS.
AND I AM NOT AFRAID ANYMORE.

Savitri

47 days, 2 hours, and 12 minutes after

Wiry keeps his balance after Holly pushes him. He whips around, facing her. For a moment, they stare at each other and I get my first look at his face: gaunt and angular, blue eyes, medium-brown hair—all the descriptors I needed for a good APB.

When she rushes at him, he grabs her wrist.

I lift the gun and point it at him, at his chest. "Don't you touch her!"

Wiry goes rigid. Every muscle stops. *Good. Good.* His fear washes mine clean.

"Get your hands off her," I say slowly.

His fingers spring open. Holly steps back, out of his reach, and pushes close to me. She clicks something on the gun—the safety. I swallow and nod.

I had eight million questions and now I can't think of a single one.

"Look, look. My hands are off her. Okay? Just walk away." Wiry's hands are up. "I haven't done a thing."

Holly steps toward him and her arm flies. He grunts when she hits him. She shakes her hand out and winces. He brings his hand to his face and it comes away a sweet red.

Holly walks behind him and then puts both her hands on his shoulders and pushes him down, down, down. He sinks to his knees. She keeps her hands on him, his body contained and under control, but her eyes seem suddenly vacant. Her jaw goes slack. And I know she's not with me—she's somewhere else again. And me . . .

Well.

I'm on my own.

The gun starts to shake. I hate holding this thing.

He looks up at me. Pure hatred. *It's mutual.*

"What the fuck do you want? Who are you anyway?"

Sometimes when you're so deep inside your own reality, you forget. I've had him in my head for forty-seven days, but he has never seen me. And Holly, with her head shaved, is not recognizable. I try to keep my hands from shaking, but the muzzle wobbles.

"The guy you killed? I'm his girlfriend and that's his sister—the one you shot."

"I didn't shoot anyone, bitch."

If Holly could do it, then I can too. I lift my finger off the trigger, raise the gun, and smack him with it. The reverberations jolt through my arm. *God, guns go off all the time. What am I doing?* But then a blossom of red opens on his head and my panic subsides. *Blood for blood.*

"I watched you."

"Prove it," he says. He lifts his head a little and his lips curve.

"Listen," I say. *For once, let me lie convincingly. For once.* I get out my cell phone with one hand, the gun still aimed at his head. His picture is on the screen. "See this?" I say. "I can send this to the cops, who have your fingerprints from the car. Do you want CPD after you? They will hunt you down and then not even your gang, not even the Serpents, will—"

He barks a laugh. "Not my gang. I'm not their kind. No, no. Too white for them, they said."

"They said?" I repeat. Which means that he has at least had contact with them and . . . and they . . . rejected him? I take a guess. "Did you fail the . . . ?" What did Holly call the initiation? "The beatdown?"

"The beatdown was a fucking setup. They wouldn't ever let me in. I stood up through the whole thing. And still . . . too white. Assholes are sorry now." He is biting off every word.

They're sorry now? The word *setup* cycles through my head and the

226

whole thing clicks. How do you pay back a big, indestructible gang? You get another big gang to take them on. The wrath of CPD that rained down on the Serpents was predictable, and Wiry planned for it, using CPD as his weapon of revenge.

"You set them up." I shake my head.

That's why he took their hair, because it is what the Serpents would do. He knew it would throw the cops right on them. That's why he shot up the Dana, spraying it like a gang hit.

Which means I'm not dealing with a dim-witted thug. I'm dealing with a strategist. Who I have cornered in a dark alley. My stomach hurts.

I grip the gun tighter and glance at Holly, but she is still . . . absent.

He looks up and down the alley and then he smirks.

Revenge from behind a shield. Coward. "But then why did you leave her alive?"

His smirk falls. "Did she look alive after? To you?"

Blood pooling in her eye. "No."

"So you *were* there. You're the witness the cops have been jawing about, huh?"

He looks me over, sizing me up. I shrink back and my heart is beating so loudly that I think of "The Tell-Tale Heart"; I'm giving myself away too. His body scan continues. Maybe he's wondering how I would fare against a bullet. Finally, his eyes rest on mine.

"I've been looking for you," he says.

A chill spreads from the top of my head through my shoulders and down each vertebra. *He'll kill me if he can; I've offered myself up as a target and he has a good reason.* My question finally floods into my head.

"Why them?"

He shrugs. "Why not them? You all came strolling through the neighborhood like you fucking owned it. And the cops . . . oh, they care when a rich white kid is gunned down by a black gang. And then they turned out to be a cop's kids. Bonus."

"Bonus?"

"And look at you . . . you aren't going to shoot me, are you, little girl? You're shaking." Then he shouts, "Give me that phone, bitch!"

Dear Bullet, metal to metal, find the iron in his blood. Signed, the girl who did something.

I hold his gaze and my finger finds the trigger.

Which is when Holly starts screaming.

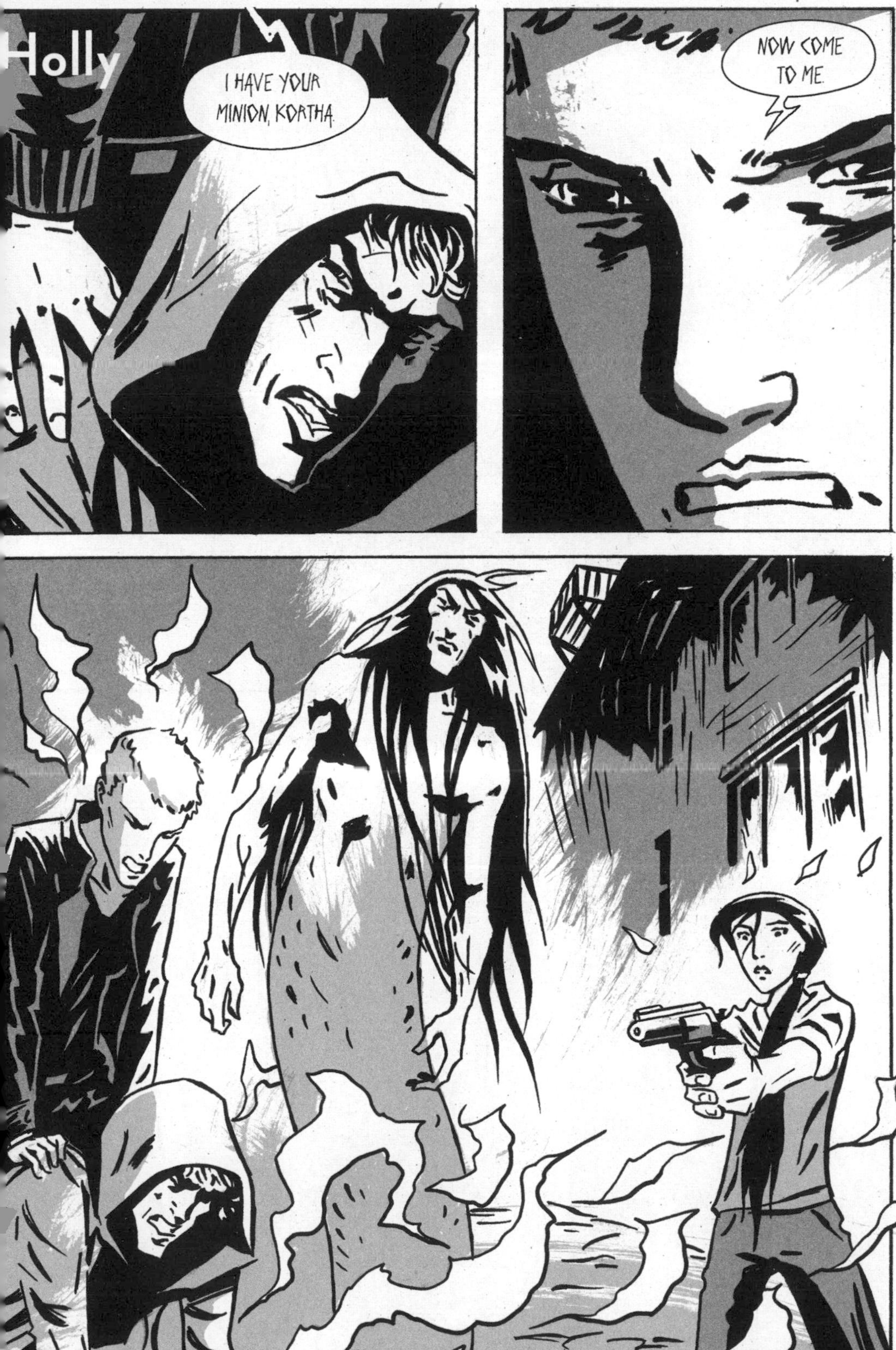
I HAVE YOUR MINION, KORTHA.
NOW COME TO ME.

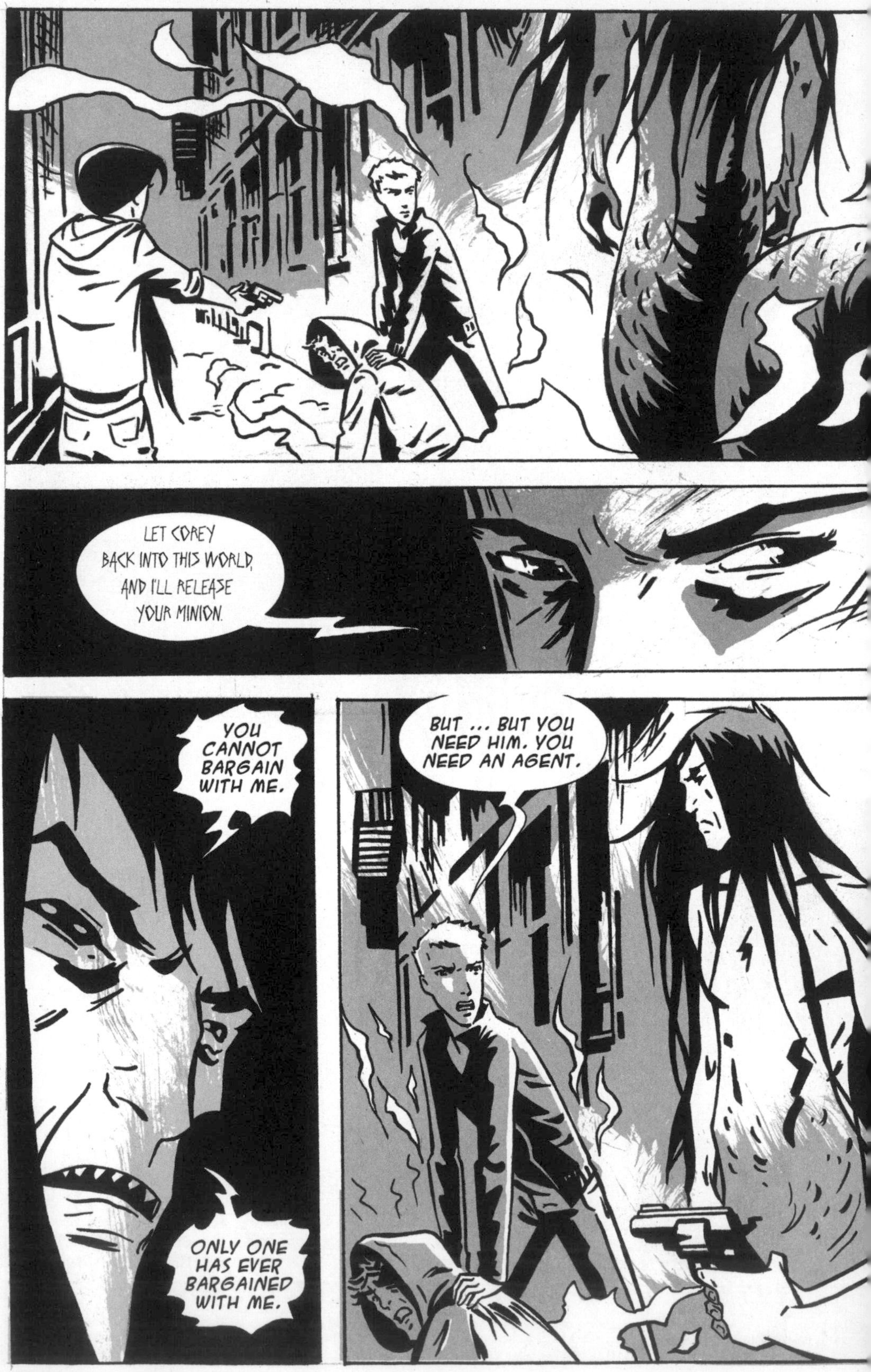
LET COREY BACK INTO THIS WORLD, AND I'LL RELEASE YOUR MINION.
YOU CANNOT BARGAIN WITH ME.
ONLY ONE HAS EVER BARGAINED WITH ME.
BUT ... BUT YOU NEED HIM. YOU NEED AN AGENT.

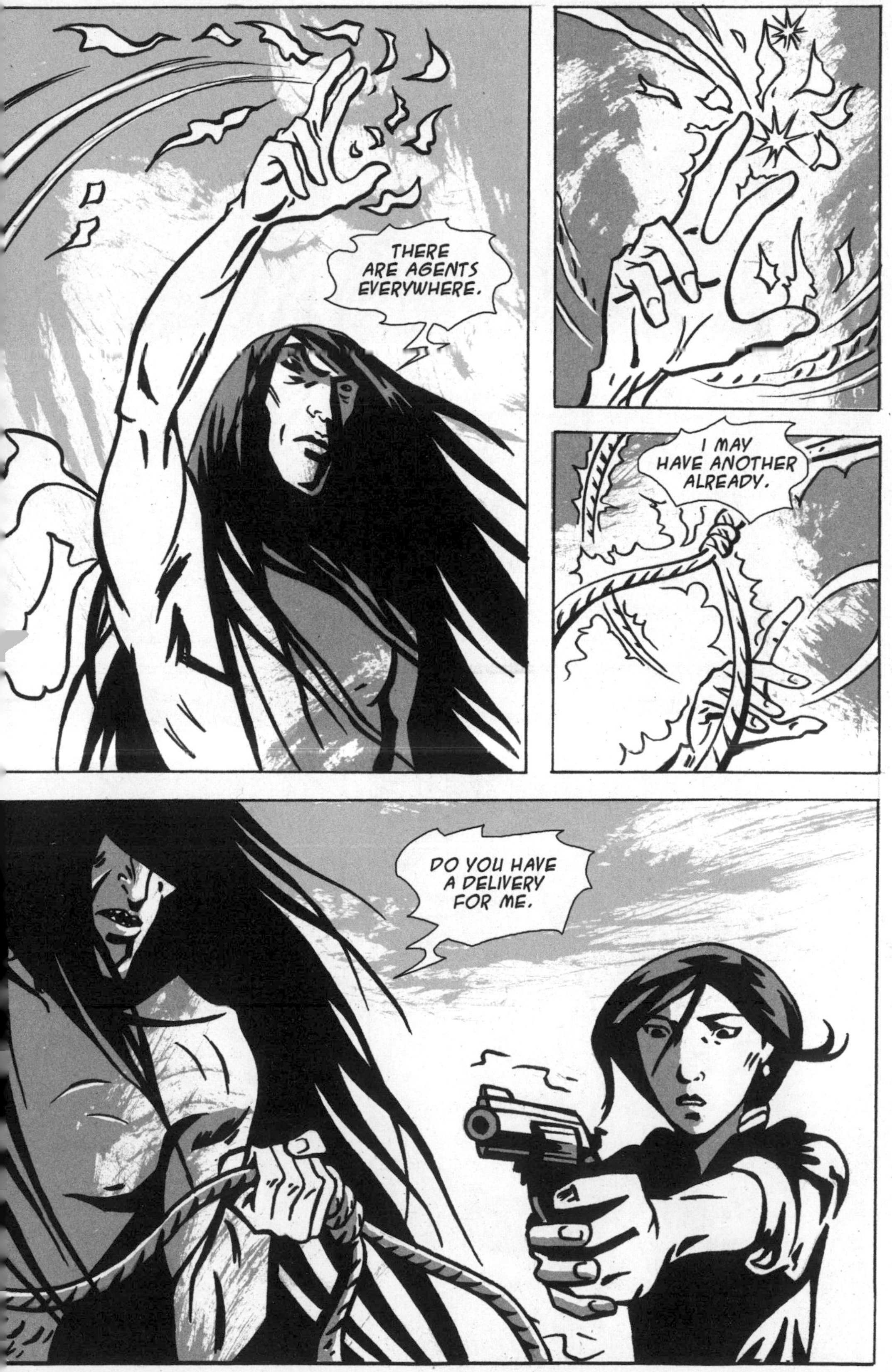
THERE ARE AGENTS EVERYWHERE.
I MAY HAVE ANOTHER ALREADY.
DO YOU HAVE A DELIVERY FOR ME.

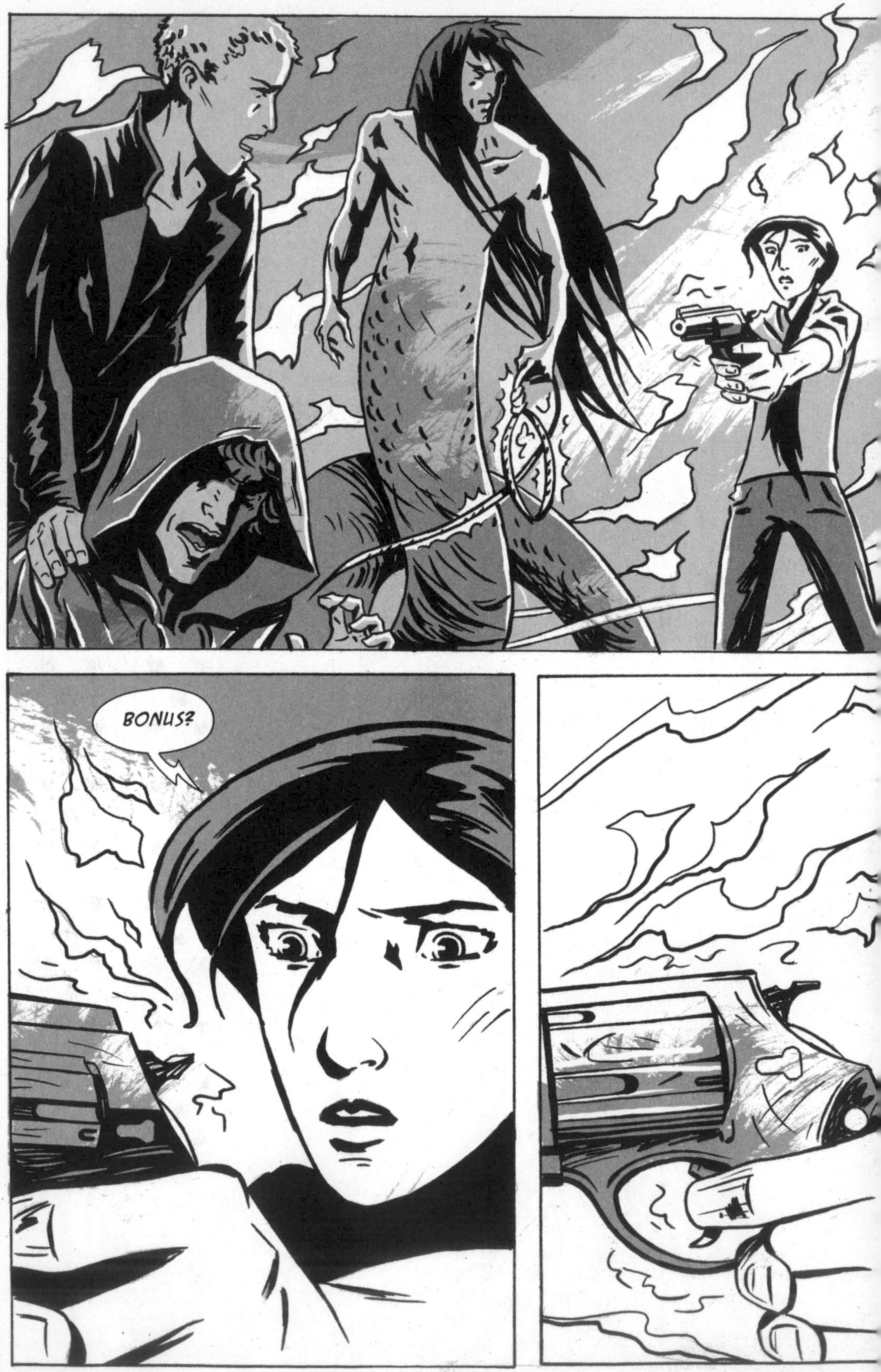
BONUS?

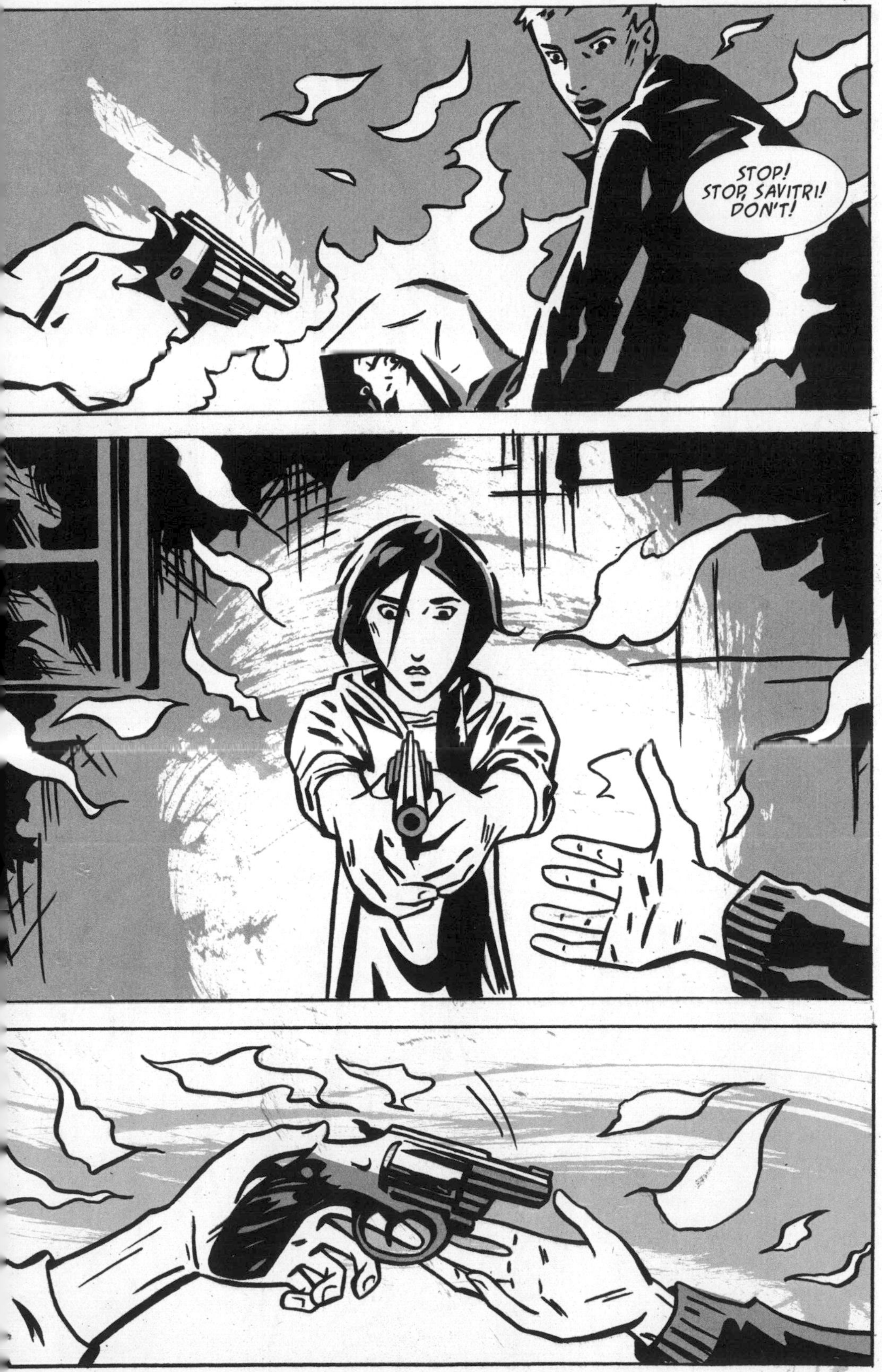
STOP!
STOP, SAVITRI!
DON'T!

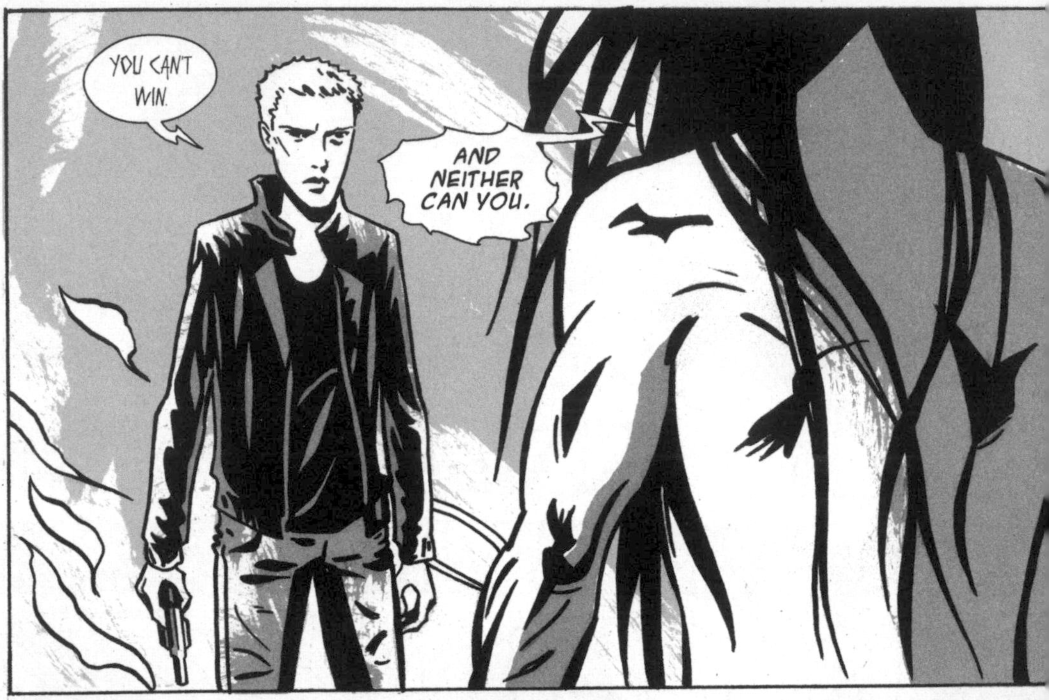
YOU CAN'T WIN.
AND NEITHER CAN YOU.

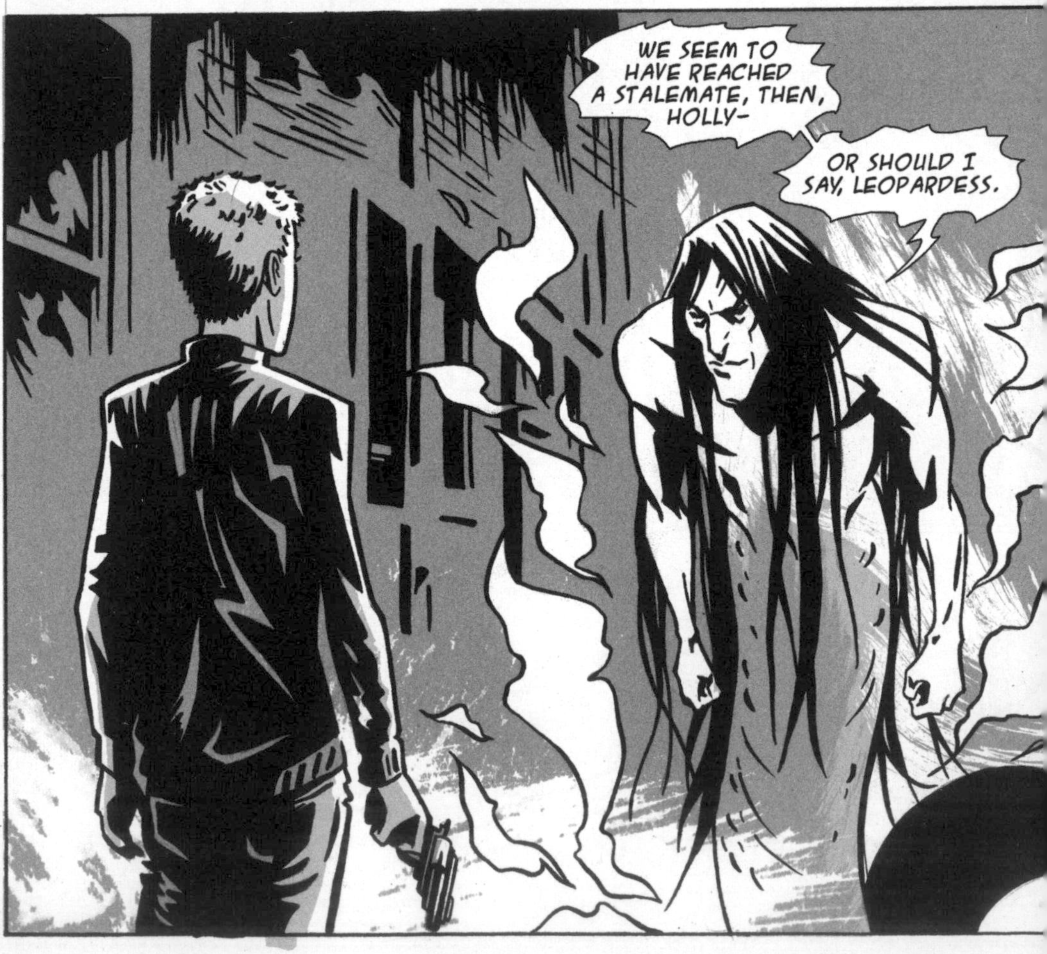
WE SEEM TO HAVE REACHED A STALEMATE, THEN, HOLLY-
OR SHOULD I SAY, LEOPARDESS.

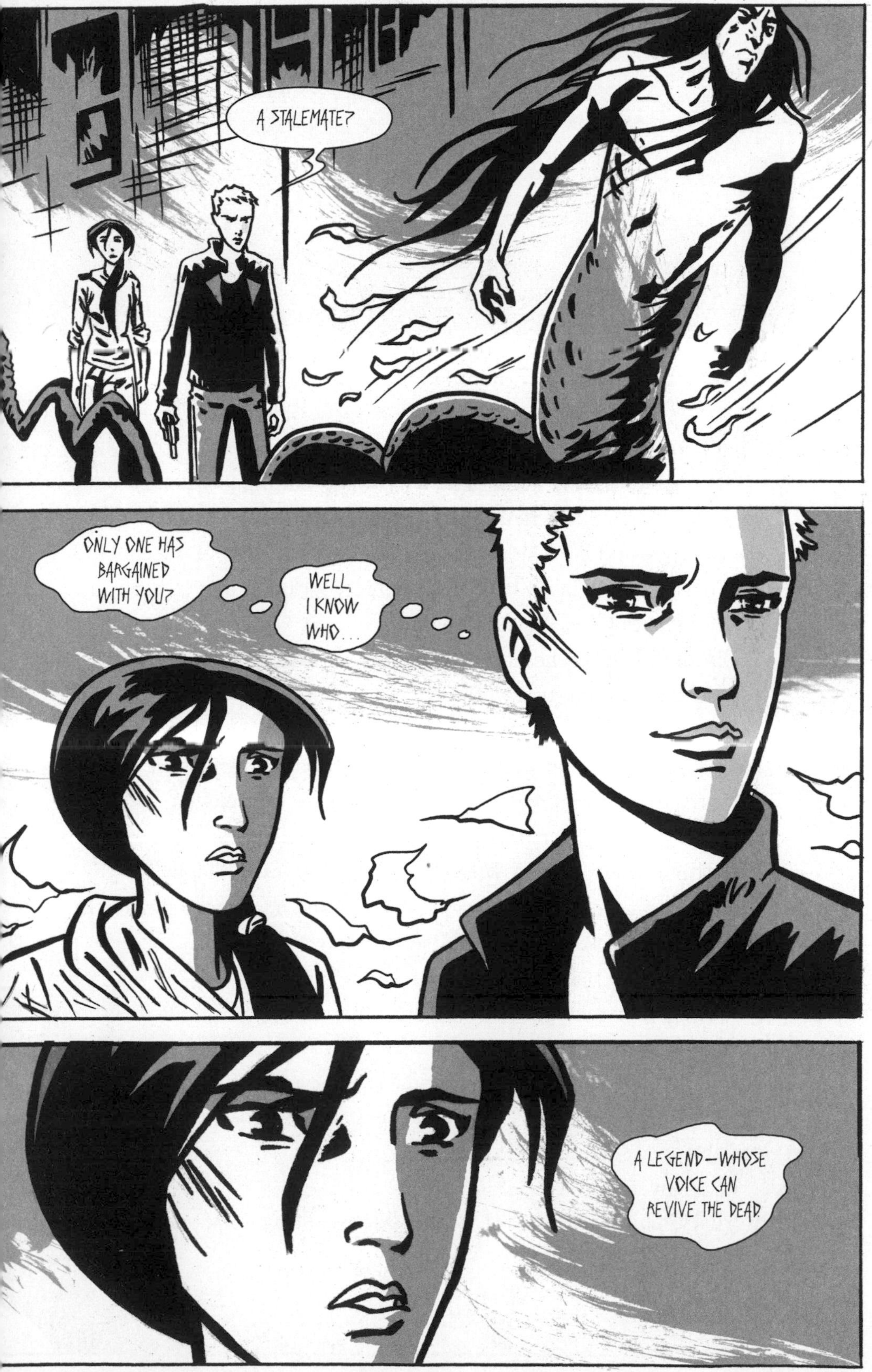
A STALEMATE?
ONLY ONE HAS BARGAINED WITH YOU?
WELL, I KNOW WHO . . .
A LEGEND—WHOSE VOICE CAN REVIVE THE DEAD.

Savitri

47 days, 2 hours, and 17 minutes after

"Stop! Stop, Savitri. Don't!"

Holly's words ring in my ears. Wiry waits, leaning forward. His blue eyes are dead, but he is flesh and sinew and muscle and bone and blood. He is alive—and if I take that from him . . . what parts of myself will I kill? With this gun in my hand, I'm barely recognizable as it is, barely the girl that Corey loved. My finger uncurls.

When Holly reaches for the gun, I let her take it.

Holly says, "You can't win."

In my peripheral vision, I see Wiry spring to his feet. He rushes into me, knocking my arm back and me down. Something clatters behind me. I try to grab him, but I miss. I turn and see him pick up whatever fell . . . my phone. He races to the mouth of the alley.

"Wait!" I scream after Wiry. As if that would work. "Holly!"

Holly stares past me, her eyes vacant. I stand up and grab her by the shoulders and shake her hard. She registers me.

"Are you all right? What are you doing?" I say.

"I'm . . . I'm saving you."

I look her over—disoriented and lost. But Wiry will disappear, like a termite into wood, completely unfindable. Worse yet, Wiry could . . . no, Wiry *will* come after us. And he has my phone. So we are completely findable.

I sprint.

Oh God, oh God, oh God. We've made everything worse.

236

Wiry is running in a straight line down the street, his sneakers pounding out a trackable rhythm. He's got a lead, but I push my muscles into high gear. My vision tunnels down to him while the world blurs. He glances back, sees me, and accelerates, but he's not fast enough; I follow him—far enough back to keep out of danger, close enough not to lose him. I need to track him, not catch him.

We've been at it for seven long blocks when I see the first car, blue light flashing in the window. Wiry stops dead and looks around, his eyes wide. *Dear Wiry, do you know how it feels to have your muscles lock up? To cling to an unbearable moment because you know that the next moment is only going to be worse?*

Well . . .

You do now.

He glares at me and my lips curve.

A police car races past and hops onto the sidewalk in front of Wiry. Wiry tries to slide through the narrow opening between the fender and the building. But Meade opens the car door and wrestles him down. My muscles pop like fireworks. Sirens cut through the air, chorusing each other. So many that it sounds like a symphony.

"Are you sure?" Meade asks me.

"I'm sure," I say, still gasping for breath.

"She's crazy," he says. "She tried to kill me. She pulled a gun on me."

One thing I've learned about the law. It is not about justice; it's about what can be proved.

"What gun?"

I put my hands on my knees and breathe while I watch Meade read him his rights.

I watch Meade handcuff him.

I watch Wiry shoved around as Meade frisks him.

I watch Wiry's blue, wide eyes dart back and forth—wild and terrified.

And watching has never felt better.

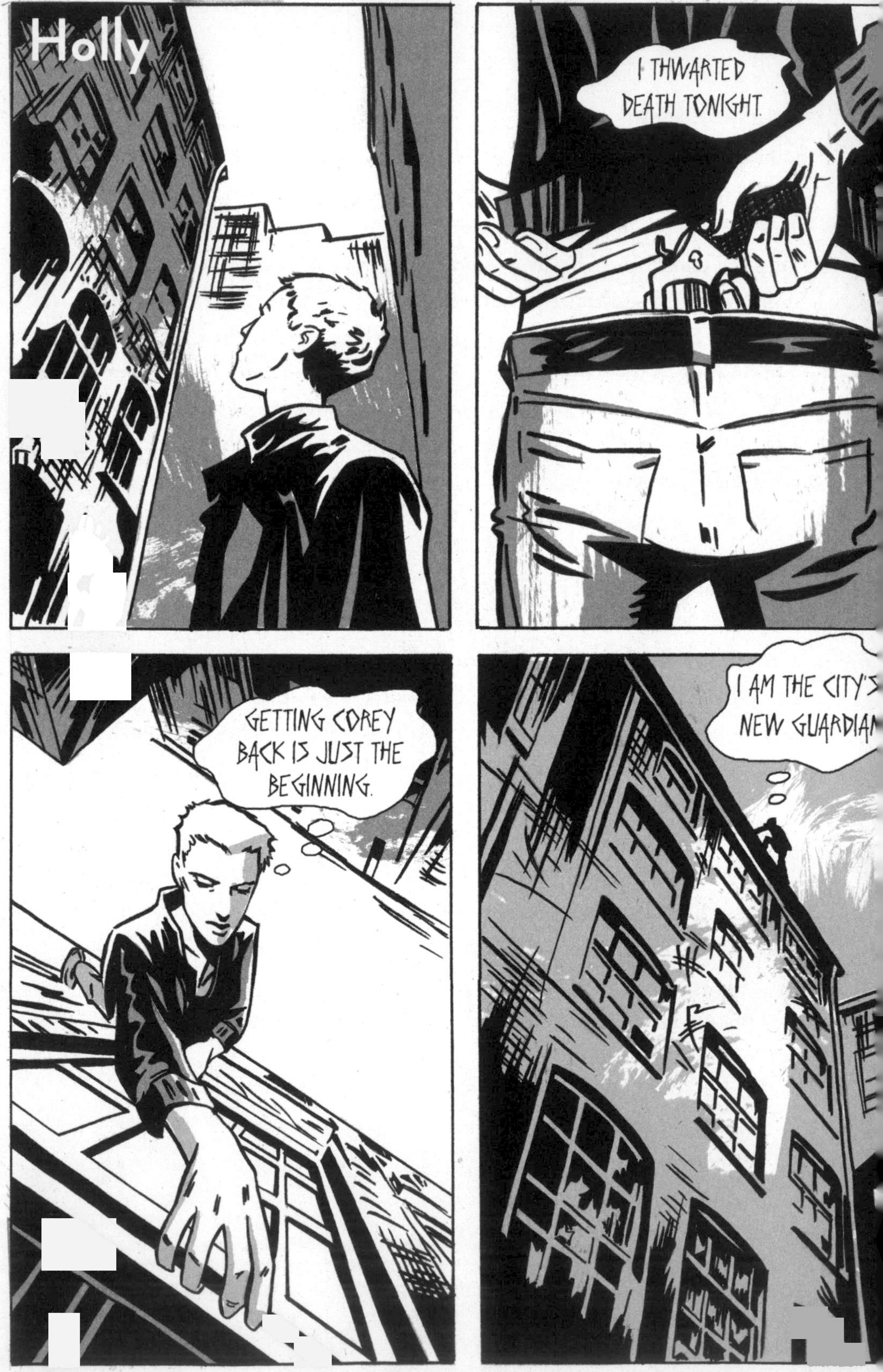
Holly
I THWARTED DEATH TONIGHT.
GETTING COREY BACK IS JUST THE BEGINNING.
I AM THE CITY'S NEW GUARDIAN

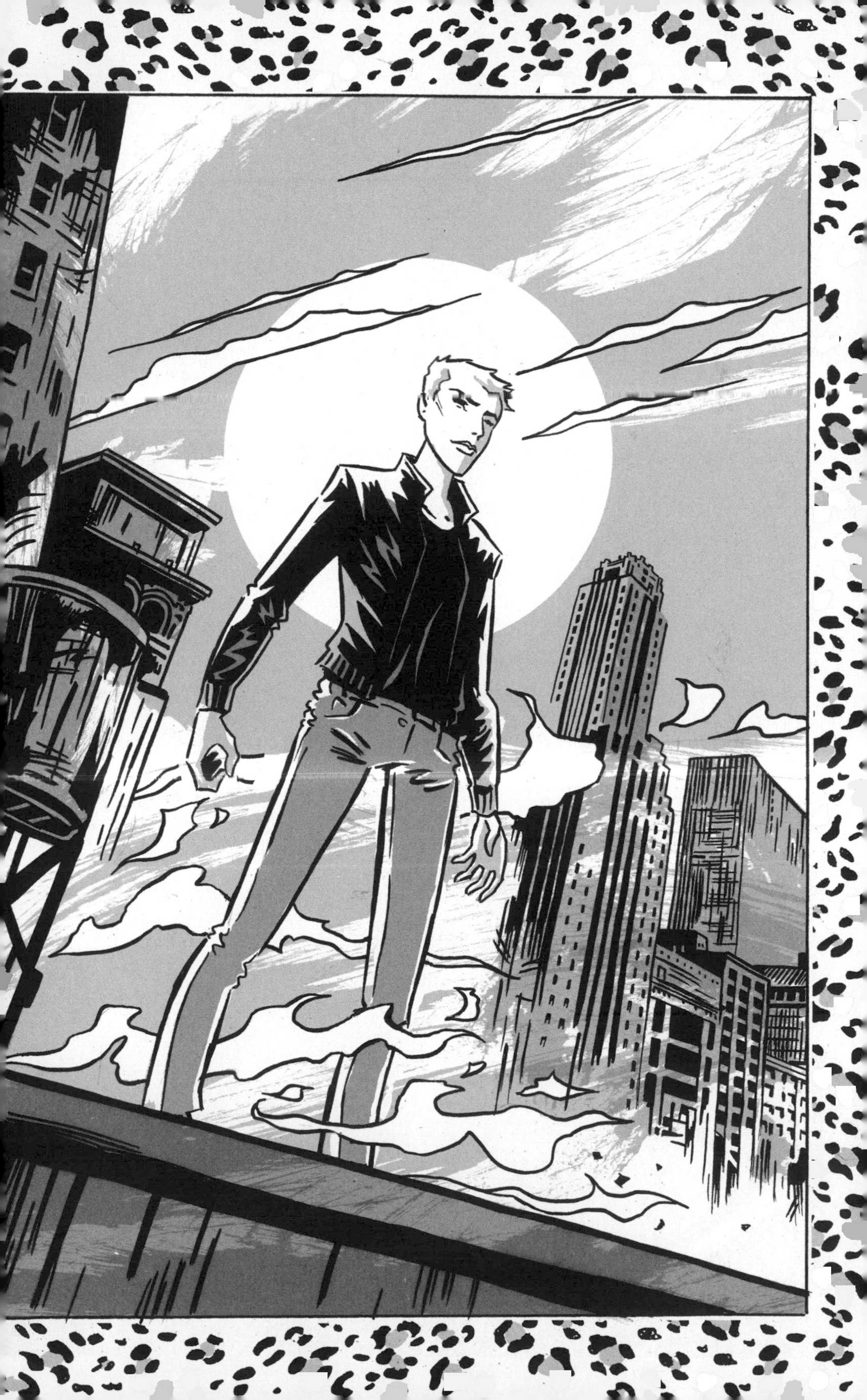

I AM THE LEOPARDESS.
LET THE NEW ERA BEGIN.

PART III

Savitri

One hour after I watched Wiry get cuffed and locked into a police car, time resumes at long last—I'm no longer listening to the minutes tick past. The media, reporters in dark suits, and the bloggers in jeans were buzzing through the street when Meade drove me to the station. Technically, I've been demoted from witness to suspect because of Wiry's accusation.

When we're in the claustrophobic interrogation room again, I give the cops the story Holly and I concocted when we first started doing stakeouts—we were there to run. I sip water without spilling it. While I talk, I wonder about Holly. Where is she? What did she do with the gun? It is strangely familiar to be here, to be answering questions and worrying over Holly.

"So, you just happened to see him?" Meade says, his voice automated. When I nod, he says, "Okay."

I don't think he cares about Wiry's accusation.

Magruder, on the other hand, has her hands on her hips. "Seems a little coincidental, don't you think?"

"The world is a random place," I say.

Meade straightens up. "Why would he run from two girls?"

Magruder and I share a look. "He ran when I took his picture and sent it to you. I didn't want him to get away, so I followed him."

"And the gun?"

I fold my hands and hope I can pull off another lie.

"Where would I get a gun?" I ask.

"Holly's in the other room, you know," Magruder says.

My shoulders come down. Holly is okay.

"She has another story. She told us about her father's gun. We found it in her car."

I smile. In this life where nothing is stable, where someone can shoot you for no reason at all, where you can corner a killer and not pull the trigger, there is one thing I'm sure of: Holly would never betray me. I don't care how freaked out she is. Never.

Tonight, I have looked into the eyes of a killer. I have nearly become one myself. I don't scare quite as easily as before. "There was a gun in the car?"

Belatedly, I remember that my fingerprints must be all over it. And maybe Wiry's blood from when I hit him. My throat goes dry and I sip the water.

"So that's your statement?"

Too late now.

I force myself to nod. He says they'll be right back. I sit in the room by myself and am quiet, thinking through the night. I deliberately push away that I was ready to kill someone, even if only for a moment.

Wiry has been captured. He will live behind bars with the scum of the earth for the rest of his life. May it be long and thorny.

When Meade returns, he says I'm free to go. He reaches out his hand and shakes mine.

"CPD thanks you," he says, formality resumed with the case closed.

I rush out to find Holly, but my mom is waiting for me. The police must have called her. She wraps me in her arms, and I inhale the scent of Issey Miyake perfume and hospital antiseptic that her sweater carries. When I rest against her, my cheek pressed against the scratchy wool, I realize I'm going to have to lie to her. Some more. I wet my lips, and my shoulders stiffen enough that she lets go of me. She strokes my head and asks me if I'm all right.

"Is Holly here?" I ask.

She sighs loudly. "Of course she is here. She's in another interview room."

When she tells me we should go home, I say I want to wait for Holly. My mom says nothing; she turns on her heel and walks to the elevator. I'm forced to follow her.

We stuff ourselves into a tiny spot in the crowded elevator, inhaling the scent of starched uniforms. My mom radiates anger. The enforced silence of the elevator gives me two floors to think of what to say, but little is coming to mind. I pull my jacket sleeves over my hands, and my fingers worry at the cuffs. When we get to the parking lot, she is stiff and says she'll bring the car around. Clearly, she can't even stand to be near me right now. And if I think too hard about it, I might realize she is right.

The elevator dings again and the doors open. Holly and her parents walk out. As soon as I see her—her cocky swagger—I remember what we've done for Corey.

"Holly!" I say. I throw my arms around her. "So?"

"So, we make quite a team, don't we?"

I laugh.

Mr. Paxton grabs her arm and starts to pull her away. His jaw is set hard and implacable and Trisha keeps glancing at me. Holly jerks her arm from him.

"Let's go."

"Oh, Ron, really," Holly says. I start when she uses his first name.

"You can call me 'Father' or 'Dad.'"

She shrugs. "Father's just mad because we found Wiry when he couldn't."

"No, Holly," Mr. Paxton says, his tone leaking rage. "Let's be clear on this, Holly. I'm mad because you took my .38 and because you put me in a position where I either had to lie for you or let you get arrested, Holly."

A stone of shame—heavy and hard—clogs my throat. I swallow it down, even if it isn't mine.

Her head leans toward me and she says quietly, "He told them that he was the one who left his gun in the car."

I nod. I underestimated Holly; she is even more strategic than I am.

She didn't want to take my car. She knew her father would protect her and, by extension, protect me too.

"Thank you, sir," I say.

He turns on me. "Oh, don't think I'm just mad at her, young lady. Are you trained in weapons? Don't you know how easy it is to lose control of a gun, to be killed with your own weapon? What if he had his knife? Or *his* gun?"

"But that's why we needed a gun of our own," Holly says. "We couldn't go after him unarm—"

"You shouldn't have gone after him at all! What were you thinking?"

The parking lot echoes.

I glance at Holly, who has a smirk on her face.

Before she mouths off, I start. "We were thinking that the person who killed your son shouldn't get to walk free. We were thinking that I'm the only one who saw him and so I'm the only one who could recognize him. But you're right. Tonight was . . ." *terrifying*, I don't say. "Too much. We were lucky and we're—"

"No, we're not. I'm not apologizing for finding him." Holly crosses her arms over her chest and says, "Did it escape your notice that neither of us got hurt? Tonight we proved that we can handle ourselves."

Trisha snorts and shakes her head.

Sergeant Paxton says, "You want to know what you proved? You proved that you needed your daddy to bail you out." He turns to me. "Honestly, Savitri, I thought you were smarter than this. I hate to say this after everything you've done, but I don't want you at our house anymore."

"What?" I say. Inadvertently, my hand finds Holly's arm.

"For a little while," Trisha jumps in. "Just for a little while."

She and Sergeant Paxton exchange a look.

"Holly couldn't have chased this down without your help."

"Thanks for the confidence in me, Ron," Holly says. "We did this together."

She puts out her fist, but I hesitate; I don't want to get her in more trouble. But when I look at her, the gap that has been growing between us is gone.

Let them be mad. Holly can handle it; Holly can handle more than I thought, apparently.

Our knuckles meet, and we hiss: *ssshhaw*.

* * *

But it was easier to stand up to Mr. Paxton, with Holly at my side, than to deal with my mom once we are back at the house. On the ride home, I watched her face slowly slide through emotions—puckered-forehead and tight-lipped anger to mouth-breathing worry to breaths-deep-past-the-sternum calm. By the time we get home, she is ready to listen. Which may be worse than anger. How do I explain myself?

She heats up a dinner for me, though I tell her I can't eat. My stomach feels heavy, stones of shame. I sip from a glass of water, letting the clear, clean liquid wash through me.

She sits across the table from me and says to tell her everything that happened—how I ended up running after a killer. I want to revert to the story I told Meade, but she and the Paxtons will exchange notes. So I tell her we'd been looking for him, hoping to get a picture the police could use. But that Holly brought a gun, and when he saw it, he ran. I leave out the rest.

She gets up and paces the length of the kitchen, mouth-breathing.

"Thank God you're okay. But you can't do that. Ever again. You can't be around guns." She touches the top of my head.

I think of the gun's muzzle shaking while I rested my finger on the trigger. I think of Corey's blood, alive under my hands, and the long river of black in Holly's CT scans. And I promise my mom. No, no more of that. Not ever again. The thousands of ways things could have gone wrong make my mouth go dry. *Thank God for Holly. Thank God she stopped me.*

"Two phone calls from the police about my daughter is my limit."

247

I apologize and she tries to smile.

When I tell her that the Paxtons are so mad they don't want me over there anymore, she just nods and says it makes sense. "Holly brings out the worst in you."

"Mom, that's a horrible thing to say."

"Horrible or not, I don't hear you denying it."

"She wasn't the only one looking for him."

"Holly put you in danger tonight, Savitri. She brought a gun without telling you about it because she knew if she had, you wouldn't have gone with her. I won't have her manipulating you. If it weren't for her—"

"If it weren't for her, Corey's killer would be out on the street—" I edit myself. Better for her not to know that Wiry was looking for me; she's been mouth-breathing enough. "This is exactly what Corey . . . what I needed. And you're judging Holly like a criminal, instead of a hero."

"Oh, God, Savitri. Don't say that. She's not a hero. Don't idolize her; she's just a girl who thinks she's invulnerable. And that . . . that makes her dangerous."

I pick up the glass and sip from it. When I put it down, it slides on the condensed pool of water. I can't really refute my mom's point.

In fact, she wanted to go after a killer with or without a gun. In fact, if I want to know how I ended up facing a killer with a gun in my hand—I have an answer. But if I tell my mom that, I won't be helping my point, so I'm silent. Which I guess she interprets as anger, because she says, "Let's just say I'm glad that Princeton is far away."

I snort. "I know you've never liked Holly; I know you think she holds me back, but back from what? From a well-planned life that may never happen?" I swallow. Wiry was looking for me. I might as well rip the Band-Aid off and endure all her disappointment at once. "Mom, I'm not going to Princeton. I'm staying right here."

"You can't change your whole life for Holly. You can't ruin your future."

248

Holly's the one who kept me from ruining my future. "It's my future. Not yours."

"Oh, stop that. That's ridiculous. I've never pushed you. You've been the one who—"

"I'm not saying you pushed me; I'm saying you are pushing me now. Like it or not, Holly is my priority."

"But *her* priority isn't *you*."

"You're wrong, Mom. You're wrong." I say it hard and forcefully because I suspect she is right. "I gave it time, like you asked. But now I'm sure."

My mom stands up. She slowly, deliberately smooths the creases in her pants.

"Savitri, forget for a moment how hard you've worked, forget for a moment how hard I've worked, and listen to me. If you don't go to Princeton, you will regret it."

"What ever happened to 'you can go anywhere, you can do anything'?"

"It's a poor choice. With a long impact. Sometimes the job of someone who loves you is to tell you when you are making the wrong choice. Be mad at me. Be furious if you want. That's not important. I need you happy and I need you safe."

She swallows loudly and her eyes look unusually large. Though I've never seen her cry—not even when my dad disappeared slowly, not even when she saw me after the shooting, not even now—I know that this expression is a harbinger of tears.

"Princeton will open doors. Holly is a path to nowhere."

She leaves and I sit in the kitchen with my fingers sliding up and down my water glass, carving straight lines through the condensation.

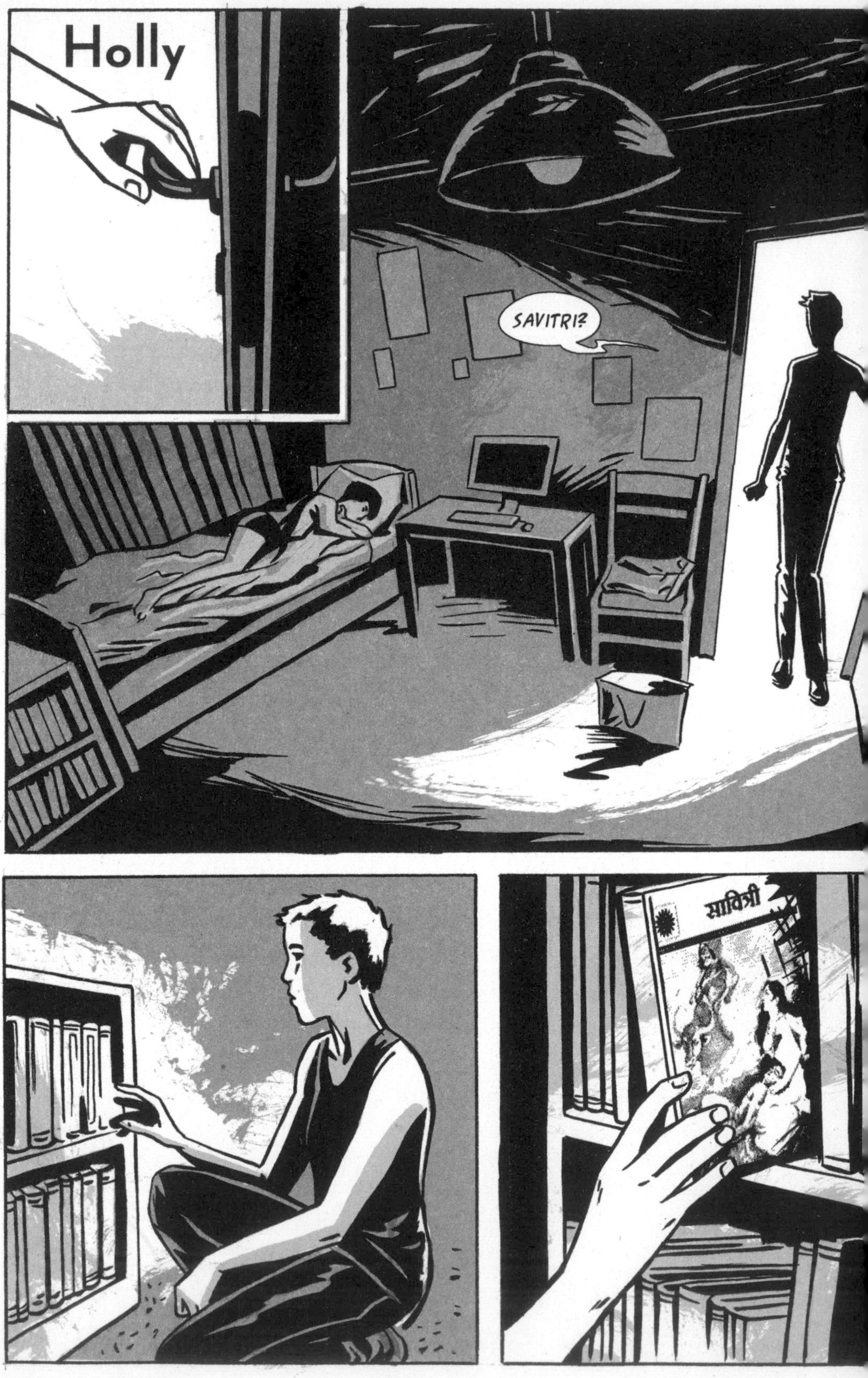
Holly
SAVITRI?
सावित्री

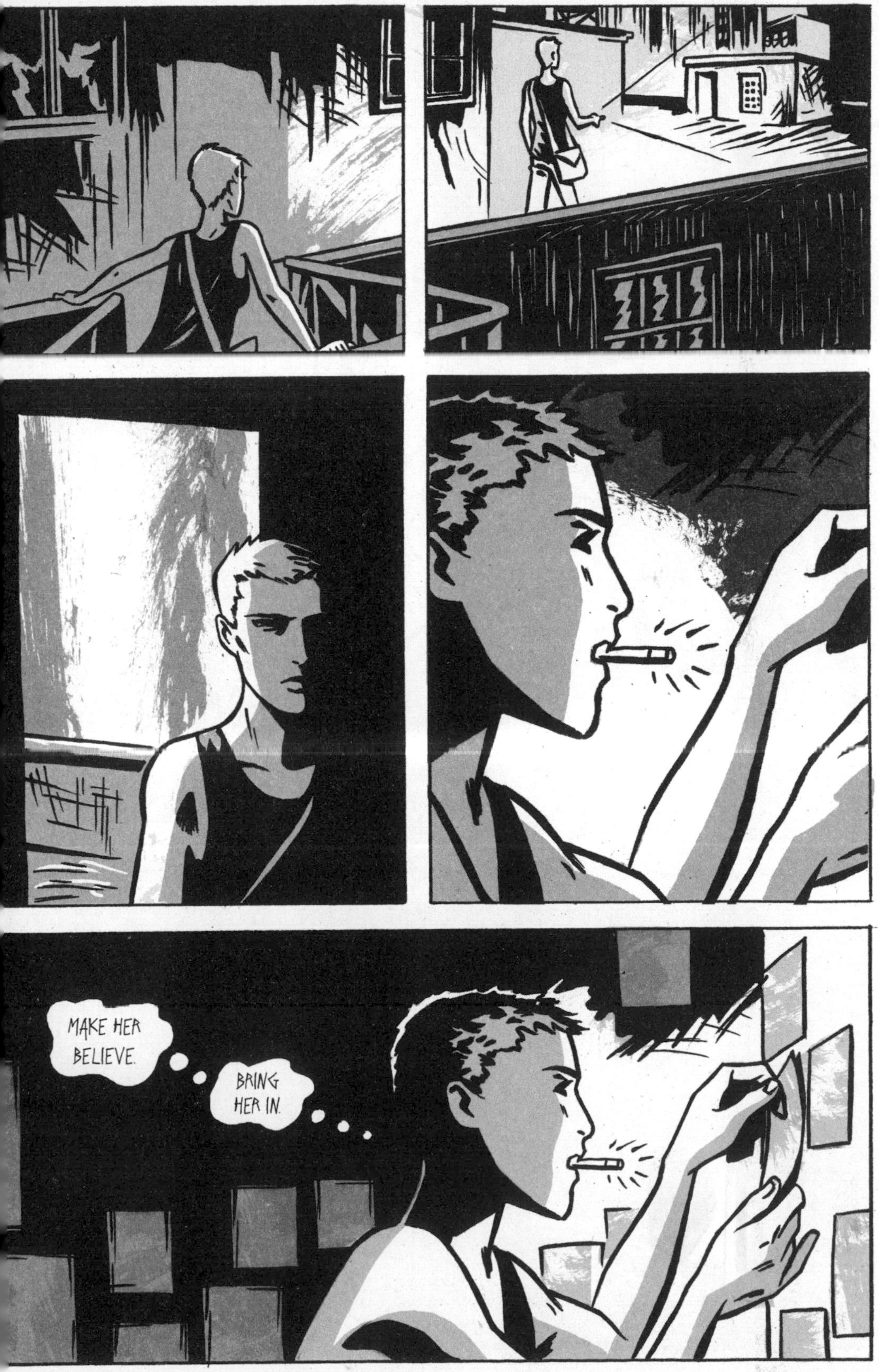
MAKE HER BELIEVE.
BRING HER IN.

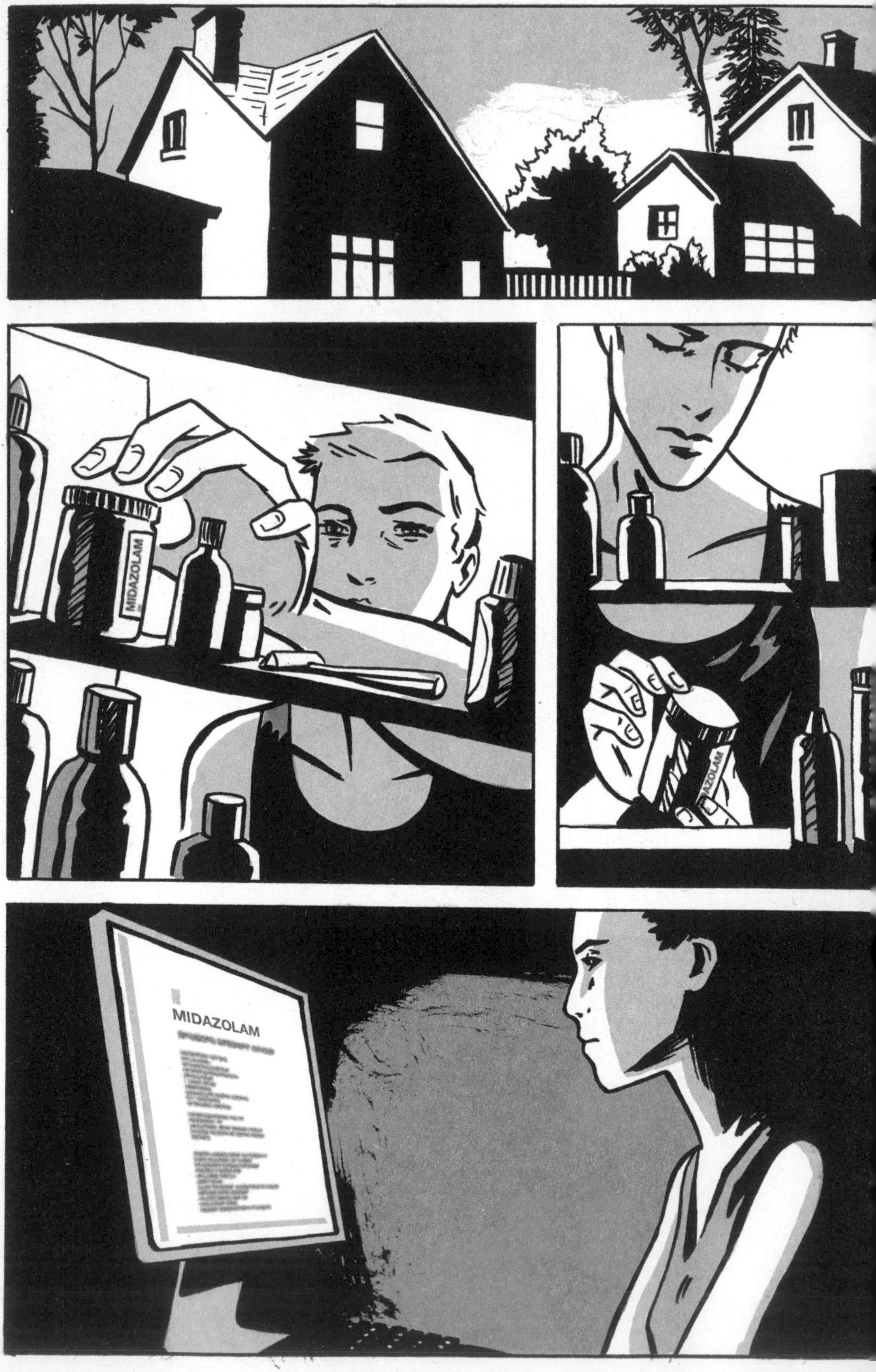
MIDAZOLAM
MIDAZOLAM
MIDAZOLAM

Savitri

The next day, I sleep late, stay in pj's, and eat microwave popcorn and mints for breakfast. While my mom runs errands, I curl up on the couch and try to replace images from last night with images from bad movies. But I keep rubbing my forefinger as if I could erase the pressure of the cold metal trigger.

Holly. I reach for the phone that's resting on the side table to call, but I stop. She'll only tell me everything is okay now, so what difference does it make that for a moment last night I considered murdering someone, that I had to be walked back from the precipice. Holly's never been one for guilt, but after last night, I doubt she even knows what it means.

Upstairs, I look for my *Savitri* comic and can't find the one in Hindi, so I resort to the English iteration, and when I finish reading it, I lie on my bed and rest it against my chest. When did revenge become my goal? The moment I picked up the gun? The moment I pointed it at him? Or when he said, "Bonus"? My throat aches—too tight for too long—but tears won't come.

When my mom comes home, she hands me a new cell phone since my old one is locked in police evidence. I don't quite manage a nod. She sits on the bed beside me. "What is it, beta? Is there something else?"

"I don't know," I say. I sigh and squeeze my eyes shut tight. If I tell her how I cornered and pistol-whipped Wiry, she'll truly hate Holly and, worse, she might even hate me a little. "Last night is just hitting me now, I guess."

I pull the covers over myself and shiver anyway while my stomach twists.

That night, when I try to sleep, I turn up my earbuds and blast the music, but that doesn't shut out the images—the knot of bodies, the blood crawling stitch by stitch up my sleeve. I thought that finding Wiry would stop this, but I'm still caught in questions: Nothing I could have done? Really? Nothing? No way I could have helped Corey?

There must have been something. *Please, God, let there have been something I did wrong, some way to lay Corey's death at my door.* I stand up and try to pop the walnuts in my spine. What am I thinking? Why do I want to claim responsibility? Why do I want to have stones of shame in my stomach?

When Wiry froze last night, he was hanging on to a bad moment because it was better than what was coming. And that's what I've been doing all this time. I've been hiding out here, reveling in the luxury of guilt.

Because there is something worse than the fact that I did nothing—there's the fact that there was nothing I could do.

Maybe there is nothing between a bullet and us. Maybe "safe" is an invention to help us sleep each night.

Which is bad enough.

But even worse, last night I could have been the one firing that bullet.

The damage we do to ourselves, by our own hands, sometimes that's even worse than what's been done to us.

And then the nausea gets so bad that I do end up racing to the bathroom.

After, I brush my teeth, but I can't erase the taste of acid and mint in my throat.

* * *

254

On Monday, I'm back at school. Somehow the attention around me no longer grates. People aren't trying to borrow my mourning; they are just trying to figure out what happened, and this time, I can frame the truth. I take my lunch inside the cavernous and loud cafeteria. The smell of limp vegetables and whatever passes for meat rises. I sit down with Kessa and the other kids from Speech. She slides over and smiles. They lean in, and I know they want to ask but that my withdrawal has set up a barrier only I can bring down.

So I tell them the lie I told CPD. At least I'm telling them something.

"Was that Holly with you?" Kessa asks. "She looks so different. How is she?"

"She's relieved that he has been caught," I say. It's a different sort of lie. The truth is, I don't know. No contact yesterday or, so far, today. Which is strange. I tilt my head from one side to the other, trying to stretch out the clenching shoulder muscles, walnuts growing.

After school, I start home. The cloud cover is thick and dark and the air promises that rain will return. When I pass the playground, Josh is hanging from the red metal dome. All four of us used to train here. I could never quite get up the courage to do a trick that Holly and Corey both thought I could manage—a flip from the top.

When Josh sees me, he swings down and walks over.

"I never come down here anymore," Josh says. "I stopped after Corey and I fought—reminded me of too much."

I nod. I put my hands in my hair, gathering it into a ponytail so it is up and out of my face.

"You know," Josh says, "I never meant for what I said to Ellie to get out to everyone. I was just confiding in a friend who turned out not to be a friend."

"Why didn't you tell us that in the first place?"

"You didn't give me a chance. And then I was pissed that you wouldn't give me a chance. It was stupid; I should have gotten over it before . . ."

Josh will always have unfinished business with the dead. He can't get absolution from Corey, but Corey and I were together in slicing him from our lives.

"We were wrong," I say, "about you."

"Is that an apology?"

"Would you like a card with it? Flowers?" I say.

He smiles and his shoulders slide down. "Thank you."

The sky starts to trickle and I put up my umbrella. He ducks under it just before the rain becomes a deluge. On the walk back to my house, we talk over the tintinnabulation of the drops striking the nylon. He asks me how Holly is now and I tell him the truth. Josh has proved he can be trusted. So I tell him everything—how Holly went wooden and I was left with a gun pointed at a killer, how she tuned back in and stopped me and then seemed fine after the arrest.

"Maybe that's what she needed to . . . be able to move on."

"Maybe that's what *you* needed. After the funeral, you sort of . . . stalled out."

"I have not. If you use the Kübler-Ross model, I've been through denial and have just passed through anger now that the guy is finally in jail. Even according to the Bonanno model, which is more accurate, I'm on the right trajectory. Sort of."

Josh's face is working hard to stay blank. His mouth quivers.

"What?"

He breaks out laughing. I cross my arms over my chest and sigh. If I were in New Jersey, I wouldn't get this crap.

"You can't study your way out of pain. No matter how many charts and graphs you do."

"Holly, on the other hand," I say, not wanting to have *that* discussion.

"Oh," he says loudly, so animatedly that I could paint a lightbulb over his head. "You've been waiting for Holly? And you won't keep going until she catches up?"

It is this simple: there's a difference between leaving Holly and leaving Holly behind.

"I want to make sure Holly is okay. Corey would want me to look out for her."

"You can't plan your life around what he'd want. You need to run at your own rate—get over the obstacles in your own way."

"You know," I say, "freerunning makes you so wise, so Zen."

He hesitates and then says, "I'll text you my comeback as soon as I think of it."

When he goes, I fish out my keys. As I unlock the door to my house, I decide what to do: I'll pick up our McDonald's meal, and this time, this time, I'm not going to say anything to contradict her; I'm just going to listen.

A horn beeps and I jump. Holly's in the car. I laugh—back to where we could read each other's minds and moods effortlessly. The headlights cut a path through the darkness, and raindrops race through the beams.

"I was just coming over," I say.

"I couldn't wait to show you. Your day is sooooo long. How do you stand it? Get in." Holly bounces in her seat.

My smile fades in the face of her incongruous exuberance.

Holly always drives fast, but tonight she seems particularly aggressive, pulling unnecessary moves, sliding around cars, checking her mirrors too many times. I'm just happy when the rain stops—almost as fast as it started—and she turns off her windshield wipers. She cranks up the music and sings along. We approach a red light, and our speed does not change.

"Holly," I say.

The white line of the intersection rushes at us.

"Holly!"

I brace my arm against the dashboard and push my feet against the floor.

"You want to help me get Corey, don't you?"

"Red light, Holly. Stop!"

257

Just as the nose of our car enters the intersection, the light flips to green, but she has to slam on the brakes as a car, turning left, slips by us.

"Sav, chill." She rolls her eyes. "The lights are timed."

"For thirty-five miles per hour," I say as we approach another. "And if you can't go that, maybe I should drive."

She looks at me aslant and accelerates. On the highway, I have to fight to keep my fear out of my muscles, out of my voice. By the time she takes the Halsted exit, I'm shaking.

Why are we back here?

"Wait," I say, "what did you say about Corey?"

"What?"

"Back there, at the red light."

"I can't explain it here. Once I show you, you'll understand. I promise."

I try to tell myself my stomach is roiling because of her driving, that there's no other reason to be afraid.

Did she just ask if I wanted to help get Corey?

When we get into the UIC area, we pass streets fast—Throop, Polk, Taylor—until we're almost at the podium building the three of us ran to that night.

She finds parking at the end of the block and we scale a building. She takes off—full sprint. I follow her, jump after jump. I try to slow down, set up jumps, concentrate. But I end up chasing her, my muscles driven by panic, my breath fast, sweat coating my skin. *Maybe her energy is at 110 percent because she is celebrating,* I tell myself, but even I don't believe me.

When I leap and land on the podium building, she is gone. Blood pumps through my ears and I scream her name.

"What?" she says. She is standing at the back of the roof with her hand on the door of the gardening shed. "Jesus, don't scare me like that. Where did you think I was?"

Four stories down, on the asphalt.

She looks behind her and to both sides, as if someone is watching us, before opening the door. Then she smiles at me. From inside, she gets out a small flashlight, grabs my arm, and pulls me inside the shed.

"This," she says, her voice loud and confident. She flicks on the flashlight. "This is it."

The circle of light shines on all she has done to the walls.

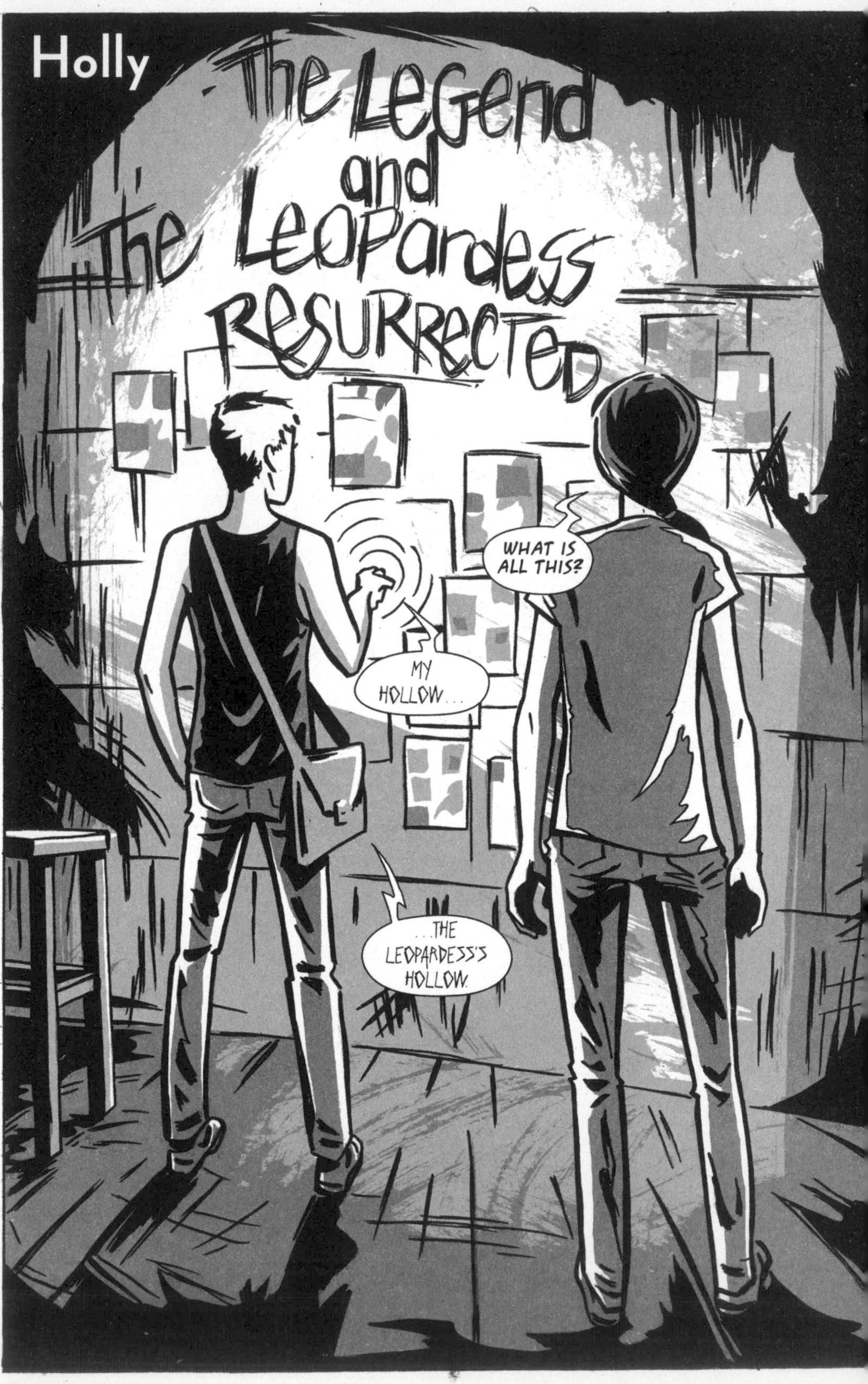
Holly
The Legend and The Leopardess Resurrected
WHAT IS ALL THIS?
MY HOLLOW...
...THE LEOPARDESS'S HOLLOW.

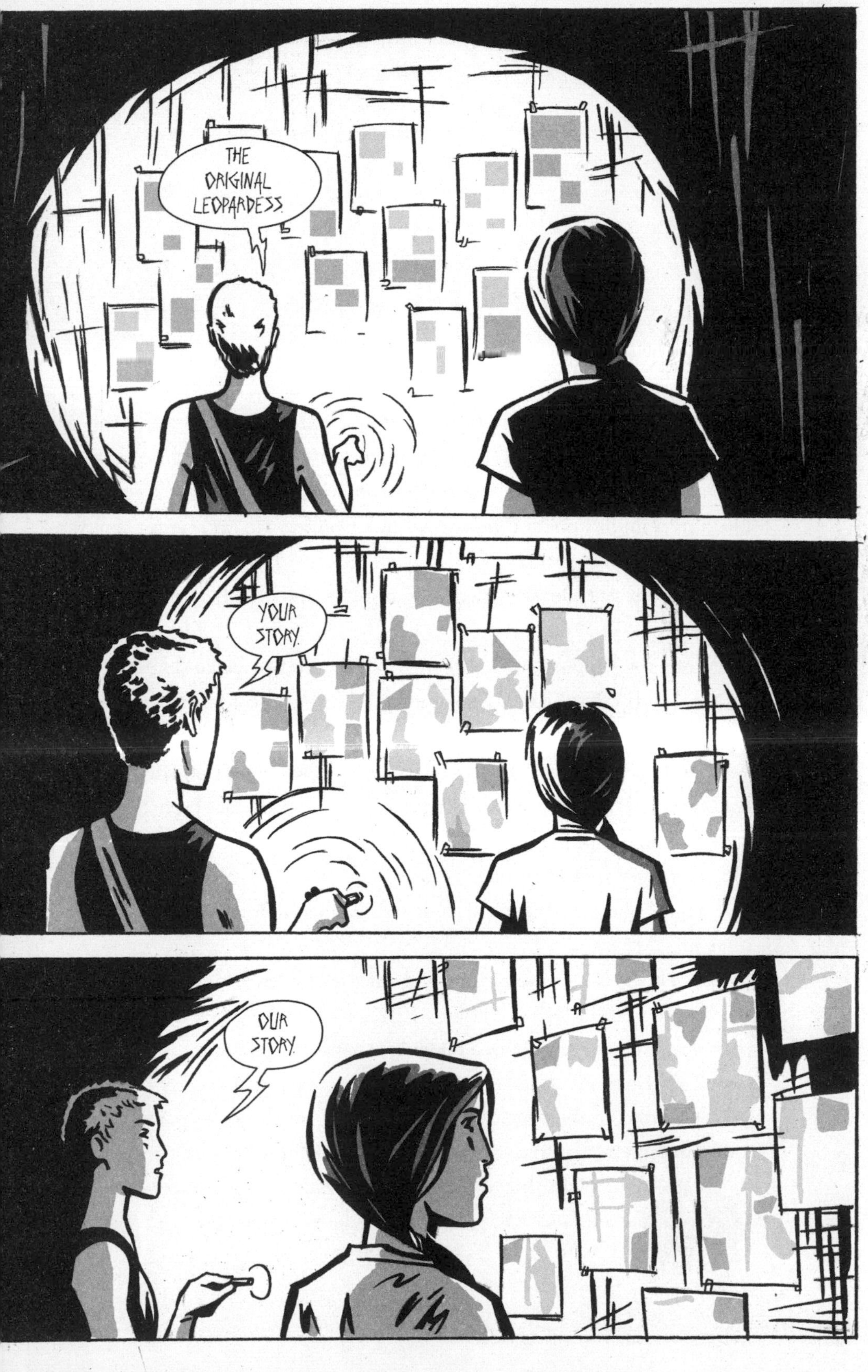
THE ORIGINAL LEOPARDESS.
YOUR STORY.
OUR STORY.

Savitri

That room, plastered with my own Savitri comic torn from its binding and pasted up in a sick imitation of her hospital room—and worse yet—those chicken scratchings. I try to make sense of the farrago of ink: a figure that I think is a man, but the bottom half of his body looks vaguely like a river and I wonder if he's drowning. *Do I want to help her get Corey? Is this what she meant?*

And I'm outside the shed, my muscles moving before my brain catches up.

Holly was slipping away, slipping underneath the ice, and I didn't see it. No, I did see it; I just didn't understand it, chose to believe I could rescue her, but loyalty and good intentions aren't a lifeline.

She is slower out of the shed. And when she comes out, she has our traditional McDonald's meal. She hands me a bag of cold French fries.

"So?" she says.

I can't get anything out.

"Here," she says. "Drink this. It will calm you down. I have a lot to tell you."

When she hands me a cup filled with root beer, I spill some of it as the lid pops off. Holly's eyebrows wrinkle in concern for a moment, but then she laughs. I drink three big gulps that burn my throat. I promised myself I'd listen. *Please let there be some logical explanation.*

She walks to the edge of the roof and sits on the short parapet, one foot dangling in free space. I sit next to her with my back to the drop.

"Can you explain this to me? Let's just walk through it together."

Holly leans in and whispers to me. She tells me my voice wrapped

262

around her and rescued her from the shadow lands, that Wiry is really a minion of Death, that there is a place where Corey still lives, where he is trapped in a prison of snakes and bones. A place where we, as the Leopardess and the Legend, can rescue him and then bring him back. Yes, she says emphatically, pain transforms us all. Yes, she has become the Leopardess and I am the Savitri of legend, reborn. We have been gifted pain so we can get into the shadow lands and back out.

Dear Coma, what piece of her did you keep? Give it back.

"Say something, Savitri."

I search for words.

"Are you shaking?" she asks me.

I look down over my body and realize that my neck, my head, my limbs—everything is wobbling. I slide my butt off the edge of the parapet to the gravel roof and rest my back against the stones.

"Holly," I finally manage. "Oh, my God, Holly."

"Are you mad that I didn't tell you before? I should have, I know. I shouldn't have let you go on thinking Corey was gone forever—I know it was crushing you, and here I was above it—but I was . . . I was afraid you wouldn't believe me. And if you don't believe in this, if you don't believe in me and Corey"—her eyes narrow for a split second—"but you do. You're all in."

I down more of the soda to buy some time, swallowing hard over the lump that has grown in my throat. She gets up and jumps higher and higher, tucking her legs beneath her like a kid on a trampoline.

"We can save him. I brought Death to a Stalemate on my own. But to win Corey back, I need you."

For a fraction of a second, I wish she were right, and for an even tinier fraction, I want to follow her into her fantasy world—a place where we could stand together against Death, stand together with Corey once more.

I get up, intending to grab her by her shoulders, but I must have gotten up too fast because the world is unsteady. I momentarily stick my arms out for balance.

"Holly."

"What?" When I don't answer, she repeats, "What? Don't you believe me?"

"I don't know what to think," I say, balancing on a narrow verbal ledge.

"We can save him and come back out. We aren't Ordinary People, Savitri. We've both been blessed. You, you were born with it, but me, I had to earn it."

"It?"

"The ability to walk between both worlds. It's probably why we've been friends all along. Deep down, we knew; we could tell."

She grabs my wrist and I will myself not to flinch, order myself not to pull away.

"Let's say for a second that I did save you and that I could save Corey. What will he do for a body? You were still alive. Corey's been—"

"Don't say it, Savitri. Not from you. You have to believe. If you don't believe, I can't use you."

"Use me?"

She drags her fingernails against her scalp, leaving four red marks on her skin. "Shut up!"

She screams it down into her chest and I'm not even sure she is talking to me. And in that moment, I'm suddenly aware of just how high up we are. Four long stories. And I have to get her—get us—down each and every foot. The wind gusts and whistles through the shed. Exactly how does she think we'll get to the shadow lands?

I pick up my cup and our bag. "Let's go, okay?" I sound like I'm whining and I reach for the tone I want—bored, in control. "Let's talk more at my house. I'm cold."

"We can't. This is Our Spot. This is the last place we three connected."

I look at her, look into her eyes. They are practically sparking with plans. They are all innocence and confidence.

"Please, listen to me. I'm scared for—"

"I knew you would be, but I can fix that." She glances at the soda and asks me if I'm done drinking it.

I shake the cup and the shallow liquid pings off the sides.

"What?" I ask her. "How?"

Her gaze rests on the cup. "It's fast-acting," she says. "You'll be in and out. I researched carefully, but the dosing was a little hard to calculate because usually doctors use a needle for such a large dosage."

"What? You what?"

"I know you. You need proof. You won't believe me until you've seen it for yourself. But it's okay, Savitri. I came out of a coma too."

Cold spreads from the base of my neck across my back and around my chest, strangling me. Oh, my God.

"You said you'd do anything for those moments back. I can give them to you." She laughs, and the sound fills my head like she has an amp in my brain. "Once you're there, use your Voice. Bargain with Kortha—whatever you have to do. Just bring Corey back to us. I'll be there too, as backup. Together, we are unstoppable."

"Why would you do this to me? We were best friends," I say stupidly, and realize I just used the past tense. If we aren't best friends anymore, then what are we to each other?

If your attacker is coming at you from the front . . .

God, no.

I recognize the panic that locks my muscles, shocks my brain. But this time I don't hesitate. This time I grab my cell phone out of my pocket and dial.

Holly swipes at the phone, but I pull it out of her reach and press *Call.*

Put as much distance as you can between you and your attacker.

I run. Even though I know I'm on a flat roof, it seems to tilt underneath my feet. I close my eyes, since I can't trust my vision, and trust my body. I run what I think is about twenty feet and glance. I'm right at the fire escape. I lazy-vault the ladder, spot the walkway, and slam into it, misjudging it. My knee buckles under the force of the uncontrolled landing, but I recover my balance with a quick step.

The entire fire escape slides in my vision. There's only one way down for me. Step by step.

Holly is faster than me flat out, but I've always been better at turns. The ladder shakes when Holly lands.

Make noise.

I start screaming for help as my legs work the steps.

If I can put enough distance between us, I can get my finger down my throat. I stop once, but Holly is right behind me, screaming.

I am only one flight from the ground when my legs start to tingle as if they are falling asleep. I'm out of steps; only the ladder to the ground is left. I jump on it and hang on while it extends, riding it down. Above me, the fire escape stops shaking, and I know, know that Holly has jumped the rest of the way. She is on the ground, waiting for me. When the ladder reaches its full extension, it jolts hard. I lose my grip and slam to the ground.

The impact ricochets through my back, and my lungs stop. I just knocked my breath out, right?

I want to believe that while I gasp for air, but my throat seals tight and my vision goes. Let that noise—the long whine of a siren in the distance—be more than wishful thinking. The phone slips out of my hand, and one last thought speeds through my head:

Three minutes without oxygen . . .

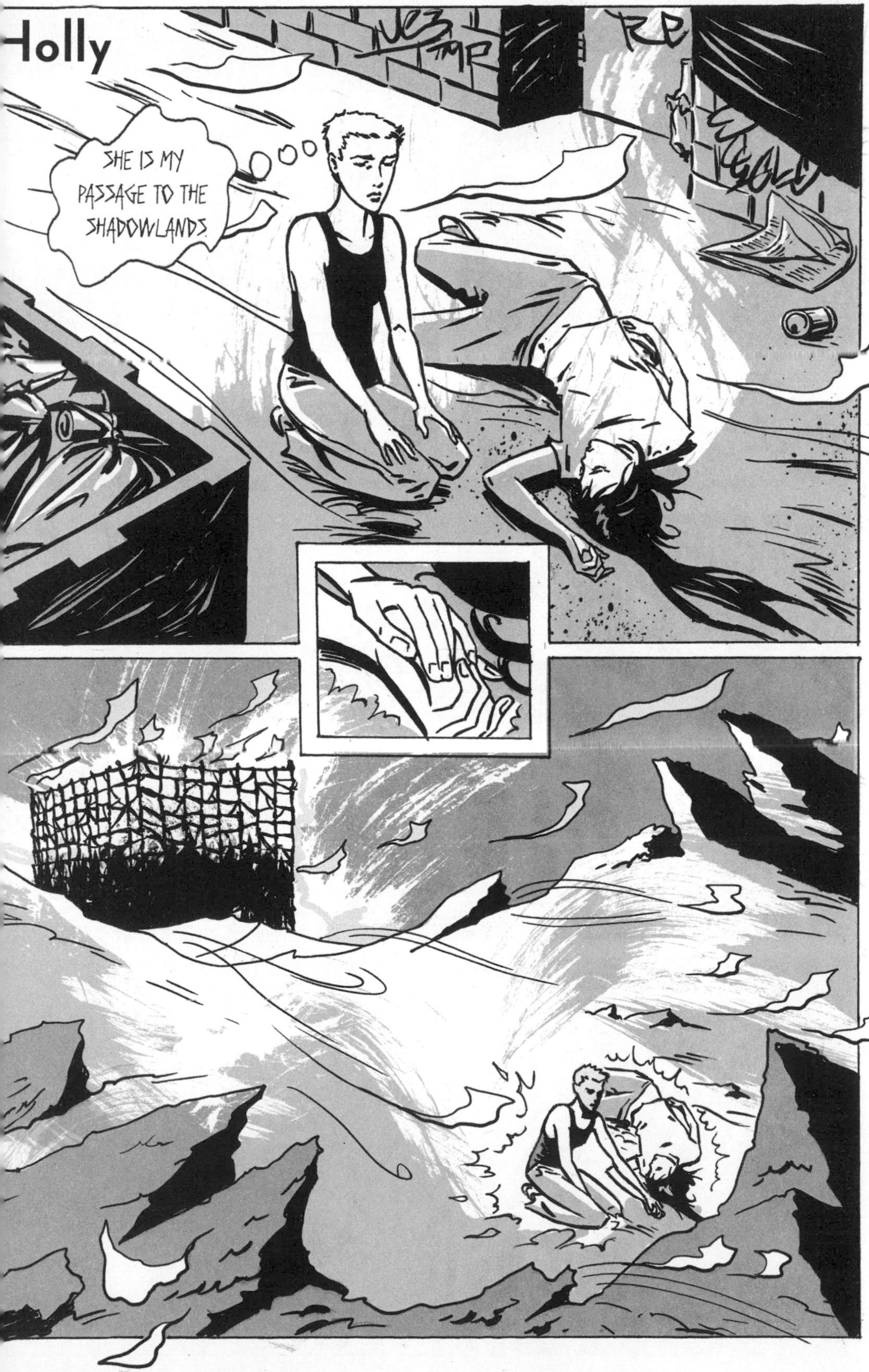
SHE IS MY PASSAGE TO THE SHADOWLANDS

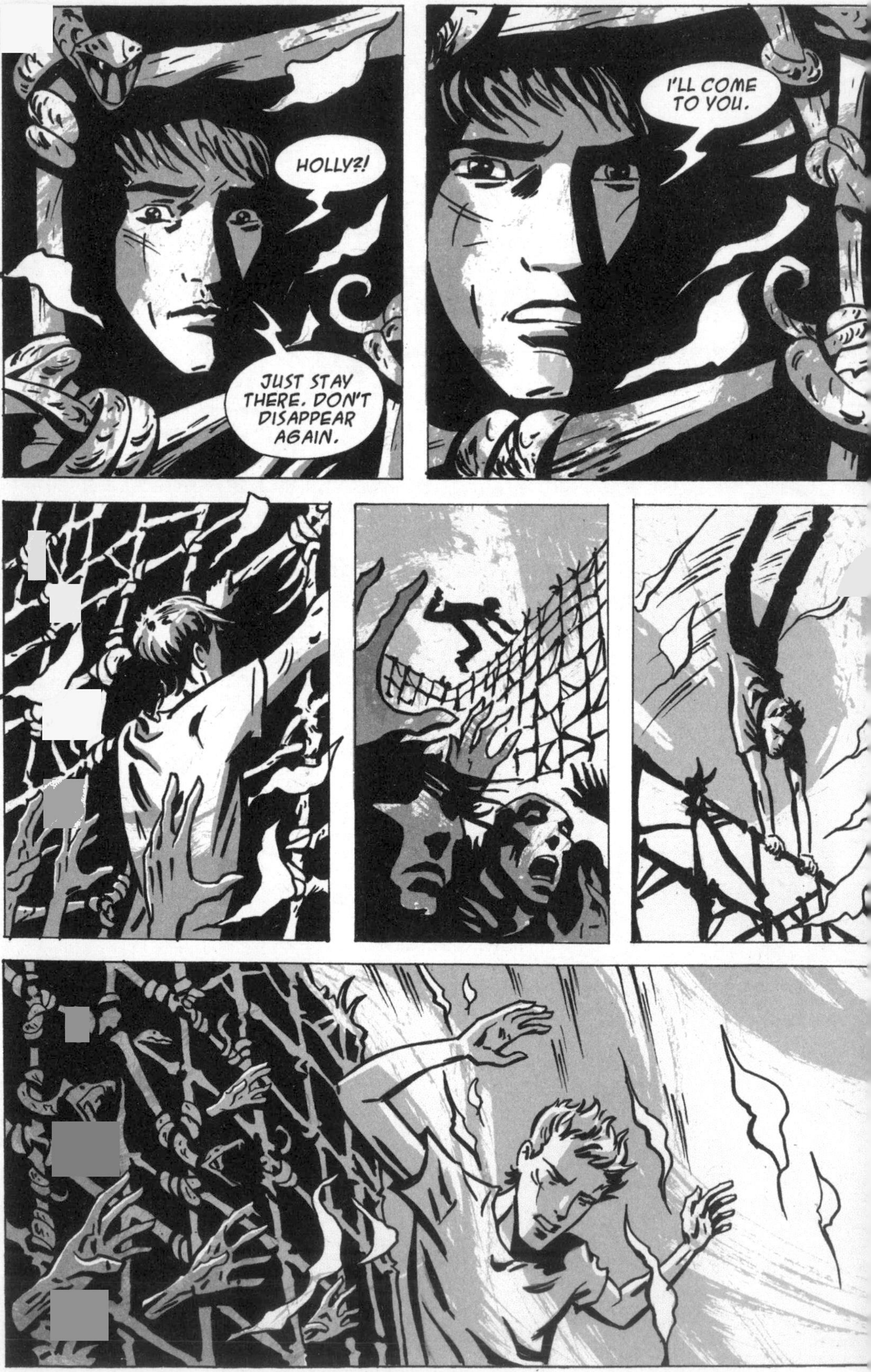
HOLLY?!
JUST STAY THERE. DON'T DISAPPEAR AGAIN.
I'LL COME TO YOU.

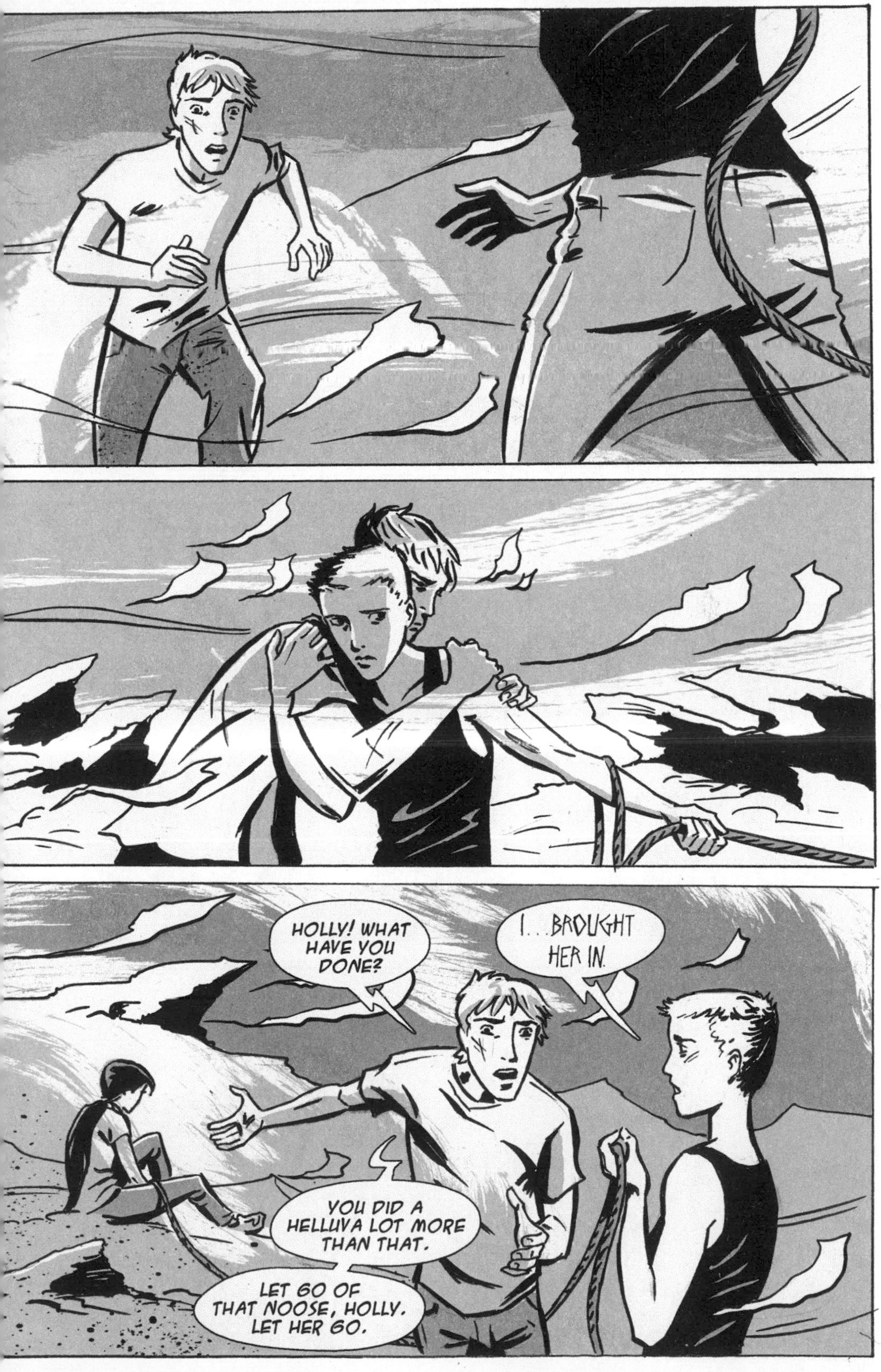
HOLLY! WHAT HAVE YOU DONE?
I...BROUGHT HER IN.
YOU DID A HELLUVA LOT MORE THAN THAT.
LET GO OF THAT NOOSE, HOLLY. LET HER GO.

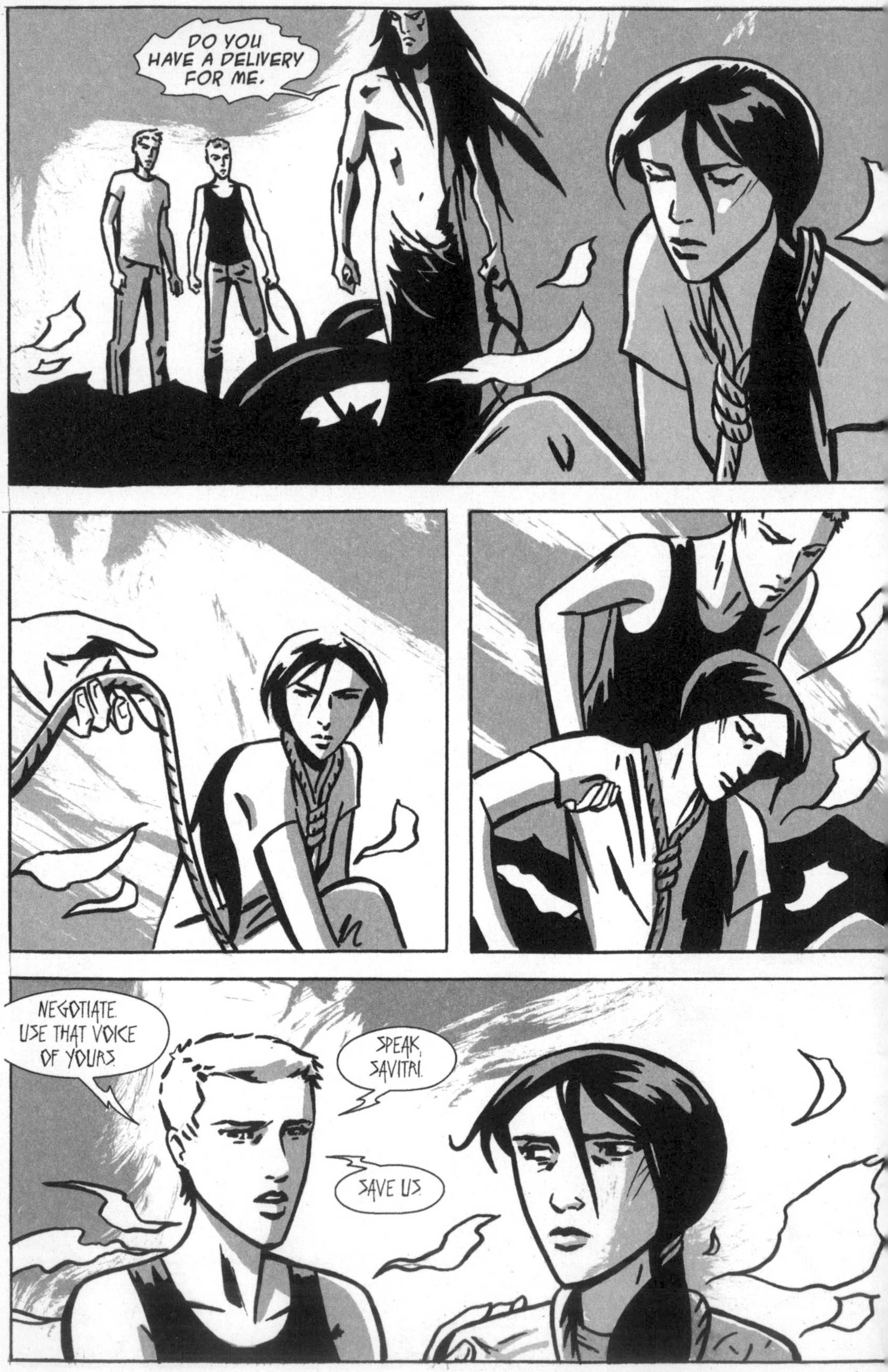
DO YOU HAVE A DELIVERY FOR ME.
NEGOTIATE. USE THAT VOICE OF YOURS.
SPEAK, SAVITRI.
SAVE US.

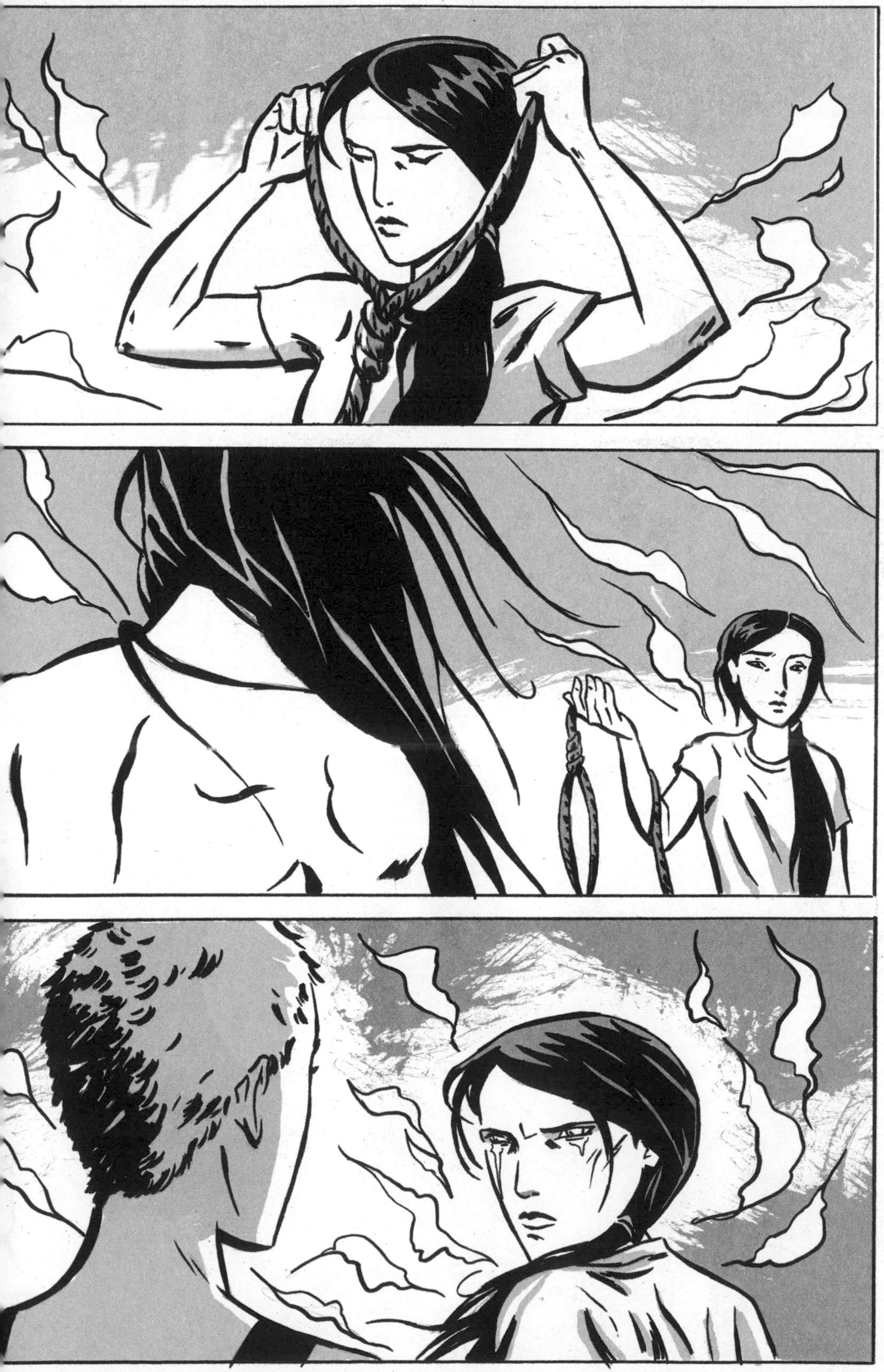

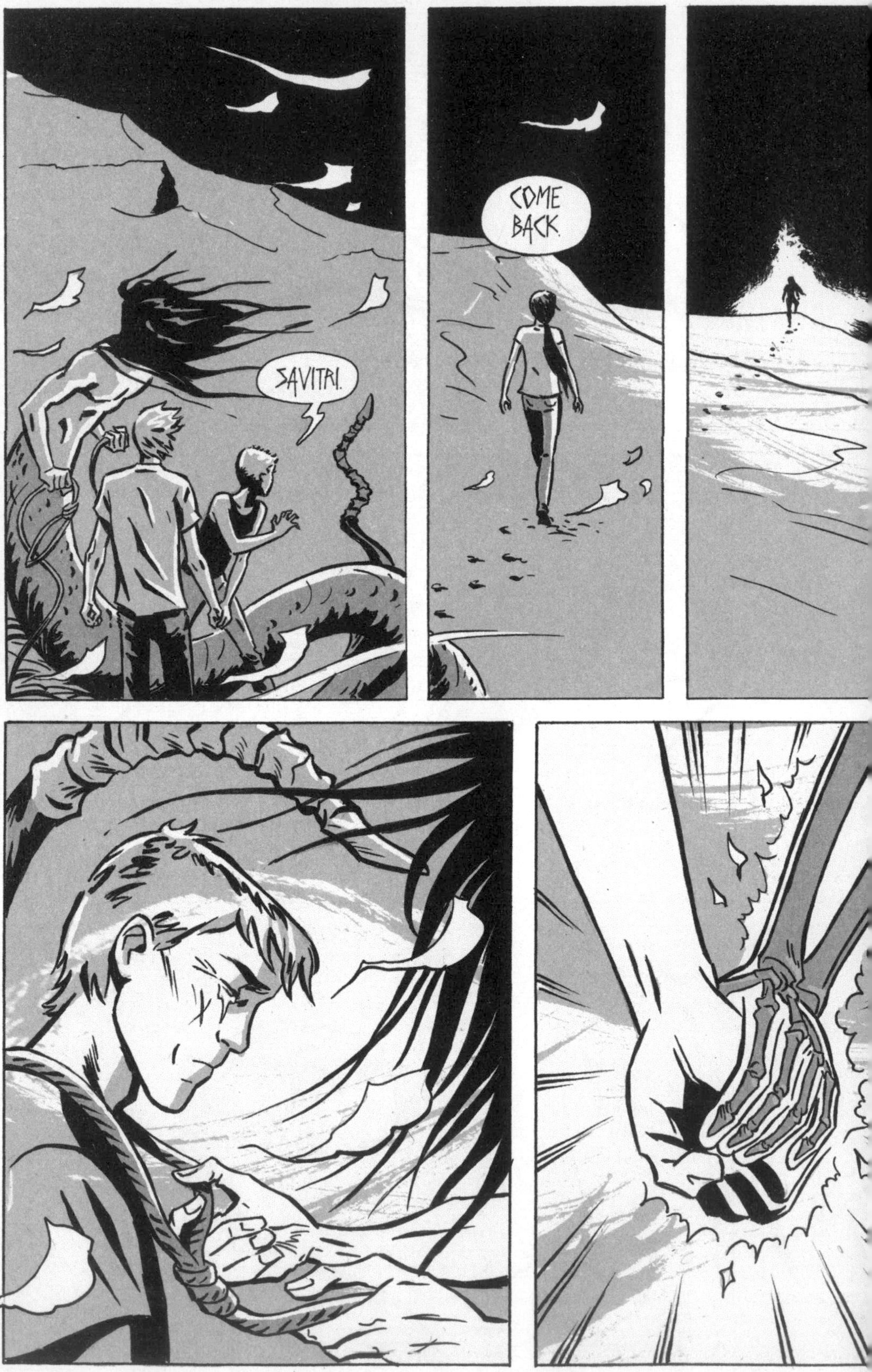
SAVITRI.
COME BACK.

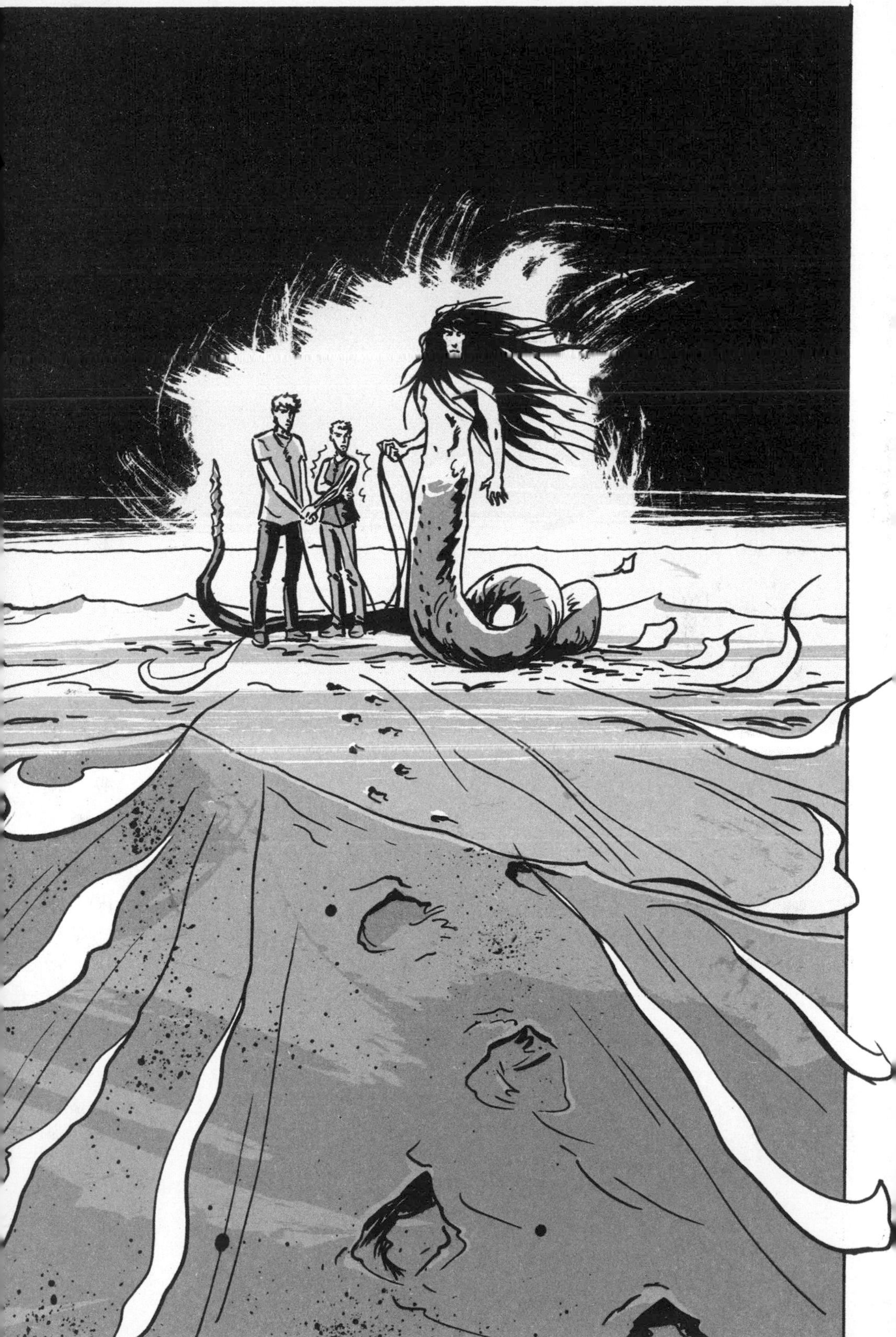

Savitri

pain.
slicing deep.
no air comes when I gasp.
Nothing but blackness and a wish:
for the knives to stop jabbing my lungs.
But the pain continues and my eyes flutter open.
Red swirls over my head in long, strange patterns.
I gasp. I get. I breathe.
Other voices slide.
"Got her."

* * *

I wake up to the familiar scent of Issey Miyake perfume mingled with an antiseptic smell. My mom sits beside me, her forehead creased and her face pale.

The hospital. Again. The white walls shine as sunlight reflects off the glossy paint. The sheets—thin but starched—irritate my arms. I'm the one in bed this time.

"Mom?" My voice is hoarser than usual.

"Oh, beta," she says, and touches my cheek with her fingers.

My head feels heavy and my limbs are stiff. I have to fight to keep my eyes open. When I ask, she tells me I've been asleep for almost sixteen hours, that I overdosed on something. How can I be so exhausted?

My voice still comes out rough. "Overdosed on what?"

"Midazolam. Sleeping pills, anesthesia. In the dose you took, it . . ."

My memory comes flooding back and I have to swallow. "Can it induce a coma?"

She raises her eyebrows. Then she says, "Or in your case, respiratory arrest."

"Where's Holly?"

When we were on the roof, she said, "I'll be there too." How would she get into the—what did she call it? The shadow lands?

My mom's mouth flattens down. Disappointment? Anger? She stands up and crosses her arms.

"Can we, for once, focus on you? Let her mother take care of her and let me take care of you." Her accent sounds stronger than usual.

She walks to the end of the bed, her back to me. But I can still see how her shoulders are curled in. She lifts a hand to her eyes.

She must have gotten a third phone call from the police.

"Mom," I say. "I'm all right."

I sit up slowly and all seems okay—no dizziness or weakness. She turns around, sits next to me, and hugs me. At first I relax into her embrace, but she hangs on so long that we move past bored and into uncomfortable. Finally I shrink my shoulders a little. Her arm muscles stiffen and she draws away, as if holding me is not her right. As always, the last thing my mother wants is for me to carry her, even for a moment.

"I am all right, aren't I?" I ask her, so that she can go into doctor mode and save us from the growing awkwardness.

"How do you feel?" She takes my wrist in her hand and checks my pulse.

I kick my feet and open and close my hands to test all my limbs. I turn my head from side to side, and the world moves slowly, since my eyes are still tired.

"Sore," I say, and try to pop my neck, but the muscles are too tight. I stretch them. How far did I fall after I lost my grip on the fire escape? Everything is so stiff—my back, shoulders, and right biceps ache.

She tells me that there should be no side effects from the drug since I hadn't been out very long, that the EMTs "restored respiratory function" quickly, using the bag alone. They ran a blood panel and found the drug; a bunch of tests found no long-term damage.

She sits down next to me and says that I'm currently on a suicide watch. Me?

Dear Doctors, I've never been the one to worry about.

"So, what happened?" she asks.

I gather the sheet into my hands and pull it up over my shoulders. I'm tempted to lie; it's so ingrained to protect Holly, but my lies haven't protected her. Or me. So I tell my mom about the root beer.

"She wasn't trying to kill me," I say. I sigh and explain.

My mother is shaking her head, her hands gripping each other—as furious as I've seen her. "Doctors give drugs in those quantities under observation for a reason," she says.

"She had her reasons, even if they were . . . well, I think she's sick, Mom. She thought I could bring Corey back from the dead by winning him back from Yama."

"She thought you were *that* Savitri?"

I nod.

My breathing becomes choppy, and for a fraction of a second I remember what it was like to get no air, how my back expanded trying to jump-start my breathing mechanically. Now I breathe deeply, sweetly, in and out of my lungs.

"Stop defending her. I don't care what her reasons were, Savitri, sane or not. What I care about is that you've been turning yourself inside out for her and she repays you with a drug overdose. I know that once upon a time, Holly was a good friend, but not anymore, not after this. Sometimes you have to let go."

I was supposed to be the good friend, the loyal one who hangs on. Can you hang on too tight? Can you hang on too long?

"At least tell me if she's all right."

"She's okay, but she's here. She was admitted here."

"Did she . . ." I swallow. "Did she hurt herself?"

"No," my mom says. "Holly is in the psychiatric ward."

Maybe it's disloyal or maybe it's the sign of ultimate loyalty, but I think, *Thank God.*

Holly

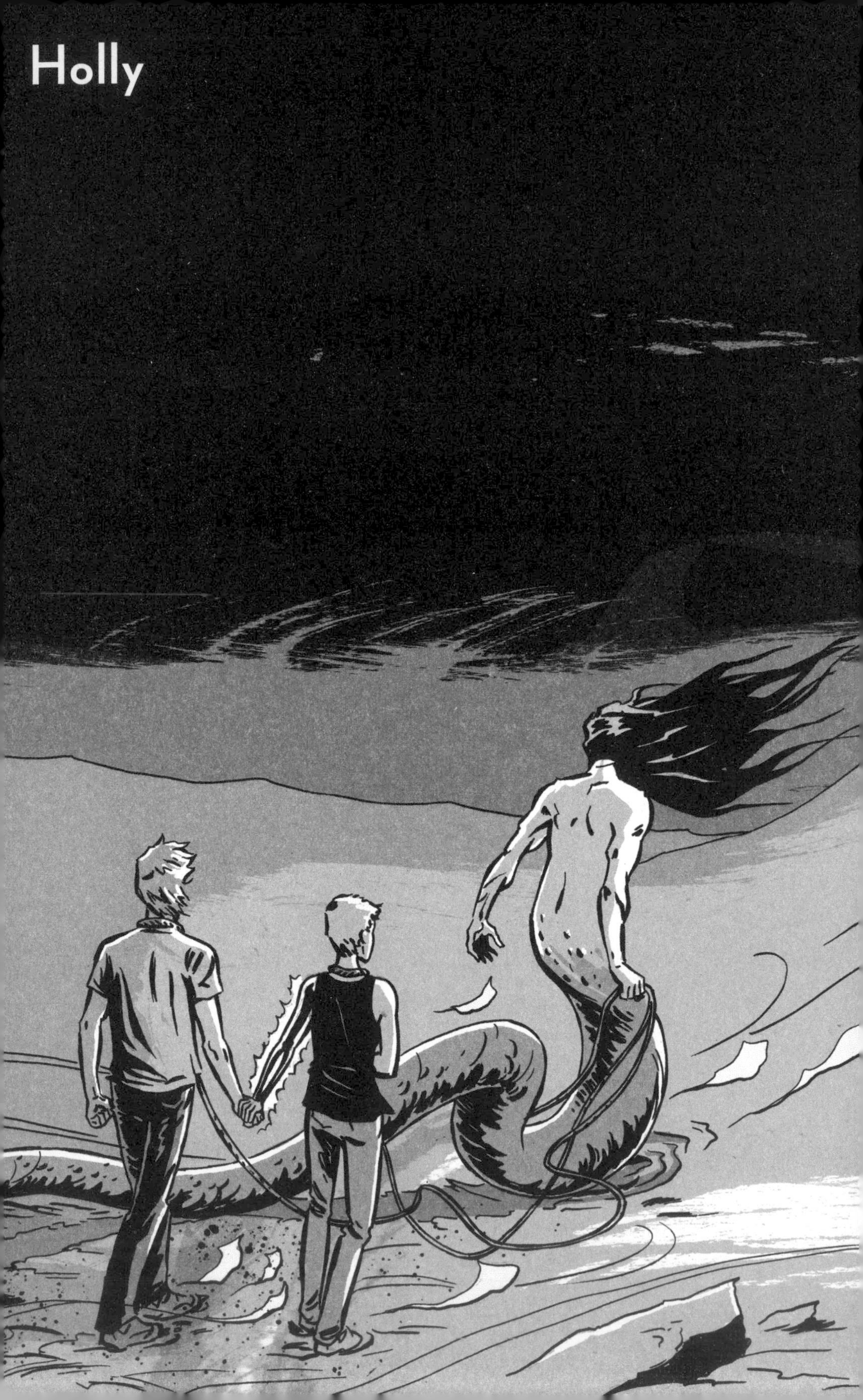

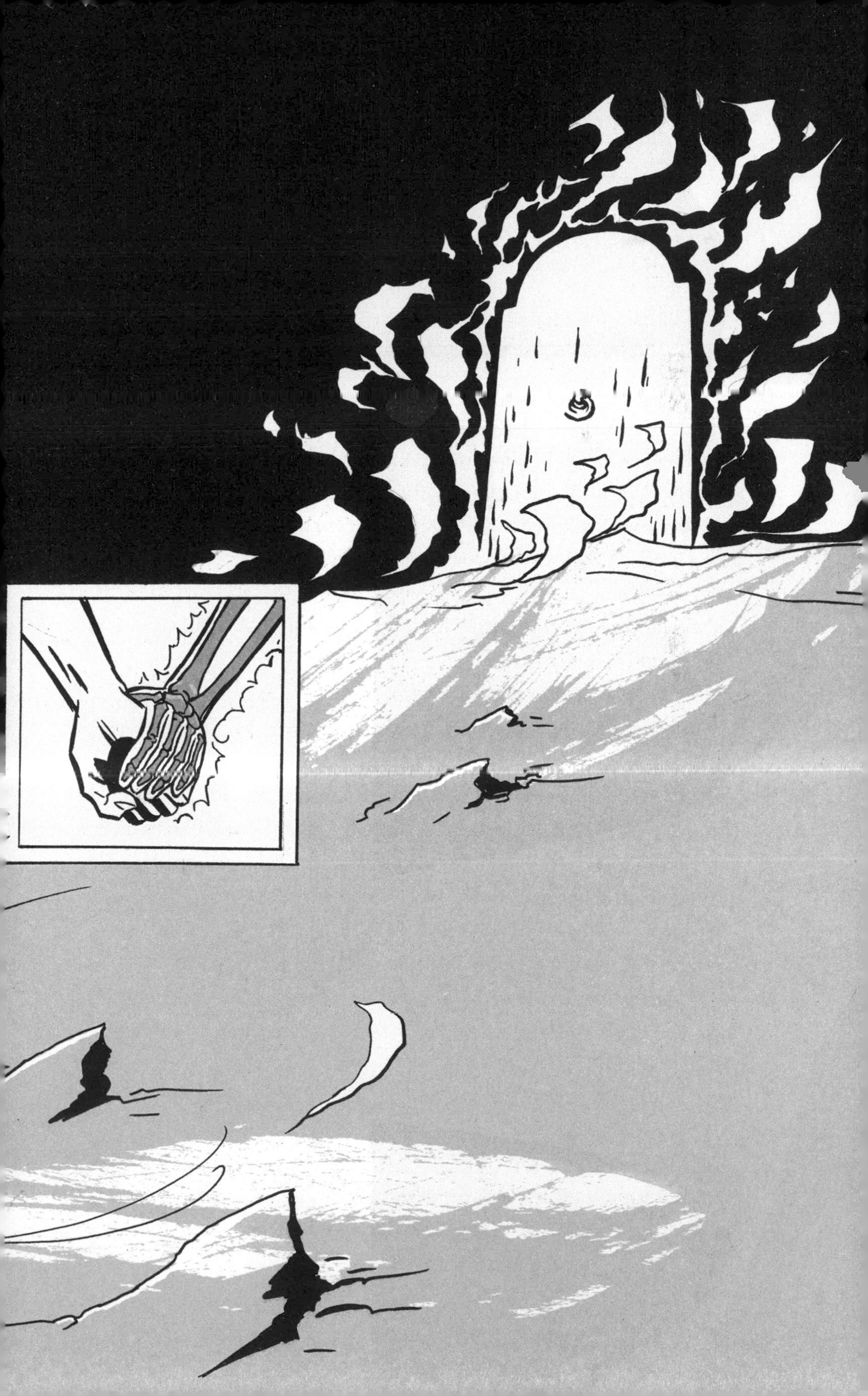

Savitri

My white cotton robe won't fit back in the bag. No matter how I fold it, it ends up in a ball. I know my mom packed everything in this duffel to get it here, so it should all fit now. But somehow it doesn't, as if my two-day stay on suicide watch enlarged it. I contemplate waiting until my mom is done talking to the doctor who signed my release, but I find new ways to shove.

Somewhere in this hospital, Holly is in a locked ward. Out of my reach, and I'm out of hers.

Dear Ambivalence, you are a murky mess.

I'm working the zipper when a voice says my name. Trisha stands in the doorway. Her hair is tied in a hurry-up bun, and she is wearing a pair of jeans and a floppy T-shirt. When my mom told me that Holly was in the hospital, it sounded so clean, so simple. As if the solution had been found. But when I see Trisha in her slept-in clothes, her body listing to the left, Holly's latest hospitalization becomes real.

"Come in," I say.

She walks as though the linoleum might break.

"I just came to check on you. And I brought you something," she says, and starts rifling through her tote bag. "Your mom said that you'd be all right, nothing permanent."

"You talked to her? Did she tell you what happened on the roof?"

"The police did."

"Oh," I say.

I want to know if she believes me but am afraid to ask. I've already talked to the police. Meade found the root beer cup and, probably at

280

Sergeant Paxton's insistence, they checked it. Although there is no proof who drugged the cup, it did corroborate my crazy-sounding story. As did the shed filled with her drawings. And Trisha's missing sleeping pills.

Of course, all that took a couple of days, while I slept in the hospital as though I was hibernating.

"I can't find it," Trisha says. She sets her bag on the corner of the high, thin hospital bed and starts unloading—energy bars, a brush, folded-up papers, a prescription slip, and one of Holly's T-shirts. She sits down on the edge of the bed and sighs. "It was a box of chocolates. They were just an excuse to come talk to you anyway."

"Do you need an excuse?" I pull at the orange plastic hospital bracelet.

"I wasn't sure you'd want to see me," she says.

I tilt my head and wait.

"I should have done something about Holly earlier. I made excuses—Corey's death, her injuries. I didn't know what was making her so hostile, but I should have seen the signs. I'm so sorry."

I can't respond; it's everything I wanted to say to her.

Trisha puts her hand over her mouth and her eyes pinch shut.

I sit down next to her and tell her what I know about Holly's world, about the Leopardess, about how heroes are born through pain. When you are hurting that much, it may be easier to crawl into someone else's skin. And whose better than a hero's? I suspect that there are times when anything, anything, seems better than the hell you are living in.

She nods stiffly. She crosses her arms and rubs her shoulders. Her voice is high and tight when she says she's still waiting for Holly to get better.

"The first medication they tried—well, it didn't seem to help. So we're on a new one now."

I search for a bright side.

"At least she's taking them," I say. "That's good, right? I mean, that's great, actually, because she's admitting that—"

"Holly doesn't have a choice right now."

"What?"

"She's . . . she's been nonresponsive since the ambulance came. She was just standing there, beside you. The EMTs talked to her, tried to figure out what was wrong with her, but she just . . . wasn't there anymore."

I remember the times she zoned out, when I had to shake her to bring her back to me. I have to swallow and clear my throat before I can speak, while I remind myself there are no shadow lands. "What does that mean?"

Trisha pauses, and when she speaks, her voice is shaky. "She's catatonic."

She lists possibilities: schizophrenia, bipolar, depression with psychotic features. Maybe a more temporary psychic break . . . A diagnosis will take time, she says.

"I hate to label her, though."

Label? I stand up and Trisha follows suit. I want to argue with her, but I can't articulate what I mean. It's not a label. Or maybe it is, but it's one she deserves. Or maybe *deserves* is the wrong word. Maybe it's one she needs—to keep her safe. To keep her friends safe.

Trisha shifts from foot to foot as if searching for balance. Then she lifts her chin and says, "It doesn't matter. Holly will come back to us. Her life isn't over; it's just going to be different."

"You can sit. It's okay," I say, feeling stupid—of course she's exhausted.

"No, thanks, I should go, but . . ." She opens her bag again. "What did I do with those chocolates? I don't know if she can hear us, but I thought maybe . . . would you talk to her?"

Conflicting thoughts flood my brain so fast that I can't even catch one. I grab on to the bed frame.

"Trisha," I hear my mother say while I stare at the white sheets and try to figure out which answer to give her. "Savitri has to concentrate on her own recovery right now, right, honey?" A hand on my shoulder makes me look up. My mom is standing between Trisha and me. I can't look at either of them, so my gaze returns to the white nothingness of my sheets. I scan the cotton hills and valleys.

"Savitri," Trisha starts.

"Sav," I correct her. *Nothing like the legend.*

"I understand if I'm asking too much considering what she did to you, but I . . . I had to try. I have to try everything."

"Of course you do," my mom says. "Come on. Let's talk outside."

Trisha tells me again she's sorry and she says we'll talk later, okay?

After they leave, I lie down on the bed and close my eyes. I cross my arms over my chest and stay very still. Maybe if I don't move—if I just lie here absolutely stock-still—maybe the pain won't find me.

*   *   *

I don't talk to Trisha later. Not the day I get home. Not the next day or even the next. I keep pulling my phone out of my pocket, but then I put it away. Once, I call Corey's phone again to hear his voice, maybe to ask him what the hell I'm supposed to do now—see Holly or stay away. I get an earsplitting three-note "jingle" that tells me the number no longer exists. I let my batteries run out.

I curl up under one of our throws and stay in front of the television; I don't eat unless my mom hands me something. I vacillate between thinking I'm the only one who can reach Holly and remembering how unreachable she is. Maybe I shouldn't even want to reach her. All this time I thought I was helping, but I was just running behind her, chasing her shadow.

My mom goes out for a birth, and when she comes home to find me in the exact same spot, her eyes narrow and she says in her Mother Voice, "Savitri, just what are you doing?"

"Report of Day Three of My Post-hospital Hibernation—" I cover my mouth. I even *sound* like Holly—too many days and nights over too many years together, our language shaping the other's voice. I slide my hand to my neck and wish I could remove my larynx. I hate the sound of my own voice—it can't reach anyone or save anything. Not in reality.

Holly's reality is so much easier that sometimes I want to crawl in it with her. *At least we'd be together.* If I could just follow her.

And that thought freaks me out so completely that I let my mom harass me off the couch and force me into the shower. I try to wash away the self-pity, stupor, and stink.

Then I get on my computer and start to search. Article after article, blog after blog, and I finally have a vague sense of what's in store for Holly if she comes back to us—medication, therapies, and constant vigilance against the nightmares in her head. Trisha is right—most mental illnesses can be managed. The typical madwoman-in-the-attic isn't actually typical. And it isn't the life of those who are treated. If Holly is treated, if she allows herself to be treated . . . what would that look like? Would we still be best friends?

I put my head in my hands as my mom's voice comes back to me: "Her priority isn't you."

Dear Psych Ward, please keep her safe. I've done all I can. Sometimes we have to let go.

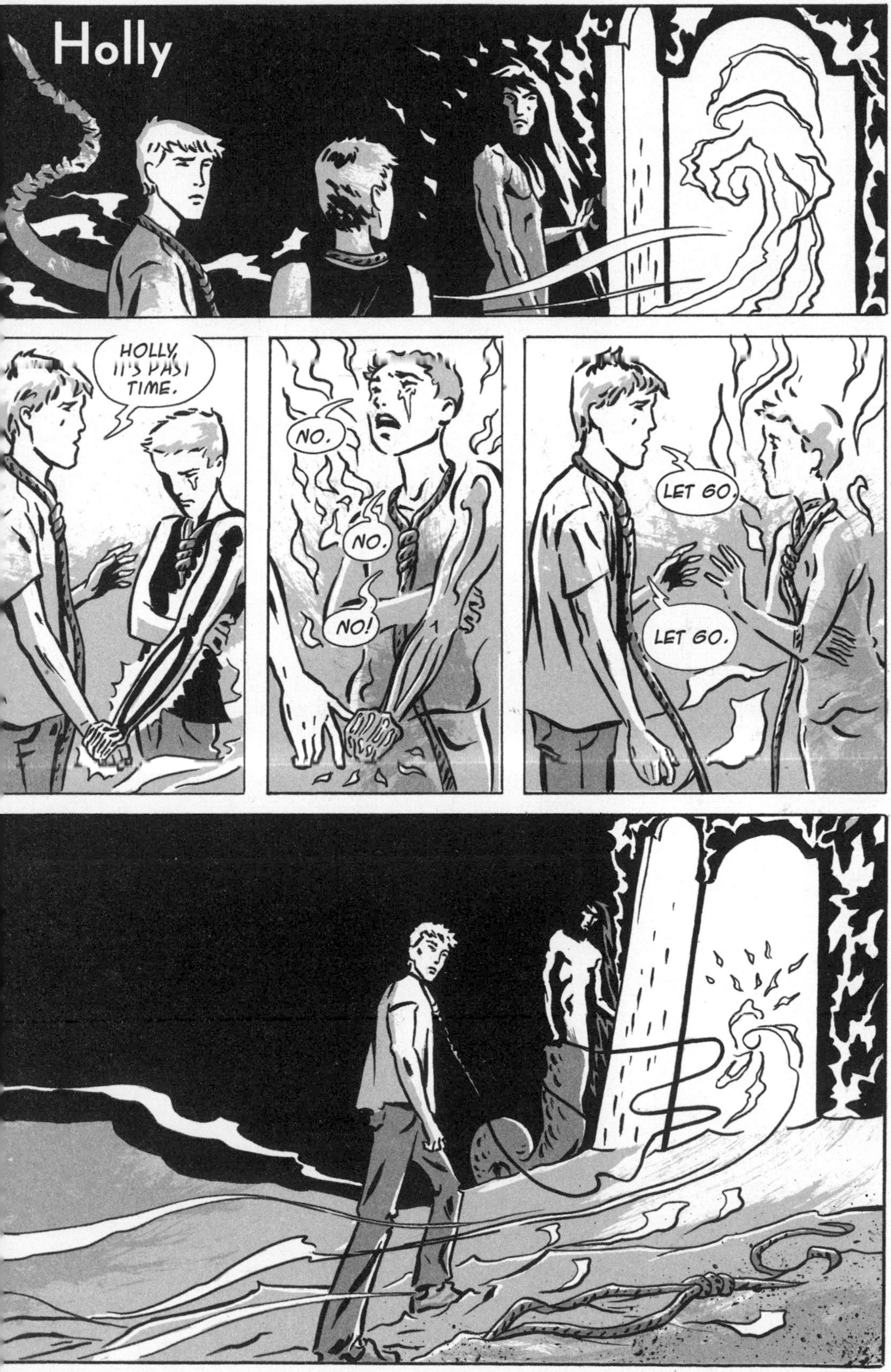
Holly
HOLLY, IT'S PAST TIME.
NO.
NO.
NO!
LET GO.
LET GO.

P
    ai
       n

       tr
         ans
           forms
           us all.

And I . . . I am not The Leopardess.
I am just Holly Paxton.

I listen for something to drag me back into the Shadowlands, something to drag me out of this reality. I hear nothing. I have no idea where Corey has gone. All I know is I can't reach him anymore. All I know is that I am alone.

Alone, but Here.
Alone, but Real.
My fists, aching from clutching too tight, open.

Savitri

The next morning, after showering and making my mom breakfast, I ask her to come with me. I drive her to the podium building. She asks about Princeton, reminding me that I only have two days left. When I say I haven't decided, she stares quietly out the window. When we arrive, I pull the fire escape ladder down for her. I've never watched my mom climb a ladder before. She uses her right foot for each new step up and her grip is tight. I grab her hand as she steps onto the roof.

She looks over the edge and then at me, lips pinched. "When did you start freerunning like this?" she asks. "I've never seen any videos of you freerunning up here."

"We've been doing it for a while. Josh used to do all the recordings, so . . . I guess . . . I really didn't mean to keep it a secret."

She sighs and shakes her head. "Well, I'd like you to stop now."

"I promise," I say, more interested in staying on the ground anyway.

The wind slices through my clothes, and my mom zips her jacket up—unpredictable spring weather.

"Come on," I say, and lead her over to the gardening shed, check my breathing, and pull open the door. I can see her drawings clearer in the midday light. My mom gazes at them, eyes wide, mouth agape.

"Yeh . . . yeh sab. Kya hai?"

And when I tell her that this is Holly's handiwork, she says, "You tried to tell me and I said . . . I'm sorry I didn't realize she was so sick."

"If anyone should have seen it, it was me," I say, sounding like Trisha. "I wanted to believe she would be okay, that I could help her. But now . . . It doesn't matter. I just want to move on."

287

"Then why are we here?"

I point to the wall with the pages of the Hindi version of *Savitri*. I peel off the tape and slowly start to bring them down. "I can't find this anymore. It's out of print," I say. "And I wanted it back. But I didn't want to come up here alone."

My mom helps me, peeling off the pages carefully. Putting my story back together. After a few pages, she moves to the other wall and stares.

"What is this one?" she asks.

"The Leopardess: Origins," I say, without looking.

I come to a stubborn piece of tape and start chipping at it with my fingernail.

"I've seen it before," my mom says.

"It was what I put on Holly's walls in the hospital. Maybe if I hadn't . . .'"

"No, honey," she says, her voice approaching behind me. "Mental illness—it's not like that. You couldn't cause it, okay? That's not how it works."

I can't get this tape off. Delicate work and my fingers aren't working. So I stop and turn around and face her. "Are you sure?"

"I'm a doctor," she says. "And I'm telling you, I'm sure."

I nod and have to work hard to keep the tears down. The luxury of guilt is being stripped away again.

When she starts pulling down *The Leopardess*, I tell her not to bother. I'm tired of cleaning up after Holly.

"And this?" she asks, pointing at the wall of Holly's strange drawings, which I can't even look at.

"Leave them," I say. *Let springtime maintenance men tear them down, bury them in a trash pile, and cremate them. Let them be in no one's head, no one's memories.*

When I turn around, she is still staring, studying them.

"Savitri, can I ask? Do you even know . . . how did she figure herself into the story? And who is this?" she says, pointing at the man with the river for legs—no, the snake half, I realize as I turn and look at it.

"That is supposed to be Yama. Or, rather, Kortha. She thought he was holding Corey prisoner in some land of the dead."

"How did she come up with the name Kortha?"

I shrug—a variant on Corey? Truth is, I have no idea what was going on in her head, no idea why in the midst of her madness she would home in on the story that cemented our friendship and twist one of my Gods into her villain. I choose to focus on this anger, this small anger, this manageable anger.

My mom makes a noise and then says, "But . . . she got it so wrong," she says. "Yama isn't a snake and Naraka isn't hell."

I turn back to the wall and look at Yama—a figure of strength, riding tall on a water buffalo. I wonder if Corey—who'd read *The Mahabharata*, who'd lit candles with me for Diwali—knew this story was sacred to me. Yes. He did.

"I know and . . . she should have known better."

"I wish she *had* known better. Corey was quite safe with Yama."

A lot of the time, I take on faith that my mom has a better handle on the world than me, but sometimes, sometimes, I see proof. I fold my arms around her.

Once I have all the pages in order, I tuck them safely in my backpack.

I look at the wall with Holly's drawings on it. In dark marker she has written: *The Leopardess: Resurrected*. Maybe it is—or it could be—Holly's story of resurrection. Maybe it's just not finished.

My mom turns toward the door and opens it, letting the air in. Holly's pages flutter.

"Wait," I say. "I've changed my mind."

When I ask, my mom helps me take down Holly's pictures and make them into their own book. And I stuff it beside mine in my backpack before we go.

Holly

Just hours on Medication No. 3 and I feel like I'm Eggshell-Walking with two images that I can't shake: Corey's hand dissolving in mine until he was gone, until I lost him, no matter how hard I held on.

And me in the Shadowlands holding a silvery rope, a thin braid that pierced my hand with thousands of small slivers. From my hand, it dipped, nearly touching the black sand before rising up and up and around Savitri's neck.

What did I do to her?

I ask the nurses and Get Nothing; I ask the doctors and Get Nothing, even when I snap at them, "Aren't you supposed to root me in reality? Isn't that the point?"

Instead, I get back, "When you're ready."

"Does that mean I killed her?" I demand. Or was the noose in my hand an illusion too? I thought I drugged her, but maybe I didn't. Maybe she's fine. Then again—she's Not Here.

Finally, I ask my parents and I get it all.

Dad says that in order to be considered guilty, I had to understand what I was doing and had to know it was wrong. Mens rea, he says. Not Guilty to a police officer, or in the eyes of the law. Or in the eyes of my parents. But maybe guilty to Someone Else.

You're either in or you're out.

It has been one week since I was on that roof with her, one week in this ward. When I was in the coma, Savitri never left. But now . . .

"Has Sav been here?" I ask, my voice quiet and body still.

Mom glances at Dad, who tells me not to worry about it.

290

"I told you that she's going to be okay," he says.

He gets a wax paper bag out of Mom's tote and hands it to me—a cold grilled cheese sandwich. The cheese is thick and gloppy, but I eat it anyway. Mom sits down with me and watches me eat, watches me chew. She smiles and it doesn't crack her face.

"What?" I ask.

"Nothing. Just good to see you eat."

Hungry is a Sign of Life. Hungry is a need. And only the Living need.

There is no way back to Corey. Tears run down my face while I bite into the soft bread. Mom wipes my cheek with her palm and wraps an arm around my shoulders. Corey is dead and there is nothing—not anything—I could have done to save him.

And that's the worst of it all.

My mom's grip is strong and I lean into her. She nearly wobbles, but holds me up. Dad puts his hand on my back.

It's not perfect, but it's better than before.

When they leave, I curl up in the bed. I pull the thin sheet over me and, still cold, get the gray scratchy blanket. I'm so tired. Damn meds.

I look at the walls; they are blank. No Leopardess. No Sav.

In the Shadowlands, the noose was in my hands; I held it, just like Wiry did. I was the one who brought Savitri there, who brought her in. I was the one who dissolved a dose of sleeping pills that would put her into a coma and then handed it to her and watched her drink it. Somehow I became the Villain when I was trying for the Hero.

I know my psychiatrist, aptly named Dr. White—white coat, white hair, pale skin, and strangely dark eyebrows—doesn't want me to think this way about the Shadowlands; I know he wants me to draw Strict Boundaries between Reality and Delusion.

But how do you Ignore your Reality, even if it isn't True? How am I supposed to pretend everything in the Shadowlands didn't happen? My memories are real. Maybe the Shadowlands are Not Real, but the ones that lie within me are. I know how to reach them and have found at least one way to stay out of them, to keep the Voice away.

Simple white pills. That keep me here. Among the Living. Among the Sane.

Sometimes, I'd rather be here.

When I sleep, I dream about Corey. I dream about his funeral. I dream about his death.

When I wake up, I have to remember that I am not surrounded by shattered glass with Corey over me, shielding me from the next bullet.

I stand up, pull my robe on, and walk into the bathroom. The cold water on my face is Real. The porcelain sink that I grab onto and hold tight is Real. Corey's death is Real.

Permanent. Unchangeable in this reality.

A reverse version of Nurse Ratched stops in and gives me an unlined journal and a pencil. My doctors told me I should draw. "You're visual," said Dr. White.

"Duh."

"Use it to your advantage."

Now I doodle a bunch of nothing—hexagons, which I color in at random. Sav would like the order. If she would just come, I could show her. *See how healthy I am? See how I'm not drawing what's in my head? See how I'm not drawing a silver rope, with a loose thread pricking into my hand, that ends in a noose? See how I'm no longer a villain?*

Hours tick by. Three visitors pass in the hallway, signaling the end of visiting hours.

I draw the noose anyway, just to get it out of me—on the paper instead of locked in my head. I only have graphite, so it comes out kind of funny—colorless and inert. I stare at it and stare at it longer.

Night comes and visiting hours are over. Time to face facts: she's not coming. And neither is he.

Options: stay in the terrible thing that's happened to me or move on.

When a nurse gives me my simple white pills that keep the Shadowlands at bay, I look at them in my palm. Sometimes I'd rather be here, and sometimes . . .

She watches me slide the pills into my mouth, but I tuck them between my back teeth and my cheek and swallow nothing but water.

* * *

The linoleum floors are cold . . . even with fuzzy, shapeless socks and
the showers run in a scalding-freezing cycle.

The days are defined by
"talk therapy" . . . and another dose of drugs . . .
        drugs . . . I don't want to take.
Pills
White cylinders, blue squares, and mauve circles dictate
                . . . everything . . .
whether I sleep, whether I can taste my food
                —metallic-tasting blue pills—
my speed.
Even how coherent
                        I slug my way through words.
In the Shadowlands, I recognized my own thoughts, recognized a voice.
In the Shadowlands, I could think, I think. Or at least . . . swiftly.
DON'T LEAVE. DON'T LEAVE.

Savitri

Tomorrow is May first. Decision day.

At school, I can't connect with Josh all day. I'm still playing catch-up, furiously taking notes, collecting handouts from teachers. I have a feeling I'll need to rely on my four-year-long spotless reputation and the fact that every teacher in my small school knows (1) how bad this year has been, and (2) that college admission is contingent on finishing high school. I spend lunch with my English teacher and an hour after school with my history teacher.

The hallways have gone silent by the time we finish. I take out my phone to call Josh as I walk down the hall.

When I turn the corner, Sergeant Paxton is leaning against my locker, a coffee cup in his hand—a stakeout on foot. He watches me measure my steps down the long hallway. *Maybe she's not okay. Maybe I should have visited her. I've done everything, everything, wrong. Please let her be okay.* Stones weigh heavily in my stomach.

"I wanted to be the one to tell you," he says.

I avoid eye contact and cradle the lock in my hand, but the combination—a succession of three numbers trained into my mind for 180 school days—has gone missing.

"Brent Owens just accepted a plea bargain."

I stare at him. "Who?" And then it clicks—Wiry. Of course. I've barely paid attention to the press coverage since the arrest. "Oh."

I let the information slide through me and unknot the muscles in my back. No trial, no courtroom, it's done. And Corey can lie down at last. But getting Wiry didn't rescue Holly or save our friendship. Maybe some things can't be saved.

"Forty years for murder one and fifteen years for attempted murder, served concurrently."

"It's not enough," I say. "Not enough for Corey."

"There are plenty of Serpents in prison and they all know how to make shivs. He'll get what he deserves."

My throat clogs tight. Satisfaction, horror, and pity fight for first place in my head.

"I never said thank you," he says.

"You shouldn't—don't have to thank me."

Silence settles. *I don't want to ask, I don't have to ask, I shouldn't ask.* I clear my throat.

I ask. "How is she?"

"She wants you to visit. I know what I said before about staying away, but—"

"That's not why." I twist the lock, but no numbers come. "I can't help her. Every time I tried to help her, I was just getting us both in deeper. We're not good for each other anymore."

25 left, 15 right? No . . . 15 left, 25 right? No . . . Oh, who knows. I drop the lock and it clangs against the door.

Sergeant Paxton makes an exasperated sound and then mutters, "You're all alike."

"Um . . . what?"

"Let me tell you what we tell all crime victims: you're alive and she's alive—living proof you did everything right."

"But Corey isn't."

"Corey made a choice." His voice gets thick. "He was a good brother. A good man. You have to honor that." Under his skin, the sinew in his cheek hardens—not with anger but with a sort of grim pride.

Somehow I hadn't thought about it quite like that.

"So," he continues, "I should tell her you're not coming, even though you know she was sick. She wasn't trying to hurt you. You know that."

I'm standing here with hands full of ashes and he wants me to go comfort the girl who lit the match?

"I can't do this anymore. I can't sink my whole life into her recovery."

"I'm not asking for your whole life. I'm asking for a half an hour of your whole life. But maybe all Holly did for you over the years doesn't stack up."

"All Holly did for me? What about what she did *to* me?" I yell.

Sergeant Paxton shifts his weight to a ready stance and I step back, shocked. *What am I doing, yelling at him?* He's not the one I want to yell at. *I can't use you,* she said that night. I'm no longer her pawn to be moved. My hands clench. Forget her.

He puts his hand on my shoulder, and somehow this gesture, this instinct to move closer when he sees someone coming apart, reminds me of Corey. "You're mad and you've got reason. Makes sense. But at the end of the day, you pick each other up and dust each other off. It's what friends do."

"The rules of friendship no longer apply."

He drops his hand and says, "Anyway, Owens is in prison now and that's thanks to you."

"Well," I mumble at the floor.

"To Corey, it would be . . . something."

I lift my gaze and look at him. "Thanks."

His footsteps fade away and I stare at what was Holly's locker—emptied out now. I put my hand on the metal door. Hard and cold.

* * *

When I get home, Josh is sitting on the bottom step of my front stoop; his elbows rest one step up, and he is leaning back, eyes to the sky. I unzip my jacket to let the warmth in. I sigh and it comes out shaky. When he sees me, he scootches over, making room, and I sit next to him.

"How are you?"

I shrug a shoulder and look away, up at the sky. Long clouds are stretched thin over bright blue.

He says he kept trying to catch me at school, but I wasn't around. I press the heels of my hands against my eyes.

"What's wrong?" he asks.

When I tell him about Holly's dad, his eyes narrow.

"Imagine if you did that to her. Do you think he'd be so forgiving then?"

I remember him in the police parking lot telling me he didn't want me at the house, and a sarcastic laugh pops out.

"Well," he says, "I guess we know where Holly gets her nerve from."

I look at him sidelong. "Aren't you supposed to be lecturing me, telling me I should be a good friend to her, a loyal friend?"

"Actually, what I said was you needed to be a friend who'd tell her when she was wrong."

"So?"

"So if you *want* to talk to her, why don't you tell her that?"

I pull the zipper up on my jacket and then draw it down slowly. "How many chances does she get?"

"As many as she has earned," he says. "Isn't that what happened with us?"

Josh showed up at the staircase to sit with me on that first day back at school, stood on top of the church roof at Corey's funeral, and said all the right things when I broke down in the hospital. He took me free-running when I needed it and told me the truth about Holly even when I didn't want to hear it.

"Yeah," I say. Corey and I should have given him space to breathe, time to explain.

"So how many has she earned?"

"Lately? None," I say. But maybe it's not about how many you earn; maybe it's about how many you need. "It would be so much simpler if I could hate her."

"You've been friends too long for simple," he says.

On the street, a car passes us, revving loudly, leaving us silent.

Josh claps his hands together and then spreads them wide. "I know. Let's do a chart. One of your Known-Unknowns?"

"Nice. Mock me when I'm down."

He laughs and then leans back on his elbows and closes his eyes. "This Saturday we're going to be working stairs and railings."

I look him over. Josh has done all the things that friends do: led the way when I couldn't see, blunted the edges when he could, and bore witness when he couldn't, when watching was all he could offer.

"Thank you," I say.

He opens his eyes and then waves a hand at me. "Yeah, yeah."

I lean back on my elbows next to him, close my eyes, and let sunlight wash over me.

* * *

That night, I call up my email and read Princeton's acceptance again. It only takes a moment to check the box and hit *Send*.

A decision. Final and irrevocable—something that won't change, no matter what she says. And that's what gets me to the hospital and to Holly.

Holly

Dr. White figured me out and started injecting me. Needles are my Least Favorite Method, so I've promised to start taking The Pills again. He nodded, reservedly, but you just know that in his mind he's patting me on my head and muttering, "Good girl." Fine. As long as he doesn't notice that I never promised anything about when I get out.

He told me to keep drawing, that it would help. So the Good Girl is sketching the noose again. This time with a colored pencil—not the pen I asked Dr. White for, but at least I can make it silver.

Movement catches my eye, and when I look up, Savitri is standing in the doorway. She looks horrible. So thin that her cheeks are starting to hollow out. So tired that her eyes look sunken. So stressed that her weight is on the balls of her feet, Ready to Spring.

I squeeze my eyes shut tight and open them again.

"Should I come in?" Her voice is removed—polite—the voice she uses with Adults, with Not Us.

I'm Out.

Doors-barred, Lights-off, Out.

Except that here she stands. Thumb worrying at her fingers. So, what is this? Pity? Revenge? Whatever it is, it's not friendship. We're past that now.

Fine.

"Well," I say. "Savitri Mathur, as I live and breathe."

I stand up and her weight shifts backward.

"Yeah, come on in, stranger. Do you like my new digs?" I sweep my arm around the closet I live in now.

I watch Sav, her eyes scanning, starting at my front door: it mimics a bathroom stall door, cut out at the bottom (Orderly-Friendly in an Emergency) and the top slants to Sabotage the Suicidal.

She looks at the cubbies and can see everything: my bras, my underwear. In Strict Compliance with the Everything in Plain Sight rule. When she spots the bathroom, her eyebrows lift—no door.

"No Privacy for the Wicked," I say. "It's like a cell," I say.

"Well . . . ," she says. Her voice is hard, and she crosses her arms in front of her chest. "Seems about right."

That's my Sav. The quiet girl who knows how to fight. I'm surprised I don't have a red welt on my cheek.

Fine. You asked for it.

"Sorry I have no red carpet for you," I say.

"What does that mean?"

"Am I supposed to be grateful you deigned to show up? After you disappeared on me?"

"I'm surprised you noticed. What tipped you off? A missing panel in your psychotic comic?"

Really asked for it.

"I've been waiting and waiting for you, and when you finally show up, you're here to yell at me? That's—"

Sav's eyes narrow and I step back. "You've been waiting for me. Really? All I've done since the night Corey died was wait for you. I've been waiting for you to come out of your coma, waiting for you to start grieving with me, waiting for you to tell me what the hell was going on."

"Oh, aren't you the best? So generous. Then again, all your waiting didn't get me that much," I say, and spread my arms out.

"You know what, Holly? You get what you give. So you tell me, what have you given?"

And with that, my anger deflates. On my paper the noose gleams silver. I close my mouth. *Shit. The things I did to her.*

"For months now, I've been your keeper, not your friend. Because you shoved me out. Did it ever occur to you that I needed you too? We were supposed to get through this together. But I was on my own. And now you tell me *I* disappeared on *you*? I showed up for you every day and I was the friend you asked me to be—turning down Princeton, following you with a gun in my hand."

Shit. The things she did for me.

She continues, "But you still wouldn't talk to me. Why didn't you let me help you? What did I do to make you stop trusting me? Is it because I didn't save Corey? Is that it?"

"What? No, Sav, no," I say. *Shit. The things I didn't bother to know about.* "I never thought it was your fault."

"Then why wouldn't you let me help you?"

Savitri—the girl who just needs answers.

I put my hands on the back of my neck and sigh. I can't look at her. "Oh, God, I'm so sorry. I was in that out-of-control moment, midair, just looking for the landing."

"I'm not talking about the Midazolam, Holly. I know you were too sick by then. I'm talking about before that. Why didn't you tell me? At the graveyard or the night I shaved your head. You knew you were slipping."

I squeeze my neck hard; she's right. I try to trace it back. Why didn't I talk to her? Humpty Dumpty on her way down.

"I was scared that if I said it to you, if I told you what was happening you'd call it what it was—crazy. And I didn't want to be that. I wanted to be . . ." I hesitate to say what's next. But isn't that what she's mad at me for? Not for how I ignored the adrenaline when I should have paid attention, pushed past the Warning Signs that Useful Fear gave me, but that I let it Silence me.

So, I say out loud, "I wanted to be Leopardess strong. But I'm not The Leopardess."

"No one's that strong, Holly—not even the Leopardess. She dresses up in a costume and chases down villains. I wouldn't call her a model of mental health."

I lift my eyebrows. That's true, actually.

She goes on. "Besides, I'm not sure it's about being strong. I think it's about adjusting your movement to your surroundings and not the other way around." Her voice quiets. "You have to let him go. Hanging on . . . it's the wrong path."

I know what she's telling me, what everyone's telling me—Corey's dead and I can't change that, can't bring him back, can't live in the Shadowlands. I'm supposed to take pills tonight—and maybe for the rest of my life—to stay here? In these surroundings? In this Real Reality?

She presses her lips together and looks away from me. "I came to tell you something. It's May first."

Princeton.

My throat closes. Just a few weeks ago, she texted me *Princeton's out and I'm all in*. It's too much to hope for now, I know.

I look directly at her. No trace of a smile or Good News. I'd bet anything that I know what's coming.

I squeeze my eyes shut, my hands curl into fists.

Sav says, "I have to focus on what comes next for me. If I stay, I stay for you. And if I go . . ." She touches my arm. "Skyping isn't so bad."

I shake her off. "I don't want a bone. Why would you keep us going after what I did?"

"It's not a bone. It's just that . . . I can't be all in. Not anymore. But we've had so many years together that I can't be all out either. So . . ."

"So?"

"So, we need something new, something more balanced."

I swallow; my muscles release one by one.

"Besides," she says, "I think I deserve to see what comes next for you too."

I nod. Jersey Girl it is then. Most of the work I need to do is mine alone. I open my breathing. Deep into my lungs. I'm going to have to see my way to safety. Without Corey. Without Sav. Some fears get respect, others get their asses kicked.

She gathers her hair up, organizing it into a ponytail. Déjà Sav. Whether our friendship survives—that's one thing. But as for me . . .

I look at her steadily.

"Seven times down, eight times up." Corey's words in her mouth.

I hold out my fist halfway between us. "Seven times down, eight times up."

Her knuckles meet mine. We hiss out our steam and our fingers uncurl and trail away from each other.

*   *   *

The window in the main room looks over the street and I watch her walk away. Her figure is small from up here on the third floor. She isn't bouncing or overjoyed, but her steps are quicker—lighter. Better.

And I did that for her; I helped her. Not such a good Villain after all.

In the Shadowlands, I can't help anyone. Not really. In the Shadowlands, nothing I do will free Corey.

Nurse Ratched, version three, who is trolling with the med cart, hands me a little paper cup of pills. My Daily Sanity Cocktail.

Kortha said, "You have to choose."

I pour the pills into my palm and stare at them.

Heroes aren't born from pain; they just make good decisions in bad moments. Corey put his body between me and a bullet. Sav tried to stand between me and madness.

And as for me, I need to find my own footing first. So I slide the pills to the back of my throat and swallow before I walk down the hall to see Dr. White.

Savitri

I tell my mom where I'm going and she asks if I want company. Another night, I tell her. As I approach the playground, fireflies glow in the twilight—hints of flame. Call and answer. I sit on the swing, twisting it tight and then drifting free to the rebound.

We grew up here together, on these swings and those bars. Maybe Holly is right: pain does transform us all. But pain isn't the only thing that made me. It isn't even the most important thing.

I had a seven-year-old girl who thought blue Gods were awesome, who peeled a second skin of glue off her hands while chattering with me. At fifteen, she flirted with a creepy counterboy for an extra milk shake when I forgot my wallet. At seventeen, she drove ninety miles per hour to get her brother to a doctor and, at eighteen, tried to reach for him while under fire.

And I had Corey—whose thumb wrapped around my pinkie while we learned wall flips, whose kisses tasted like mint and salt, who was the first to tell me to go to Princeton.

All this time, I thought I had too little left of him, afraid that I'd have nothing left of her. But they are in everything I do. Turns out I can't leave them behind.

I twist in the swing side to side. Princeton is miles away, miles of separation. Maybe we won't be as close. But maybe we'll both be stronger—a better version of us. She in her story and me in mine, bearing witness at a distance, living scrapbooks for each other.

I get up and walk to the red metal dome of crisscrossed bars that squats in the middle of the playground. I climb to the top and stand, fighting for my balance. Even though I knew I had the distance to make the backflip from here, I would stand on the top, glancing back so many times that Holly would pelt me with pebbles. "Just do it," she'd say. But my throat stayed tight.

Now I close my eyes and inhale and exhale.

Corey did handstands four flights up, Holly crawled into someone else's skin, and I swallowed stones of guilt just to hide from a simple fact: we are all vulnerable, and there is nothing between us and a bullet. It's terrifying, this life. Its precarious nature, its random un-design.

Maybe all I have is my own two feet. And the confidence that they can bear my weight when the world goes sideways. Maybe that's enough.

I look at how far the metal structure stretches behind me and spot my landing. The ground will rush up to meet me whether I'm ready for it or not. The air will whistle past me as I negotiate gravity's pull. I turn my back to the distance.

And leap.

ACKNOWLEDGMENTS

H. M. Bouwman, Trisha Speed Shaskan, and Charlotte Sullivan helped me reveal the heart of this book. They found elegant plot solutions and provided hours of book-therapy and Swati-therapy. Good friends who led the way when I couldn't see, blunted the edges when they could, and bore witness when they couldn't.

Anne Ursu, Julie Schumacher, Patrick Hueller, Laura Ruby, and Stephanie Watson helped me find the center and the edges of this novel. Deepa Dharmadhikari kept me honest. Geoffrey Sirc and Zander Cannon taught me everything I know about graphic novels from ground zero.

Rosemary Stimola's grace and wisdom cleared the rocky path, removing boulders and smoothing the grade.

Nancy Siscoe should get a gold crown for her patience and a new set of rubber boots for standing her ground on the muddy banks of this process and hauling a novel from the muck. And something else . . . like a pass with St. Peter. A round of applause for Katherine Harrison as well, who read and noticed. I bow to Knopf's copyediting, art, marketing, and publicity departments.

Craig Phillips brought all the visions of the book—soul cages and snakemen—to life, with boundless creativity!

And this book would never have come together without the astute art direction of Sarah Hokanson.

Freerunner Chad Zwadlo and his cohorts at Fight or Flight Academy answered questions, showed me their moves, and taught me the terminology and the philosophy of the sport. Dr. Anita Koshy, Dr. Robert T. Law, Lisa Wennerlund, and Susan Hess all provided their medical expertise. Police officer John Biederman gave me a long chunk of his time. Jennifer Meade and John Magruder, Chicago consultants, helped me zero in on setting. Karen Beltz entrusted her emotional insights to my imagination.

Thanks also to the many librarians, booksellers, tweeps, and Facebook friends who cheered this novel along. I had a great time writing nightly, if remotely, alongside @NyraeDawn and @JenDuffey.

The Minnesota State Arts Board and the Thomas H. Shevlin Fellowship in the University of Minnesota's Graduate Program generously gave me the gift of time through their funding—essential for any artist and particularly necessary on this venture.

Pratap and Pushpa Avasthi kept asking and supporting, no matter what.

My kids give up their mother to this crazy craft. They forgive the forgotten permission slips, last-minute tumults, and frozen dinners. They keep me going with their bright spirits and inspire me with their strength and tenacity.

John Yopp's dedication to and endurance for this novel was Iron Man limitless. Draft after draft, frenzy after frenzy, freak-out after freak-out, he never wavered. His musical ear turned slop into phrasing, his questions helped me shape a mess into an arc, and his ramrod backbone helped me find the courage I needed for this novel. Oh, and he made me pie—writerly pie.

SWATI AVASTHI (pronounced SWA-thee of-US-thee) is the author of the highly acclaimed novel *Split,* winner of the IRA Book Award and the Cybils Award.

Ms. Avasthi received her MFA from the University of Minnesota and currently teaches in Hamline University's MFA program in Writing for Children and Young Adults. She lives in Minneapolis with her husband and two children. You can read more about her work at SwatiAvasthi.com.

CRAIG PHILLIPS is an award-winning illustrator whose work has appeared on book jackets, in publications like *Rolling Stone,* and on tour posters for bands, including Foo Fighters and the Red Hot Chili Peppers. He lives in New Zealand with his family. You can learn more about his work at CraigPhillips.com.au.